The
Kosher
Butcher

The Kosher Butcher

**A
Lincoln/Lachler
Mystery**

Melvyn Westreich

Laurel
Publishing

The Kosher Butcher

Copyright © 2020 by Melvyn Westreich

First Printing: 2020

ISBN - 978-1-7347004-0-4

Laurel Publishing
24751 Sussex Street
Oak Park, Michigan 48237

Also by Melvyn Westreich

Murder in the Kollel

ACKNOWLEDGEMENT

So many people helped me with this effort. As usual my thanks to my extended Detroit family, Burt & Sharon Cohen and Joe & Carol Perecman who have always been there for me and for Carol's checking facts and doing the research of Michigan State Police proceedings. To Rivy Gordon who continues to encourage me, as she has for the past twenty years. To Phyllis Shapiro and Malkie Goldberg for helping in the proofreading and for Phyllis' terrific legal advice. To Dr. Neetzan Shtal for partially curbing my chauvinistic mind-set. Finally I must thank my wife, Ada, and my family for tolerating my hours away from them, as I toiled in front of my computer screen and for my general *mishigas*. Thank you all.

DEDICATION

To Dafna, Matan, Ayelet, Keren, Esther and
Neetzan.

Thank you for coming into my universe. You,
and your families, make me so proud. From
you I learned what makes the world go round.
View life as a cup half full or make sure that
your medical plan covers psychiatric therapy.

Author's Preface

Once again I let my deranged mind create a world where a murderer is able to do horrible things to his victim and the team of Lincoln and Lachler come to the rescue. The book is complete. It has a beginning, middle, and end but Shimon Lincoln and Dafna Lachler live on in my thoughts and I will have to see what new mischief I can get them into. But not quite yet. My next book is a romantic story that also deals in death and grieving. A bit of change for me, but Rabbi Kalmonowitz insights are still a major feature. Should be fun. I decided that in **The Kosher Butcher** all the words in *frumie-speak* (words in Yiddish and Hebrew that are liberally sprinkled in the conversations of Orthodox Jews) would not be translated on the spot. So no parentheses in the text. Instead I have added a glossary at the end for those that need it.

Prologue

THE MURDERER SAW THE APPROACHING vehicle and thought, 'Well, it's about time.'

It was unlikely that anyone but his intended victim would be coming down this dark stretch of road so late in the evening. But, you cannot rely on luck. If someone else does drive by, that person would remember him standing alongside his stopped car and he would have to abort.

The vehicle appeared to be the right make and model so the murderer waved his arms to flag it down.

The car went right on by.

'What kind of driver is that idiot Jew?' thought the murderer. 'Nearly hit me.' A moment later the brake lights came on and the car slowed and stopped. The driver had the full beard, black hat, and dark suit identifying the driver as the rabbi from the *yeshiva* academy.

"He's perfect," the murderer whispered to himself as he walked up to the car.

"Sorry about that ... I did not expect to see anyone on the road," said the rabbi apologetically as he rolled down his window.

"That's OK," said the murderer. "At least you stopped."

"What's the problem?" asked the clergyman through the window.

"I am really glad to see you," he said. "Car died and my cell phone doesn't work. Could I borrow your phone to call my road service?"

"Sure, just a second," said the rabbi searching in his pocket and handing the phone through the window to the murderer. "There you go."

"You're a life saver," he said with a smile. The murderer took the phone and began punching in some random numbers as he wandered back towards his own car. "Hey, what's this?" he exclaimed pointing towards the front of his car.

"What's what?" asked the rabbi sticking his head out the window.

"I don't believe it. Would you look at that? I never would have made it home," said the murderer earnestly.

"What did you find?" asked the clergyman getting out of his car to see if he could help.

"Right here. Do you see what I'm talking about?" said the murderer pointing at the bumper of his car.

"I don't see anything wrong," said the rabbi, leaning over to look under the car.

The murderer quickly slipped the garrote around the rabbi's neck and pulled his arms apart tightening the thin wire loop. "Now you see what's wrong," said the murderer hoisting the victim across his hip to gain leverage. When he felt he held the rabbi securely he began dragging him off the road into the low bushes.

Other than the scuffling of his heels against the ground, the rabbi hardly made a sound as he fought the pressure of the wire about his neck that was crushing his windpipe and extinguishing his life. He thrashed about for almost four minutes and then became still. The murderer kept the garrote tight for another two minutes just like the instructor in the Ranger course at Fort Benning had demonstrated so many years before.

The murderer hoisted the limp body up onto his shoulder and dumped the now dead Jew into his trunk.

He found the wallet in an inside pocket and extracted the thirty dollars in cash. 'I thought all these Jew boys carry oodles of green,' he thought to himself. He walked back to the rabbi's car and on the way retrieved the fellow's black hat from where it had fallen on the road. The murderer tossed all three - wallet, cell phone, and hat - through the open window onto the front seat of the rabbi's car.

He returned to his own vehicle and as he slid behind the steering wheel the murderer said out loud, "That went pretty well. Two down and two to go."

#

Mazel Tov

I AM NOW one happy over-stuffed *yeshiva bocher.*

We had been invited to break bread — or more correctly *challah* — at Rabbi Kalmonowitz's Friday night table and since the *rebbetzin* — in my expert opinion — is the third best cook in the Detroit ultra-Orthodox Jewish community, I knew the meal would be out of this world.

I was definitely on the money.

In addition to her being a superb cook, the *rebbetzin* uncannily knew which foods were my favorites. Tonight she served an appetizer of stuffed cabbage in a tangy tomato sauce. Yummy. This was followed by a rich flavorful chicken soup with *knaidelach* so light and fluffy that I was sure that at any moment they were going to rise up out of the golden broth like helium balloons and float away. Delectable. For the main course there was a lamb shoulder roast with those crispy little Irish potatoes swimming in gravy. The garlicky meat literally fell off the bone. Delish. Then, when she brought in the three-layer chocolate mousse dessert, topped with non-dairy whipped cream — Jews that keep kosher do not mix meat with milk — I thought I would *chalish.*

I love the word *chalish.* It is a Yiddish expression with no true English translation. It means to — pass out —

feel weak — become ecstatic — be overjoyed — and so much more.

I thought I would *chalish*.

I cannot eat another bite and I have to sit back in my chair with my belt loosened by a notch (maybe two — I lost track). Tears come to my eyes just recalling the savory meal.

Way to go *Rebbetzin* Kalmonowitz!

I mentioned before that 'we' were invited to Friday dinner and the 'we' is myself and my soon-to-be fiancée, Dafna Lachler, and her family. Her family consisted of her two daughters, Aliza and Suzie, and my future mother-in-law, Mrs. Shaindel Kalin. All the females were now in the kitchen with the *rebbetzin* arranging the leftovers and helping in the sorting of the pots, pans, and dishes. They were doing what male chauvinists would call Jewish women's work. I was sitting in the dining room with Rabbi Kalmonowitz and his two unmarried sons. What male chauvinists would dub proper behavior for Jewish men.

Hey, that is what male chauvinists would say. I would be more than willing to pitch in with the kitchen work, but the *rebbetzin* would have a heart attack. She felt it was a Jewish woman's mission in life to help her man be successful. So, she did the housework, cooking, cleaning, etc. — and seemed to enjoy doing it.

So, if she is happy — who am I to interfere?

While the ladies were fulfilling their mission in life, we men sat in the dining room discussing pithy points of *Torah* study.

Of course, that is not really an accurate depiction of the actual interplay around the table. It was more like I listened and the rabbi and his sons spouted the pithy stuff.

Rabbi Kalmonowitz sat at the head of the table in his shirt sleeves. His long black frock coat and black hat were draped across the sofa in the living room. He stroked his long gray full beard and his steely blue eyes twinkled every time one of his sons made a point concerning the week's *Torah* portion. After about twenty minutes, Rabbi Kalmonowitz stood and asked me to accompany him to his den/library. Once we got to his book-laden hideaway, he took his place behind the small study table and pointed to the chair opposite saying, "Have a seat *Reb* Shimon. What did you want to discuss with me?"

Most people know me as Sy Lincoln, but he always called me *Reb* Shimon, although I really do not deserve the title. I am not a rabbi nor am I any sort of scholar. But that was how Rabbi Kalmonowitz, as head rabbi of my *yeshiva*, referred to everyone.

Sort of a no-cost compliment.

It was like telling a woman who was older than Methuselah, that she looked so young. Or, greeting a male who was battling with his girth and could hardly squeeze through the doorway, that he appeared to have lost a few pounds.

Just a little white lie that does not cost you anything but it makes the other person feel a whole heck of a lot better.

So, I was *Reb* Shimon. Shimon is my Hebrew name.

What I wondered was — how did the rabbi know that I wanted to speak with him? I had not mentioned a thing. Dafna always says that he has some sort of sixth sense. That he can read minds and foretell the future.

I really did have something I wanted to tell him and had not known how I could broach the subject.

Something quite important.

I had rehearsed what I wanted to say over a dozen times. So, I should be good to go. But the physical act of opening my mouth and actually speaking the words to Rabbi Kalmonowitz was not easy. My tongue became sluggish and felt as if it had swollen up in my mouth.

I hesitated.

Why could I not say a simple sentence?

It was not as if *Rebbi* ever distanced himself from me or any of his students. Far from it — he was willing and eager to speak with anyone that wanted his ear. It was just that I, and almost every other student at the *yeshiva*, held him in such awe. The man was a *tzadik* and a brilliant scholar. I was constantly in fear of saying something stupid and proving to him what a dunce I am. Yet, I also knew that if I did happen to make a faux pas he would never shoot me down. That was not his way. If he felt he had to correct something I did or said, he would never do it in a way that would cause me any embarrassment. But you knew. You certainly did.

'Oh well, here goes,' I thought to myself.

My heart was thumping rapidly in my chest and I was having trouble breathing. I cleared my throat and began, "*Rebbi*, as you know I have been dating Dafna Lachler for the last five months — I wanted to tell you that we have decided to get married."

There, I said it.

At least I think I said it. I am not certain that all the words actually came out correctly. Perhaps everything had been gibberish.

That was a lot tougher than I thought it would be.

Dafna and I had decided that we were not going to make it public until we cleared it with Rabbi Kalmonowitz. That was why I referred to her as my 'soon-to-be' fiancée.

Rebbi did not say a word for a moment and just nodded his head while he somberly looked off into the distance considering my words.

Uh oh.

He is not going for it.

My goose is cooked. No engagement. No Dafna. *What am I going to do?*

The rabbi then looked at me sternly and said in a scolding tone, "*Mazel tov* and it's about time. What were you two waiting for?"

He agrees? Oh wow — I will be marrying Dafna. I cannot believe it. But *Rebbi* just asked me why we took so long, so I said in my defense, "I thought that Jewish matches are supposed to be done slowly. We did not want to appear improper."

"A *shiduch* either works or it doesn't. You knew you wanted to marry Dafna after the first week."

He was absolutely correct. I met Dafna last year when I had investigated a murder up in Lansing. After that hectic first week I most definitely knew I wanted to be with her. But for the longest time I could not convince myself that someone so wonderful would actually be willing to consider me seriously.

I looked at him inquisitively, "How did you know?"

"I did not get all these gray hairs from not observing people. It was obvious. You both come here very often for *Shabbos* dinners. Dafna is very fond of you and so are her two daughters. Even Shaindel thinks you are a fine fellow. Having a mother-in-law that likes her son-in-law is a rare commodity," he said with a knowing nod. "Have you set the date?"

"We thought *Lag B'Omer*. In two months."

"Why not in two days? Why are you stalling?" chastised the rabbi. "You're thirty eight years old and both of you are not spring chickens."

Dafna was a thirty one year old widow. Her rabbi husband, David, may he rest in peace, died of cancer almost three years ago.

I answered the rabbi, "I would have been happy with a small quick wedding but Mrs. Kalin threatened me with great bodily harm if we did not have a catered affair so that the relatives could join in the celebration and she needed at least eight weeks prep time."

"That sounds like Shaindel.   Does my *rebbetzin* know?"

"I believe Dafna is in the kitchen telling her right now."

"Very good," said the rabbi with a smile, as he stroked his beard. "And what else?"

"That's it," I said defensively.

"I think there is something more," said the rabbi raising his brow and nodding his head.

How does he do that?

"Well, there is one little thing ..."

"How little?" he asked.

I gulped down some collected saliva, "I've enjoyed my time here in the *yeshiva* and I've learned so much. But if I am getting married ... I think I have to start working again. I know enough *Torah* now to realize that I will never be a great scholar. Spending more time in the *yeshiva* would be enjoyable, but I am an old fashioned guy and I think I have to pull my weight to support the family."

"Does Dafna agree with all this?" asked *Rebbi.*

"Her business is very successful and she told me that she is willing for me to stay in the *yeshiva* for as long as I want, but to me, it would not feel right. So, I would like to drop out of the full time *yeshiva* program and try to make it to night *seder* two or three times a week." Then I quickly added, "If that is all right with you. I want to reopen my private investigator's office."

"Of course it is all right with me. Your progress here with us has been extraordinary and I am sure you now have a true love for *Torah* learning. But a life devoted exclusively to learning is not for everyone. I am so proud to have had you as my student," he said patting me on my shoulder. "When do you start?"

"I was thinking of this coming week. Would that be all right?"

"Absolutely ... and it will solve a problem for me."

"What problem, *Rebbi*? I am always willing to help."

"*Rav* Yechezkel Slater has been missing for the last month," he said mournfully.

"Everyone in the *bais medrash* knows that."

"Last year you helped us greatly when you investigated Rabbi Klein's death, but I was reluctant to approach you again and disturb your studies."

"I thought the police were handling Rabbi Slater's disappearance," I stated.

"They are, but I have been a bit disappointed in what they have been able to turn up."

"What did they find?"

"It's not what they found, it is more what they did not find. They think that Rabbi Slater left his wife and family voluntarily. That he abandoned his pregnant wife and the *yeshiva* way of life."

"That's ridiculous. Anyone who ever met him knows that that could not be the reason for his disappearance," I stated matter-of-factly.

"Exactly," said the rabbi with a nod of his head. "But the police did not know Rabbi Slater like we do. And because they think he left of his own free will they are reluctant to look further. Maybe the police are correct but it could also be that something terrible has happened. I know it has only been a month but if Reb Yechezkel is not found, his wife will be an *agunah*. Do you know what that is?"

"Yes, *Rebbi*."

For a woman to be an *agunah* was a Jewish social tragedy. So if she was an *agunah* it was imperative to free her from that status.

"Whatever the reason for his disappearance, under Jewish law *Rebbetzin* Slater will not be allowed to remarry or be free until we know with certainty what happened to him. The longer we wait the harder it will be to find out the *emes* of the matter."

"I understand, *Rebbi.*"

"Therefore I would like to hire you to investigate this case for the *yeshiva*. We will pay your usual fee. I do not want any discounts. After all you will soon be a married man and will need the income."

The reason *Rav* Kalmonowitz was offering me this job was because I had not always been a *bocher*. Up until two years ago I had never set foot in a *yeshiva* and my knowledge of Judaism — or any religion for that matter — was near absolute zero. In the days before the *yeshiva*, I had been a detective. Fifteen years on the Detroit police force and two years as a private investigator. For the last eighteen months I had been attending the *yeshiva* full time, living off my savings and investments. I kept to a rather Spartan life style and had few major expenses, but, even so, a year and half with no money coming in put quite a dent in my net worth. The hard reality was that I eventually had to make a living. I would have investigated Rabbi Slater's disappearance for free, but getting paid was even better. "Sure *Rebbi*, I'll be glad to do it."

"Good, keep me informed on how you progress."

I knew that during the day, Rabbi Kalmonowitz was in the *yeshiva* and did not take phone calls, "Should I call you in the evenings?"

"Will you be coming to *shacharis* at the *yeshiva?*"

I planned on continuing to attend the morning prayers at the *yeshiva* whenever I could, so I responded with, "Yes, I will definitely try to do that."

"Good, if you have anything to report, catch me after *davening*. Call me if you can't make it."

2

The Line

ONE HALF hour later I was accompanying the Lachler family down the fair streets of Southfield, Michigan on their way back to their home. Like so many subdivisions in suburban communities the layout of the roadways changed from one block to the next — sometimes straight and sometimes serpentine. This part of town was developed over seventy years ago for the upper middle class and the houses varied in size and cost. The only unifying feature of all the homes was that the lots were large and the lawns expansive.

Shaindel and the two girls were up ahead and I was with Dafna. Suzie, the oldest daughter, was a strawberry blonde and almost thirteen years old. Most teenage girls her age suffer from acute parental negativism, but by some act of God, or perhaps good parenting or just plain lucky genes, she was 100% positive. She loved her mom and respected her. Miracles do happen. Aliza had black hair and was a curious eleven year old who was always chattering away at full volume. Both had their mother's sky blue eyes.

It was a cold March evening and the forecasters were telling us that a big storm was on its way. They said we should be poised to receive what could be the last snowfall of the season. The air temperature was about ten degrees and making a quick calculation that meant it was twelve degrees below zero on the Celsius scale. We were bundled in heavy coats and were fairly comfortable despite the frigid wind. The only real problem was my ears. They felt like painful icicles hanging from the sides of my head because my *yeshiva bocher* outfit, black suit and Fedora hat, did not include ear protection. I was sure that if anyone, or anything, touched one of my ears it would snap right off, plummet to the ground, and shatter into a cloud of a thousand frozen particles.

I suffered in silence.

That's what macho men did. You toughed it out and if someone asked, you said, 'I'm fine.' In addition, you would never ever admit that you got your sorry self into the dilemma because you were too vain to wear ear muffs.

I looked at Dafna and could not believe that when I had first met her, I thought she was fourteen years old.

I was way off.

But in my defense I must say that anyone could have made the same mistake, because last year when she opened her door in Lansing she looked like a typical teenager. Her blond hair was in a ponytail — it was a wig — but I did not know that — and she was wearing a faded oversized Michigan State University sweatshirt and scuffed sneakers.

She fooled me completely.

But then I was introduced to her daughters and it became abundantly clear, even to a dimwit like me, that mommy was no teenager.

Down the block I heard the girls laughing and speaking loudly with Mrs. Kalin. They were hardly aware that we had fallen behind.

For the moment, we had a bit of privacy.

It felt good to be walking at Dafna's side. We were not holding hands or touching in any way — that would not be appropriate for an Orthodox couple who are not married — but I could feel the magnetic pull across the few inches that separated us.

Wonderful feeling.

Dafna is not tall — in her stocking feet she is a head shorter than my six feet — and quite thin — not skin and bones skinny — more like someone who exercises a lot or has a high metabolism, like a hyper-energetic teenager. I told you, I was fooled. But, when she is dressed in her *Shabbos* clothes, as she is tonight, there is no mistaking that she is all woman. The dark blue long-sleeved dress was a knockout. Definitely not fourteen years old.

I had not been able to take my eyes off of her all evening.

I was one lucky guy.

We walked, we talked — it was just plain nice.

Using your feet to perambulate from one place to another — commonly known as walking — may not seem special for anyone who lives in a major city, but walking has become a no-no in suburban America. In the burbs, legs are to be used for exercise purposes only — jogging, running, or power walking — so, on cold March nights, you were expected to drive everywhere. Many of the streets of our fair city do not even have sidewalks. Anyone walking in Southfield would immediately arouse the suspicion of the police or the local neighborhood vigilantes. The only exceptions to the 'no-walking' rule are the *frumies* on the Sabbath. For unless there was a dire emergency, Orthodox Jews do not use any sort of vehicular conveyance on *Shabbos*.

They walked everywhere.

If a place was too far away to reach by walking — they just do not go there on *Shabbos*.

Dafna craned her neck up to speak, her words coming out in white puffs as the warm vapor of her breath hit the freezing air, "Did you tell Rabbi Kalmonowitz that I am willing to support you if you want to stay in the *yeshiva*?"

"Yes, I did. I told him about your offer just after he gave us a big *mazel tov*."

"The *rebbetzin* wanted to know why we did not make the decision sooner."

"That's exactly what he said. And they're right. We both knew quite a while ago. We could be married already ... and tonight is Friday night," I said in a conspiratorial tone.

"There you go, talking dirty again," she said jokingly. We were referring to the Jewish custom of Friday nights being the evening when married Orthodox couples tried to be intimate. "You will just have to wait out the nine weeks until the wedding."

Two years earlier it would have been inconceivable that I could be in a celibate relationship with a gorgeous woman with whom I shared a mutual attraction. I was raised in a super permissive world. Our motto was always, 'If it feels good — and it does not harm anyone — do it.'

But that is not the way of Orthodox Judaism.

For me to revert to such a semi-monastic lifestyle was tantamount to a Bengal tiger switching to a vegan diet and surviving on berries and shoots. So you may ask, how did a firm believer — and practitioner — of the 'casual sex' credo, come to accept this 'no-touch' type of relationship?

I changed.

During the time I studied in the *yeshiva,* I observed Orthodox Jewish families. I noticed that in their homes there was a lasting mutual respect and admiration between husband, wife and even the offspring. Like most families, they did not exist in perfect harmony. Life is not like that. Sometimes joy was the rule and sometimes there was tension in the air. But no matter what, they were glad to be together. It was beautiful. It was happiness.

So I switched my philosophy of life. It was difficult —
but I did it.

Why?

Because, I wanted a piece of that happiness.

With a false bravado I responded, "I am waiting. I am
suffering, but I am waiting."

"Poor boy," said Dafna pouting her lower lip. "So next
week you start work. Do you have any prospects or cases
lined up?"

"I was planning to call all the companies and lawyers
that used to send me cases, to see if they had any work
for me, but *Rebbi* surprised me. He wants to hire me to
look into the disappearance of Rabbi Slater."

"He does?' exclaimed Dafna. "That's terrific. When do
we start?"

Whoa!

What did she just say?

No way was I going to allow her to pull that *shtick*
again. Last year she conned me into letting her help with
Rabbi Klein's murder. She is not going to do that again.

"What's this 'we' business? You have your work and I
have mine. I'm going to be doing the investigating on my
own. You stick with your computer stuff."

"But you know how mysteries interest me," she said
pleadingly. "You have to admit I was helpful in Lansing."

Of course she was. There was no way I could have
solved the case without her computer savvy. But it had
almost gotten her killed — four times — and I was not
going to let her get involved in one of my cases again.
"I'm sorry, but I can't let you be part of this investigation.
I will be doing it on my own."

She assumed a supplicant's pose pressing her palms
together and saying mournfully, "Please?"

"I will not budge on this. You are not helping with this
case," I said firmly.

Dafna cocked her head to one side and said slowly and
firmly, "Are you sure about this?"

I responded in kind, "Absolutely."

"Fine," she said curtly and then began walking more quickly towards her mother. Her heels clicking loudly against the pavement as she strode away from me.

Uh oh.

I know Dafna. When she says 'fine' in that tone of voice, it means that things were most definitely not fine. It certainly would not be fine for me. What was she planning? I caught up with her and asked as we walked, "Dafna, what are you going to do?"

"Me? Nothing," she said in mock innocence.

"Come clean," I insisted.

She stopped and turned to me, "You want to work on this case all by yourself and not share with your fiancée ... well that is just fine. But I think you will need my help."

"Just because you used your computer stuff to help solve the case last year does not mean that I will need you now. Being a detective is ninety percent footwork. Interviews, surveillance, evidence accumulation, documentation. That's how most cases are solved."

"Maybe that's the way it was in the past," she replied. "But the odds are that in this new computer-based world, you are going to need the help of some computer nerd. You and I both know that there is no better computer nerd than yours truly. So you just go ahead on your own ... but if and when you need my help ... you get it only if you make me your partner in the case."

She was absolutely correct, she was the best. Possibly the best in the whole country. All the local police forces, state police and even the FBI, used her services. She had security clearances up the whazoo.

But all that was irrelevant.

I had to keep her safe.

"I won't need your help so you can just forget about it. I'm sorry I even told you."

"Suit yourself. But now you know my condition for helping you."

"Case closed," I said firmly.

"No, the case is just getting started. But, even if I don't get involved, you have to do everything you can to help poor *Rebbetzin* Slater. She must be going out of her mind."

"Of course I will do everything I can," I said. "I would not do anything less."

"You had me fooled. After all, you turned down my assistance," she said with a shrug of her shoulders. "But that's only temporary. You'll come around."

With that, Dafna marched up her driveway, went into her house and shut the front door behind her. That left me — her now official fiancé — standing alone on the sidewalk.

I was in trouble.

Deep trouble.

I stood staring at Dafna's closed front door trying to decide what to do.

She had just drawn a line in the sand and was daring me to cross it.

This was going to be a problem for me.

Almost five years ago — it was my last year on the force — I sustained a gunshot wound. I spent quite a few months in rehab and one of the shrinks diagnosed me as being 'confrontational' — meaning if someone makes me angry, I react immediately and directly. Not a bad trait for a cop who had to routinely deal with the scum of the earth.

But this was Dafna.

A whole different story.

So, what were my choices? I could cross the line and grovel. Thus, forever relinquishing all authority for making decisions in our future family and forfeiting my position as 'the man' of the house. Or, I could cross the line and stand my ground, but I would be in the dog house for who knew how long.

I was flummoxed and angry. I knew that massive amounts of adrenaline and testosterone were coursing through my veins, inundating my brain, and clouding my judgment. It was a bad idea to make decisions in my overwrought state.

Wrong or right I needed to do something.

I took the easy option.

There would be no decisions now.

I began trudging back to my own condo, four blocks away.

I needed to cool down.

The problem with my fiancée would have to be solved after *Shabbos*.

As I walked I reflected on the fact that I truly loved Dafna and I was sure that the feeling was mutual. This was just a small hurdle on the way to the altar. It will pass.

I hoped.

How do I get her to talk to me again?

I had a problem.

3

Barbecue

SUNDAY AFTERNOON, I was still in trouble.

I arrived at this conclusion without having to rely on any of my superb deductive skills.

It was obvious.

We had just begun the Jewish month of *Adar*, and the holiday of *Purim* was four days away. Dafna was baking — big time — and her kitchen looked like a war zone. But she had known that this was going to happen and had organized things accordingly. She planned a barbecue at her house for this afternoon. At her house but not in her kitchen. She made me responsible for everything — I was to bring all the meat, salads, sides, and trimmings — and do all the cooking on the outdoor grill. Under no circumstances was I to enter her kitchen. Absolutely no trespass. The meal would be prepared and consumed in the back yard — as far as possible from her kitchen — even if everyone had to bundle up in winter parkas and sit in the rain under umbrellas.

So, here I am fixing dinner in Dafna's backyard and she is still not talking to me.

I can see her and Shaindel through the big kitchen window as they move around in the fog of flour created by the Lachler bake-a-thon. There were piles of cakes, cupcakes, strudel, cookies, and brownies everywhere.

Ten different flavors, ten different icings. All this to fulfill the Purim requirement of *mishloach manose*. Or as they say in Southfield — *shlach manose*.

The official requirement for this *mitzvah* was to give any two types of prepared foods to any two friends. So with two Oreo cookies and two Hershey bars, you were done. That is what I was going to do. But no woman in the community would do that. They each gave dozens of elaborate *shlach manose*.

Dafna was no exception, so even though she was extremely busy with her computer business, she would never take the shortcut of using purchased pastries. That was the reason that there were baked items on cooling racks all over the kitchen and raw dough on baking sheets or batter in cake forms spread out on the dining room table.

And why we were banished to the backyard.

It was quite chilly and the skies were cloudy but there was no precipitation as yet. The steaks, hamburgers, and hot dogs were sizzling over the bright red charcoal and just about ready.

Dafna's daughters were setting the picnic table with all the salads, condiments, drinks, plastic cutlery and plates that I had brought over. They laughed and spoke exuberantly as they worked. Normally I cannot cook to save myself but for some reason barbecuing is the exception and is something I can do. It is probably an expression of some primitive male trait handed down from the caveman. Since I was the designated grill master, I made my official announcement declaring the meat to be officially ready. Medium rare on the steaks, well done on the hamburgers. I transferred all the meat to the serving platters and invited everyone to come to the table.

Mrs. Kalin took a break in her baking and was now in the backyard. She called back into the kitchen for Dafna to join us and my fiancée came through the back door beating at her apron and creating a cloud of flour. Without looking in my direction she took a seat as far away from me as she could. She was still only an arm's length away but she behaved as if it were a mile.

This was ridiculous.

I deliberately asked Dafna, "Would you like a piece of rib steak or a burger?"

No reaction. She treated me like I was just a distracting breeze. I was of no significance.

I turned to Shaindel, "Would you ask your daughter if she would like a steak or a burger."

Even though Aliza and Susie were still quite young, they knew what was going on and began to giggle. Mrs. Kalin also thought this was all a hoot. With a sly smile she asked Dafna, "Steak or a burger?"

"Who prepared the food?" Dafna inquired of her mother.

Of all the nerve. Here I am sitting three feet away and she was the one that asked me to organize this whole shebang.

Shaindel said immediately, "I'm fairly certain that all this meat was grilled up by your *chassan*. He is sitting right over here. You can ask him yourself."

Dafna answered, "No need. He probably did everything all on his own, without asking for help from anyone. But you know how that usually turns out. I think I'll just have salad. Poor fellow. That's just the way he is. He can't help himself."

I was definitely in big trouble.

4

Missing Person

MONDAY MORNING after prayers I called the Lachler household to see if I was out of the doghouse, but there was no change. Dafna was not taking my calls.

The only ray of sunshine was that as of this morning I was officially back in the investigation business.

I decided my first priority was to speak with *Rebbetzin* Slater. After all, if the police were of the opinion that the rabbi left voluntarily, I had to make my own assessment of her part in his disappearance. But so far, I was not having much success in arranging a meeting. I explained to *Rebbetzin* Slater that Rabbi Kalmonowitz had asked me to look into the case, but for every suggestion I had for us to meet, she came up with an excuse. She was busy just then. Her schedule was getting full. She had a doctor's appointment. It was not convenient.

Obviously, the woman did not want to speak with me.

In my adult life there have been a number of ladies that have made a conscious decision to cut off all communication with me, but usually they got to know me first. Dafna was a prime example.

I told the *rebbetzin* I would call again.

Strange and suspicious.

Since the interview with *Rebbetzin* Slater was not on my immediate agenda, I decided that my next move would be to somehow convince the police to share whatever information they had collected concerning the rabbi's disappearance.

Not an easy task.

As a general rule police officers considered private investigators to be the equal of carrion eaters in the wild. PIs did not hunt on their own, took the best parts and left the mess for someone else to clean up. The only PIs who got a bit of help were the ex-cops who still had connections, but that too was limited. My private investigator license and carry permit were current, but it was four years since I was a detective on the Detroit police force. I had closed my investigation company almost two years ago when I went to study in the *yeshiva*, so that left me with few viable contacts in the local constabulary.

I figured that the jurisdiction of Rabbi Slater's case would be a mess. His residence was in Southfield and the car had been found abandoned on one of the local streets. The Oakland County Sheriff's Department were also involved since this all happened in their county, but they were probably not conducting any kind of active investigation. The state police also got into this hodgepodge, because the little used road where the car had been found was in fact officially part of an entrance ramp for the I-696 freeway and thus under their jurisdiction. In addition they were always consulted in missing persons cases.

I knew that none of them would be overeager to share information with an outside investigator. To them, I was butting in where I did not belong.

Rabbi Slater's wife must have filed the initial police report with the Southfield police. Therefore they would be the ones to instigate the missing person investigation. I decided I would start with them.

Eventually I would have to speak with all the other law enforcement agencies, but I would take one step at a time.

Throughout my career on the Detroit force and in my private work as an investigator I had never worked true missing persons cases so I was a bit ignorant about the nuts and bolts or the etiquette of a formal MP investigation. I figured that it could not be much different from my PI work of tracking down debtors that were hiding from the people to whom they owed money. The big difference was that with these voluntary skips we knew the missing person was hiding but still alive. With a true missing person, anything was possible. From my experience I learned that if a person did not want to be found, and planned the disappearance properly, that person could literally vanish off the face of the earth. The only way to find a MP that wanted to stay hidden was if the missing individual made a mistake. Like using a credit card. Or contacting family or friends. Or receiving a traffic violation. Or getting admitted to a hospital.

There were two more reasons for my decision to start with the Southfield police. It was over a month since Rabbi Slater had disappeared and their MP division had already made its initial assessment of the case. Rabbi Kalmonowitz told me that they had reached a decision that the disappearance was voluntary and that Rabbi Slater was not truly an MP. So, although the case was not officially closed, it was not really an ongoing investigation and was on the back burner of their unit. In addition, many years ago the present Chief of Police in Southfield had been a partner with my old boss from the Detroit Detectives Division, Lt. Mike Gleason. I contacted Mike and he said he would make a few calls to the various police departments and smooth the way for me.

Most likely, that was why they even agreed to talk to me.

Southfield police headquarters was located adjacent to the city administration building, court house, and library in a two-story red brick and glass building on Evergreen between Ten and Eleven Mile Road. I climbed the wide concrete stairs to enter the dark lobby of the station. I told the duty officer in his bullet-proof glass reception booth that I had an appointment with Detective Sergeant Alice Chandler. He made a call and then told me that she would be right down. The duty officer gave me a visitor's pass on a lanyard and warned me that it had to be worn at all times while in the station. Sergeant Chandler came to the front desk and personally escorted me up the stairs to the second floor Crimes Against Persons Unit.

I pride myself in being able to make a quick read of most of the people I meet. It is a knack I have. While I was recuperating from my service injury, one of the shrinks told me that I probably analyzed body language, tone of voice, and other subliminal signs to make this assessment. That could be the way I did it — I have no idea if he was correct. This talent had been extremely beneficial when I was a detective. It helped me identify people that were lying and those that were telling the truth. It also allowed me to make a snap decision as to which of the people I encountered would best be handled by taking the friendly route and those that needed threats and pressure to come around. And finally — and most important — it let me know which people I could rely on in a crunch and warn me about the ones that required that I watch my back. It was a very useful tool and it rarely let me down.

But, Sergeant Chandler confused me.

The face did not jibe with the walk. It just was not appropriate.

Her face — she was a pretty woman with big gray eyes. There were no major or minor wrinkles showing and I guessed her age as early thirties. She was about

five feet seven inches tall in black loafers and carried
around 130 pounds. She wore a long sleeved flouncy
beige blouse and tailored black pants. Even though her
outfit was not skin tight, I could tell that she was not
runway model skinny nor was she pin-up babe
voluptuous. The best term would be solid. Her hair was
muddy blonde, cut fairly short and styled with most of
the hair parted to the right side of her head. At first, it
looked like she was not wearing any cosmetics but that
was deceiving. When I studied her face more closely I
saw that her makeup had been applied expertly. I was
pretty sure that her police salary did not allow for a
private cosmetician, so I had to assume she did all her
own makeup and hair styling. Most mornings, when I
was on the job, I barely had enough time to shave and
splash water in some intimate places. This lady had to be
spending at least fifteen or twenty extra minutes every
morning to get her glamour look.

So was she vain? A light weight?

I had no idea.

Then there was the walk.

The walk — it was the walk of an athlete. Someone
with a toned body. Shoulders back and feet ever so
slightly splayed outwards, she moved with a low volume
swagger. Maybe a professional dancer, gymnast, or
martial arts person. The walk exuded confidence. It was
a statement — 'I am the queen of the roost' and if need
be, 'I can kick your *tuchis* to prove it.' Given her career
choice, martial arts were probably her specialty. I had
seen many women just like her at the *dojo*.

So was she a lightweight coquette or a heavy weight
conqueror?

She climbed the stairs effortlessly and I followed
behind. I can now attest that nothing on Sergeant
Chandler jiggled. Like I said — solid. I would not be
surprised if she had a better six-pack than I did. It was

probably better than what I had when I was in my prime as a Marine.

The wedding ring on her left hand told me nothing, because nowadays it did not mean that she was married to a man.

I was keenly aware that a *yeshiva bocher* — certainly one who was about to be married — was not supposed to go around making such critical judgments of female anatomy, but since I was back being a private investigator, I had no choice but to investigate.

Purely for professional reasons.

The detectives division of the Crimes Against Persons Unit turned out to be just a large room with five desks — only one was occupied. "Welcome to the Missing Persons Bureau of the Southfield police," she said with a sweep of her arm, as she took her seat behind one of the desks.

I took a chair beside the desk and said, "Thank you for seeing me."

She leaned back in her chair, laced her fingers together and rested them on her abdomen as she asked, "So who the hell are you?"

I was confused.

Not more than an hour ago we had spoken on the phone and she knew I had just given my name to the duty officer in the lobby. *Did she suffer from short-term memory loss?*

"I'm Sy Lincoln."

"I know your name and I know you are a private investigator," she said condescendingly. "I just don't know who *you* are. I did not expect —," she waved her hand up and down indicating my *yeshiva bocher* outfit.

Oh yeah. The unofficial uniform of all *yeshiva bocherim* around the world. Black suit, black shoes, black tie, black Fedora hat. Sort of a cross between *Men in Black* and the *Blues Brothers,* but without the sunglasses. Those in the know will spot the white fringes of my little prayer shawl hanging from my belt. A *yeshiva bocher* is easily recognizable in any crowd.

The *yeshiva* had no strict rule as to how anyone was supposed to dress. However during my time in the institution I wanted to fit in and so I had adopted the *yeshiva bocher* 'uniform.' I suddenly realized that now that I was back doing investigative work, the 'Blues Brothers' outfit was not going to be very inconspicuous and would definitely not be appropriate for surveillance work. That is why detectives did not wear uniforms. But for now, I felt more comfortable in my *yeshiva* clothes, so I was unsure what to do.

I would have to speak with *Rebbi* about that.

One step at a time.

"Well, yeah, my outfit... I am ... I was studying at the *yeshiva*."

"I'm a detective ... I figured that part out. What I don't understand is why a *yeshiva* student was studying my behind so intently as we climbed the stairs or why my Chief called me in this morning and said I was to roll out the red carpet for you. He said I was to treat you like the Governor. Anything you wanted. The last time he sent up warning flags like that, we were investigating the break-in at the home of the daughter of the state Attorney General. He has never been this cooperative with a private investigator."

"As far as studying your behind ... I want to apologize ... I was ..."

"Yeah, I know. You are an investigator. Just doing your job. What about the red carpet treatment?"

"He and my old boss, Mike Gleason, used to be partners on the Detroit PD."

"Oh, I get it now," she said with a nod of her head. "That explains things. The chief has mentioned Lieutenant Gleason. So you were a detective before going private. The old boys club at its best."

"It can't hurt."

"So, what do you need?" she asked with a wave of her palms.

What I needed was for Sergeant Chandler to cooperate fully. The problem was that all cops — myself included — were power and control freaks. It is the old, *'Hey, I am the police. Ergo, I have power over you.'* They could push around civilians and anyone with a lower rank. For any cop, the lowest persona on the law enforcement pecking order was the private investigator. Carrion eaters — remember. Therefore, even though her boss told her to cooperate, she could still make my life miserable. I decided I would use the 'super-confident' ploy. I would make her think that I handle missing persons cases all the time and *as usual*, I expected her to give me all the material I needed.

Full of false confidence, I said, "I was asked to look into Rabbi Slater's disappearance. I don't want to get in your way. So, if you could just give me the missing person file and the information you collected in your investigation, I will be out of your hair."

"You want the *missing person file*," she repeated seriously.

"Yes, I do."

The sergeant did not speak for almost a full minute and just sat there smiling at me.

Something was not right.

I must have made some sort of mistake. But what could it be?

How did I know that I made a faux pas?

Easy.

All the police forces of the world do pretty much the same thing. They are the ones who are given the responsibility of dealing with the people that have difficulty with the 'thou shalt not' rules that society imposes. Most of the day they encounter folks who have problems with 'thou shalt not litter' or 'thou shalt not park here' and stuff like that. But occasionally they must deal with violent people that have trouble with 'thou shalt not murder' and 'thou shalt not maim.' Since you could never know when you might encounter one of the murderers or maimers, cops are always wary. They are on guard whenever they are in contact with the public. If a cop got friendly with the wrong guy at the wrong time, he could get dead real quick.

Because of this constant wariness and tension, almost all cops have a compensatory macabre sense of humor. They joke around, *kibitz* and make sarcastic comments amongst themselves. However, when asked to function in an official capacity they will always appear quite somber. Cops will smile if it is appropriate for the situation but this will vary with the police force. City cops smile less than suburban cops. Probably because there is less to smile about. Urban police are swamped with gangs, drug trafficking, family disputes, vice, etc. So that makes them a little short on the manpower that might be available to devote time to the PR work necessary for improving the rapport between police and the city's inhabitants.

In other words, being friendly.

In the suburbs, the population expected more of their police and they usually got it.

Southfield cops were different.

For lack of a better definition, let us just say they were *uber*-professional.

The Southfield police followed regulations. They did everything by the book. Their blue uniforms were always immaculate. They never approached dangerous situations without appropriate backup. They responded respectfully and appropriately to all who addressed them and they did a damn fine job of keeping the Detroit crime ambience from creeping into their city.

But there was one thing that the Southfield police did not do.

In all contact with the citizens or visitors to the community — they did not smile.

Whatever the situation — investigating a crime or giving a ticket — the corners of their mouths never curved upwards. Even in the most ludicrous of situations — and citizens can get into some really crazy problems — they never showed signs of mirth. They were always 'professionals.' Most probably when the captain ended his morning briefing he would tell his squad, "And when you are out there ... remember ... do not smile."

So why was Sergeant Alice Chandler sitting there looking like the proverbial Cheshire Cat from Alice in Wonderland?

She leaned forward, placed her elbows on the desk, interlaced her fingers and asked, "When did you go to the Academy?"

What did that have to do with anything?

"About eighteen years ago," I said truthfully.

"That explains it," she said, still smiling.

"Explains what?"

"I'm making an educated guess that you have never worked missing persons."

I could see that my 'over-confident' tactic has not been a resounding success.

"No, I did not," I answered defeatedly.

"When you went to the police academy the NCIC manual did not even exist," she said. "My guess is that right now you don't know your elbow from a hole in the ground when it comes to what we do here. So ... at the behest of my chief ... I am going to give you the Cook's Tour."

"Thank you," I said in humble appreciation.

She began her lecture, "Someone goes missing in Southfield it gets reported to the Duty Officer who gathers the basic 'who, what, and where' and he passes it along to me or to Sergeant Langley. They sent us to the NCIC course for missing persons, so that here in

Southfield, the two of us are the MP contacts for Oakland County, the State, and the FBI."

"What exactly is the role of the NCIC in all this?" I asked out of ignorance.

Almost mockingly she said, "I'm sure you know that the NCIC is the National Crime Information Center, a division of the Criminal Justice Information Services of the FBI and is located in Clarksburg, West Virginia. That's where all the fingerprints are kept and ... the National Missing Persons database."

I knew about the NCIC, but did not know their connection with missing persons. "Are they involved in this case?"

"Yes and no," she said. "If the person who disappeared is classified as an MP, we fill out all the forms ... and there are a ton of those ... and it all gets shipped to the state police in Lansing and the National MP database at the FBI ... the NCIC."

"What do you mean *if* they are classified as an MP? If someone disappears, doesn't that automatically make that person an MP?" I asked.

"It is not against the law for a person to disappear, if that someone does so voluntarily and ... very importantly ... if there is no danger that he or she will harm themselves or others, by their disappearance."

"So, if someone disappears, and the family is greatly concerned, but there is no chance of any harm, you don't look for them?"

"Not only don't we look for them, we would be breaking the law if we did. People are entitled to their privacy."

"So, you do nothing?" I asked incredulously.

"I wouldn't say we do nothing. We investigate. First we make a distinct division between adults and minors. Minors are subdivided into kids ... up to age thirteen ... and adolescents ... up to age eighteen. Almost all missing minors are classified as MPs. We arbitrarily say that all kids are in danger from their surroundings. We also send out an AMBER Alert."

"I've heard of that, but how does the system work?" I asked in ignorance.

"It's a voluntary cooperation between all the police agencies and the media, to let people know a particular child is missing. It is an acronym for ... America's Missing: Broadcast Emergency Response."

"Is it effective?"

She looked around her and said in a low voice, "Between you me and the lamppost ... it works if the child was taken by an angry parent or a family member. You know, a family squabble. But if a kid is snatched by a stranger ... meaning someone who is out to do the child harm ... then no. The kids still stay missing or worse. We call the alert because when a kid goes missing we don't know who took the child and it makes the parents think we are doing something."

"And with adults?"

"With adults we check to be certain there was no crime involved with the disappearance. Abductions, property damage, threats. Then we look for any indication of possible bodily harm. Self-inflicted or from any other source. We check for things like notes left by the person signaling suicidal tendencies or possible medical conditions that might cloud a person's judgment or need treatment. These include dialysis, mental illness, cancer treatment, insulin ... medical conditions. Then we look for external threats to the person who disappeared."

"Like heavy debts, family problems ... stuff like that?" I ventured.

"Yeah, just like that," she said, with a nod of her head. "Once we've got the person placed in an appropriate niche, we re-interview the family member who filed the complaint and get personal information that might help tell us what was going on with the person that disappeared.   Credit   card   and   bank   accounts, employment status. All this gets into the file."

"And where is that kept?"

"At first, in our department, but it does not stop there. After the initial investigation we try to determine if the person who disappeared qualifies as an MP. If it is obvious that the person made a voluntary exit from society and they're in no danger, we put the file on hold. If it is obvious that it is an MP case, we proceed according to the NCIC protocol. If we are undecided, we continue the investigation until we come to a decision."

"What do you do if it is an MP?"

"Protocol is to gather pictures, finger prints, medical and dental records, x-rays, determine if there were any body accoutrements ... if these things have not been done already."

"What is a body accoutrement?" I asked in ignorance.

"You know ... body art."

I still had no idea. "Define body art?"

"Tats and piercings," she said in explanation.

"Oh, I see," finally understanding.

"They can be very helpful in identification. And of course we obtain DNA samples. Everything gets sent to the state and the FBI, but the DNA stays right here. We don't process it. Too expensive. But, it is available if and when it might be necessary."

"Like with an unidentified dead body," I ventured.

"You got it. You must be one hot shot detective. I bet they called you Sherlock when you were on the force," she said sarcastically.

"I was the number one hot shot in the division."

"I can tell," she said, nodding her head.

"What exactly would convince you that a person took off voluntarily?"

"A note saying, 'I'm leaving. Don't try to follow me.' Usually works for us."

"I see what you mean."

"Here in Southfield, we have a small detectives division and handling missing persons is not my only assignment. So even if a person is not officially declared an MP, and if there is no sign of the person after one month, copies of all the information we collected, are passed on to the state and federal MP divisions and everyone hopes for the best. Any case we get is never officially closed until the person is found, but many became cold cases and the only activity in the file is the automatic computer scans that look for traces of that missing individual. If they surface anywhere in the USA ... hospitalization, death, criminal charges, credit card activity ... the name gets flagged, it rings a bell and everyone gets a heads up. Us, the state, and the Feds."

"So what is the status of Rabbi Slater's disappearance?" I asked.

Sergeant Chandler flipped open the tan folder on her desk and read from a computer print-out, "Forty-three-year-old white male. Married ... wife's name is Leah ... with five kids and a sixth on the way. Five feet nine or ten, 180 pounds, brown eyes and brown hair and full beard with some graying. Circumcised. Had a femur fracture a few years ago so he has a scar on his left thigh and a steel rod on x-ray. No other surgeries or scars. No body accoutrements. Disappeared on February 18 of this year ... that would be thirty five days ago ... He was dressed in the regulation black suit, tie and hat, white shirt and was supposed to be on his way home from a late study session at the *yeshiva*."

"There is no regulation that says he had to wear a black suit," I said, correcting her.

"I know that," she said admonishingly. "He called his wife at 22:35 but never made it home. At 04:22, the next morning a Southfield patrol unit found his abandoned car on Jefferson Street near Lincoln, which was on his normal route back to his house. The car was unlocked with the keys in the ignition. His wallet and cell phone were on the front seat. The phone and wallet showed a few partial prints from the rabbi and some prints from the patrol officer that found them and the property master at the station."

"So the items were not bagged at the scene."

"Correct," she said with a nod. "There was no reason to do it."

"I see your point ... no evidence of a crime."

"No cash in the wallet but all the credit cards were still there."

"Perhaps, there was a robbery. The cash was gone," I ventured.

"Possible, but the wife said he never had more than thirty or forty bucks on him and as you well know, cash has been known to disappear on the way to or from the property room."

"Yeah, I know." An embarrassment to any police force.

"There was also a black fedora hat, apparently his, on the seat. There were no signs of violence. He has not used his bank and credit card accounts since the disappearance. No one has reported seeing him. None of the cab companies or limousine services had any pickups in the area. The nearest bus stop is almost a mile away and the bus drivers do not remember any white males, with a beard or without."

"Was anything found near where the car was discovered?"

"Our patrol officer ... Officer Cummings ... did a standard search while he waited for the tow truck, and I went back there two days later and searched the area myself. Nothing was found," she said.

"It has been over a month," I said logically. "So this is a cold case."

"You got it. We have passed all this on to the state police and the FBI."

"I heard you have decided that this is a voluntary disappearance. How did you come to that conclusion?"

"Everything is patterns nowadays. The shrinks and FBI analyzed thousands of cases and they tell us there are patterns in the behavior of missing persons that can give us clues. Basically, leaving all his identifiable belongings ... the phone and credit cards ... are the biggies. Plus he left his hat. That supposedly is also a big thing in ... his ... your religion." She looked at my outfit and said quickly. "No offense meant."

"None taken."

"All he had to do was shave off his beard, get a change of clothes and he would have been virtually unrecognizable. He could go wherever he liked. Everyone we spoke to insists he had no psychiatric or medical problems. To us, it looks like a voluntary skip."

"But he had just spoken with his wife and said he was on his way home," I argued. "He also had plans for the next day at the *yeshiva* academy. He never ever mentioned that he was unhappy with anything or that he needed a change in his life. To me, that does not sound like he was planning to leave suddenly."

"Sorry to disagree," she said shaking her head. "Actually, it does. That's exactly the way voluntary skips do it. They have everyone convinced that everything is fine, so that no one will try to stop them."

5

Mary Lou

I WANTED to speak with Officer Cummings, but he was still out on patrol and not due back at the station for a few hours. Waiting was not an option because I had another appointment on the other side of town. I had to bicycle over to the Lincoln Office Building at Greenfield and Lincoln — AKA 10 ½ Mile Road. My re-opened investigation business needed office space and they had an appropriate vacancy.

Why was I bicycling?

Simple.

About ten months back, during the murder investigation in Lansing, my beloved two-year-old SUV was blown to smithereens. Once I got back into my study routine at the *yeshiva,* I discovered that I could get by with just my bike and for the rare occasion that I needed wheels, I borrowed, Ubered, or rented. Now that I was going back to work, I would obviously need some sort of motorized conveyance. But, for now I only had two-wheeled transportation.

Peddling along with the ambient temperature hovering in the low teens is not the most pleasant of experiences. I was wearing a heavy parka, had a woolen cap pulled down over my ears and wore well insulated mittens. My Fedora hat was stored in special carrier on the back fender. But the cold wind still buffeted my face. My eyes were running and I had lost sensation in my nose. The Artic breeze also ran up my pants legs and chilled me to the core.

Duh, I think I need a car.

I chained my bike to the hydrant right in front of the office complex, switched my woolen cap for my black hat and entered the building.

Thank goodness — the lobby had a well functioning heating system and I could feel the warmth sinking into my bones.

A pleasure.

From across the hall I heard someone call out, "Sy, is that you?"

I would recognize that voice anywhere. It was hoarse and high pitched like a jet engine firing up. It was also loud and piercing and so was Mary Lou Evans.

A sight for sore eyes.

To say that I was happy to see her would be an understatement.

Mary Lou had been my secretary for the two years that Lincoln Investigations, Inc., had been up and running. Parting with her was probably the hardest thing I had to do when I closed my office. Besides being a terrific secretary, she was an absolute genius when it came to organization. She had run the whole place and me as well.

But that was not all.

Before she switched to office work, she had put in her twenty years on the Pontiac police force and then worked six more years as a PI. She only fully retired when she got an ultimatum from her husband. He was not happy that she was putting herself in danger and they did not need the income. It was her career or their marriage.

It was a no-brainer.

She picked the marriage.

However, her dad and three brothers had been cops, so police work was in her family's blood. It was tough for her to abandon the field of law and order entirely. She felt she had to use her expertise, so she went to work as a secretary and then administrator for one of the largest security firms in the state. That was where I met her and was very impressed. To this day I do not know how I lured her away from her former employer, but I am surely thankful that I did. Her uncanny ability to deal with the unavoidable police bureaucracy cut my work load tremendously. It was like having a second detective on my staff. Without her, I definitely would not have had the success that I had.

Mary Lou still kept her PI license and carry permit current. I am certain that if I looked in her bag I would find her 'Baby' — a 38 caliber Smith & Wesson snub nose 'Chief's Special' — she did not go anywhere without it.

She was sixty-two years old, but you would never have guessed it. I am privy to this fact only because I had seen her date of birth when I signed her social security forms. She had seven married kids and seventeen grandkids and was looking forward for that number to escalate. All of her family were devout Catholics, and she, more than anyone else, encouraged me to go to the *yeshiva* and find religion. On the few occasions that we discussed the merits of Judaism versus Christianity, she would say that the only difference between us was that the Jews were expecting the Messiah to come, while Christians were expecting him to come *again*. One of us was bound to be correct. When he (or she) does finally show up — someone is going to be in for a rude awakening.

She was short, just a tad over five feet, and the only thing in her appearance that could be considered 'normal' was the large silver crucifix that adorned her neck at all times. She had the metabolism of an active teenager and the unflagging energy of a whirling Dervish hyped up on speed. So, even though she ate everything, often and in large quantities, she was as skinny as a rail—almost anorexic looking.

I loved Mary Lou like a — mother — sister — friend — take your pick — and her stylistic quirkiness never bothered me. Some people, who did not know her, thought her a bit strange.

Her hair was always cut short, and today it was rather sedate — one half being bright orange and the other half purple — with sparkles. She had three or four massive earrings adorning each of her ears — because she thought they were cool.

Body accoutrements, if you will.

She was dressed in a long loose patchwork jacket made from a variety of different fabrics. There were bright swatches of pink, green, and yellow against a dominant background of fire engine red. Under the jacket, was a blue Tigers T-shirt over a washed denim skirt and her feet were shod in what looked like unlaced 'Desert Storm' army boots. Instead of a purse she had a burlap sack tied with heavy sisal rope hanging from her shoulder.

Rather sedate for Mary Lou.

Even though she was quite passionate about her self-expression in her manner of dress, she was a bit of a prude in just about everything else. Her moral compass unfailingly pointed true north. She did not drink excessively or use drugs and would harangue anyone that did. She married her husband, Andrew, forty-one years ago — she calls him Andy — and had no tolerance for philanderers or adulterers. I know Andy — there are no signs that he is either one. He had been a CFO for a large auto parts factory. Fifteen years earlier he took early retirement when the CEO of his company would not listen to his advice on how to save the firm from foundering. He cashed in all his stock options — before the company failed — and invested wisely. So besides being a genius in finance and a whiz at repairing just about anything mechanical or DIY, he was also extremely wealthy.

So here was Mary Lou yelling at me from across the lobby, "Sy, is that you?"

Her apparent confusion was understandable since she had never seen me in my *yeshiva bocher* outfit. For the last three years I had been a guest at her Christmas dinner, but whenever I went over, I ditched the Blues Brothers get-up and opted to wear jeans and a sports jacket.

"Mary Lou, good to see you."

Arms spread wide, she rushed towards me, "Come over here and give your *shiksa* a big hug."

I never actually got a chance to move in her direction, because before I could convince my legs to overcome inertia, she had already slammed into my body.

I said she was a whirling Dervish.

She stood on her tippy-toes and got her arms around my six foot frame.

Then she hugged me like there was no tomorrow.

Quite a sight for all the people waiting in the lobby.

One 'uniquely' dressed, skinny, Catholic, hippie grandmother and an over-aged *yeshiva bocher* locked in an embrace.

When I finally got out of her clutches I said, "Mary Lou, you did not have to come here yourself."

We spoke every couple of months, so I knew that at present she was not working in the security field. Her cousin's Birmingham based industrial baking company had needed her help, so she stepped in as the office manager. Not only had she reorganized the administration of the company, she also did the books, payroll, and much of the office work for the mid-sized company of 103 employees. In most firms they would need at least two or three people to do all the work that she did. But, for her it was a breeze and she liked the challenge.

I called her yesterday and I told her I was looking for someone to take on the duties of running the office of the re-opening Lincoln Investigations, Inc.

She promised to ask around.

When I mentioned that I needed office space in the Oak Park or Southfield area, it was amazing the way she was able to rattle off what was available in both cities and then gave me her recommendations. Then she added that I was absolutely useless when it came to haggling and I was bound to pick a bad location or overpay for whatever I chose. So she volunteered to set up the appointments and then come with me to look at office space.

As usual, Mary Lou was correct. I did not know how to haggle.

We rode the elevator to the seventh floor and entered the offices of Earnest Salzer, CPA. Four years ago, the accountant had leased one third of the seventh floor, hoping his firm would expand to fill the large quarters.

He had been overly optimistic.

Now he needed to rent out the three rooms at the end of his suite to help pay the bills.

"When I said you did not know anything about picking offices, I meant it. Leave this to me," insisted Mary Lou.

We met with Mr. Salzer. I told him my name and hands were shaken. Mary Lou began talking to the CPA and after that I never said a word.

Earnest showed us around, all the while directing all his comments to Mary Lou.

Naturally.

When she was in the room everyone did that.

After the tour, we went to the CPA's private office and Mary Lou got down to business — she was now calling him Ernie. She haggled over the rental price and what we would get for the rental money — use of the wash rooms, office equipment, utilities, etc. When she was satisfied, she announced, "We'll take it."

Good old Ernie went off to get the rental agreement and I turned to Mary Lou, "Is that wise? I have not seen the other properties. I might get a better deal elsewhere."

"I already looked at the other two properties. One is a dump and the other has a huge construction project going on right next door. This is much better. You have your own entrance to the offices. You get the use of all his major office equipment and that will save you a bundle. If Lincoln Investigations is successful ... and I am sure it will be ... you can get more office space in this same building. So that's convenient. Besides I like the ambience of the office. The staff is happy here."

When did she have time to see the other properties? Typical of Mary Lou.

"Why is the ambience of the office so important to you?" I asked.

"If I am going to work here, it is vital. I can't work with bad vibes."

What?

Did I hear her correctly?

"What about your job at the bakery?"

"My cousin knows I only took the job on a temporary basis to help him out. I got things pretty much organized there. And working for you was always such a hoot. Much better than ordering fruit toppings and arguing with the health inspectors. So do I have a job?" she asked coyly.

"Of course you do," I stammered. "You're hired. Tell me how much I have to pay you."

"Boss, you suck at negotiations," she chastised. "Never say that to an employee."

"You're right," I agreed.

"I'll let you know my salary demands. I don't come cheap," she insisted.

"I know that."

I also knew that she loved her work and would do it even if she did not earn a dime.

"OK, now that we have that settled, I will get to work. I'll call the phone company to have phones put in, order some stationary, and get the company account activated at the bank. I'll need a couple of computers, scanner, and printer. Got to have a sign on the door. Make keys and about a dozen more items. Anything you need?" she asked.

I thought for a moment, "I will need a car?"

"I'll get you a lease," she said.

"I usually buy my car," I answered.

"Better for taxes. You'll lease. If you fall in love with the car you can always buy it."

"Oh yes, I almost forgot," I added. "In eight weeks I will be getting married."

That stopped her.

"Are you kidding me? You 'almost forgot'," she said mimicking me. "The great Sy Lincoln is getting out of circulation? Who is the poor unfortunate woman?" she asked jokingly.

"Her name is Dafna Lachler. She lives in Southfield."

"*Daphne* I can say, but there is no way I can say Lahahler. How do you Jews make that sound?"

"It's like trying to clear your throat."

"I'll work on it," she said with a smile.

"Mary Lou, this is terrific."

"Have we got any business lined up?"

"I will be calling my old contacts that sent me clients, but meanwhile I've got one case. I'm investigating the disappearance of a rabbi from the *yeshiva*. But other things should start coming in."

"Until they do ... just to keep busy ... I am planning your wedding," she said with certainty.

Whoa.

What just happened?

There was no way I would allow Mary Lou to have anything to do with planning my nuptials. The problem was not whether she was capable of organizing a wedding — it was just that Mrs. Kalin would have a conniption fit.

"I don't think my future mother-in-law will go along with that."

"Flaming fiddle-sticks."

Mary Lou was just chock full of earthy expressions.

But cuss words were not in her vocabulary.

She once told me that they had been beaten out of her when she was nine years old by Sister Theresa at the Academy of the Sacred Heart School for Girls. To this day, Mary Lou is a firm believer in the 'spare the rod spoil the child' school of child discipline. She feels that if corporal punishment, in controlled and appropriate doses, had been administered to the spoiled kids of this generation, it would have saved quite a few young adults from languishing in our penal institutions. For her, the purpose of the stick was not to inflict pain. It was there to reinforce the feeling of disappointment expressed by the responsible adult, for some misdeed made by the child. Today's kids are just confused. The stick cleared things up quite nicely.

It also stopped her from using cuss words.

"Mrs. Kalin, my future mother-in-law, is a tough cookie," I insisted.

"That's fine ... because I am just an old softy."

"Yeah, right," I said sarcastically.

"I will work with her and just be there to help modify any ridiculous suggestions that might crop up," she said innocently. "God knows your own mother has not got a clue about planning weddings. I've done seventeen. My seven kids and ten nieces and nephews."

"My mother-in-law wants to be in charge," I insisted.

"Of course she does. Jewish, Christian, Buddhist, Muslim ... every mother-in-law wants to be in charge of their daughter's wedding."

"It's a second marriage. She has two daughters," I added.

"Wow ... you are going to be a dad. Then, it is even more important that I get started on the wedding. We want it to come off without a hitch."

I could not see Shaindel agreeing to collaborate in the planning of an ultra-Orthodox Jewish wedding with Mary Lou. "Mrs. Kalin wants to make all the major decisions. I don't think this is going to work."

"Sure it will," she said assuredly. "Whenever I feel that a radical change in plans is necessary, I get the other person to believe that the change was their idea. Never fails. Why do you think you and I got along so well?"

"This is going to be a religious Jewish wedding. I don't think you understand."

"What's to understand? You send out invitations. You hire a caterer ... a kosher one. You gather all the guests together with the bride and groom and an officiating rabbi. Have a party and then instead of saying, 'congratulations,' you say, 'mazel tov.' What don't I understand?"

"This is different."

"Then I will adapt. I always adapt," she said with confidence.

"Yes, you surely do," I agreed.

"Meanwhile, I've got to get back to the baking company and start to pass the reins to the other people in the office. I'll be here off and on for the next two weeks and then full time after that. I still have my old Rolodex and the Access files from two years ago, so we are all set. Tell your future mother-in-law I will give her a call."

I envisioned the cataclysmic encounter of Shaindel with Mary Lou and I decided to be firm.

I would be as immovable as the Rock of Gibraltar.

"I absolutely forbid you to call Mrs. Kalin," I said sternly.

"Tell her I will call after supper this evening."

A rather large pebble has just fallen into the Mediterranean Sea.

"Are you listening to me?" I demanded, trying to get her to see reason.

"Certainly, you want me to set up the office and get you a car. Text me your mother-in-law's number. Anything else?"

It was no use.

"Mary Lou ... thanks ... give my best to Andy. Tell him he better treat you right or I am going to steal you away."

"I tell him that all the time. Just don't let *Daphne* know about us. Tell your future mother-in-law ... maybe around eight o'clock."

6

Partner

ON THE WAY out of the office building I called the
Southfield station and they told me that Officer Cummings
could see me in about twenty minutes. I once again
bundled up in my warm coat and stowed my hat in the
rear bumper carrier. I climbed onto my bike and
furiously pumped my way back to the Southfield Police
station. I was not used to doing so much pedaling on one
day, so in addition to the rather unpleasant hypothermia,
my behind was getting a bit sore. When I got off the bike,
I could feel the strain in my glutei and I walked with a
bow-legged limp. It was becoming obvious that I needed
wheels powered by a combustion engine.

Officer Cummings was just signing out and would be
with me shortly. That gave me time to review the short
printout of the case file that Chandler had given me. The
rabbi's abandoned car was found on the west side of
Jefferson Street, 0.3 miles from its intersection with
Lincoln. The keys were in the ignition and his phone, hat,
and wallet were on the seat. There is no overnight
parking on most of Southfield's streets, so the car was
towed to Able's Towing yard, and was released to the
family after they paid the impound charges.

Officer Cummings was a uniformed policeman of my height and build but around ten years younger. He was now off-duty but courteously took the time to tell me whatever he could about finding Rabbi Slater's car. My *yeshiva bocher* outfit did not faze him in the least.

He was courteous — but no smile.

What did I tell you?

My snap assessment was that he was a competent policeman and someone I could rely on in a pinch. He was the kind of cop that did most things by the book, but had enough leeway and enough compassion to let things slide when he felt it was appropriate. Nothing truly illegal, but sometimes it was better not to make the arrest or write out the ticket. All in all, a good cop.

Cummings told me that he remembered the incident quite clearly and performed the standard search around the vehicle before the tow truck arrived. Nothing suspicious was found. I asked all the pertinent questions but got nothing new.

So far, a big fat zero.

My next scheduled stop was going to be at Dafna's house. *If I was still a pariah … there could be trouble.*

For the fourth time that day I climbed aboard my trusty bike to once again traverse the breadth of Southfield while I gallantly faced the icy hordes of the Michigan winter. If I was going to freeze at least I could be poetic about it.

It was definitely getting colder and the skies were more ominous.

The storm was coming.

As I pedaled, I called Mary Lou on my cell phone. I asked her to set up appointments with the state police and Oakland County Sheriff's Department. I had to cover all the bases.

Why did I not call them myself? Because now I had an administrative assistant. Not a secretary — that is passé — an administrative assistant.

My behind was sending me semaphore signals. I was in agony from bouncing up and down on the little hard bicycle seat in the freezing wind and I anxiously asked her if there was any chance of getting me that car real soon.

Good news.

She informed me that she had secured a good deal on a lease for a new Ford Explorer XLT with 4 wheel drive. The bank said it was all set. I could pick it up at any time.

Is Mary Lou terrific or what?

When Dafna was not mad at me, we usually spoke three or four times a day. Since Friday — not a word. I had to assume that she was still — perturbed with me. So, I was a bit apprehensive when I leaned my bicycle against her garage door. This meeting had been arranged over a week ago ... before Dafna's ultimatum. The three of us — Dafna, Shaindel and I — were supposed to sit down to try and hammer out some of the nuts and bolts for the wedding. She had not called to say the meeting was cancelled, but I knew that this could get awkward.

I entered the Lachler household, where I was enveloped by life sustaining warmth — *Thank God.* In addition I detected some delicious cooking smells wafting from the kitchen. That was where I found Shaindel fussing over some pots on the stove. In a somber tone she informed me that Dafna was still not talking to me.

She was having a tough time restraining herself from breaking out in laughter.

How were we supposed to communicate about the wedding?

And, if that was not enough, now I had the added problem of having to tell the two of them that Mary Lou intended to 'help' plan the wedding.

I did not know what to expect or what to do.

Mrs. Kalin said in an overly dramatic tone, "Dafna is down in the basement with her computers."

Time to enter the lion's den.

And what a den it was. This was not some little cubby hole with an old computer.

It was Dafna's business. Her disc repair company.

Did I tell you that Dafna — my soon-to-be wife — is a computer genius? Well she is.

Home computers came into this world in the 80's and grew up in the 90's and so did Dafna. Even as a little girl she had been a computer nerd. When she was first married, she would help friends — with less computer savvy — retrieve information from crashed disc drives and other media. She was good at it — better than good. Dafna did the impossible. Soon complete strangers began bringing her broken disc drives and other failed data storage devices and were willing to pay good money for the service. That was the start.

By word of mouth, it became known that if a regular disc repair service said your information was irretrievable, there was still a good chance that Dafna could get most, if not all, of it back. It did not take long until some of the larger national disc repair companies were sending Dafna their 'impossible' jobs. She became known in the trade as the 'Disc Lady.' Her reputation grew and many of the computer experts affiliated with government agencies began asking for her help. Usually it was to retrieve material 'erased' from confiscated discs that were being investigated for criminal or security reasons. Her customers included major corporations and most of the law enforcement agencies within 500 miles. The FBI and congressional committees were frequent users of her service. Even the CIA and NSA had each asked for her help. When those two particular discs were in her house they had Marines, from the Selfridge Airbase, camp out in her basement until the work was finished.

When she first started getting overtures from prestigious governmental and non-governmental institutions they pointed out that although she personally could obtain the necessary security clearances, her small basement workroom did not offer the security they needed for their 'delicate' work. The information that was contained in their special discs could not fall into the wrong hands.

So, with their approval and at their direction, Dafna dug up her backyard and built an underground extension to her basement. The contractor put up high plastic tarps around the property so that the neighbors would not know what was being built. They were told that Dafna was trucking out all the dirt because she was contemplating putting in a swimming pool. Thick reinforced concrete walls were constructed and a heavy steel door was installed. The whole extension was buried under the lawn and none of her neighbors ever asked why there was no swimming pool.

Access to this extension was only through the massive steel portal in her basement. An elaborate security panel, of Dafna's own design, would allow entry only after entering a digital identity code and getting a retinal scan confirmation. Powerful one way positive pressure air-conditioning units were installed to relieve the heat generated by the computer equipment. Her neighbors probably thought that the humongous compressor located behind her backyard shed was for a gargantuan meat freezer somewhere in her house. Fire sensors were scattered around the room and if needed they could trigger the dispersal of fire retardant powder and gases. Not water. Water would ruin the electronic equipment and discs. If there was a power outage, there was a one hour battery back-up for the entire room. For anything longer, there was an emergency power generator inside her garden shed, with enough fuel for a week.

The cost to build the extension was enormous — even more than the house — but this way she could work at home, and her income from the special services·more than compensated for the cash outlay for the construction project. People wanted and needed the 'Disc Lady.' They paid her well.

Dafna and I have never discussed how much money she has in the bank, but since she already outstrips me in brains, looks and personality, I am not going to let a little discrepancy in our net worth bother me now.

The heavy steel security door was left open for me and I could see the double tier of computer terminals — about 20 or 30 — on three walls of the space. Almost all were chugging away on their own, analyzing and repairing discs and other types of failed data archival equipment.

She had a tool area at the back containing a drill press, band saw, and other hand tools which might be needed to open damaged disc casings. In the center of the room there was a contaminant-free clean box where she dismantled discs. Dafna was in her little laboratory area, at the far corner of the room, where she did all sorts of magical electronic stuff.

She once attempted to explain some of the things that she does, but for me it was like hearing a foreign language. I am a total dunce when it comes to things cyber. I feel I have reached a pinnacle in computer prowess when I am able to retrieve my e-mail without erasing half of the messages.

"Hi," I said to get her attention as I flopped into one of the empty chairs.

She looked up for a moment and returned her eyes to the computer screen. "Oh, it's you," she said, as if she had just discovered half a worm in her apple.

I am dead.

How am I going to get out of this?

"Dafna! Come on. You know I can't let you be part of this investigation."

"Oh, really? And why is that?" she said without looking up.

"Client privacy."

"You are trying to use the old client privacy ploy on me?" she asked in disbelief. "Who is your client?"

"Rabbi Kalmonowitz," I answered honestly.

"Exactly!" she said emphatically. "And did *Rebbi* specifically say that he does not want me helping you?"

"Well ... no ... but ..."

"But, what? You can ask *Rebbi*."

"There is also *Rebbetzin* Slater," I said defensively.

"OK ... and did *she* say I should not help you?"

"Actually ... I ... haven't ..."

"Have you even spoken with *Rebbetzin* Slater?"

"Well ... you see ..."

"You have not, isn't that right?"

"No, I haven't," I answered in defeat.

"I bet she won't agree to see you."

"She said she is very busy."

"And she will remain busy every time you call."

"She said sometime later in the week."

"Later in the week, she will say next week."

"How do you know?" I asked.

"You haven't got the foggiest notion of how women like *Rebbetzin* Slater think. She will never see you."

"What do you mean?"

"If I don't miss my guess, when you called her you said something like ... you are a private investigator sent by Rabbi Kalmonowitz and would like to come over and speak to her about her husband's disappearance," she said.

"That's right."

"Well, guess what? There is no way the *rebbetzin* will see you without another woman being present."

Yikes! She's right. "I forgot about that."

"You have to tell her you will be bringing a woman with you. A woman that will be assisting you. One that will be privy to all the facts in the case. Your *partner*," she said for emphasis.

"I get the feeling that you're referring to yourself."

"What a terrific detective you are."

"But why would I do that?"

"Because you need my help," she said smugly.

I was not going to let her wheedle herself onto the investigation. I would be adamant, "I can handle this case on my own."

"Maybe. But can you handle my mom?"

Whoops — what is she talking about? "Your mom loves me."

"She sure does. Right now. And she is also so excited about planning *your wedding*." She paused and then said emphatically, "Your *first* wedding."

What? Shaindel did not know?

For me, these nuptials were technically considered a first marriage. I say technically, because you could not really count my three-year marriage to Bethany as a real marriage. We got hitched when I left the Marines. I was twenty years old and she was eighteen. What people nowadays call a starter marriage.

The definition of a 'starter marriage' is a period of time spent with an initial spouse, in which you learn what marriage is all about, so that you can do a better job at your next attempt.

Our last year together had been a constant battle. We parted as friendly enemies and I heard that she now has a family up in Flint. The reason our matrimonial vows did not really count was because she was not Jewish. According to Jewish law — *halacha* — taking a non-Jewish wife is not legally binding. So technically, this will be a first marriage for me.

What I feel for Dafna is totally different from what I felt towards Bethany. I know now that with Bethany I had never really been 'in love.' It was more like we had been 'in lust.' When the lust part dwindled and cooled — and then froze over like the Antarctic — we discovered that we really did not have much going for us.

Dafna was a whole different deal.

A big deal.

Dafna knew all about my first marriage and I had assumed that she had related this information to her mother.

Telling Shaindel about Bethany at such a late juncture was going to be a big problem.

Like the start of World War III.

"You never told her?" I asked in disbelief.

"Not in my job description. Part of the client privacy rule. I don't break that rule. Not ever," she said wagging her finger. "So, you are on your own with mom."

"You have to help," I insisted.

"You want my help ... you know what you got to do ... partner."

"That's blackmail," I protested.

"It sure is," she said with a nod. "So, am I in?"

"I have to ask *Rebbi*," I said in defeat.

"So, ask."

There was still the problem of Mary Lou — a nice Catholic lady — wanting to be part of the planning for our ultra-Orthodox Jewish wedding. How do I broach the subject? "There is one more thing."

"What would that be?"

"You know my mom is more than happy that your mother is handling all the preparations for the wedding."

"That is why it is just perfect, since my mom does not like to share in the planning of her projects."

"Yeah ... but you see ... there should be someone from my side to ... coordinate ... my ... the groom's side of things."

"That is reasonable. Who did you have in mind? Your father? Your sister?"

The idea of my dad trying to hire a Jewish band or deciding who would say the seven blessings under the *chupah* or just about anything related to a Jewish wedding was absolutely ludicrous. My married older sister lived in New York and would be even worse. "No, not anyone from the family."

"Then who?" asked Dafna impatiently.

I had no choice but to spill the beans, "My secretary."

"Your secretary? Since when do you have a secretary?"

"I have an administrative assistant since this morning."

"You met this woman this morning and now she is going to be the one to *coordinate* your side of things for the wedding. Are you crazy?"

"I've known her for a few years. She was my secretary before I went to the *yeshiva*."

"This administrative assistant of yours ... that you just hired this morning ... is she like young and ..."

My goodness. *Do I sense a bit of jealousy?*

"She's an older woman ... but don't tell her I said that ... and she is a grandmother ... and Catholic."

"Catholic? You really must be losing your mind. Even if Mom was willing to let her help, your secretary would not know the first thing about planning a Jewish wedding."

"You don't know her."

"It is not going to work," insisted Dafna.

"You want to be in on the case ... you also have to help me tell your mom about my secretary. Take it or leave it."

Dafna thought for a moment and then said, "I'll take it. Did you get the case file?"

I knew from experience, that Dafna was dying to read every scrap of information. So, I handed over the CD containing Rabbi Slater's file so she could make a copy.

"One thing more. If you are going to help me you have to keep everything you learn secret."

"Are you kidding? Look around you. This room is packed with secrets. I eat secrets for breakfast, lunch, and dinner. I have security clearance from the biggest firms in corporate America and all levels of government. The Pentagon sends me stuff. Have I ever leaked a secret to you or anyone?"

"How would I know? Have you ever leaked a secret?"

"Can't tell you. It's a secret."

Dafna inserted the disc into a drive and her hands flew over the keyboard. She punched a few buttons and her computer whirred for about twenty seconds. The disc popped out and the screen went black. She handed back my original disc. "Let's go and get this over with."

7

SUV

I CLIMBED the stairs feeling as if I was going up to the gallows. Mrs. Kalin raised her eyes from the pot she was tending and asked, "Are you two communicating again?"

Dafna said, "Shimon, has seen the light. We are talking."

Shaindel looked at me inquisitively, "We will be eating dinner in about an hour. Will you be staying?"

This was not really a question. More like a low key order. Not that I would ever refuse one of her meals. I told you, she was a terrific cook. What was interesting was that Shaindel had acquired all of her culinary skills from Dafna over the last three years. That was when her son-in-law had passed away, and she had come out from New York to help Dafna by taking over the cooking and housekeeping. She learned to follow Dafna's recipes and the food was delicious. She was definitely the number two cook in the community.

My ability to rank cooking skills stems from my unique experience of having been a dinner guest of about 85% of the two hundred or so *balabustas* that make up the ultra-Orthodox community. I know from whence I speak.

The reason for the plethora of invites stems from my having been an unusual *yeshiva bocher.*

Up until today I was a student at the Detroit *yeshiva gedola* in nearby Oak Park. I even dressed in the typical *yeshiva bocher* uniform. But, unlike most *bocherim,* who are college age — late teens to early twenties — at 38 years old I was the oldest *bocher* in the *bais medrash* and I was an eligible bachelor.

In the eyes of all the women of the community, that last part was written in capital letters and flashing lights.

That was the key.

I overheard some of the *frummy* women describe my unmarried status as *a shandeh* or *nebach.* My *Yiddish* proficient friends tell me the words mean 'a disgrace' and 'pathetic' respectively. They further explained that it was not me who was a disgrace or pathetic, but the community for allowing me — a bachelor — and an older one at that — and one who apparently possessed a modicum of the social graces — to go around without a spouse.

A vacuum.

The worst kind.

Nature — and all Jewish homemakers — abhor vacuums.

Especially an older unattached vacuum.

So the *balabustas* affiliated with the *yeshiva* arranged for me to be invited for meals so that I could be unofficially introduced to unmarried older single females. The women I met came in all varieties: never married, widowed, or divorced. They could be a: sister, niece, grand-daughter, or friend. I figure I have been informally introduced to almost two hundred available women over the last two years. Nothing ever came of it.

The only good side of all these dinner invitations was that it gave me my unique perspective to evaluate the relative cooking skills of the different Jewish homemakers whose homes I visited. I can say with certainty that not all *balabustas* are equally talented in the kitchen. My unofficial research indicates that most are OK cooks. Some had specific dishes that were terrific, but in general their meals were just palatable and/or nourishing. But there was also a small group of remarkably superior cooks and an equally small group of absolutely dreadful ones. The superior cooks created banquets that were the true essence of a culinary experience. Taste bud extravaganzas. However, the dreadful ones served meals that could be dangerous to your health and well being. They were to be avoided at all costs.

Trust me — *Rebbetzin* Kalmonowitz, Mrs. Kalin, and Dafna are the top three cooks.

"Be glad to stay for dinner," I answered.

"Great," she said. "Let me turn off the gas. We'll delay the meal just a bit so we can sit down and do some work on your wedding."

I had not eaten anything all day, and I was starving. Luckily Dafna read my mind. She began setting out coffee cups and then brought in a serving platter with thick slices of marble chiffon cake. One of my favorites.

Hey ... the meal was delayed. I needed something to tide me over until supper.

The cake was Dafna's recipe, so that meant that it was out of this world and Shaindel knew how to prepare it perfectly.

An investigator needs sustenance to investigate.

I took a seat next to Dafna and Shaindel brought over a half a dozen thick file folders. Her wedding plans.

I speared a substantial chunk of cake with my fork and effortlessly hoisted it up to my mouth. It was light as a feather. I closed my lips around the tender morsel and felt how it melted on my tongue. Sweetness, chocolate, warmth, smooth — heaven. I took a swig of coffee and I was ready to face the problems of the world.

Well, not quite yet.

First, I had to polish off the rest of my cake — then I could confront the debacles of the universe.

Mrs. Kalin took a sip of her coffee and said, "First let us set the date and time."

Dafna interrupted, "Mom, there are a few very important things that you have to know about Shimon and the plans for this wedding."

Thank God she was helping me. I do not know how I would be able to do it on my own.

"And what is that?" asked Shaindel inquisitively.

Dafna nodded her head a few times trying to find the right words and then turned to me and said, "Shimon, tell her."

She was chickening out of telling her mother. *What about our deal?* She suckered me. *She gets to be my partner and I get shafted. When Shaindel finds out that I had been married before she is going to kill me. And then when I get to the part about Mary Lou, she will resuscitate me so that she can kill me again.*

How will she take that?

I am dead.

Double dead.

I began tentatively, "Mrs. Kalin —"

"You know my name is Shaindel," she insisted. "Mrs. Kalin is my mother-in-law, she should live and be well."

"Shaindel," I said. "As you know I have re-opened my investigation business."

"I heard. I wish you great success," she replied.

"I have been lucky enough to get back my old secretary ... I mean administrative assistant ... and she is like a really good friend ... and ..."

Dafna interjected, "Shimon, would you tell her already."

I held up an open palm to indicate that I would get to the point directly.

Unfortunately, I did not know how to do that.

Instead, everything just came tumbling out of my mouth, "And she wants to help plan my wedding and she is Catholic and a little weird ... but she is really nice ... and I was married before ... for three years ... when I was twenty years old and she was a *shiksa*. So that's it. Do you want me to leave?"

Mrs. Kalin said calmly, "Why would I want you to leave. We still have to plan your wedding."

What. "You are OK with this?"

"Sure," she said.

"What I said does not bother you?" I asked incredulously.

"No," she said simply.

"There is no problem with me being married before?"

"Dafna was also married before, and your first wife was not Jewish, so that does not really count."

"You know about Bethany?"

"I did not know her name, but yes. Your mother told me."

"When was this?"

"Last month when you brought your family over to introduce them to us."

I should have thought of that. My mother was not one to keep secrets. "And you are fine with my secretary wanting to help plan the wedding?"

"Certainly," she said calmly with a nod of her head. "She can *want* to plan the wedding to her heart's content. But, she is not coming within a mile of this *simcha*."

"She said she will call after dinner."

"When she calls I will be perfectly civil to your secretary and I will explain to her ... something that you do not seem to be able to grasp ... that she cannot participate in the planning of the wedding."

I turned to Dafna, "Help me here."

Dafna shrugged her shoulders and said, "I said I would help you tell my mother about your secretary. I did not say I would help convince her to go along with the idea."

Mrs. Kalin was giving me an unflappable smile and I knew there was nothing I could say that would convince her. Then I realized that it was not my problem. Mary Lou was the one that had to get Shaindel to go along with the sharing of the wedding plans.

An unstoppable projectile meeting an immovable object.

"My administrative assistant's name is Mary Lou."

We had a delicious dinner of beef stew with hefty zesty chunks of meat, little carrots, sweet peas, and sliced potatoes, in a thick tomato sauce.

About half way through the meal it began to snow. The big storm that everyone was expecting had arrived.

Typical Michigan weather — if you do not like it — stick around for five minutes, it will change. March snowfalls are fairly common in our state. The white stuff was piling up in the streets and I knew I would have a very difficult time peddling my bicycle way over to the car dealership on Telegraph Road. So, I left my bike in Dafna's garage and asked her to give me a ride to the dealer.

When they brought out my car it was not exactly what I had expected.

Most leased vehicles were of the vanilla variety. Meaning they only have the bare bones standard features, so that at the end of the lease period they would be easy to sell in the used car market.

This was not a vanilla Ford SUV. This was a specialty order.

It was an inky black, Ford Exhibition XLT-Max SUV four-wheel drive, with a huge engine — AKA gas guzzler — a super high clearance, all terrain tires, a front winch with a hundred feet of cable and a fully equipped light bar on top. In addition it had a three inch steel roll bar just behind the front seats that connected with another three inch steel pole running forward through the middle of the car and down the center of the windshield and on through the dashboard to connect with the steel body frame below. This was not a car for driving in the suburbs. This was for someone exploring the outback that was afraid of falling into a canyon or an abyss.

The salesmen saw me looking at these unusual features and explained that it had been ordered by the Bloomfield Heights Safety Division, but budget cuts forced them to cancel the order. The car had been sitting on the lot for three months, so the dealership decided to put it out on lease.

Most of the exotic features were way over the top for me — but I loved the car on sight.

I think that somewhere in the holy book of Ecclesiastes, it says: 'If thou giveth any red-blooded American male a muscle car, thou shalt see him smile.'

I smiled.

Thank you, Mary Lou.

"Pretty Snazzy," said Dafna, as she inspected the car. "I hope you can keep this one from blowing up."

"I doubt if a missing person case will have the same dangers as a murder."

"Yeah, maybe so ... but during the investigation ... let's use my car. I will feel safer," she said.

"Don't be silly. It will be perfectly fine."

"Still, please say *tfilas haderech* whenever you drive her."

8

Special delivery

I WAS in heaven.

The car drove like a dream. There was already two inches of snow on the roads but my powerful car was pushing its way through as if it were a bright summer's day. Plastic sheeting still covered all the interior surfaces but I was not going to touch them for now. Today, I would just enjoy the new car smell.

Terrific.

I parked in front of my condo and gave the vehicle a fond pat, wishing the car well for its first exposure to Michigan snow.

Once I got into my warm snug home, I turned on my coffee maker and switched on my laptop. I had homework to do.

I booted up the disc with all the information concerning Rabbi Slater's disappearance and dutifully read every document, going through each scrap of evidence very carefully. Then I did it again — and again — and again.

Nothing jumped out at me.

Everything seemed straight forward. Anyone that has ever actually read a routine police report knows that they can be extremely boring. I had to fight to keep my eyes open. After three cups of black coffee and reading it all for the umpteenth time — I was exhausted. I knew that if I was not alert I was just wasting my time. So, at 11:00 p.m., I turned off the computer and went to bed. Even with all the caffeine streaming through my veins, sleep came immediately.

A catchy tune interrupted my slumberland interlude. For a moment I thought I was a budding Beethoven composing melodies in my sleep, but then I realized it was the ringtone from my phone. The clock said — 12:03 a.m.

What the heck?

Only one hours sleep.

Who was calling me in the middle of the night?

The ID screen on my phone indicated an unknown caller and I said groggily, "Hello."

"Shimon, get dressed and get over here."

It was not Dafna's phone but it sure was her voice. I was suddenly awake.

A flood of horrible images went through my perverted cop's mind and they all featured her, or her family, and all sorts of deranged mayhem. "What happened?"

"You wanted that interview with *Rebbetzin* Slater?"

"Yes."

"Now is your opportunity."

"At midnight?" I asked unbelievingly.

"Have you looked outside?"

"No, I was sleeping."

"There is about fourteen inches of ice and snow on the ground and there are drifts of up to three feet. None of the streets have been plowed," she said excitedly.

"Sounds very picturesque, but what does this have to do with *Rebbetzin* Slater?"

"She's gone into labor and this is a sixth child and it won't be long until the birth. Her husband is missing and she can't get a cab or an ambulance. Our cars don't stand a chance in this snow. You have that big, new, four-wheel drive tank. Get your behind out of bed and get over to the Slater house right now."

She hung up.

No discussion.

Once again she was giving me a command and I was expected to obey.

Of all the nerve.

I decided I would show her who wore the pants in this — family.

So, I got my butt out of bed and dressed quickly, just like she said. No time to lose.

The roads were really treacherous. If, in the early evening, it had been a heavy snow, it was now officially a Michigan springtime blizzard. The huge snowflakes appeared to be the size of silver dollars and were the wet clumpy kind that stuck to anything and everything. The headlights reflected off the snow and even with my wipers going full speed the visibility was just a few yards. Greenfield Road, normally a six lane thoroughfare, was down to a single pair of white ruts running in each direction and even that was partially blocked with at least three fender benders. The 4 wheel drive and studded tires allowed me traction that most of the other vehicles did not have. I was able to negotiate my way around the traffic jams by going through the pristine streets that had as yet not seen a snowplow. Normally the drive would take two minutes, tonight it took over fifteen.

I pulled up in front of the Slater house. The front door opened almost immediately and through the heavy snowfall, I saw three, maybe four, people moving as one big mass towards my car. They were all bundled up in blankets and heavy coats, so I had no idea who they were. The back door opened and one individual climbed in.

It was Dafna.

She helped a woman, wrapped in blankets, climb into the back seat and then slammed the door.

Dafna said, "Shimon, this is *Rebbetzin* Slater. Leah, this is Shimon Lincoln. Now drive," she said loudly.

More commands.

So, I drove.

That is, I tried to drive.

My car had no problem powering its way through the snowy streets but it was slow going because there were so many more accidents and the roads were virtually impassable. I had to back track four or five times, only to get to another impasse.

The usual travel time to the hospital was around six minutes. We had been driving for over 45 minutes and we were nowhere near the medical complex.

Rebbetzin Slater was in labor. Oh, was she in labor.

In the movies, American pioneer women are depicted as stoically enduring the pangs of childbirth by biting on a leather belt or clenching the sheets in their fists. They never let out a whimper or uttered a single cry. Those were real heroines.

But, this was not the movies and *Rebbetzin* Slater was not one of those heroines.

She was laying flat on her back on the rear seat of my car, knees splayed apart, shrieking at the top of her lungs. Her yelling was so loud I am sure the hospital had to know we were on the way. With every contraction she squirmed and thrashed her arms and legs, then threw her head back and went rigid. At this point she would wail like the dickens until the contraction passed. I am no obstetrician but it was obvious that the contractions were coming fast and furious. It would not be long until another Slater baby would make its appearance on this earth.

Problem was, we were still far away from the hospital.

"It's coming, it's coming," she was screaming now.

Dafna was sitting on the floor and leaning between the *rebbetzin*'s legs saying, "Take deep breaths."

I had no idea why she thought that taking deep breaths would slow down the baby's imminent arrival.

"More deep breaths."

Atta girl Dafna.

If I thought the *rebbetzin* had been bellowing loudly before, it was nothing compared to the caterwauling that she was doing now. It was like having an air raid klaxon screeching next to my ear.

I would be deaf for a week.

I heard Dafna say over the screams, "Shimon, you have got to help."

"Help in what? I'm driving."

"But we aren't getting anywhere, and the baby is coming. You were a policeman, didn't they teach you about this in your first-aid training?"

Eighteen years ago, when I was at the Police Academy, a retired obstetrician had shown us an instructional video and gave us a lecture on how to deliver a baby in an emergency situation. But, as a detective, I had little exposure to women in labor. So, up until this very moment I had never utilized that esoteric bit of training. All I remembered was that the lady screams and you let her do all the work. The job of the policeman was just to catch the slippery kid before it fell on the floor. Fat lot of good I was going to be.

"I don't remember a thing," I said in all honesty.

"Whatever you know about birthing is certainly more than me. I have always been at the other end. Park the car and get back here."

More commands.

Of all the nerve.

I pulled into an unplowed parking lot of a closed strip mall and put the gearshift into park, but left the motor running so the heater would keep us from freezing. I climbed into the back seat and closed the door to conserve the warmth. The back seat was crowded. The screaming *rebbetzin* was still on her back and the bottom of her nightgown was matted with blood and other bodily fluids.

I forced myself not to imagine what this was doing to my upholstery.

My car was not even one day old.

Dafna was crouching between the front and back seat, patting the *rebbetzin*'s head, "Big breaths. Big breaths."

Dafna definitely had the situation well in hand.

I pulled off my gloves and lifted the nightgown. Through the gore and blood I saw that the baby was coming.

How did I know?

The training film I has seen so many years ago was inching its way up from my subconscious. I put my hand on the woman's abdomen and felt the contraction begin, "Push down now. Hold your breath and bear down. Push the baby out."

To my utter surprise Dafna stopped demanding more breathing and the *rebbetzin* stopped her screaming.

She began to push.

The baby's head began to emerge but it did not come out.

I was elated, "OK, take a rest. Now you can breathe. With the next contraction we are going to get that little bastard out of there."

Uh oh, maybe I should not have said 'bastard', in front of the rebbetzin.

Too late now.

Dafna looked up at me disapprovingly as she stroked *Rebbetzin* Slater's head.

Yeah, definitely a bad choice of words.

The *rebbetzin* was resting, trying to gather her strength. The contraction started and I told her, "When I tell you to ... hold your breath and push."

She was now panting loudly, but stopped for a second to say, "OK."

I waited until I felt the contraction reach its peak and then I yelled, "Now. Push!"

The *rebbetzin* held her breath and then pushed down with a grunt. The crown of the scalp started to come out and then in one quick rush the entire head emerged. I was supporting the little calabaza, sensing a feeling of awe, when almost immediately, the rest of the baby slid into my hands along with a large gush of amniotic fluid. It was all I could do to keep the little slippery sucker from falling on the floor.

Just like they told me at the academy.

It was a boy and he was crying softly. No need to slap the kid's behind. Dafna handed me a large clean towel and I swaddled the child and handed it to her. The umbilical cord was still attached and I could not find any string to tie it off, so I ripped off a piece of plastic film from my ruined upholstery and did the deed. A knife or scissors was needed to cut the cord but that could wait until the placenta was delivered. If it did not come out the mother could bleed to death.

I felt the *rebbetzin's* abdomen and sensed another softer contraction. I pulled gently on the cord and the placenta plopped out. Lots of blood.

"Dafna, give the kid to his mother to hold. You have to press on her abdomen to massage the uterus so that it will contract and stop the bleeding."

"What are you going to be doing?"

"I going to try and get us to the hospital."

The *rebbetzin* held her baby boy in her arms, lifted her head from the seat, and with a smile on her sweating face said, "Shimon, thank you."

We made it to the hospital at 1:45 in the morning and Dafna, the *rebbetzin* and the baby were hustled into the emergency room. Only a small portion of the hospital's parking lot had been plowed and I had to park my car at the far end. When I finally got to the ER, everyone thought I had been injured because of all the blood on my coat. Once I assured them I was fine I was directed to the maternity wing.

I was a little worried about Dafna.

From past experience I knew she could get through the toughest of situations like a trooper. But the moment she was out of danger, and the adrenaline rush was over, she could go into meltdown mode. Like a balloon loosing air slowly. Support was required for just a few minutes. A hug and reassurance was all that it took. The tears would fade and she would revert back to being a tough girl once again.

I was worried about how she was holding up.

I found Dafna in the waiting room.

"The baby is being checked by the pediatricians and *Rebbetzin* Slater is in the delivery room," she stated authoritatively.

Good — the balloon is fully inflated.

"Why is she in the delivery room?   She already delivered," I said.

"They said it was just to be safe."

I am sure safety is their only consideration.

I mentioned previously that I had once sustained a gunshot wound and I was in the hospital for almost three months. That little episode started me on a journey of trying to find myself. It led to the *yeshiva* and where I am right now. But, during the time I spent in the hospital and rehab, I learned that if you wanted to remain fiscally sound, hospitals are places to be avoided. Doctors can do miracles and they need hospitals. But, healing centers are expensive to run, so the administrators gouge the patients and their insurance carriers to the limit for every service they provide. The only things covered by a patient's outrageous daily room charge are the meals, the change of linen and the toilet paper. Everything else is extra.   It is the only place in the universe where an aspirin tablet costs six bucks and a box of tissues runs fifteen dollars.

Most likely, *Rebbetzin* Slater was in the delivery room just so that they could tack the charge onto her bill, "Yeah, just to be safe."

"Shimon, thank you," she said emotionally. "You were terrific."

"Yeah, I guess I was," I said in all modesty.

"Now, please go home. There is nothing more for you to do here. Get some sleep and try to find the baby's father."

I got to my condo at three in the morning but I knew I would not be able to sleep just yet. The adrenaline rush of the evening had not abated. I sat on my couch drinking a glass of milk and it slowly sank in.

I had just helped bring a new life into this world.

Amazing.

9

Mufti

TUESDAY MORNING, I slept late.

Hey, I earned it.

I showered and went to the later prayer services at the *yeshiva* and was able to catch Rabbi Kalmonowitz in his tiny office before he had to go to class. I had two questions to put before him. The first was whether it would be appropriate for me to wear 'regular' clothes while I did my detective work and the second was whether I could allow Dafna to help in the investigation.

Before I had a chance to ask my questions he congratulated me for coming to *Rebbetzin* Slater's aid and delivering her baby. He said I earned a whole bunch of *mitzvahs.*

To my question about wearing street clothes, he told me that the *yeshiva* outfit, is not intrinsically holy, but like any uniform it had a purpose. Unlike the police or military, it is not meant to dehumanize the individual or to be an aid in learning to obey commands. *Rebbi* explained that the main purpose of the *yeshiva bocher* uniform was to allow others to identify the student and to keep him from transgressions. Anyone who might see him in a moment of weakness might not specifically know who the transgressor was but he could identify him as an Orthodox Jew and thus the sinner's action would be a blot on all Orthodox Jews. This is known as a *chilul*

HaShem. No one wants that to be on his conscience, so it helps the *yeshiva bocher* stay on the straight and narrow. Heavy stuff.

An additional benefit of wearing the simple, clean, modest clothing was its ability to help the *yeshiva* student reach a higher spiritual level. It teaches him that he should use personality, hard work, and brains to make him stand out and not rely on expensive, stylish or attention grabbing clothing.

Rabbi Kalmonowitz told me that clothes do not make the man — they can only help. I did not need the *yeshiva bocher* outfit to be an upstanding Jew. He ended the topic by saying that since in my situation such a uniform would hinder me in my job, there was no problem for me to work in less conspicuous clothing. He told me, "Use your *sechel,* think modestly, and work towards *kiddush HaShem* in everything you do and things will be fine."

Concerning Dafna, he first inquired as to whether I thought she might be in any real danger if she helped me. I thought for a few moments and had to admit that the chance of harm was slim. He then asked me if I knew the term *'shalom bayis.'* I told him I knew the translation was 'peace in the house' but actually meant marital harmony. He informed me that there was no bigger blessing for a man or woman to have a spouse that supported and encouraged their work. If a couple could work together, it was an even greater blessing. He ended the discussion by saying, "Accept this gift your future wife is giving you ... but keep her safe. Perhaps with two pairs of eyes, things will be seen that others have missed."

I drove back to my condo. The temperature had risen into the forties and the storm was now just a constant heavy rain that was melting most of the snow. The white stuff was disappearing rapidly and only remained where it had been pushed into mounds by the snowplows. My first job was to get out the soap, detergent and deodorizers to try and remove the gore from my back seat.

Luckily my condo had a car port for every tenant so I did not have to work in the rain. I tore out all the soiled plastic sheeting and found that body fluids and blood had slithered into a multitude of unreachable crevices and niches. I scrubbed, sluiced, and washed down most of the interior. One hour later I had cleaned up the worst of it, but the car would never be the same.

My new car — my one day old vehicle — smelled like a hot summer's day in the back room of a meat market with a dozen Department of Agriculture health violations.

I stowed all the cleaning paraphernalia and took another shower. Then I set up my coffee machine and grabbed myself a bowl of cornflakes. I pulled out Sergeant Chandler's CD again and put it into my laptop. The rest of the morning was spent reading and re-reading the file. That was the hardest part of any investigation. The constant nagging feeling — 'What did I miss?' It looked to me that Sergeant Chandler and the Southfield police had done a thorough investigation and I could see no loose ends.

I called Mary Lou and told her I was sending her an e-mail containing Rabbi Slater's personal information and told her to contact the Skip-Trace Company in Los Angeles. This firm monitored all the usual financial institutions, health services, and legal listings that might reveal the whereabouts of a missing person. There were half a dozen companies that would do similar investigations, but Skip-Trace had one unique advantage. For a hefty fee, they offered an additional service where they could be a bit pro-active — AKA do illegal searches. They had the wherewithal to hack into major data banks to look for a particular individual. Since 9/11, everyone was expected to have some sort of ID, so if someone used his ID to rent a room, enter a museum or whatever — even if he used cash — that ID got entered into some sort of database. If he was in the system, Skip-Trace would find him. I wanted them to do a search from the date the rabbi disappeared and keep the inquiry active until we told them to stop.

I knew that the preliminary search was going to cost over $5,000, but I was not going to charge the *yeshiva* for this expenditure at this point. My savings were not vast, but I could handle the cost for a couple of months. Then I would decide if we would continue.

I was hungry again but as usual my kitchen larder was a bit on the anorexic side. Meals, with real food, came my way when I got invited to someone's home or I mooched them from Dafna. My cornflakes breakfast was a memory and my stomach felt like it was gnawing its way through to my backbone. I suddenly realized that the Jerusalem Pizza store was no longer a twenty minute bike ride in the pouring rain.

It was only a two minute drive in a warm dry car.

Praise the Lord for modern forms of conveyance.

Ten minutes later I was sitting in the shop chomping my way through two slices with mushrooms and extra cheese and sipping from a can of Coke.

Ahh — the simple pleasures in life.

I thought about the case and realized that I was less than a quarter mile from where the rabbi had disappeared.

Perhaps, I should go look at the area.

Why did that seem like a good idea?

After all, both Officer Cummings and Sergeant Chandler had already searched the scene and it was almost five weeks since the disappearance. It was very unlikely that I would find anything.

I had to think about that some more.

As I was devouring the second slice, my cell phone began playing *Hava NaGilah*. The ringtone signified it was from Dafna.

I smiled — Dafna.

When I thought about her I always smiled.

I was a basket case.

But it felt good.

She informed me that she had just spoken to *Rebbetzin* Slater and she agreed to allow me to interview her in the hospital. She would discuss her husband's disappearance on the condition that Dafna was also there.

Way to go, Dafna!

I suppose my small part in the delivery of her newborn son also had something to do with her consent. Special deliveries get special consideration.

I gobbled down the last of the pizza and exited the store. I had to make a stop at the kosher carry-out before I could go to the hospital. If there was no food available at home tomorrow I would be very hungry.

<u>**10**</u>

Cookies

I ARRANGED with Dafna that we would meet in the hospital parking lot at exactly 3:30 p.m. so that we could discuss strategy. This would give us enough time to confer and get to the maternity ward just at the start of the afternoon visiting hours. The interrogation had to be conducted using a specific game plan and it was imperative that I speak with her before we went in. She had to learn how to work as a team. There was an art to interviewing people in pairs and she was sorely lacking in experience. I could not have her ruining the meeting.

I pulled into the hospital lot exactly on time and parked near Dafna's car. The rain was still coming down in buckets and I had to pull up the collar of my coat to sprint over to her vehicle. I opened her passenger door and hastily climbed in, "When we get to see *Rebbetzin* Slater let me do the questioning."

Dafna turned in her seat and sat there staring silently at me. Then she said, "That's it? You just jump in the car and start giving orders. No 'Hello' or 'Hi' or 'How was your day, Dafna?'"

"Oh, yeah. Sorry," I said in mock contrition. "Hi Dafna. How was your day?"

"No, that did not work," she said admonishingly. "Try again. Say it with feeling."

"What's going on? This is not some sort of game. We are on a case."

"Which will turn into a homicide in about two minutes because I might just murder you," she said with conviction. "Haven't you noticed that no matter how busy I am, whenever you come in, I always take the time to acknowledge that I appreciate seeing you? I always say 'Hi' or 'Hello'."

What was going on here?

"Unless you are in the middle of working out a glitch in a computer program. Because then the world could explode and you would not notice," I stated.

"Well ... yeah ... except for times like that," she agreed. "So where is my 'Hello'?"

I put a broad smile on my face, looked longingly into her eyes and said slowly and meaningfully, "Dafna dear ... how was your day?"

She considered what I had said for a moment and replied, "OK, that passed. But just barely." Then without skipping a beat, she said excitedly. "Wasn't that totally awesome last night?"

"Yeah, I suppose it was," I said nonchalantly, as if I delivered babies every day.

She looked at me in disbelief and then punched my shoulder, "You're so full of it."

"Now that we have that out of the way ... when we are in with the *rebbetzin* let me do the talking. Don't try to second-guess me. After I finish, if you think there is anything I missed, that will be your opportunity to ask whatever questions you think pertinent."

"Are you implying that I don't know how to be a good assistant?" she asked indignantly.

"Not at all, but it does take some skill. Reading mystery novels is not considered on-job training."

She made a mock bow of acquiescence and said, "Learn I must from Master Yoda."

"Very funny," I said with an equally mocking smile. "But there is one thing I want you to do."

"What's that?"

"When it seems right, I will ask to leave the room."

"You want my permission to leave the room?"

"No, of course not."

"Where are you going?"

"I will say that I am going to the restroom," I said. "But what I am really doing is leaving the two of you alone."

"Terrific interrogation tactic. Remind me to write that down so I won't forget it."

"Would you cut that out," I chided. "When I leave the room I want you to ask her about their sex life."

"Whose sex life?"

"Her's and the rabbi's."

"Are you out of your mind?" she said in disbelief. "That is not a topic that is ever brought up in conversation by anyone in the *frum* community. I can't do that."

"Well, I certainly can't do it and it is a question that has to be asked."

"No, it is not a question that has to be asked. It implies that there may have been something wrong in their ... relationship ... and that maybe the rabbi went looking for ... the greener grass in somebody else's lawn."

"Very nice metaphor."

"Thank you. I thought it got the point across."

"I will think about what you just said every time I mow the lawn."

"But that is crazy. Anyone that met Rabbi Slater knows that that could not be the reason. They were a perfect couple."

"Perfect?" I asked.

"Well, not perfect, but they were happy together. You could see it. There is no way that the police are correct. That he got up and left Leah with five kids and another on the way. I won't ask a question like that. It is a waste of time."

"You are probably right and it will most likely be a waste of time. But, we cannot assume anything," I lectured Dafna. "I have been doing this for a long time and if the police think he took a walk, there must be some basis for their assumption. As investigators we have to ask all the questions in order to be sure we can eliminate them as possibilities. Sometimes you get surprised by the answers and sometimes an answer to one question can lead us into another unrelated area that will help solve the problem we are facing."

"OK, but I am going to be so embarrassed bringing up the subject."

"I will get the ball rolling by bringing up other possible domestic problems. Then when I take the bathroom break, it will be 'showtime' for you."

Rebbetzin Slater was in a semi-private room and luckily the other bed was vacant. Now that she was not screaming and flailing her arms and legs, I could see that she appeared to be around thirty-something years old and was dressed in a loose fitting, long sleeve, floor length, purple caftan that did not hide the fact that she could lose about twenty pounds above and beyond the residual plumpness of the pregnancy. Her eyes appeared to be brown behind her thick spectacles and she was a tall woman. Very likely over five foot ten. I have no idea about the color of her hair since every strand was hidden under a head covering that looked like a humongous purple sock.

She had arranged cups of diet Coke and a small plate of cookies on the bedside table and proffered them to us, "I can't thank you enough for everything you did last night. Have a cookie. I made them myself. The kids brought them over."

Dafna declined but since I wanted to build up a rapport between us and show her that I was an easy going *mensch*, I reached for a cookie. Dafna took in a quick breath and shook her head ever so slightly, as if warning me about something.

What could it be?

I devoutly recited the appropriate blessing for the cookie out loud — just showing off — and they both answered, "Amen."

I popped the small cookie into my mouth and bit down.

Now I knew what she was warning me about.

I had forgotten.

Rebbetzin Slater was one of those Jewish homemakers that were totally inept in the kitchen. I had once been a dinner guest in their home and the one meal had been dreadful.

The cookie was vile.

More than vile.

I have no idea how anyone could make sugar and flour taste so bad.

My tongue clung to the roof of my mouth. My cheeks were puckering inwards, all my saliva was drying up and tears were welling up in my eyes.

I forced a smile to my face and looked about frantically to see if there was any way I could spit out the glob of terribleness. I could not even ask to take my break now, because opening my mouth would make the cookie from hell move about. There was no convenient refuse receptacle and that left only one option.

I had to swallow.

Oh my God.

I smiled some more and then held my breath as I pushed my tongue backwards in my mouth in the hope of forcing the mass down my gullet.

My esophagus rebelled.

It would not accept the putrid lump. It was now a battle between my tongue and my gullet.

I had to impose my will over my rebellious gastro-intestinal tract. Sweat beaded on my forehead and I felt like an Olympic weightlifter trying to hoist a two-ton barbell above his head. I finally succeeded in forcing the congealed offal down my obstinate esophagus.

I desperately reached for a cup of diet Coke.

Residual cookie still lingered in my mouth — blah.

I quickly mumbled the appropriate prayer for the drink and washed away most — but not all — of the cookie's horrible taste.

I turned back to the *rebbetzin*, smiled and said, "Delicious."

"Thank you," she said. "I can give you the recipe."

Dafna looked at me and said with a broad smile, "That would be great. If Shimon likes them so much, I will make sure to prepare them for him after we are married."

"That's right," said the *rebbetzin*. "I should have given you both a big *mazel tov*."

"Thank you," I said graciously.

I can be gracious when it is necessary.

Now to start the questioning. I have to take it slow. A successful interrogator's most important skill is the ability to get the subject to trust him by beginning the conversation on an entirely different topic and then gradually moving and molding the discussion so that the one being questioned hardly realizes that they are being pumped for information. Dafna should just sit back and observe the master at work.

I took another sip of Coke and began to open my mouth.

Before I had a chance to say a word, Dafna said, "Leah, we have to ask you questions regarding Yechezkel's disappearance."

There goes all the subtlety.

The *rebbetzin* nodded and replied, "Of course, that is why you are here."

"Good," said Dafna. "First I want to ask you if you two were having *shalom bayis* problems with the marriage."

The *rebbetzin*'s eyes hardened and she said angrily, "How can *you* ask me that. You are behaving just like the police. And I thought you would show real concern. I think something terrible has happened."

"You may be right and we will keep that in mind," said Dafna, trying to calm the *rebbetzin*. "But as investigators we cannot assume anything. We have been doing this for a long time and if the police think Yechezkel left voluntarily we have to look for the basis of their assumption. As investigators we have to ask all the questions in order to be sure that we can eliminate them as possibilities. Sometimes we get surprised by the answers and sometimes an answer to one question can lead us into another unrelated area that will help solve the problem we are facing."

It looks like the pupil is trying to up-stage the teacher.
Not happy Master Yoda is.

Leah was mollified, "I see. The police never explained it to me as you just did. I am so happy that you will be looking into this."

Dafna shook her head ever so slightly from side to side, "Think nothing of it. It is the least we can do. So back to my question. Was your marriage a happy one?"

I decided that I was not going to stop Dafna and would let her proceed on her own. It would not take long until she realizes that without my help she is not going to get very far. She wants to play hard ball — game on.

I will gloat the gloat of the ages.

But for the next thirty minutes, Dafna posed incisive questions covering just about everything we needed.

I never opened my mouth.

Her questions were succinct and she asked for appropriate elaboration when necessary.

My impression was that *Rebbetzin* Slater was speaking the truth — or at least the truth as she saw it.   There were absolutely no major problems in their marriage. He was a good husband and was also dedicated to his work as a teacher at the *yeshiva*.

Sometimes too dedicated.

He might go down to the basement on some chore and then not come up for hours because some *sefer* had snagged his attention and he had to read it through. Sometimes he would lose himself in thought when he contemplated a Talmudic issue.   This was not a big problem if it happened at home, but twice it had occurred while he was driving back from the *yeshiva* and he was halfway to Port Huron before he came out of his reverie.

I had to admit it — Dafna was doing great.

I guess Master Yoda will not need to show her the way of the force.

She had a natural knack for seeing the problems and asking the right questions.

As expected, marital intimacy had as yet not been addressed, so I took this as my cue to ask directions to the washroom.

I gave them a good ten minutes and when I returned, Dafna and the *rebbetzin* stood talking amicably near the nurses station.

Dafna held up an envelope, "Leah, prepared a list of all their acquaintances and family as well as all the different credit card and bank accounts that they had"

"Terrific. So I guess that will be all," I said. "If we have any more questions, we will get back to you and if we have any information, we will be in contact."

"Thank you so much Mr. Lincoln. Rabbi Kalmonowitz said that if anyone can help, it would be you."

"I am very flattered, but most of the work is being done by the Southfield police. We will see what we can do."

"I just want you to know that I appreciate it and so does my family," she said somberly. Then she handed me a paper sack, "I saw you enjoyed the cookies, so I packed them up for you. The kids can bring me more from home."

I looked down at the toxic package in her hand.

I was trapped.

There was no choice but to take the bag and say with a smile, "That was so thoughtful of you. Really, I don't know how to thank you enough."

As we sauntered down the hall I tried to drop the bag with the cookies from hell into a trash can but Dafna whispered into my ear that *Rebbetzin* Slater was watching. We left the hospital and it took all of my self-control not to call 911. I wanted Emergency Services to deliver a hazmat suit and a ten-foot pole so that I could keep the paper sack as far from me as possible.

Dafna got into her car and since the rain had finally let up, I stood at its side. She rolled down her window to say, "That went well."

Reluctantly I said, "You did good."

"Ooh, Master Yoda gives compliments to young Jedi knight."

"Cut the crap," I admonished. "Your questions were to the point and you handled *Rebbetzin* Slater perfectly."

"So what do you think?"

"First, you have to tell me about their sex life."

I could see Dafna squirm a bit but she finally said, "He would say 'Thank you.'"

"Who would say 'Thank you'?"

"Rabbi Slater. They had mutually enjoyable sex and when they completed their marital duties, he would always say 'Thank you.'"

I knew that Dafna was referring to the Jewish law that both a man and a woman have the duty of affording sexual pleasure one to the other. Sounds like there were no problems but I needed to ask, "So there were no problems with kinky sex asked for or refused?"

Dafna was turning beet red, "I asked and the answer was definitely no problems."

What a trooper. I knew how difficult it had been for her to ask.

"So, from what you just said, even though the Southfield police think he is a voluntary skip, our opinion is that they are wrong. Something happened to the rabbi."

"I agree one hundred percent," she said.

"Yeah, but what happened to him?" I asked.

"What are the options?"

"Abduction —" I ventured.

"For what reason? No one has any money to pay a ransom."

"Someone did him harm."

"Why?" she asked.

"Pay back ... bad debt ... personal grudge ... jilted lover ..."

"Rabbi Slater? He would not harm a fly. Did not gamble. She told me he had no major debts and did not owe any money to anyone. All indications are that there was no outside romantic interest. Nothing fits."

"Yes, but he has disappeared. What do we do?"

"Maybe you should speak with Rabbi Kalmonowitz."

"I did, this morning," I stated.

"What did he say?"

"First he okayed me wearing regular clothes for the investigation."

"That's going to take some getting used to."

"And he said it would be all right for you to be part of this investigation ... so long as I keep you safe."

"I told you he would agree," said Dafna gloating. "Did he say anything about the case?"

"He just said, and I quote, '... Perhaps with two pairs of eyes, things will be seen that others have missed.'"

"Is that what he said? Really?"

"Yeah, really."

"Exact words?" she asked.

"Yeah, exactly."

Dafna nodded her head rapidly and said, "That means we are supposed to be out looking for something."

"That's what we are doing. We are looking for a solution to the rabbi's disappearance."

"No. No. Rabbi Kalmonowitz does not make unnecessary statements out of the blue. If he said something, his words have meaning. I think we are supposed to be looking for something physical. Actually looking."

"You really believe that? That his words have some hidden message?" I asked with interest.

She nodded in the affirmative, "I told you that when *Rebbi* says something will happen ... it happens. You can take it to the bank."

"Where do you see 'You can take it to the bank'? He did not predict anything."

"You just don't understand. *Rebbi* is special. He won't admit it because he is not a *Chassidic* rabbi. But he has that same ... God-given ability. What he says has special meaning even if he is not willing to acknowledge it himself. It is our job to figure out what his words mean. So, if he says two sets of eyes will see something ... he means we have to look for something."

OK — I will go along with this.

"So, what do you think *Rebbi* meant?" I asked.

"How about Rabbi Slater's wallet?"

"What is there to search in a wallet? There was no money and none of the credit cards were missing."

"Maybe we have to search the accounts. Was there any unusual activity? How about his bank account? Any strange movement of funds in or out?"

"Sergeant Chandler checked those things."

"When did he do that?"

"It's a she, and she did it almost immediately and it was a thorough job. There is no evidence that the rabbi was running up debts or getting unusual sums of money. Nor was he making unusual purchases."

"Maybe everything was done with cash. Then there would not be a paper or computer trail."

"You're stretching it beyond belief. What is this *everything* you are talking about?" I asked. "There is no evidence that *anything* was going on, much less in cash. This is Rabbi Slater. Not a hard-nosed bad guy."

"You're right," she agreed. "I got carried away."

"Too many mystery novels."

"So, it is not the wallet. What about the phone? Maybe I should check the phone, see what messages and calls were made?"

"She did that as well. No unusual phone calls or messages. Nothing strange on his WhatsApp. She even had the memory card checked for erasures. Big fat nothing. And don't tell me he could have had another phone."

"How about the car? Where is it?"

"Right this minute it is sitting in the driveway of the Slater house. The car was checked by the police. Nothing unusual. They even looked for fingerprints ... which is unusual since it was only examined a week after his disappearance ... but the family insisted. The Southfield police found dozens of prints but they are of no use. Some they could identify as being from the Slater family. And they also could identify Officer Cummings ... the patrol officer who found the car ... and the tow truck operator. The rest were smudges and chocolate smears that looked to be from kids in the carpool."

"What's left?" Dafna said out loud. "Did anyone check the area where the car was found?"

"Yes, Cummings did, and Chandler also made a search."

"Did they find anything?"

"Nope."

"What time of the day did they do the search?"

"I don't know when Chandler did her search, but Cummings found the car at about four o'clock in the morning. It probably took a couple of hours until they towed the vehicle. So, I guess he did his search at around dawn."

"It's now a little over an hour until sunset. The light will be coming from the opposite direction. We should look there. Maybe we'll find something that was missed."

"Slim chance of finding anything after five weeks. It has rained or snowed at least five times and we just got through a snow storm and it rained all day."

"*Rebbi* said to look ... and have you got anything better to do?"

I had no leads and no idea how to progress. Another look would not hurt.

"I'll go with you ... but I have one condition."

"What is your condition?" she inquired warily.

I extended the paper sack, "You take the cookies in your car. I don't want to be anywhere near them."

11

Spectacles

ACCORDING TO the police report, Rabbi Slater's car was found on the right shoulder of Jefferson Street facing south, three tenths of a mile from where it crossed Lincoln. I told Dafna to park her car at a convenience store close to the intersection and I waited for her to join me in my car.

My poor — poor — car.

After all the scrubbing and cleaning, my one-day old car no longer had the terrific brand new car smell.

It was all gone.

The smell that is so addicting to all red blooded American males.

Apparently, women cannot properly appreciate this unique pleasure that comes with owning a new car. Perhaps there is a defect in the female nasal apparatus and it is impossible for them to smell the intoxicating vapors. It could be that for some strange reason they are unable to get their jollies from inhaling the fumes of automotive solvents and virgin plastic.

That would mean that new cars are basically wasted on women.

An interesting epiphany.

"Where was the car found?" asked Dafna climbing into my car and arousing me from my profound analysis of the male/female new-car equation.

"Three tenths of a mile from here," I answered reflexively.

"How do you know?"

"Because that is what it says in Cumming's report," I said, stating the obvious. *She should know that.*

"How did he determine how far it was?"

"What are you getting at?"

"Did the cop measure it with a tape measure? Did he drive his car and check the odometer? Did he get a GPS positioning? Or maybe he eyeballed it and made an estimate?"

Good point. *Why had I not thought of that?* Gee, isn't it great fun to be shown up by a neophyte. "I don't know. We'll just use the old odometer," I answered testily.

I set the odometer screen to zero — these new cars are really something — everything is digital. I drove slowly until the display showed three tenths of a mile and stopped.

"Do you see the problem now?" she asked.

At first I was not sure what she meant but then it became obvious.

Even if the car was parked as the cop said at the three tenths mark, was it at the beginning of the third tenth or the end? When they built the adjacent freeway they razed all the homes on Jefferson Street and shifted the actual roadway so that it could function as a temporary access ramp. Eventually the new ramp was built and this part of Jefferson reverted back to being a local street and curved through what had been the backyards of the neighborhood. Because there were no homes on the road and its slow serpentine course, it was little used. Beyond the narrow gravel shoulders of the roadway, the area was wooded with a fairly dense growth of bushes and weeds. There were no buildings nearby so there was nothing to help determine the position of the Rabbi's car. If we wanted to be thorough, we would have to search almost three hundred yards of roadside and we still could not be certain if we were even in the right place.

"Yes, I see the problem," I said. "But I can't think of how we can determine the exact position of the car, so I suggest we just start searching the entire area starting from the beginning of the second tenth and we'll continue until we reach the end of the forth tenth."

"Big job. We only have about an hour until sunset and we are only two people," said Dafna logically.

"Do you have a better suggestion?"

She looked around for a few moments and then made some sort of mental decision as she turned to me, "What was the rabbi's phone number?"

I reached into the back seat to retrieve the printout of the case file, "I have it here," I said.

"Never mind," she answered. "It was 248-734-8582."

I keep forgetting her photographic memory.

Dafna started punching buttons on her phone, "Write the number down, so you have it available."

Show off.

She kept hitting keys and doing things for about four minutes. I gave her the rabbi's number whenever she asked for it and soon she exclaimed, "We're in luck ... the phone was on." Then she returned to do some intense work on her phone and after another three minutes said, "We're way off. Start the car and drive."

She had no authority to tell me what to do.

I was the boss here. "What do you think you are doing?"

She looked up from her screen and said sternly, "Just drive."

"Yes, ma'am."

I drove ahead slowly for about half a mile until she said, "Stop. This is where the car was found."

The digital screen now read eight tenths of a mile.

"How do you know that? Have you got a crystal ball in that phone?"

"No crystal ball. The rabbi's phone was left in the car, presumably for a number of hours. The phone had been on during that time. I just did triangulation between the different cellular towers and checked the GPS coordinates for the rabbi's phone during that period of time. It was right here."

I was astounded, "You can do that with your phone?"

"Well, my phone allows me to contact my computer at home and my computer can do that."

Dafna's ability with computers was mind-boggling, "Amazing."

"Thank you, kind sir. All in a day's work. It was nothing," she said with false modesty.

"Don't get a swelled head."

"How could the cop have been a half-mile off?"

"It happens. He could have written eight tenths of a mile in his notes but when it came time to transcribe it into the computer his written numeral eight might have looked like a three to him."

"Reasonable."

"Now that we know where the car was abandoned, let's start looking."

"How do you want to do this?" she asked.

I turned to Dafna and said, "Something is bothering me. Cummings looked around the scene when he found the car, so whether it was at the three tenths or at the eight tenths mark was irrelevant, because unlike us, he had the actual car to tell him where to look."

"Obviously."

"We have to assume that the standard Southfield police search is what they teach at the academy. So that means he checked twenty-five yards in front and behind the car, on both sides of the road."

"Is that the standard?"

"If no crime is suspected that's it."

"So what is bothering you?" she asked.

"Why did the rabbi stop here? It is not near any transportation."

"Was there anything wrong with the car?"

"Perfect working order."

"Maybe he met someone, and he or she, drove him from here."

I held up my index finger to make a point, "But we believe that it was not a voluntary skip. So, that does not make sense. I ask once more, why did he stop?"

Dafna thought for a minute, "Late at night ... he would stop if someone had car trouble and needed help. That is what Rabbi Slater would do."

"Exactly," I said waving my finger. "Now, if he stopped to help, he could have done it two ways."

"What two ways are there in stopping to help? You stop. You help."

"Did he stop behind the car that needed help or after passing it?"

"It could be either one," said Dafna logically.

"Yes, but think about Rabbi Slater. It is a dark road, he is coming back from an intense study session with the students at the *yeshiva.* He is alone in the car and ...," I looked to Dafna to finish my thought.

"...And his mind is wandering. He probably would not immediately notice that someone is asking for assistance until he was almost on top of him. Probably scared them both."

"So where would he stop?" I asked Dafna.

"Further down the road. Could be even fifty or a hundred yards until he stopped."

"I doubt it was that much, but thirty to forty would be reasonable."

"What difference does it make?"

"Think about it. If something bad happened to the rabbi ... and it was done by someone else ... that someone must have taken him away. That would require force, because if the rabbi was awake he would be fighting him and if not he would have had to carry him."

"So what?"

"So, the perpetrator would probably try to do whatever he did as close as possible to his getaway vehicle."

"I see your point," she said.

I switched to my dramatic sotto voice for effect, "So he gets his victim to stop ... and somehow lures the rabbi near his car ... and does the deed."

"Very graphic. Thank you."

"So where do we look for evidence?"

"Everywhere."

"Of course. But where should we put the emphasis?" I asked Dafna.

"In the forty yards behind the rabbi's car," she said logically.

"Give the lady a Kewpie doll."

"What's a Kewpie doll?"

"I have no idea."

Since we felt that Rabbi Slater had probably passed the stopped vehicle, we decided to search the one hundred yards behind the position of the rabbi's car and the fifty yards in front. We would work together, with Dafna on one side of the road, and me on the other. The road had a six-foot sloping gravel shoulder. We would check the shoulder and another two yards into the bushes, including the area under all the vegetation and leaves.

It was slow going and everything off the roadway and gravel was muddy and slippery. The car was found on the west side of the road and that was the side I searched. We were fifty yards behind the position of the car and I looked across the road to Dafna's side. She was bent over examining some dense weeds when a ray of sunshine broke through the cloud cover. Suddenly I saw a flash of reflected light near Dafna's foot, "What's that?"

"What's what," she said squinting into the sunset.

"In those weeds. About two feet behind your left foot," I said pointing as I approached her.

Apparently she also saw something because she bent over.

"Don't touch anything," I commanded. I tried to move quickly but I did not make it in time.

"It's a little late for that. Sorry," she said holding up a pair of black horn rimmed glasses.

Exactly like the glasses Rabbi Slater wore.

"OK, don't move. And don't handle the glasses any more. Keep your hand just as it is."

"I'm sorry," she said. "I have read enough mystery books to know not to touch evidence."

"No, it is my bad. I should have told you how to deal with anything that we found."

"What do I do now?" she asked.

"Just stand where you are. I want to take some pictures."

I pulled out my phone and shot multiple photographs to show the exact spot where the glasses were found and its relationship to the surroundings. I then used my phone's GPS to find the exact position. When I had the entire area covered from every angle, I allowed Dafna to return to the road and get into my car. Since I did not have an evidence bag and did not want to add my fingerprints to the glasses, I told Dafna to hold them just as they were, and we drove to the Southfield police station.

On the way I called Sergeant Chandler. She was not on shift but she said she would call the duty officer and he would take the glasses and process them. I was to leave copies of all the pictures I took of the area along with the GPS coordinates. The duty officer would also get Dafna's fingerprints and put them into the system because she had touched the glasses.

Before I hung up I said to Chandler, "You do realize that if these glasses are indeed the rabbi's, it means a crime may have been committed."

"I figured that out on my own, Sherlock," said the sergeant.

"So does the rabbi now become a missing person?"

"If they are the good rabbi's spectacles, he is definitely going to be designated as a missing person."

"Well, you know —"

Chandler interrupted me, "There is a good chance that I will be spending over four hours filling out the ton of forms for the NCIC, so if you say 'I told you so', I will bestow upon you the curse of the wicked witches of the Southfield police."

"There are witches on the Southfield police?"

"I am the wickedest witch and I run the coven. You do not want to get on my bad side."

"My lips are sealed."

"Once everything is processed, we will tell his wife what we ... what you found. But, that probably won't be until tomorrow."

"Can you let me know if you are going over there? She just had her baby and they are still in the hospital. I'll try to get someone from the community to be there with her if you tell her."

"No problem."

Chandler was a good egg.

The paperwork and processing at the police station took about two hours.

I did not expect it to take less. The wheels of justice grind very slowly.

"Wow, we really did something," said Dafna as we left the police station.

"Yeah, it looks like we discovered that something very bad happened to the rabbi."

Dafna turned and looked at me questioningly, "What did you just say?"

"Something very bad happened to the rabbi," I stated again.

"No, the first part."

"I said it looks like we discovered something happened."

"That's right. Why didn't I think of that?"

"Think of what?" I asked.

Dafna was eager to get home, because she had an idea and wanted to check something on her computer.   No matter how much I pressured her, she refused to tell me what it was.

Just shows you how we were equal partners on the case.

Her excuse was, "You don't want to know."

12

Noise Maker

WEDNESDAY MORNING, I went to *minyan* at the *yeshiva* and I told Rabbi Kalmonowitz about finding the glasses. He immediately understood what it signified and told me that he would arrange for his wife to be at the hospital if the police were going to tell *Rebbetzin* Slater any bad news.

I was hungry, but there would be no breakfast this morning because today was *Ta'anis Esther* - a fast day. From sunrise to sunset Orthodox Jews took no food or drink. So, that meant no soda pop and no bagels or any kind of *nosh* until the sun went down. The rabbis at the *yeshiva* taught me that fasting nourishes the soul. I suppose they are correct — but I sure could use a cup of coffee right about now.

Dafna and her family were at their home working like little beavers putting the finishing touches on all the *shlach manose* for delivery tomorrow on Purim day. Unlike Dafna, I was not having any brainstorms and could not think of anything to do that would help uncover the whereabouts of Rabbi Slater. So, I spent most of the morning in my new office — the rental furniture had been delivered — calling all my old contacts to tell them that Lincoln Investigations was back in business.

Private investigators offer a variety of services to the public. Usually they do things that are not within police jurisdiction or the things the police would like to do but money and man-power limitations do not allow. Most of my former clients were businesses and legal firms but there was the occasional walk-in.   My practice investigated things like potential jurors, background and fact checking for business deals and court cases, authenticating CV's, locating people that owed money to others, and finding people whose whereabouts were unknown, like heirs mentioned in wills or people that disappeared. I had a few successes with cases involving industrial theft and espionage, but those were the rarity. The big money maker for most private investigators was getting the goods on unfaithful spouses, but I never tried to attract those cases. It made me feel like a voyeur and I avoided them whenever possible. I also did not design or install security systems nor did I do bodyguard work. I liked to investigate and I was good at it.

Everyone I contacted was optimistic that they would be able to send some business my way in the not too distant future. I could not tell if they were sincere or if it was just something you said to be polite. Like telling someone, 'Let's have lunch sometime', when having a meal together is the farthest thing from your mind. I could only hope.

By noon, I had worked my way through my old client list and since I really had nothing else on my agenda and there would not be any lunch, I decided to go to the *yeshiva* to participate in a Talmud class.

I found it very enjoyable. This is kind of unusual because when I was in high school I was the super expert at ditching lecture classes. Gym and laboratories were OK, but I just could not concentrate or even sit still during lectures. Modern day educators will probably tell you that I have some sort of learning disorder. So I have no idea why I am able to concentrate in the *yeshiva*. I suspect it is because it reminds me of detective work. I find it very stimulating to unravel the challenging mental conundrums and the logical progressions of the text. Whatever the reason, I had no problem being attentive.

I was going to miss my *yeshiva* life.

When the lecture ended I noted that even though today was a fast day, and everyone should be in a somber mood, there was a jubilant air of expectation at the *yeshiva.* Most likely that was because tonight was Purim. A big deal in the Orthodox calendar.

The motto of most gentile holidays is, 'eat, drink and be merry. ' Jewish holidays were more like, 'eat until you burst, drink to moderation, and no merriment.' Well, maybe there was a little merriment, but the emphasis was on Torah study — that was always a biggee — goodwill and good deeds to others and do not become an obnoxious inebriated Neanderthal while celebrating the day. Added to this wet blanket approach was the fact that almost every one of the Jewish festivals had some sort of unique additional requirement that further dampened the 'eat, drink and be merry' aspects of the celebration. *Yom Kippur* — no eating, drinking or worldly pleasure at all. *Rosh HaShanah* — extremely long services, not to mention the inevitable appeal for donations to support the synagogue. The Sabbath — no smoking, no cooking, or use of electricity — need I say more? *Sukkot* (Tabernacles) all meals have to be eaten outside in a temporary hut. Passover — no bread or leaven — not even a trace — only *matzah.* Even the regular kosher foods, eaten the year round, were not permitted. Hebrew holidays were akin to winning a million bucks in the lottery only to be told the prize would be awarded in pennies.

Purim is the exception.

This is our one 'eat, drink and be merry' holiday.

Not only were all the Neanderthal antics allowed, they were encouraged. You had to eat a fancy meal and you had to drink. I am not talking about soda pop — really DRINK. On Purim everyone was expected to imbibe enough alcohol to at least get a buzz. Some rabbis say that you are required to get sufficiently drunk so that you will confuse the prime characters of the Book of Esther — the despised Haman and the beloved Mordechai. For me that was four beers or two glasses of wine. I am a quick drunk.

There was one additional requirement. You had to be in synagogue to hear the reading of the *Megilah* once in the evening and again during the day.

Purim commemorates an event that took place ages ago when the Persian king, Achashverosh — the head honcho — allowed the Jews to protect themselves against the hordes that were intent on killing them. If he had not given his permission, the Jews of the Persian Empire — quite a large chunk of the world in those days — would have been decimated. This turnabout of events — where Jews come off as victors — apparently prompted the tradition that on this special day Jews behave differently — out of character. They eat to excess, drink until they are sloshed, poke fun at their elders, and in general have a good time. The kids — and some adults — wear costumes, but these are not like the Halloween getups. Jewish kids run around dressed as princesses, angels, brides, policemen, soldiers, super heroes, etc. No witches, goblins, skeletons, or other spooky characters for our Hebrew 'trick-or-treat.'

The Purim evening service at the *yeshiva* was a sight to behold. All the men and women had been fasting all day and you would naturally expect that they would be in a hurry to get home to get something to eat. Instead, they sat waiting patiently for the holiday to officially begin. The costumed kids and their mothers were also there in throngs, all eager for the reading of the *Megilah*. The reader, one of the rabbis, was wearing a sultan's turban — part of the *Purim shtick* — and the kids loved it. He unrolled and folded the *Megilah* and waited for silence, because even though frivolity is the rule on this day, everyone was required to hear every word that he chanted. The silent congregation concentrated on the reader and he began. He read for about five minutes until he reached the name of the notorious arch-villain of the book — Haman (pronounced — Huh Mon).

My parents were, and still are, six-day Jews. They are members of the Reform synagogue but only attend services six days a year. They go for a couple of hours on each of the two days of *Rosh Hashanah* and again on *Yom Kippur*. In addition, they go for about one half hour on the three festival days to say the memorial prayer for my mom's parents and my dad's mom. Six-day Jews. Every once in a while they would try to convince me and/or my sister to come along but we usually found some way to get out of it. On those rare occasions that we were forced to attend, I always found the services to be staid and proper and totally boring. So, up until three years ago I had never been in any kind of synagogue for Purim. It was only when I started attending the *yeshiva* that I witnessed the phenomenon that takes place when Haman's odious name is uttered during the reading of the *Megilah*. To say I had been surprised would be a huge understatement. Pandemonium does not adequately describe what occurs.

Imagine a New Year's Eve party. Everyone waits with great anticipation for the lighted ball at the Times Square tower in New York City to hit the bottom of the column. Once that ball makes contact everyone starts screaming 'Happy New Year,' fireworks go off, noisemakers are sounded, and people yell one to the other. In short, unbelievable noise. Now take that noise and triple it — or perhaps quadruple it. That is what happens when the name 'Haman' is chanted in the *yeshiva*. All the kids come equipped with some sort of noisemaker and wait eagerly for that terrible name. As soon as it is chanted they all tear into it. The little ones use feeble stuff that they shake, bang, or spin. Not much noise, but they go at it with amazing gusto. However, the older kids come equipped with stadium horns, huge noisemakers, and even electronic amplifiers. Everyone else boos out loud or stomps their feet.

Deafening.

So tonight, every time the reader recited Haman's abhorrent name there was raucous noise for about twenty or thirty seconds, sometimes longer. The congregation went from absolute silence to an earsplitting cacophony every few minutes. Why anyone should find enjoyment from raising the decibels to a 'wake-the-dead' level, I have no idea. But the kids had a great time.

So did I.

When the evening service was completed all the congregants were a bit tuckered but in good spirits. Just like everyone else, I headed home to get something to eat.

He that plans ahead — does not go hungry. The fried chicken dinner I purchased yesterday at the take-out was waiting in my fridge. I transferred the food from the Styrofoam container to my plate and nuked the food in the microwave. While it was warming I poured myself a large glass of Coke. The real-thing, with sugar.

After the welcome 'ding', I retrieved the stuff from the oven and juggled the piping hot plate to my table.

It smelled great.

I said the appropriate blessing, grabbed a hunk of chicken in my hand, dunked it in my favorite horseradish sauce and I had it almost to my lips, when I heard *Hava NaGilah* on my phone.

What did Dafna want?

I took a savage bite of the hot chicken and then reluctantly dropped the rest onto my plate. Using a paper napkin I wiped the drippings from my hands and took my phone from my pocket. Mumbling over the scalding hot food I was chewing I said, "Hello."

"Shimon," said Dafna demandingly loud. "Please get over here now."

I assume she meant her house, "What's the problem?"

"What's the problem? What's the problem?" she repeated excitedly. "A skinny little woman just walked in. She has purple hair and is dressed in what looks like a clown suit. And she is not dressed for Purim. The lady says she is here to plan our wedding. You need to come ... now," she demanded.

"I was just sitting down to eat ..." I tried to explain.

"Now!!!!"

Mary Lou had arrived.

13

Rip Off

NEXT MORNING was Purim day and I had not planned on going into work, but after the prayers and the required *Megilah* reading at the *yeshiva,* I went to my new office anyway.

I had to confront Mary Lou.

I wanted to chew her out for going to Dafna's house when Shaindel had specifically told her not to come. In addition, last night she put me in a particularly awkward position. Since I was Mary Lou's boss, I had no choice but to spend most of the previous evening defending her. Now I wanted to ball her out.

I knew she would be at the office, because that was the way she worked. Before I closed my firm, she used to get in at six a.m.

I saw her sitting in the corner of the room unpacking a shipment of stationary. Her back was to me and she apparently did not hear me enter.

Of course she did not, I am trained in stealth.

I am a professional.

That is why they pay me the big bucks.

Her hair was now canary yellow with a bright red tinge.

When had she had time to change the color of her hair?

She wore a black T-shirt under light blue bib overalls. The legs of the outfit were cut off well above the knees and red and white barber pole stockings covered her legs. Her feet were shod in pink ballerina slippers.

She did dress like a clown.

I took one silent step forward.

Then without turning around Mary Lou said, "Good morning, Mr. Lincoln."

How did she do that?

"Mary Lou, look at me."

"Yes, Mr. Lincoln," she said, as she swiveled her chair in my direction.

Uh oh. She never calls me Mr. Lincoln. It is always Sy or boss. Never Mr. Lincoln. *What was she playing at?* "I am thoroughly pissed off at you," I said angrily.

"Mr. Lincoln!" she said in a scolding tone.

"What?" I snapped in return.

"Mr. Lincoln, please don't use cuss words. Say, 'I am thoroughly *annoyed* at you.'"

What the heck? No way. "I am not annoyed, I am pissed. There is a big difference."

"Mr. Lincoln, we are all God fearing people in this office," she said in a saintly tone. "Cussing should have no part in our lives."

"OK. I am not p... the p-word ... with you. I am annoyed. Very annoyed. You had no right to show up at Dafna's house unannounced."

"Pardon me, Mr. Lincoln, but I had every right."

"How can you say that? They told you not to come."

"That is correct, but when they told me not to come, I told them in return that I was still coming. So they knew I would be there. Maybe I was not invited and maybe they were not happy that I came. But they knew I was coming so it was not unannounced."

"Why didn't you tell me you were going to do that?"

"Would you have allowed me to go?"

"Definitely not," I said decisively. "I would have demanded that you keep away from them."

"There you see," she said, as if pointing out the obvious.

"See what?"

"You would have asked me not to go. So there was no point in telling you."

"What?" I asked angrily.

"What is the problem? Everything worked out for the best."

"How do you see that," I said dumbfounded. "We were arguing for over an hour."

"We were not arguing. We were discussing the issue ... very heatedly."

"Shaindel was practically yelling. She never yells."

"But we came to an agreement. That's what is important."

"As I remember, the agreement is that you have nothing to do with the planning of the event. You will be Shaindel's assistant, doing all the gopher work and she will do all the planning and make all the decisions."

"That's right," she said innocently.

What was she plotting? Mary Lou was never anybody's assistant.

"When you planned all your nieces' and nephews' weddings ..."

"Extraordinary affairs," she commented wistfully.

" ... were you the official wedding planner?"

"Of course not," she insisted. "I told you, the mother, or mother-in-law, always wants to be the official planner."

"So what did you do?"

"I was always just the *assistant.*"

So, that was it.

She would be the *assistant.* Somehow I had the feeling that it was going to be a case of the tail wagging the dog.

I was still p... the p-word ... but I knew that she would never intentionally sabotage my life.

I am just an old sucker.

"OK, you are forgiven," I said solemnly.

She smiled and said contritely, "Thank you, Mr. Lincoln."

I am going to kill her.

No, I am not. She is a dear and I need her on my side, at least until the wedding is a memory.

"Boss — two things. Skip-Trace messengered over the preliminary report on Rabbi Slater. It's on your desk."

I knew that Mary Lou had already read it, "What does it say."

"Nada, nothing, and zilch. Not a trace of the rabbi. How long do you want to keep the account open?"

Skip-Trace charged for the preliminary report and then a daily charge for searching all the databases for the missing person. It was not cheap. Now that we had evidence that something bad might have happened to the rabbi, it might just be a waste of money. I decided to wait until we had definite proof. "Keep it open until I say to close it. What was the second item?"

"Frank Macon called. He has some work for you. Here is his number," she said holding out a yellow post-it note.

This could be the start of my new/old business. The problem was that since I am basically a one man firm, I could not work on too many cases simultaneously. So, before I decided if I could handle anything else, I called Sergeant Chandler to get an update on the Slater case.

She told me that the glasses had been examined carefully and the prescription and some smudged fingerprints showed that they were indeed Rabbi Slater's. Chandler also surprised me by stating that the investigation of the disappearance of Rabbi Slater was no longer being handled by the Southfield police. It would now be under the jurisdiction of the Oakland County

Sheriff's Department and the state police — mostly the latter. The reason for the shift was partly because this was commonly done in missing persons cases and partly because the Southfield police chief did not like the snide comments the state cops made about the Southfield force needing civilians to find evidence. The police chief's exact words were, "If you guys think you can do better ... be my guest."

Chandler did not object to the shift in responsibility. She would not be the one who had to fill out all the NCIC forms and someone else would take on the unpleasant duty of going to the hospital to inform Mrs. Slater. She added, that the county CSI team, using my GPS coordinates, went over the stretch of road where the glasses had been found and did not find anything else that would help determine the whereabouts of the rabbi.

Chandler also told me that if I needed anything more concerning Rabbi Slater, I should contact Lieutenant Nealy at the state police post on Ten Mile Road and he would send the request on to Lansing. "He's a real gem," she said sarcastically.

Chandler did not elaborate.

There had been no new information in the past 24 hours and there was no one I had to contact. So for now, the rabbi's disappearance was dead in the water and I was not generating any income to pay for my new office. Perhaps I did have time to see what Frank Macon wanted from me.

I sat down on my new chair behind my new desk in my new office. Mary Lou had rented all this stuff — we could always buy later — and had done a terrific job in setting it all up. She remembered all my likes and dislikes and the office was almost perfect. It needed a picture of Dafna and the girls for my desk. And then — as Goldilocks so aptly put it — it would be just right.

Frank Macon was a lawyer who specialized in corporate law and represented many medium to medium-large sized firms in Lower Michigan. The City of Detroit might be in financial straits, but the suburbs were bustling with business and Frank Macon's law practice was quite prosperous. His secretary answered on the third ring and put me through to her boss, "Sy, thank you for returning my call. Glad to hear you are back in business. I missed you."

"What can I do for you, Frank?"

"I am not really sure," he said hesitatingly. "I represent a firm that thinks they are being ripped off."

"What do you mean, 'they *think* they are being ripped off'?"

"They are pretty sure someone is stealing from them, but they don't know how it is being done."

"I assume when you say 'ripped off', you mean losing money. I suggest they get an auditor to follow the money trail. That's the best way. You don't need me."

"That's just it. The auditors went through the books with a fine-toothed comb. The profits and sales are just about the same as in previous years."

"But you just said they are being ripped off. I am confused."

"Welcome to the club," said the lawyer with a muffled laugh. "Could you contact the owner of the company and let him explain his problem. If you think you can help, that would be terrific."

"Sure, have someone scan the file and send the stuff to my e-mail. I will check it out and if it looks like I can do something I will give him a call."

"It's on the way."

The material arrived twenty minutes later and I printed it all out. Since I had some time to kill before the obligatory — and much anticipated — festive Purim meal at Dafna's house, I quickly looked through the papers. The Alkay Company manufactured high-end doors and windows for luxury commercial structures — hotels, office buildings, etc. The firm had been around since 1987 and was privately owned. It had 183 employees and their average annual sales were almost 300 million dollars. There was a seven percent fluctuation of this amount, plus or minus, every year for the past five years.

That is a lot of doors and windows.

Corporate profits were running at about 30 million per year with a fluctuation directly related to the sales figures — if more product was sold there was more profit for the firm.

So what was the problem?

The president of the company, Albert Kowalski, was convinced that someone was stealing their product. He just did not know the who, what, where or how much was being taken.

I could see why this was driving him crazy. There was no paper evidence that anything was being stolen and the company was not suffering any loss in profits.

Maybe the president should think about retiring?

I called the number given to me by the lawyer's office and Albert Kowalski answered himself. He sounded like he had all his marbles and we set up an appointment for early the next day.

The meeting had to be early. Tomorrow was Friday and I had to get ready for the Sabbath.

14

Bozo

WHEN I arrived at Dafna's house on Purim afternoon I thought I had mistakenly entered the UPS logistic center for the Lower Peninsula of Michigan. The entire living room was filled with in-coming *shlach manose* that other people had sent to the Lachler family. Dozens and dozens of assorted food parcels of all sizes were on the tables, sofas, and chairs. There were fancy packages with colored cellophane, artsy-craftsy containers, cardboard boxes, and just plain plastic bags. All of Dafna's outgoing stuff was in the kitchen, which still resembled a Cosco warehouse. She was furiously making more parcels, "Be with you in a little while. I still have another fifteen left on my list." Her full list had over 150 names. Dafna had lots of friends but had whittled down her list of pending *shlach manose* by shipping parcels all morning. Her daughters were still out on their bikes making deliveries.

Shaindel was in the dining room sorting through the parcels received and was separating all the food items into three groups. Stuff that would not keep and had to be eaten soon went in the first pile. Stuff that would not spoil or could be frozen went on the next mound. It was still a month before Passover and everything would be consumed by then. The third group of foodstuffs was almost exclusively homemade victuals and baked goods. These were items prepared by certain *balabustas* whose track record showed that they were sorely lacking the minimal level of culinary skill to prepare food that was edible. All this stuff was deemed a possible health hazard and not fit for human consumption. After carefully recording all the dangerous items in these risky *shlach manose,* they were dispatched to a large round rubbish barrel that sat at the side of the table. The precise inventory of the terrible stuff was necessary so that Dafna could wax eloquent about how much she enjoyed what she had received. I recognized a bag of *Rebbetzin* Slater's cookies in the bin.

Shaindel put me to work packing freezer boxes and *shlepping* them down to the basement. People came and went all afternoon. Some were delivering more parcels and others just stopped by to say hello. At about five in the afternoon all the deliveries had been made. The received goods had been sorted and stored away, and we were finally ready to sit down for the required festive meal.

"Time to set the table for the *Purim seudah,*" announced Dafna.

"How can I help?"

"Aren't you forgetting? I told you about our family's *minhag.*"

Oh my goodness, I forgot.

In Dafna's family the *Purim seudah* was a costume party. Anyone who wanted to partake had to be in full costume. Putting on a small face mask or a funny hat did not fill the bill. She warned me about this when I was invited and I had planned accordingly.

"Slipped my mind for a second," I apologized. "I have to go back to my condo to get my costume."

Shaindel chimed in, "It better be good or no meal."

It was going to be good.

An uncle of one of my dad's friends used to have the Bozo the Clown franchise for the Detroit area in the 70's and 80's. He made a living appearing on the local TV, opening shopping malls and stuff like that. When the superheroes and the internet took over the media in the 90's, Bozo was retired. I remember, when I was a young kid, he once surprised me by taking his costume out of mothballs and performing at my birthday party. When he died, his nephew — my dad's buddy — inherited the costume and he was the one who agreed to allow me to use it today. It took me almost fifteen minutes to put on the whiteface and makeup, and another quarter hour to get into the costume and put on the wig. I could not don the massive red shoes until I got to Dafna's house because if I wore them I would not be able to drive.

The huge red wig forced me to drive with my head tilted to the right but I made it to the Lachler house without wrecking my car. I put the clown shoes on over my own, checked myself in the mirror and walked up to the door.

I rang the bell.

Aliza opened the door, took one look at me and burst out laughing. Suzie joined her and began screaming, "Ima come here. It's Bozo. Just like in the cartoons."

Shaindel came to the door first. She took one look at me and said laughingly, "Now, that is good. You earned your meal."

Dafna joined the family at the door and totally cracked up.

So far I had not said a word. I just stood there.

I looked at them and asked, "How did you know it was me and not some nut dressed in a clown costume."

Dafna was the first to respond, "It is a nut dressed in a clown costume but we also saw you get out of your car."

I forgot about the car.

My superb detective skills show themselves once again.

"Come on in, everything is ready," said Mrs. Kalin.

I followed them into the house galumphing along in my oversized shoes.

Everyone was now in costume.

Suzie was a fairy with gauze wings attached to her back. Aliza was dressed in a doctor's outfit with a stethoscope draped around her neck. Shaindel had gone for the cowgirl look and was wearing a ten gallon hat, plaid shirt and leather skirt with fringes. Dafna's outfit was the most unusual. She was wearing a gray wig with a bun in the back and a long floral dress. Granny glasses were perched at the end of her nose. Old Mother Hubbard if I ever saw one.

I was hungry and we almost made it to the dining room when my phone rang.

It was Mary Lou, "Boss, I just got a call from the state police on Ten Mile Road. There is a Lieutenant Nealy over there who wants to speak with you. Write down his number and give him a call."

"How do the state police have your number?"

"I called them to let them know our office number and I also left them my cell. So give him a call."

"I am just about to sit down to dinner with Dafna's family. Can it wait?"

"The way he sounded ... I don't think so. Better talk to him."

I punched in the cop's number and he came on the line, "Nealy, here."

"Lieutenant, hi. This is Sy Lincoln. I was told to call you."

"Yeah, Lincoln," said the Lieutenant in a gruff voice. "You wanted something from the state police and I was told to give it to you. Come over and get it."

"I appreciate this Lieutenant Nealy. Would it be OK if I come in about two hours?"

"No, it would not be OK," he responded angrily. "I was told to give you this ASAP, so you get over here ASAP."

"How about in a half hour?"

"If you are not here in ten minutes, I am out of here and since I will not be around this weekend, you won't get the stuff until next week."

I thought how ridiculous I looked in my Bozo outfit, "Thing is, Lieutenant, I am not really dressed to come to the state police at this moment."

"So put on a pair of pants and get over here," said Nealy.

"It's not a matter of a pair of ..." There was no point in continuing because the lieutenant was no longer on the line.

I did not have a choice. I made my excuses to the Lachler family, took off my clown shoes and drove over to the station.

Although the state police have jurisdiction in the entire State of Michigan they have little interplay with the citizens of any particular community and most of the routine police work is done by the local constabulary. The state police handle problems for citizens far from any incorporated town, or that involve more than one county or if the problem involves traffic jurisdiction on one of the many interstate highways.

The state police post on Ten Mile Road is convenient to the I-696 Freeway, which connects with most of the major interstate routes in southern Michigan. By chance it is located immediately adjacent to the girls' school of the ultra-Orthodox community in Oak Park, so I have often passed this station but have never gone in.

I do not know of anyone that has ever gone in.

I parked in one of the visitor spots and approached the duty officer. He took one look at my clown outfit and broke out in a big smile. He was allowed. He was not on the Southfield police force. I told him my name and he gave me a visitor's badge. I got directions to the commander's office at the rear of the building. He told me I was expected and that I should go right in because the lieutenant's administrative assistant was not in today.

The outer office was empty and I knocked on the closed inner door bearing the prominent title in gold lettering, 1st Lieutenant Bertram Nealy.

"Come on in," someone bellowed from within. This was not a, 'Hi, how can I help you? - come on in.' This was more like a, 'Who is here to bother me now? - come on in.'

I entered the office and saw a police officer sitting behind an oversized super neat dark wooden desk. He was holding a mug of coffee in his hand and had his head bent down perusing a file. The center of the desk — about eighty percent of the polished surface — contained nothing but the file he was looking at. Everything else — the stuff that normal people scatter helter skelter on their desks — was arranged in small orderly piles aligned to the edges. There were no pictures, trinkets, doodads or old coffee mugs with pencils on the lieutenant's anally retentive work surface.

Lieutenant Nealy had a single silver bar on the collar of his dark blue state trooper's uniform. He looked to be in his early forties and his brown hair was shorn in a military like buzz cut. Even though he was sitting, he looked tall and lanky. His ruddy skin and angular facial features made me think that there must be some Native American heritage in his past. It looked as if his uniform had just been starched and ironed with him in it. *His shirt did not show a single unintentional crease.* There was a peaked officer's cap hanging from a hook on the back wall between the numerous plaques and accolades for the lieutenant personally and the station. Three file cabinets were at the right side of the room and two straight back wooden chairs were positioned in front of his desk. That's it. No decorations or pictures anywhere. The place was all business.

Nealy looked up from the file and took in my clown outfit. For just a fraction of a second, the expression on his face was like he had just seen a creepy crawly thing in his salad. It was gone in a flash and he put on an exaggerated compensatory smile as he asked disparagingly, "Are you Lincoln?"

My instant assessment of Lt. Nealy.

This guy was not too happy to see a clown come into his office. But I do not think that he would be any different even if I was not in the harlequin get up. Like maybe he was not too happy with his present assignment. Or maybe he had been passed over for a promotion. He also impressed me as the type that was known in the jargon as a 'hard-ass.' The kind of cop that could make your life a living hell if it suited him to do so. He was never your pal, but always your boss. I made this evaluation from only hearing him say, 'Come on in' and 'Are you Lincoln?.' Maybe I was wrong, but I still had to be on my toes.

"Sy Lincoln," I said.

"They said you were from that Ya-Shee-Vah. So, what are you? A rabbi or a clown?"

"Just Sy Lincoln. I'm no rabbi," I said extending my hand.

There was a moment's hesitation but he shook my hand across his desk and responded formally, "Have a seat."

"Thank you," I said.

"Would you like something to drink? I can get you a cup of this bad coffee," he said politely, gesturing with the mug.

"No thanks, I'm fine."

"Suit yourself." He waved his hand up and down in my direction and asked, "Why the clown outfit?"

"Today is a Jewish holiday. Like Halloween."

"Are you sure you are not a rabbi?"

"Positive. I am absolutely sure I am not a rabbi."

"Headquarters said that you are some kind of private investigator. You a former cop?"

"Detroit police ... fifteen years."

"And you want information on some rabbi that disappeared."

"Five weeks ago."

"Yes, I was just looking at the file they sent in from Lansing. You must have some sort of pull up there because they asked me to deliver it personally. They had me come in from a scene just to give this file to you and I have to be downtown in an hour. I am not usually yanked around like a yoyo just to be a messenger boy for a clown."

I have no clout with the state police, therefore it probably meant that my old boss, Mike Gleason, must have asked for a favor up in Lansing. So that was why he was pissed, "I appreciate any help I get from the state police."

"What's your connection to this case?"

"The head rabbi asked me to see if I can locate Rabbi Slater."

"Does that mean that they are not satisfied with what the police have been doing? Is that it?"

"It is not that ..."

"I really couldn't care less," he said, cutting me off. "I don't have any personal information on the incident. Those cases are not handled on the post level. You would get more information from the ..." he stopped to check the file, " ... Southfield police. Sergeant Chandler."

"I've already spoken with her."

"And did she give you all the info?"

"Yes, she did."

"So, having me come in special to be your messenger boy is all a big waste of my time?"

"I did not ask that ..."

Nealy did not let me continue, "The state police have not really done any investigating in the case and I don't know how we can help you."

"I just wanted to be sure I have all the information that is available."

"You want information?"

"Yes."

"The file says that they think this was a voluntary skip. Why are you getting bent out of shape for a voluntary skip?"

Obviously Lieutenant Nealy did not know about the glasses we found. So, I began, "There has been a new ..."

He cut me off with, "I don't give a rat's ass about the whole case, but, I can tell you one thing. Don't work yourself up into a sweat. People sometimes just pick themselves up and disappear without telling anyone. It happens all the time. My secretary ... she's a civilian ... just suddenly stopped coming in three weeks ago and left me in the lurch. She did not call me, or anyone else, to explain why. She was just gone. No reason. No one knows where she went. Not even her family. You just have to accept the fact that some people just need a change and the only way they can get it is by making a complete break and not looking back."

"I can assure you that this was not the case with Rabbi Slater," I stated emphatically.

Once again the lieutenant would not let me continue, as he quickly stood to his full six foot two height and said with a false smile, "Well, I'm not going to argue with you about whether he did or did not make a skip. So, I wish you well and here is your copy of the file. But, it is exactly the same as the information in the Southfield file."

I sensed that he was dismissing me and I stood as well, "Thank you for seeing me."

"Just one more word of advice," he added sternly. "This appears to be a simple skip. Don't go making a mountain out of a molehill. If you try to second guess the police you'll only make yourself a nuisance and a bigger clown than you already are. And having been a cop yourself, you know people in law enforcement do not take kindly to people who are a nuisance."

"Thank you, lieutenant. I appreciate your concern."

The bastard just threatened me.

There I go again, using the term bastard. Totally inappropriate for a *yeshiva* student. But as I walked out of the state police post — big clown smile painted on my face and bright red hair on my head held up high — I was totally pissed off.

Another expression I should not be using — but it fits so well.

I climbed into my car and slammed the door.

I just sat there staring out the windshield. I needed to calm down. I am confrontational, remember.

Once my blood pressure returned to normal I started my car and drove back to Dafna's house. I got my brain sorted out by reminding myself that today was Purim. The most fun day on the Jewish calendar. Good friends, happy family and a terrific meal awaited me.

15

Stolen Car

AND WHAT a meal it was.

It was spectacular for two reasons.

First, because unlike other Jewish holidays, where you cannot cook and all the foods have to be prepared ahead of time, today everything was fresh and either right off the stove or just out of the oven.

Second, because Dafna and her mother are such terrific cooks and everything was just sooooo — good. First course were ever so thin crepes filled with tangy peppery salmon, topped with a thick onion-garlic sauce. Then they served a rich vegetable soup with homemade noodles. The main course was a prime-rib roasted with lima beans. Sounds like a strange combination, but believe me it was delicious. Dessert was my favorite — chocolate mousse.

I was in heaven. Nealy was forgotten for now.

I took doubles and triples of everything. Today I did not have to feel unduly embarrassed about pigging out with the food, because this was an obligatory meal. I figured the more I ate the bigger the *mitzvah*. Besides, did I mention it was so — so — good?

Finally, when I had my gluttony under a modest amount of control, I leaned back in my chair and closed my eyes in total contentment.

I think they will need a crane to get me up from the dinner table.

"Shimon," said Dafna. "There is something I want to show you."

Coming out of my postprandial stupor I thought, 'More food?'

I mumbled, "What? ... What did you say?"

"I want to show you what I found."

Oh yeah. She had her computer looking for something.

We went down to her sanctuary.

She hit a few keys and turned the screen in my direction. "Take a look at this."

A grainy picture came up on the monitor showing a dark street and the rear of a white sedan with its brake lights illuminated. "What am I supposed to be seeing?"

"After we found the glasses, you said, 'We discovered that something very bad happened to the rabbi.'"

I nodded my head, "That's right and that is why we handed it all to the police."

"Yes, but I got to thinking. If we assume that someone did something bad to the rabbi. That means that that person had to have his own transportation. After all, Rabbi Slater's car was still there."

"Obviously," I stated.

"So whoever did this would not want to leave behind any evidence which could possibly indicate that something bad happened. Because if there were any clues he knew that the police would immediately try to spot his vehicle near the scene of the crime. But everyone with any brains in their head knows that just about all the major roads around here have traffic cameras so their car would be captured on the video cameras ... *discovered* if you will ... either coming to or going from the scene."

"So what?" I said. "Whoever did this knew there were no cameras on Jefferson Street and the traffic cameras on the major through streets take pictures of thousands and thousands of cars."

Dafna held up her palm like a traffic cop, "One second. You are correct, but it still does not alter the fact that the car that took Rabbi Slater probably went down one of those main streets and the image of that car had to be caught on camera."

"Big deal," I stated. "Even if the car was photographed we have no way of knowing which car it is."

"Maybe we do."

"OK," she just got my interest. "Explain."

"Like I said, the person that did this had to know there would be cameras. Unless he is a complete idiot, I am sure he did not want any of the cameras to photograph his own car and certainly not his license plate number. Because that would connect him with what happened to Rabbi Slater. So what could he do ...?" she asked looking for me to supply the answer.

I thought for a moment, "He could have used a stolen car."

"Right, but there is a problem with that. If he was driving a stolen vehicle, and it had been reported to the police, a cop might spot the car and run the plates and he could get stopped. Too dangerous for him," she said.

"Yeah, that would be troublesome," I agreed.

"So how could he still use a stolen car?" she asked rhetorically.

I thought for a moment, "If the stolen car had different plates."

"And where would he get such plates?" she asked again.

"From a wreck or maybe steal them from another car."

"Exactly."

"Wait a second. You're saying he switched plates, but if he was swapping plates, why didn't he just put them on his own car?"

"Because, his car would still be photographed near the scene. Too close for comfort," she said.

"So you propose that he used a stolen car with different plates."

"That's what I figure he did."

"But, he would still be driving a stolen car, so, he would have the same problem," I argued.

"When you were a cop and you saw a suspicious car, did you check plates or the make of the vehicle?"

"Almost always, the plates."

"So, he was fairly safe."

I saw what she was getting at, "Then unless he got stopped for some reason, no one could easily identify the car as being stolen."

"Correct," she said with a smile. "So if we see a stolen car or a car with the wrong license plates, on one of the traffic cameras ... it could be the car that was transporting Rabbi Slater from the scene."

"It could be. But, so what? We can't isolate that car because it would be lost in all the thousands that went by."

"Not really lost," she said. "What I did was look at all the cars that traveled down the main roads that access Jefferson Street between 10:30 at night, when Rabbi Slater called his wife, and 4:30 in the morning, when the car was found."

"What do you mean you looked at? Did you hack into the Oakland County Traffic Center's computers? Are you crazy? You know you broke the law. You could be arrested."

"Yeah, yeah, we'll get to that," she said dismissingly.

"What do you mean, 'We'll get to that'?"

"It's only a technicality. I have security clearance for all the counties in Michigan. I just did not ask … permission this time."

"But … but…," I stammered.

"First, look what I found," she said pointing to the car that appeared on the screen.

"What about the car?"

"A car just like that was reported stolen from Somerset Mall on the evening of the disappearance. The next morning, it was recovered a mile away from the mall just off Big Beaver Road."

"Did you also break into the police computers? I don't believe it," I said in exasperation. "Now you crossed the line. You are just going to love the Huron Valley Correctional Facility for Women. They have an exceptional *Shabbos* program."

"We'll deal with that problem after we find Rabbi Slater," she said nonchalantly.

What am I going to do with her?

I am going to marry her.

If she does not wind up in prison for a trillion years.

But that is Dafna. She does not think about herself.

A good *neshama.*

"Is this the car that was stolen?" I asked pointing to the picture on the screen.

"Maybe," she said. "This was shot on Greenfield road at 11:02 in the evening. So the time is right. Now look at the license plate. The plate we see is for a dark blue 2010 Honda Accord. This is a white 2014 Chevy Cruze."

How she could tell the exact model and year on such a grainy picture was beyond me. But I knew she had all sorts of enhancing software so I figured she knew what she was talking about.

How did she know that the registration was incorrect?

She must have hacked into the motor vehicle registration computer as well.

Better look up when they have visiting days at Huron Valley.

"What do you think of that?" she asked.

I had to admire the genius of the maneuver, "Stolen car with a different stolen plate. Clever. If the car was reported as stolen its plate number would be in the system. But with another plate on the car it would be almost unrecognizable on a routine check."

"What do you think?" she asked.

"I think I have an anonymous tip for Sergeant Chandler," I said.

"Why anonymous?"

"Because if I tell her you hacked into the system you could go to jail."

I called Chandler and she answered immediately. I heard kids screaming in the background, so I guess I caught her at home.

"Hi, this is Sy Lincoln."

"Mr. Lincoln, to what do I owe this unexpected and unrequested chat. Since we talked only this afternoon, you know that I am no longer involved with your missing rabbi."

"I know, but I thought you would be interested in hearing this anonymous tip and you can pass it on."

"Anonymous, like I did not hear it from you."

"Exactly."

"You thought wrong. I do not want to hear your tip. Call Nealy at the state police."

"Nealy does not like me very much."

"Hey, I don't like you that much either."

"Have you got a pencil."

"Call somebody else," she insisted.

"You have sworn an oath to help and protect the citizens of Southfield. It is your duty."

"Get out the fiddles and wave the stars-and-stripes, I'm already holding back the tears," she said mockingly.

"Got a pencil?"

"I am going to regret this."

"At 11:02 p.m. on the evening that the rabbi disappeared, there was a white 2014 Chevy Cruze, seen going south on Greenfield at Ten Mile Road and its plate number was UNZ-783."

"That's it?" she asked.

"Yup."

"I assume that you are not just reporting that one of your neighbors is guilty of some sort of moving violation. Is this connected with the rabbi's disappearance?"

"Could be."

"You mean, you don't know?" she said in exasperation.

"I said it could be. If nothing comes of it then no foul. If it does ... well ..."

"And you are not going to tell me how you got this information or from whom?"

"No, it is an anonymous tip."

"Lincoln, if I pass on this bit of information, and it pans out, they are going to be all over me. I have to know where you got the tip."

"I can't tell you. Trust me. There is a good chance that it might help find the rabbi."

"You know they will figure out it is from you or your girlfriend, *Mrs. Lackler*."

Cannot blame her for mispronouncing the name. I do not do much better. But how did she know about Dafna? "What makes you say that?"

"Because the state police in Lansing told me about you two solving a case up there last year, that's why. They are well aware that *Mrs. Lackler* is some sort of computer genius. And I don't have to use any of my sharply honed detective skills to figure out that someone took an illegal peak into the computer that houses the traffic videos and who knows what else."

"It is still an anonymous tip."

"Suit yourself. I'll run it through traffic. If it rings any bells, I will pass it along."

16

Doors

AFTER ALL the food I packed away at the *Purim seudah,* it was no surprise that I woke Friday morning feeling bloated like the Goodyear blimp. Somehow I was still able to drag myself to morning prayers at the *yeshiva.*

I sensed that everyone was staring at me.

Thing is — no one really was.

I looked around the large *bais medrash* and saw that all the other worshipers were either concentrating on the words in their *siddur* or were praying devoutly with their eyes shut.

My head was playing tricks on me.

Why did I feel like a fish out of water?

Today was my first day back in civilian clothes. The Blues Brothers' uniform would be used on *Shabbos* and holidays. My present outfit consisted of a dark green polo shirt under a tan zip-up sweatshirt, light brown corduroy slacks, and dark blue Nikes. My black Borsalino was hanging from a peg in my foyer and a Tigers cap covered my head. I looked very trendy.

Rebbi told me that no one in the *yeshiva* would care what I wore — but apparently I did.

I felt as if I was out of uniform. And if you do not wear the uniform you are not really part of the team.

Of course this was not logical, since as a detective on the Detroit police force, I rarely wore my uniform and I was certainly part of the team.

I was dressed this way because this morning I had my meeting with Albert Kowalski. Wearing my *yeshiva bocher* outfit might just make him a bit uncomfortable.

I had to learn to control my own paranoia.

Alkay Incorporated was located in a modern industrial park on Thirteen Mile Road in Warren. The entire complex was walled off with cyclone fencing topped with coils of ominous razor wire. Anyone stupid enough to climb over this fence would come away cut to ribbons. Visitors only had access to the administration building. All the manufacturing areas and storage facilities were behind the offices and could only be reached by getting clearance from a security guard at a separate gate.

My initial assessment was that the security arrangements for physical access to the plant were satisfactory. It was not at Fort Knox security level but it was still pretty good.

I parked in a visitor's spot in front of the two story administration building and went in to the security desk. The guard called someone and I was told to wait. He then gave me a green visitor's badge attached to a lanyard. I placed it around my neck and he told me that I had to wear the tag while I was on company property and to return it when I left.

A young woman came down the hall and told me she was Mr. Kowalski's assistant and to follow her. She did not introduce herself by name and I could not read it from her little yellow ID tag, because she apparently was a firm believer in the 'If you've got it ... flaunt it' school of life. Her name tag was not on a lanyard and was intentionally pinned in an already prominent area of her upper torso. Polite gentlemen were expected to avert their eyes from this anatomical area. Careful scrutinization of her yellow tag would be considered to be in poor taste.

Even though no one has ever accused me of being a polite gentleman, this was certainly the expected behavior for an engaged Orthodox gentleman — even if he was part of an investigation.

Albert Kowalski was waiting in his office and asked me if I would like something to drink.

Kidneys must be hydrated at all times, so I accepted his offer of a soft drink.

Mr. Kowalski asked Miss Yellow Tag to get me the beverage. The boss man of Alkay, Inc., looked to be around sixty years old and was almost entirely bald except for a fringe of gray hair that went around the back of his skull and continued forward as long sideburns. He was wearing a long-sleeved white shirt with thin blue stripes, gray trousers, and no tie. There was a large picture on the wall showing a much younger and thinner Albert Kowalski, decked out in a football uniform, jumping in the air catching a pass. He was about six feet tall and his commendable paunch gave me a clue that his football days were long gone. A minute or two was spent discussing the weather and the chances for the Tigers having a good season. His assistant, with the eye-catching yellow badge, returned with my Coke.

What was my initial impression of Albert? Good honest hard-working man. Probably built this company up from scratch. Kind of man that his word is his bond. You treat him fairly he treats you fairly.

Albert got down to business.

"Somebody is stealing from us."

"That's what Frank told me. I saw your auditor's profit and loss sheet, along with the assessment of your entire inventory and they look fine. What makes you think someone is stealing from you."

"Frank said you were a good detective."

"Thank you."

"And so am I."

"Then, maybe you don't need me."

"Do you know how I know that we are being ripped off?"

"Right now, I have no idea."

"I did not tell Frank, but last week I happened to be in New York. And I was near Times Square where Zeelon Corporation, one of our biggest clients, is putting up a super duper luxury hotel. For the past ten years they have been buying windows and doors from us for most of their projects."

"So far, sounds good to me."

"Luxury office buildings and hotels need luxury doors and windows. There are a lot of low-end door and window manufacturers but in the high-end market there are only seven major players and we are one of them. A cheap door unit runs about $700 to $1,000. Quality doors run three to four times and even ten times that amount."

He opened a desk drawer and handed me a large plastic embossed booklet which showed what they produced. "Our company makes five basic styles ... and only five ... of windows and doors. We make them in all sizes, but there are only five styles. Each model also comes in five different finishes and many many colors. If one of the styles is not selling well we will consider developing a new one, and that happens about every three to four years. Bringing in a new style costs a tidy bundle, and that is why we only have five and do not change very often. By keeping the number of styles steady we save money on retooling and design. That way we can sell a really good door or window for a really good price ... cheaper than the other companies. That has been my marketing strategy since I opened this place."

I studied the different types of doors and window frames. I could see why his product was indeed high-end. His items seemed to have solid construction, good materials, heavy steel framing, sound and fireproofing, and were compatible with a multitude of decors.

In short they made a unique, quality product.

"That's what we produce," he said proudly.

"Where does the theft come in?" I said handing back the catalogue.

"I'm getting to that." He put the booklet back into his drawer. "About two ... maybe three ... years ago I read in the trade papers that Zeelon got the contract to construct this fancy hotel in Midtown New York ... real close to Times Square and the theater district. I was really excited for them, because we sold them doors and windows and that meant we would make a tidy profit. You following me so far."

"Zeelon ... tidy profit."

"So, I was real happy to see the order from Zeelon for 3,000 doors and 6,000 windows. About a twelve million dollar order."

"That's a lot of doors and windows. Congratulations."

"The thing is ... that was it."

"What was it?"

"That was their entire order. It does not make sense. A hotel like that needs close to 6,000 doors and 12,000 windows. Around twenty-five million dollars. They never ordered any more. There was just the one order."

"Maybe they ordered the rest from one of your competitors?"

"Possible, but unlikely," he said wagging his finger at me. "First of all we are a lot cheaper. Second ... you change your door company you change the style of your rooms. No architect or interior designer is going to go along with that. Guests in fancy hotels like to see a consistency in the décor. They know that they will get the same kind of room if they check in a year from now."

"So what did you do?"

"Well ... I said I was a good detective."

I thought for a moment, "So, last week you did not just happen to be in New York. And you did not just happen to be near Times Square. You went there to snoop."

Albert pointed his finger at me, "Bingo."

"And what did you find?"

"I found my windows and doors."

"But what about the rest of the hotel?"

"I found my windows and doors in the entire hotel."

"3,000 doors?"

"No, 6,000 doors."

"So, the hotel is finished and all the doors are yours?"

"They are still in the middle of construction. About 60% completed, but I saw where they keep their stock and what has been installed. I could not count them exactly, but I can make a good estimation. There were 6,000 doors and 12,000 windows."

"Your product?"

"No question about it," he said. He reached into his desk drawer and handed me a packet of pictures, "You can keep the pictures ... I have other copies. Those are my doors and windows."

In each of the photos there were piles and piles of cartons with the Alkay logo, "And you did not sell it to them."

"Not the second half."

"Could this stuff be some sort of Chinese knockoff? Stuff that looks like your product?"

"That kind of junk could maybe fool a simple contractor But I make this stuff and I recognize what I manufacture. Those are Alkay doors and windows."

"Do you have accurate records of how much product you make and ship?"

"Very tight control."

"So why don't you just see who bought that type of door and look among them for your thief?"

"The model door that Zeelon ordered is our best seller ... Zephyr style, Pueblo tan color and glossy finish ... it's our lowest priced model and accounts for over 40% of our sales. That's hundreds and hundreds of orders. Still we looked. Every box has a serial number. We know when it was made. We know where it is stored here in the plant and we know when it was shipped and to whom."

I looked at a few of the photos and noticed that in several pictures the labels with the serial numbers appeared quite legible. "Did you check out the serial numbers that can be seen in the pictures?"

"Of course we did. Checked every one we could read."

"And what did you find?"

"Every number matches with the stock Zeelon purchased from us."

I pointed to the pile of pictures, "So where is the stolen stuff?"

"I figure the bastards were smart enough to first install all the merchandise they ripped off from us and left the legal stuff to be put in last."

"But to do that would require a logistics operation of huge proportions," I argued.

"Stealing twelve million dollars from me made it worthwhile for them."

"So, even though you have not seen a single pilfered item ... you are still convinced that they stole twelve million dollars worth of doors and windows."

"Absolutely."

"OK, let's say that is so. Did you check to see where the product was stolen from?"

"Sure."

"And?"

"Well that's the reason I need you. Every window and door that we made for the last two years is accounted for."

"No one has been stealing product from the people you sell to?"

"I called all the major buyers and they have not reported any large losses."

"Did you call the Zeelon Company and ask them about the discrepancy?"

"Of course not."

"Why?"

"I don't want to let them know I am on to them. I don't want them to be able to cover their tracks. I want to catch those bastards."

"So where do you think Zeelon is getting your product?"

"That's what I want you to find out."

I thought for a moment. *Could I help this guy?* There was probably a very logical reason for this discrepancy in the door and window orders. *Still, what was going on here?* "I'll give it my best shot," I said.

"Here at the plant, no one knows that I want this investigated except you, me, and Frank Macon. So, we're going to introduce you to everyone as a security expert who has been called in to do a routine evaluation of the security measures in the plant. I'll have my secretary show you around," said Kowalski as he picked up his phone.

"You want me to investigate, but to be honest with you, I may be wasting my time and your money. I'm willing to bow out at any time if you think that is the best way to go."

"Thanks for being so open about it. Frank told me that you are a reliable and capable investigator. So, if you get to the point where you think that no crime has been committed against Alkay, please let me know as soon as possible."

"You can count on it," I said.

Miss Yellow Tag took me on a tour of the main features of the plant. We went through the administrative offices, the production facility, and the storage buildings.

The visits were cursory and I knew I would need to spend more time in each area.

We wound up at the security office. She left me with Ace Bigelow, the fellow in charge. I knew his real name was Horace because I read it on the little yellow card hanging around his neck. I am allowed to look in that area if it is a man who was 60 years old and a former Birmingham policeman. He told me that the rest of his fifteen-man crew had no real police experience and he trained them in basic security measures and protocols. The crew rotated to cover the plant 24 hours in the day. The actual security arrangements for the company had been prepared by a security firm and at first glance they appeared to be adequate.

Initial assessment of Ace. Good policeman. He most likely had not been the sharpest cop on the Birmingham force, but he would be thorough and do things by the book. I also sensed that he was honest and a hard worker. He took pride in keeping his crew as professional as possible. You could trust him.

Horace explained the nuts and bolts of the security measures in place at the company. I could not see any obvious problems in the protocols. But, if someone was stealing from the company, then it was quite possible that these standard security arrangements were just not good enough.

I learned that one of the security guards was on duty at the loading bay at all times and all product was checked off on his iPad before it was loaded onto the trucks. All the manifests were checked again by the guard at the gate. The trucks were also weighed as they entered and left the plant to be sure that whatever was supposed to be on the truck was there. Nothing more and nothing less.

There was 'real time' computer control for all product and this list was updated instantaneously. The main office and all the salesmen knew exactly how much product was in stock and available at all times.

After about thirty minutes, Kowalski's assistant came back and she helped me explore all the nooks and crannies that could possibly hide a door or a window. I checked buildings and sheds around the plant. Closets, niches, storerooms, and containers. I spent a total of four hours exploring, but when I left, I was in the same position as when I had arrived — large numbers of doors and windows were being stolen and I did not have an inkling as to how it was being done.

Before I left the plant, I stopped back at the security office and Horace handed me a stack of DVDs. These were copies of the videos for the last six months of the six surveillance cameras that covered the warehouse, loading docks, and gates. So that meant I had three years of video to review. I had no idea how I would be able to scan so much video footage.

I looked forward to the coming *Shabbos.*

Perhaps the quiet and rest would jump-start my brain so that I might get some insight as to how Alkay was getting ripped off.

17

Dojo

I ATTENDED *Shabbos* services at the *yeshiva* and slept in my own condo but I spent the rest of the time with Dafna and her family.

Shabbos is unique.

What makes it special?

It builds families.

The Sabbath starts on Friday at sundown with the lighting of the *Shabbos* candles and ends at nightfall on Saturday night. During these twenty-five hours, Orthodox Jews go to synagogue (three times), eat fancy meals (three are required), and enjoy each other's company. Jewish law adds further restrictions regarding the actions that may be performed on *Shabbos*. Religious Jews cannot use wheeled transportation and cannot turn on any electrical items. So, there is no TV or radio. No iPhones or tablets. No electronic anything. It also meant that no one goes to the mall to take advantage of some unbelievable sale. No one has to get to a ballgame because someone's favorite team is in town. No one has to go back to their place of business to catch up on work they did not finish during the week. You just stayed home with your family.

My grandfather, Morris Lincoln (nee Moshe Levinsky), is now 91 years old and still going strong, living in a retirement village on the Gulf Coast of Florida. He used to come to visit every couple of years and one time he told me that when he was a kid, he felt that the start of the Jewish Sabbath was like being locked away for a 25-hour jail sentence. At age eighteen he rebelled against his parents and Orthodox Judaism, changed his name to Lincoln, and refused to observe the Sabbath in any way. Grandpa Moshe had three kids and two followed in his boycott of Orthodox Judaism. But my Uncle Bernie, somehow returned to the fold, observing *Shabbos* and attending services at the Young Israel Synagogue. His son, my cousin Steve — a successful contractor — is also a member. Grandpa still cannot figure out where he went wrong. Grandma Ethel passed away ten years ago and Grandpa now lives in sin with Norma, a 83-year-old spring chicken, from New York. Norma is not religious in the usual sense but she still insists on lighting *Shabbos* candles every Friday night. It probably drives Grandpa crazy.

I have only been Sabbath observant for two years, but for me it feels nothing like being incarcerated. When *Shabbos* starts I can sense how it envelopes me with an almost tangible aura of spirituality. I cannot explain it. It just feels good.

So on this particular Sabbath I ate great food, relaxed body and soul, and enjoyed Dafna and her family.

Soon to be my family.

All during the day some of Dafna's friends dropped by to say hello and chat. Most people in today's electronic age do not remember that before the advent of iPhones, tablets, Facebook, Instagram and Twitter, people would do that. They would communicate by talking one to the other — in person — without any texting or posting. Unbelievable.

The Jewish Sabbath builds families.

After evening prayers on Saturday night I said good bye to the Lachler family and went back to my condo, changed out of my black suit into jeans and a T-shirt, grabbed a beer, turned on my computer, and inserted a DVD. I put the machine at fast speed — I had three years of Alkay video images to review. After four hours I had done three weeks on just one camera. I was fighting to keep my eyes open, so I called it a night.

Next morning after services I put in another three hours, but looking at videos of the empty Alkay factory — even at a fast speed —was extremely boring. At noon I cashed it in and went to the *dojo* of the Detroit Kodokan for my weekly workout.

As a youth, the educational system had dubbed me — for want of a better term — a problem student. I was the kind of kid whose report card was liberally sprinkled with the comment — 'does not reach his full potential.' I was probably ADD or ADHD or some other fancy initial syndrome. The educators in my schools — plural, because I was expelled from several — never figured out how to educate me. In desperation my folks indulged me in the one thing that interested me. Martial arts. They sent me to several martial arts schools and even hired private instructors. I became quite proficient, earning black belts in Judo, Aikido, and Karate. Each sport required a different mindset — discipline. So when I played one sport, I had to concentrate to keep my moves correct for that art. Interestingly, when I needed to defend myself as a street cop I used a combination of all three in a harmony that I cannot explain.

Ten years ago, my Judo *sensei,* Nakamura-san, formally asked me to come by on Sunday afternoons to help instruct his advanced Judo class. I could not refuse and I now try to make it every week. It gives me satisfaction to help train his students and keeps me from getting rusty.

I spent the first hour doing warm up exercises with the students. Slow and easy. The next hour was instruction. The *sensei* showed them the proper way of making a particular move and I worked with individual students showing them how to finesse each move in a way that would be appropriate for each of them. In the third and fourth hours bouts were organized between students while the others watched from the side. Nakamura-san judged these contests but after each bout we both commented on the success or failure of each of the moves made by the pair. The final bout, as usual, was me against one of the advanced students. The majority of these guys and gals had brown belts and most times I won. Today I lost, but that was the way it was in sport. Win or lose, it certainly helped to keep me on my toes.

When I returned from the *dojo* I showered and changed into casual clothes. I glanced at the pile of videos that awaited me.

It was daunting.

I called Dafna.

I needed her help.

I gave Dafna all the known facts about the possible theft from Alkay and how I had to check the equivalent of three years of security videos to see if there were unusual comings or goings from the plant. Anything that might indicate how product was being smuggled out of the warehouse.

She listened patiently and then said simply, "Same deal."

"What deal?" I inquired.

"I help you ... you let me work on the case."

"You are already working on Rabbi Slater's disappearance."

"I meant the theft from the Alkay Company. So ... if you want my help ..."

"Come on now. That's not fair."

"I never said I was fair. You want me ... you gotta pay the price."

I considered my options. Sit in front of the computer bored out of my head for a year or two, or spend a few days and afternoons with Dafna at my side.

No contest.

"I agree," I said reluctantly. I just had to be careful that Dafna stayed safe. The case involved quite a few million dollars and things could get very hairy, very fast.

"Good," she said. "As I see it we have three problems. The first is reviewing the actual videos to see if there is any unusual activity. That's the easy part."

"That's easy? There are three years of video on the DVDs."

"Hold your horses," she said. "I'll explain in a moment. The second problem is checking to see that what we are looking at is genuine. Someone could have stolen half the plant and then spliced in old footage to cover the activity."

"How do you check that?" I asked.

"Luckily there is a dual time stamp on most videos. The first is the visual legend that prints the time and date on every video image. That can be faked. But there is also a digital time stamp and it is extremely hard to alter."

"But it could be done."

"Yeah, but there are only a half dozen people in the world who know how to do it, so it is unlikely."

"Are you one of them?"

"Yes, but why would a thief waste his time doing that? It is very time consuming and it would be easier to just destroy the video."

"The third has nothing to do with the videos. You need to check the computerized records for receipt of raw materials, production, and shipping. Someone could be making a whole heck of a lot of doors and windows and then erasing it all from the computer production records. Then they could be smuggling them out of the plant. I have to look at the company's computer system."

"I'll arrange it," I said. "But the first thing we have to do is check the videos. Can you do that?"

"Sure. Leave it to my Playstations."

Dafna had figured out a way to hook twelve Sony Playstation IVs in line so that they functioned like a super computer. They were sitting on the shelf behind her computer and appeared innocuous. Few people knew the power residing in that stack of game machines.

"How can Playstations do that?"

"From what you told me it would be almost impossible to steal the product by going through the normal shipping and handling done through the loading docks. So if the videos are genuine, it is extremely unlikely that we will pick up anything unusual during the working day. We have to assume that the best possibility is that it is being moved during the off hours. That is what makes my work easy."

"This will be easy?"

"It's like reverse facial recognition."

"Whose face are we looking for?"

"The face we want to see is the empty plant. Anything else would be abnormal. Should be a breeze for the Playstations."

I nodded my head as if I understood what she was talking about, "Yeah, a breeze."

"My program will recognize what the deserted plant looks like. If there is any movement or action, that segment will be extracted and saved. It will also automatically check for the digital time signature to be sure all images are really what they say they are."

"How long?"

"Bring over the DVDs. I'll need about two hours to write the program and then another seven to ten hours for the computer to go through thirty-six months of video images. You will still have some video segments that you will have to review visually.   Maybe an hour or two of recordings."

Three years in seven hours?

Unbelievable.

A breeze she says. How does she do that?

Tomorrow morning Dafna might just give me the first clue as to how someone could be stealing from the plant, "Terrific. Thank you very much."

"My pleasure ... partner."

<u>18</u>

Threats

IT WAS now Monday morning and a week since we started looking for Rabbi Slater. So far we had found his glasses and the suspicious car on Greenfield road from the night of the disappearance. Unfortunately there were no further 'Aha!' or 'Eureka!' moments from us or the police, therefore we still had no idea what actually happened to him.

I was eager to find out what Dafna's computer search had turned up on the Alkay case so I mooched a breakfast invitation for after morning prayers. The fact that my kitchen cupboards were as bare as the Alaskan tundra in the dead of winter and that I could look forward to delectable victuals at Dafna's house, had no bearing on my decision.

I knocked on her door and heard a scampering of feet. Aliza and Suzie dressed in their school uniforms, pulled open the door and screamed happily, "Shimon!"

The girls were a delight.

I asked solemnly, "Princess Suzie, Princess Aliza, is the Queen Mother at home?"

I always referred to them as royalty.

Aliza giggled and held up her hands to cover her mouth. Suzie just smiled widely suppressing her mirth. She was trying to act mature.

They were a good audience. Both of them did not tire of my *shtick*.

"*Ima*," screamed Suzie. "Shimon is here."

Dafna came to the door, "Get ready for school, girls. Your car pool will be here in a minute."

The girls ran off saying over their shoulders, "Bye Shimon."

"You know, my girls really love you," she said.

"Ah ... a good start. Perhaps I can hoodwink their mother into loving me as well."

"I have been hoodwinked ... hoodwinked but good," she said fondly.

"You have made my day, fair lady," I said with a formal bow.

"Come in. I suppose you would like something to eat."

Is she kidding?

Is the Pope Catholic?

"I could do with a little bite of something to tide me over," I said humbly.

"Almond scones and scrambled eggs with cheese. How does that sound?"

How does it sound? It sounds as I was about to enter the Garden of Eden to sample from the Tree of Life.

"I am willing to give it ... a taste ... just so you will not be offended by my refusal."

"You are too kind."

"I know."

The scones, with crunchy bits of toasted almond, were light and flaky. Sliced and slathered with butter, I could eat a million of them. The fluffy eggs were augmented with a mixture of two types of molten cheese — zesty and mellow — that blended together fabulously. This ambrosia flowed over my tongue and exploded into a taste sensation that slid effortlessly down my gullet. I can become very emotional when someone feeds me good food. I could not help myself and polished off three portions. I am a pig — sometimes.

Perhaps — often times.

Breakfast culminated with blueberry muffins and one of those capsule coffees, heavily dosed with half-and-half.

Hey, I am a hard-working man. I am entitled.

We finally made it down to her computer work area and she handed me a disc, "These are all the unusual segments from the six cameras we were looking at. Whenever something came up on one of the cameras I automatically brought it up on the other five cameras to try and get another view of what happened. Altogether, 780 separate incidents."

"That's quite bit."

"Luckily, the vast majority ... over 500 of them ... are when a security guard wandered into the field of view of one of the cameras. The other two hundred or so make up a total of 72 minutes that have to be reviewed. There was no monkey business with the time stamp, and that means everything we see is genuine."

She slid the disc into the drive and booted it up. Besides the security guard captures Dafna's program had detected between 40 to 50 incidents that had triggered each of the six cameras. There were a few stray dogs and cats running around the plant. Wind had knocked over cartons a few times. In one scene a forklift suddenly rolled backwards in the middle of the night and crashed into the loading dock. There were a few nearby lightening strikes. All in all — nothing. No unusual activity that indicated that any raw materials had been smuggled in or product smuggled out of the plant in the last six months.

We finished checking the videos and I said to Dafna, "So no product left the company, other than whatever went through the normal shipping procedures."

"It's always possible there is a secret tunnel somewhere, but highly unlikely. So I agree with you," she said with a nod of her head.

I was contemplating our next move when my phone rang and I recognized Lieutenant Nealy's angry voice, "Lincoln, is that you?"

Of course it was me. *Who else would answer my cell phone?* The state police lieutenant was not in a good mood.

"Yes it is. And a good morning to you too," I said cheerfully.

"Get your rear end in gear and get over to my office," he demanded gruffly. "And bring your girlfriend, *Mrs. Lackler*, with you as well."

"What is this in reference to?" I asked innocently.

"It's in reference to obstruction of justice, you losing your license, *Mrs. Lackler* going to jail ... that's what this is in reference to. Get over here now."

He hung up.

My — my — he is not a happy boy scout.

An obviously displeased Lieutenant Nealy was waiting for us in his office. He impatiently motioned to the two chairs facing his desk and we sat down.

No offer of drinks or refreshments. Very ominous.

"Have you seen this?" he asked, passing us a copy of the Oakland County News opened to a middle section. I had not seen the publication because the small local paper came out on the weekend and neither myself nor Dafna had a subscription.

There was a short article stating that Rabbi Slater was now considered a missing person and that the police were following up on a possible stolen car involved in the disappearance. It also mentioned our names — both me and Dafna — and stated that I was a private investigator helping the police.

Someone had leaked the story to the press and I was pretty sure I knew who it was.

"Do you know the expression 'Shit rolls downhill'?" asked Lieutenant Nealy rhetorically. "Well, the shit has begun rolling. My captain chewed me out. Chewed me out really fine. Do you know why he chewed me out?" he asked again. "Because you two have been meddling in things you should not."

"All we did was ..." I began.

"All you did was try to show up the Southfield police and the Oakland County Sheriff's Department. They all called the inspector for District 2 who spoke with our captain. Who spoke with the lieutenant colonel in Lansing. Who spoke with the colonel. Now you have the entire state police pissed off at you. The colonel started the shit rolling and it came all the way back down to me, simply because I had spoken to you that one time. So now you have me pissed off as well."

"There really was nothing ..." I tried to say.

"Not only that, when you were here last week you already knew that the rabbi's glasses were found. But you did not tell me. You came in dressed like Bozo, but you made me out the clown," he said angrily.

"I tried but you would not ..."

"You didn't try very hard."

"Look, I'm sorry and I ..."

"I do not want to hear that you are sorry. I want you to listen to me and understand what I am saying. You are a licensed private investigator in this state, so officially I can't tell you what to do, but if you try this crap again, we will bring you up on charges for willfully contaminating a possible crime scene, obstruction of justice, and we will rescind your license so fast your head will spin."

What the hell was going on here? I did not work for the government — at any level — so he had no right to push me around. I answered defiantly, "Who are you kidding? I was a cop. There is no way you could yank my license or convict me on any of those charges."

"Maybe not," he said with a smile. "But even if we can't make the charges stick you can be assured that your name will go on our big brown list and your days of having any kind of cooperation with any police force in this state will be over."

That he could do.

Big problem.

The cop then turned to Dafna, "We have proof that you illegally hacked into numerous restricted state and local computers. The only reason you are not up on charges is that the computer folks in the Lansing headquarters say that you are a big help to them in many cases. But if you do anything like that again I will arrest you in the blink of an eye."

Dafna looked stoically at Lieutenant Nealy and said simply, "No, you don't."

"No, I don't, what?" snapped the cop.

"First of all, I don't know who you think you are talking to. I am not your employee. As a matter of fact ... you ... as a state employee ... you work for me. So, I advise you to change your tone."

"Now look here ..." began Nealy.

Dafna cut him off with, "I'm not saying I did or did not do whatever you said I did, but you certainly do not have proof that I did anything illegal," she said with conviction. "Ask Jane Fuller, in the IT division."

Atta girl Dafna.

"Who the hell is Jane Fuller?" asked the cop.

"She is just about the brightest person in the state police IT division and the state's expert in detecting illegal entry into government computers. Call her and she will tell you that there is no such evidence," said Dafna confidently.

Nealy had been bluffing and Dafna had called him out. If he was not pissed before, he sure was now.

Time to call it a day.

Rising to my feet, I said, "Thank you Lieutenant. If that is all, tell the higher-ups that the message was received loud and clear." I tugged at Dafna's sleeve, "Let's go. I think the Lieutenant is done with us."

Dafna stood and turned to me, "Aren't you going to ask him about the car?"

The veins on Nealy's neck were bulging dangerously and he looked like he was about to explode.

"I think we will save that question for another day," I said as I pulled her out the door.

Dafna was furious, but I kept her in check until we made it to the parking lot, then she let go with a vengeance, "Did you hear that? He was threatening us."

"He sure was," I replied.

"Of all the nerve. He had no right to talk to us that way."

"His boss ... and all the brass of the state police ... gave him permission."

"Then, they had no right to do that. We are law abiding citizens."

"Well, not exactly," I said, hedging a bit. "You did break into a whole bunch of government computers illegally."

"But, they don't know that. They are only guessing."

"Are you sure, there is no proof of your break in?"

"One hundred percent," she said with confidence.

"Could you detect if someone broke into those computers."

"Certainly."

"Then, so can they."

"No, they can't."

"Why not?" I asked.

"Because they do not have the hardware, software, or talent to discover how I get into computer systems. There are only a dozen people on the globe that could."

"OK, so you're in the clear. Even so, they can make both our lives miserable if they are so inclined, so I guess we cool our heels for a while and just work on the Alkay account."

"Where did the newspaper get the information about the glasses and the car? Do you think your sergeant from the Southfield police told them?"

"I'll ask her but I'm pretty sure it was not her."

"Then who?"

"Did you tell your mother?"

"Tell her what?"

"About the glasses and the car."

"Well ... she did ask me how we were doing ... and ..."

"... and you told her. Did you remember to tell her not to tell anyone else?"

Dafna seemed a bit embarrassed and finally said, "I guess I forgot."

"So if she spoke to one of her friends ... and that information somehow got to a reporter from the paper .... and that reporter just happened to call her ... she would be more than eager to tell them how her brilliant daughter helped the police."

"She would not do that," she said without much conviction.

"You know she would."

"But that still did not give that lieutenant the right to scold us. He just made me so angry."

"I know how you feel," I said in agreement.

"I have a good mind to ..."

"No, you won't. Stay clear of Lieutenant Nealy. Don't get into his computer. Don't sabotage his pension fund. Don't do anything. Is that clear?"

"Absolutely clear. Don't I do everything you ask?"

Yeah, sure.

19

Bris

TUESDAY MORNING bright and early I called Mr. Kowalski at his home and arranged for Dafna to check the computer system at the plant later in the morning. He said he would set it up immediately.

We were not available during the early morning, because today the Slater baby was eight days old and we were to be guests at his *bris*. We were not invited to the ritual circumcision, but we were still going. Why? Because in the Orthodox world no one is ever invited to a *bris*. It is an old Jewish custom that you only *inform* people about a *bris* — no *invites*. Something to do with excommunication if you are invited and do not show. So, the parents let people know that their eight day old male child would be undergoing his life changing genital alteration at a certain time and place, and they would be happy to see them there. *Rebbetzin* Slater had called twice to tell us that she would be delighted if we came.

We had to go.

The occasion was more sad than happy. It was happy because another young baby was being ushered into the Jewish faith and sad because the pall of his missing father hung over the event. The circumcision was to be held in the *bais medrash* of the *yeshiva* and would commence immediately after the morning prayers. Women, other than close family members, rarely came to these early morning affairs, but not so for this *bris*. Practically all the wives of the *yeshiva* teaching staff showed up to offer moral support for *Rebbetzin* Slater.

The *mohel*, one of the young rabbis in the community, chanted the prayers to start the ceremony and the baby was brought into the hall. People were honored by having their names called out and then they helped pass the young tyke on to the next person being honored until he reached the central *bima* and the 'Seat of Elijah.' The name for this special chair was based on the Jewish tradition that even to this day the Prophet Elijah comes to witness each and every *bris*.

Rabbi Kalmonowitz was the *sandek*, and the kid was set on his lap. His job was to keep the fidgety kid still while the *mohel* wielded his blade. Men crowded around the *bima* to get an unobstructed view of the proceedings. This little unsuspecting baby was about to get his manhood manhandled and the thought made me a little squeamish. I had no interest in getting a ringside seat and found a place well behind the crowd.

The kid is in for a surprise. He thinks he came here for his birthday party.

The people gathered around the *bima* chanted the appropriate blessings, the baby gave a short but loud wail, a wad of wine soaked gauze was placed in the infant's mouth, and the youngster went silent again. The deed was done. Another babe has joined the Hebrew faith.

Now came the post ceremony blessings and the naming of the baby. The *mohel*, holding the brand-spanking new Jew in his arms, recited the Hebrew phrase '... and his name shall be ....' He turned to *Rebbetzin* Slater to get the name. She whispered in his ear and he announced, "His name shall be Shimon ben Yechezkel."

What was that? My name is Shimon. I turned toward *Rebbetzin* Slater and she smiled at me.

She named the kid after me.

Wow.

There was a traditional ceremonial meal following the circumcision and I stuffed myself with bagels, cream cheese, and lox. Jewish soul food. My gluttonous tendencies were revealed once again.

A special grace was said after the meal and once completed I drove Dafna to the Alkay plant. We went directly to Mr. Kowalski's office.

He took us to the computer department, and Mr. Hurly, took over. The supervisor gave us a fifteen minute explanation on how the system worked. I had a feeling that his entire lecture was superfluous for Dafna, but she appeared to be listening attentively. When he was done, Dafna asked for a computer terminal and the passwords to the restricted areas of the system. Once again I knew the passwords were unnecessary, but Dafna wanted him to think that his security was adequate. She took a seat at the computer and began hitting keys. Screens came up for a moment and then disappeared, only to be replaced by others. I had absolutely no idea what she was doing, but with her photographic memory she just needed a glance at the screen to absorb all the information.

Forty minutes later she logged off and said, "As far as I can see. No one is fiddling with the computer. All production is automatically logged into the system, and all product is followed until it reaches the customers. The production machines and assembly line are not working in unrecorded overtime and no product is being smuggled out."

I had to ask, "Are you sure?"

"Shimon, what did you just ask me?" she said with a surprised look on her face.

My bad.

She was sure.

Dafna asked for a tour of the plant to familiarize herself with the layout and once again friendly Miss Yellow Tag was there to show us around. After seeing the plant, I drove Dafna back to her house because she wanted to be there when her girls returned from school.

I pulled into her driveway and said, "So we are dead in the water with Rabbi Slater's disappearance and have no inkling of who is ripping off the Alkay Company."

Dafna thought for a moment and then said, "Are we sure that someone is actually stealing from the company?"

"Mr. Kowalski saw a few million dollars worth of his product at the new hotel that had not been paid for. I don't think he made that up."

"Maybe he was mistaken. The doors could come from another firm."

"He was certain that he recognized his stuff."

"Still ... it could be," she said getting out of the car and heading for her door.

I put the car into reverse and was backing down the drive when I saw Dafna bend over to retrieve a large yellow envelope on her stoop. She looked at it and then signaled for me to stop. I shifted the car into park and asked, 'What's that?"

She held it up in the air and shouted, "It's addressed to you."

I went to her and took the envelope, "Let me see." It was a standard manila envelope about 8 by 11. It had no bulk and felt empty. I pulled the string that opens the package and found it contained a single folded sheet of paper. Printed on the page was a short message with a picture. The message said, 'Don't stick your nose where it does not belong.' The picture was of Shaindel, Dafna and her two daughters standing in front of their house. All I could say was, "Shit."

"What's the matter?"

"You might as well read this," I said handing her the page.

After a moment Dafna said, "That's us. This picture was taken this morning, when we went to the *bris*. Where have you been putting your nose?"

"Well it is either the Alkay case or Rabbi Slater. I am not exactly swamped with a whole lot of business."

"How could it be about Rabbi Slater's disappearance? No one knows you are looking into that."

"What are you talking about? Your mother blabbed to the newspaper. The whole world knows."

"Oh yeah, I forgot."

"I doubt if it is the state police, because Nealy already reamed us out about that yesterday. They don't have to warn us twice."

"I don't think they should have warned us the first time," she added angrily.

"So I think it probably is the Alkay case."

"But, I thought you said no one at Alkay knows you are looking at the stolen stuff."

"We know about it, and obviously so does Mr. Kowalski. Ace in the security office and Hurley in computers probably have an inkling and Miss Yellow Tag might know."

"Miss who?"

I felt color rising in my cheeks as I said, "Kowalski's secretary."

"Why do you call her Miss Yellow Tag?" asked Dafna and then she stopped to think for a second. "Oh, I see why," she added nodding her head.

I was in trouble. I wanted to change the subject as soon as possible, "And there is one other person that probably suspects that we are looking into theft of Alkay product."

"Who's that?"

"Whoever is actually stealing the product. He must know Kowalski would eventually catch on."

"What are you going to do?"

"I am going to figure out which case this guy wants me to drop."

"Are you going to abandon either one of them?"

"Hell no," I said vehemently. "I am going to find the bastard. The picture and the fact that they delivered a letter for me on your doorstep is a warning. If I keep up my investigation your family may be harmed. Nobody threatens my family."

<u>20</u>

Choo Choo Train

PERHAPS I should simply drop both cases. Maybe that would keep Dafna's family safe. But all things considered it really was not an option. That meant I now had to solve both cases. We were stymied on the rabbi's disappearance and I could not see any way to progress. So I spent all day Wednesday at Dafna's house going over all the facets of the Alkay file. She was able to do high resolution scans of all the pictures that Albert Kowalski had shot of his product at the hotel construction site in New York. Then I pulled each one up on a computer screen and enlarged them to their maximum and examined every visible square inch of the photo.

All the readable serial numbers seen on the boxes in the pictures checked out as legally purchased merchandise.

Nothing seemed unusual.

Dafna combed the internet databases for all the information available about the Alkay and Zeelon corporations.

Again nothing.

That was not exactly correct. There was something. Like an indeterminate itch. Some bit of information that I had processed was bothering me. The trouble was I could not figure out what it could be.

I was frustrated and depressed by our lack of progress. The only good thing that came from all our work was that it allowed me to spend a day with Dafna. Not a bad way to pass the time.

That night I tossed and turned in my bed with the Alkay case keeping me from sleep. I must have dozed off in the early hours of the morning because my phone awakened me. It was six o'clock in the morning. *Who was calling me so early?* I looked at the caller ID on my phone screen — it was Dafna's home phone. "What's up?" I asked.

"Rebbetzin Slater called me a few minutes ago and told me that the Southfield police are back in her house looking for something. They won't tell her what it is. Could you call your sergeant friend and see what's going on."

"I'll take care of it."

"Love you," she said.

"Love you too," and I hung up.

Big smile on my face. *She loves me.* Wow.

What did the police want at the rabbi's house at the break of dawn? It was six weeks since the disappearance. *Why had they gone back?*

I tried Sergeant Chandler's cell phone but she did not answer. Then I called *Rebbetzin* Slater who picked up immediately, *"Rebbetzin,* hi. This is Shimon Lincoln ..."

"Shimon?" she said cutting me off. "The Southfield police are here and they won't tell me what is going on."

"What are they looking for?" I asked.

"They are not exactly looking. They are spraying powder on things and examining it with a magnifying glass."

Fingerprints? Now, after so long? Everything would be smudged or obliterated.

"*Rebbetzin*, is there a woman police officer with the cops?"

"Yes, she said she is a sergeant."

Had to be Chandler. "Try and get her to talk to me on the phone."

I heard the *rebbetzin* talking to someone and after a few moments Chandler came on the line, "Lincoln, I can't talk to you," she whispered. "The only reason I am answering you now is that this is not my phone. If someone found out I spoke to you, I could get canned."

"Look, I already know you are looking for fingerprints."

"Cannot confirm or deny," she stated.

"So, if you are looking for prints it normally means that you either have his body ... alive or dead ... or you have a print on something that makes you suspect it was the rabbi."

"Cannot confirm or deny," she repeated.

"But neither makes sense. If you have the body then you have other identifiable things ... like the big scar on his hip ... and do not need to look for fingerprint confirmation. And if it is an item with a print, why the hush hush."

"Lincoln, I'm busy. Take all your speculations to the state police."

"Something tells me you need something specific," I ventured. "Tell me what it is. Maybe I can help. I have resources."

The sergeant did not answer for a moment and then she whispered into the phone, "A thumbprint."

"You need the rabbi's thumbprint?"

"Right thumbprint. Can you get me one?"

I thought for a moment and had a brilliant idea. I was pretty sure I knew where I would find a good thumbprint of the rabbi. "Yes, I think I can do that for you," I said. "But you owe me. Where do you want it?"

"Whatever you do, don't bring it to the station. When will you have it?"

"Give me a couple of hours."

"Meet me by the choo choo train in the Oak Park city park at ten o'clock. Don't wear the Blues Brothers' suit."

Five minutes after ten I parked my car on the street opposite the park and grabbed the package from the seat next to me. I took the trail to the famous choo choo train. A brightly colored wooden locomotive — built to one third the size of a real one — that has brought joy to generations of Oak Park children.

I positioned myself next to the short ladder leading up to the engineer's position on the locomotive and looked around for Chandler. I knew I was a little late but I was fairly certain that the sergeant would not leave without the requested thumbprint.

"Lincoln," I heard someone call softly. I looked up and saw Chandler bent over under the canopy of the cramped engineer's compartment of the toy train. It was a funny sight. The train was scaled for little kids and she looked like Gulliver in Lilliput.

"Don't look at me," she instructed.

I turned my head away immediately and said, "You cannot be too comfortable in there. I guess you do not want anyone to see you meeting with me, that's why you had this meet in Oak Park."

"I always said you were some sort of genius in the investigation department," she said sarcastically. "Did you bring it?"

I raised the small package, "I have it here."

"Put it on the floor of the train and leave. What is it?"

"It's the rabbi's phylacteries."

"His what?" she asked.

"It's a body accoutrement that we Jews use, only we don't punch holes in the skin. They are used in the morning prayer service. There are leather straps and nice shiny lacquered boxes for the arm and head."

"Nice shiny boxes that will have nice shiny prints?" she queried.

"Exactly. They are also called *tefillin.*"

"How come we did not find them when we searched his house?"

"Because they were not in his house. He said his morning prayers at the *yeshiva* and kept them there in his lectern in the study hall."

"I owe you one."

"Why are you so uptight and secretive about this whole thing?"

"The captain had his ass chewed off by the state police for not having recovered adequate prints. And then he chewed my ass."

"It ... always rolls downhill."

"Exactly. That's why we went back."

"Why didn't the state police just come themselves? They have their own crime scene guys."

"I can't tell you. Everyone has put a lid on anything to do with this case."

"What did the rabbi do? Steal the plans for a nuclear weapon?"

"Can't tell you."

"And what's so special about getting a thumbprint?"

"I can't tell you. Honestly, if I could I would."

I believed her. But I also knew that there was something weird going on.

"When you can tell me, will you give me a call?"

"I promise. Maybe some of your old buddies downtown could be of help. Now, would you please leave so I can get out of this torture chamber."

As I drove away I considered what I should do with this new bit of information. Obviously something had changed concerning Rabbi Slater's disappearance. The police had some sort of evidence that required fingerprints. It was six weeks since the rabbi had gone missing and if he was dead and his body had been left exposed to the elements it could have deteriorated badly. Normal putrefaction did quite a bit of damage and opportunistic predators could have done more. Small carnivorous animals liked to start with the soft bits or protuberances like ears and fingers.

Perhaps they had the rabbi's body and the only remaining finger was the thumb. But that still did not make sense because there would be other methods to identify the rabbi. His dental x-rays, an x-ray of the corpse to show the big metal pin in his leg, blood typing, and of course DNA sampling.

So maybe, no corpse.

It could be they had a print from a crime scene and it rang a bell with the rabbi's prints that were now in the NCIC. That made more sense, since it was very likely that the partial prints Chandler had originally lifted around his house were inadequate and the match was not conclusive. But where would the rabbi's fingerprints show up that would interest the police?

Also, why was Chandler getting the prints? She told me she was no longer on the case and that it was now the baby of the Oakland County Sheriff's Department and the state police. So who was calling the shots? Who put the whole case under wraps?

Finally, what did she mean when she said to ask my buddies downtown? Did someone on the Detroit PD know anything?

Someone out there must know what was going on in this case, but it certainly was not me.

I had no idea as to who might be able to help, but my first call was to my old boss, Lieutenant Mike Gleason, Chief of Detectives for the Detroit Police. If the Detroit Police Department was dealing with Rabbi Slater's disappearance, he had to know about it. We shot the breeze for a few minutes and then I thanked him for all the calls he made to help me in the investigation of Rabbi Slater. He said he was more than happy to help and wanted to know if there was any progress. So I told him what I knew, including the sudden need for fingerprints and the secrecy. He quickly figured out all the possible reasons for the odd request but he had no concrete information. He did come up with one brilliant idea. If the case involved getting fingerprints from a corpse, I should call Timmy Tech.

His real name was Timothy Spangler and he worked as a laboratory technician at the Wayne County Medical Examiner's Office. The detectives gave him the nickname of Timmy Tech and his ability to uncover evidence was respected by all the staff of the medical examiner's office and the police. Getting prints off of a fresh corpse is fairly straight forward. But once the body begins to decompose it is a whole different story. All body tissues breakdown eventually.

'Ashes to ashes' and all that.

But different body tissues degrade more rapidly than others and it can be accelerated even more by environmental factors: Rapid temperature changes, immersion in water, dehydration. One of the tissues most affected are the fingers because of their vulnerability and composition. Along with this change in the fingers comes a dramatic change in fingerprints. The ridges and valleys disappear and the definition of the whorls is lost. Getting a print from deteriorated fingers is an art and Timmy Tech was the master.

He knew all the tricks to enhance and visualize prints in deteriorated corpses. Some of the techniques that were used by forensic pathologists all around the world were methods he developed. His latest 'magic' used a program developed by NASA to spot geological formations on Mars. He adapted it to scan fingers that appeared to have absolutely no signs of any prints. The program he designed could detect elevation changes of one hundredth of a micron and make a virtual plot of the missing fingerprint with all its ridges and valleys.

In short, when it came to forensic fingerprints — he could work miracles.

If the corpse was in Wayne County and they needed finger prints, Timmy Tech would know about it.

Timmy was an easy going unassuming fellow who loved his work with a passion. He was an older bachelor aged around fifty-five who put in lots of unpaid overtime whenever a case caught his fancy. He was an average guy — height, weight, coloring and I probably would not recognize him in street clothes because I only saw him at the medical examiner's office where he always wore green scrubs under his long white lab coat. There was always a disposable lab cap on his head and latex gloves on his hands. He wore glasses but he was constantly removing them to fit on surgical loupes for his work.

When I was on the force, Timmy Tech and I became friends. Not, 'let's go have a beer' type of friends but we shared an interest in fantasy books. Our ongoing mutual passion had been the 'Wheel of Time' series. Fourteen volumes and almost twenty years — a long time. Whenever we met we would review how the plot was progressing. It was fun and for me, it relieved the tension of being in a place filled with dead bodies. All the corpses and their spare parts did not bother Timmy. He even ate his lunch at his lab desk.

Just thinking about that gives me the heebie jeebies.

I called the Wayne County Medical Examiner's Office and got put through to Timmy Tech's lab. "Hi, Timmy. Sy Lincoln here."

"Sy, how the hell are you? They said you retired and went private."

"That's right."

"What are you reading lately?" he asked.

For a few minutes we tossed around the merits of the various fantasy books now on the market and when I thought it appropriate I commented innocently, "I hear you did some more of your magic and pulled a thumbprint out of the air. Nice going."

"How did you know? It was really tricky. Lots of putrefaction. So I did an acrylic mold in situ and then did the scan on the mold. It was the only finger that was readable. The prints on file are only partials and not very good so I recommended that they try to get a new thumbprint to compare."

Bingo!

"What was the reason for the putrefaction?"

"Apparently freezing and thawing. Same on the other hand. But the other two were in a lot better shape."

What other two? What is he talking about?

"You mean the feet?"

"No, the other two hands. There were four hands."

"Are you saying there were two victims?" I asked in shock.

"No, there were four victims. They brought me four hands. Four right hands."

21

Invitations

TIMMY TECH'S revelation fell on me like a ton of bricks.

What was I supposed to do? I was between a rock and a hard place.

Even if I assumed the worst, I could not act or do anything that would allow this information to escape to the media or the general public, because of the possible repercussions for Chandler and Timmy.

It seemed to me my best option was to brainstorm with someone smart.

That meant Dafna.

After all she was my — no, not my partner — my assistant, on this case.

I called her cell, "Hi, it's me."

"I figured as much. Since I can see your name on my screen."

"I want to come over."

"No problem," she said warily. "Is this about what the police wanted at the Slater house? Why do I get the feeling that you are coming with bad news?"

"I'll tell you when I get there."

Dafna was dressed in her old faded Michigan State sweatshirt and a denim skirt. She had furry orange slippers on her feet and a kerchief covered her hair. Shaindel had left fresh coffee on the machine and had heated some apple strudel — just so I would not go hungry.

Mrs. Kalin knew that I was crazy about her strudel.

"Where are the girls?" I asked.

"My mom took them to the mall a little while ago. Enough stalling. What did the police want at the *rebbetzin's* house?"

We sat at the kitchen table drinking coffee and munching strudel while I told her why Chandler had returned to the rabbi's house. Then I gave her all the information that I had gotten from Timmy.

Her first reaction was, "Oh, my God."

After the initial shock wore off she began to systematically analyze all that we knew.

Typical Dafna.

The obvious conclusion that had to be considered from the discovery of the hands was that Rabbi Slater was no longer amongst the living and had gone on to a world that was only goodness. But that was not a sure thing. First, because a definite match with the rabbi's print had not been made. Second, a single hand was not absolute proof that the rabbi was dead.

She also immediately understood why whoever was in charge put such a tight lid on the case. There would be a media circus of astronomical proportions when it was learned that the state police had recovered four amputated hands in a trash barrel at a McDonalds in Wyandotte. The cops would want to have a good handle on the case before it went public.

But how should *we* proceed?

We were both eager to do whatever was necessary to help catch the person that did this — whatever 'this' was. But we could not do anything because if anyone found out that I was privy to this information, Chandler and Timmy Tech could both be fired.

A real dilemma.

Two hours of brainstorming and we could not come up with a good plan of action. We decided we needed help from a real expert. An expert we could count on to give us good advice. That meant talking with Rabbi Kalmonowitz. I would inform him about the hands and hopefully he would help us decide what should be done.

We were still stymied, but the strudel had been delicious.

Friday morning, I caught *Rebbi* after *davening* and told him I needed a few minutes of his time. He took me to the small kitchen area near the dining room to make himself his first coffee of the day. One sweetener, no milk. He offered me a cup.

There were over two hundred young men studying in the *bais medrash* and they needed their caffeine to stay alert for the long hours of learning. So, 24 hours in the day free coffee was available in the kitchen. But coffee was expensive and the ever frugal *yeshiva* administration decided long ago that so long as the word 'coffee' was written somewhere on the label, it was good enough for the students. They supplied a dark brown mystery powder that came in two pound cellophane bags. After having been a cop for so many years, I thought I could drink just about any kind of coffee. As long as it was hot and had sugar, I was happy. Caffeine was what made a police officer's world go round. But, this stuff tasted like a combination of the black crud you scraped off your burnt toast and turpentine. Utterly disgusting. I could not bring myself to drink it.

"Thank you, *Rebbi.* I'm good."

We settled into his small office and I gave him the grim news about the four hands found by the police and the possibility that Rabbi Slater was dead. I also told him about the warning letter and that I felt it was most likely related to my other case.

He listened intently, and then asked, "Can you be certain that they were warning you about your other case?"

"Certain, no. But it is the only thing that makes sense."

"Sense to you, maybe. But not to the person that is threatening you."

What was Rebbi telling me?

"But Dafna and I have not been making any kind of progress in Rabbi Slater's case lately. So why would someone be warning us about that? No, I am pretty confident it involves this other case. There is quite a bit of money involved."

Rebbi nodded his head. "You say that the police are not certain that one of the hands belongs to *Rav* Slater," he said sadly, looking to me for confirmation.

"That is correct. No definite identification yet."

"So for now we will not tell *Rebbetzin* Slater. It would be extremely painful for her and even if they do verify that one of the hands is from her husband it is not enough for her to sit *shiva*. It would be different if they had found a vital organ."

I explained the problems that could develop if people knew I was aware of the 'four hands.' He told me not to do anything about it just yet and ended our conversation with, "The work of the righteous is done by others."

I had no idea what he meant.

Since there was little I could do just now about the mystery of the 'four hands', I went to my office hoping to accomplish two things. First — to once again examine all the pictures that Kowalski had taken, review all the information in the file, and check the financial reports for the Alkay Company for the last ten years. Second — and most important — come up with a 'Eureka' type of discovery that would solve the Alkay case. I was able to complete the first task but the second evaded me completely.

That itch gnawing at the back of my mind was driving me crazy.

There was something in the stuff I had just reviewed that was wrong but I could not discern what it could be. The who, what, where of how the company was being ripped off was still a mystery.

Mary Lou came into the office while I was in the middle of my review. She was winding down her work at the baking company and was giving me more time. Today she had long blond braids — obviously some sort of hair extensions — tied with large pink satin bows. She was wearing a long mock sheepskin vest over a bright yellow T-shirt and pants that look like jodhpurs which were tucked into high black boots. A go-to-church outfit for Mary Lou.

"Cancel the Skip-Trace on Rabbi Slater," I told her. "Odds are he is not about to check into a motel somewhere."

"What happened, Boss?"

Mary-Lou was my administrative assistant and she had to know. I filled her in about the four hands and the warning letter.

She simply nodded her head, "So it looks like this is a murder."

"Most likely, but I cannot do anything about it for now. So I want to move ahead with the Alkay investigation. Call the Net-Worth company and have them check out the top guys at Alkay. Let's see if anyone is putting away or spending more than they should."

The Net-Worth company had the ability of finding hidden bank accounts and investments for just about anyone in North America and a good part of Europe. Sort of like a turbo credit check. In addition, they could 'unofficially' look into IRS filings. Totally illegal, but often quite helpful.

"How far down the food chain do you want them to go?" she asked.

"In administration, from under Kowalski down to the division managers; in production, to the foremen; and in sales, do just the sales manager."

"Will do," she said eagerly. "I have a couple of things for you to look at."

"What now?"

She handed me a large envelope and said, "First off, Shaindel wants you to OK the invitation proofs."

As I opened the envelope I asked, "Why didn't she show me them herself. I was at her house last night."

"She did not want to get into an argument with you, if you did not like them."

"What is there not to like? It's only an invitation."

I slid the contents out onto my desk and examined the proofs. Nice heavy cream stock, embossed letters, classic Jewish symbols running along the margins — Stars of David, doves with olive branches, candelabras. Nice. I read the text in English and although a bit formal for me, it was satisfactory. Kind of funny to see my name in print on a wedding invitation. When I married Bethany there were no written invites.

I began the difficult task of deciphering the Hebrew text. It took a few moments and then I found what Shaindel was worried about.

The problem.

Just in front of my Hebrew name someone had added the abbreviation for the word '*Reb*,' so that my name read '*Reb* Shimon Lincoln.' This honorary title in front of someone's name did not mean that the person was a certified rabbi but it did signify someone with some standing in the *Torah* world.

No way was that going in front of my name.

I knew how inadequate I really was in the study of *Torah*. Every time I joined a study session at the *yeshiva* my ignorance exhibited itself in all its glory. I did not deserve the honorarium and would be embarrassed if anyone saw that title in front of my name.

"Did you know about this?" I asked Mary Lou.

"They mentioned something about a little 'rabbit' thing in front of your name in Hebrew. But I can't read Hebrew and I don't know what that means."

"Yeah, that little 'rabbit' thing."

"Is that a problem?"

"You tell Shaindel, I will not have that title in front of my name," I insisted.

"She told me that was what your rabbi called you. So she contacted him and he said that is what they should put on the invitation."

Indeed, Rabbi Kalmonowitz did always call me *Reb* Shimon. Of course, he did that with everyone. So, if he said that is what should be written on the invitation, I really did not have much of a choice.

"Do you still say that you did not know about the 'rabbit' thing?" I said accusingly.

Mary Lou held her arms out palms up, "Boss, what is your problem? It's only an invitation. Would it hurt you to make Shaindel happy? So, what should I tell her?"

"Tell her ... everything is fine with the invitation."

"There is one more thing," she said warily.

"Now what?"

"Mrs. Kalin wants to know how she should manage her leaving Dafna's house."

"What are you talking about? When is she leaving?"

"She realizes that once you are married to Dafna it would not be ... appropriate for her to live there anymore, and wants to know how you want to handle it."

I had never considered Shaindel moving out. She was part of Dafna's home and family. How dense could I be? Dafna and I had decided that because her computer business was based in her basement fortress it was only logical that I would move in.

But Shaindel was right. When I took up residence, it would be awkward if she stayed. We would just be asking for trouble. Husbands and wives sometimes — had disagreements — and they were very often hot tempered misunderstandings. Settling these disagreements would be so much more difficult for the couple if the mother-in-law was always present. I also could never move about the house freely. There was no way I could run out to get the paper in just a robe over my underwear. Yeah, Shaindel was on the money. She would have to leave. Funny thing, I did not want her to go.

"Did she say what she wants to do?"

"Apparently she has been thinking about this quite a bit. She came up with three options."

"I'm all ears."

"Number one, she returns to her house in New York. She would just not renew the lease for the people living there now and she would go back."

"Don't like that option. Aliza and Suzie would go bananas."

"Option two, she rents an apartment near here or moves into your condo and would come to visit as often as she could."

"Better, but not that great. It would look like I was tossing her out on her ear."

"Option three, build an extension onto Dafna's house … a separate living area with its own entrance. Then she would have her own place and you and Dafna could have privacy when you needed it."

"Which one did she prefer?"

"Boss, are you kidding me? Obviously she hopes you will go for number three."

"What did Dafna say?"

"Shaindel has not broached the subject to her. She wants to settle it with you first."

A wise man once said that mothers-in-law should be considered distant relatives. The more distant the better. But I really liked Mrs. Kalin and did not want to take her away from Dafna and the girls. A nearby apartment was nice but I knew it would be terribly inconvenient for both Dafna and Shaindel. So the house extension made sense. Besides, if I found that having her so close was causing problems, I could always ask her to give us a little more breathing room.

"I'll speak to Shaindel about the problem."

"What are you going to tell her, Boss?"

"I am going to tell her about my cousin, Steve, who is a hot-shot building contractor. If anyone can get the permits and build the extension before the wedding ... it's him. I am pretty sure he will do me this favor."

Mary Lou smiled. "Good decision."

"Did I really have a choice?"

Mary Lou smiled at my predicament and then switched the subject by pointing at the material spread out on my desk, "How is it going with the Alkay case?"

"Big fat zero. I have no idea how someone has been able to steal the windows and doors."

"Would you like Andy to have a look at the books?"

Andy, or Andrew, Mary Lou's husband had been a CFO and was an accounting whiz. If anyone could spot a discrepancy in the books it was him. "Do you think he would mind?"

"He just finished ripping out and replacing all the plumbing in the kitchen, so his DIY handy-man addiction has been satisfied for a while. He gets a kick out of discovering the business secrets of other firms. He'd love it."

I made a copy of the disc that held all the financial records of the Alkay Company and gave it to Mary Lou. She gathered up the proofs for the invitation, "Don't let the wording of the invitation get you down. They mean well and now they owe you."

"Owe me for what?"

"Like if I can't convince your mother that it is inappropriate to come to an ultra-Orthodox Jewish wedding in a strapless gown," she explained.

"Does she really want to do that?" I asked in horror.

"I'm working on it."

For now I could not do anything to help solve the mystery of the rabbi's hand — if indeed it was his — so I went back to looking at the Alkay books and pictures, again and again.

What was it that was bothering me?

22

Cooperation

AFTER EXAMINING everything for the umpteenth time, I closed my eyes, leaned back in my chair, and let my mind wander. I was trying to think out of the box to come up with some brilliant idea as to how to progress, when my phone rang.

"Lincoln, this is Nealy. Could you come to the state police post on Ten Mile at eleven o'clock this morning?"

Very strange.

There was no anger in his voice. No threatening tone. In fact, he was downright cordial — almost a supplication. *Was this the same Lieutenant Nealy?* How strange and what did he want?

"How about you tell me what this is all about?" I asked.

"We'll tell you both when you get here," he replied.

"Who else is invited?"

"You and *Mrs. Lackler*."

What did they want with Dafna? We had not been conducting an active investigation into anything remotely related to the Slater case. At least, I was not doing anything. *Did Dafna break into the computer of the Oval Office?* I would not put it past her.

"Do I need to bring a lawyer?"

"No, *this time* you can leave the lawyer at home."

I called Dafna and she told that she had already been contacted.

What was going on?

Five minutes to eleven I pulled into the parking lot of the state police post and parked my car near Dafna's utilitarian Chrysler van. She got out of her vehicle and we walked together towards the entrance. Today she was wearing a straight, down to her shoulders, blonde wig. It went perfectly with the well cut navy business suit and low heeled navy pumps. Dafna looked great. But, then again in my eyes she always looked terrific. Every time I saw her I felt an indescribable warm feeling. A feeling of completion.

I held the door to the station open for her, "Do you think the reason they called us here has anything to do with the hands?" I asked.

"I'm sure it does," she answered calmly.

"If they bring it up, make sure to act surprised."

"How do I do that? Flutter my eyelashes and pretend to faint?" she said jokingly.

"Stop kidding around. We could be in big trouble."

"Unlikely. You told me Nealy said we did not need a lawyer."

"Never trust a cop."

"How about ex-cops? Can I trust them?" she asked.

"Especially not ex-cops."

We were escorted to a small conference room and found four men in blue. Lieutenant Nealy and three more ranking officers of the state police. Everyone stood when we entered. Hands were shaken and introductions were made.

The head honcho, with two gold bars on his collar, was Captain Forrest, the commander of the CID — Criminal Investigation Division. The next one down the pecking order was Inspector Richards, the head of the Homicide Task Force. He had a silver and blue bar on his collar. The final newcomer was another first lieutenant named Jarron, the head of the detective unit for the 2nd District — Wayne, Oakland, Macomb, and part of Washtenaw counties. The first two were based in Lansing and Jarron had his office in Detroit Public Safety headquarters in downtown Detroit at the old MGM Casino building, on Second Avenue and Michigan.

Pretty hefty.

What did they want with us?

Captain Forrest began, "We understand that you are investigating the disappearance of a Rabbi Slater."

"That's right. His employer hired me to look for him," I answered.

"I also understand that you uncovered some evidence near where his abandoned car was found which suggests that this was an abduction."

"We found his glasses," added Dafna.

"Yes, his glasses," said the captain.   "You also discovered that there was a Chevy Cruze with the wrong license plates driving away from the scene of the abduction."

How did they know that we were the ones that found the car? Time to bluff. "Oh really, there was a Chevy Cruze?" I asked in fake innocence.

"Mr. Lincoln ... we know it was you. It was also in the paper a couple of days ago."

"Were they connected?" asked Dafna eagerly.

I guess we are not going to be bluffing our way out of this.

"We located the Chevy you discovered. The lab went over the car very carefully and came up with trace evidence that indicates that the rabbi had been in the trunk of the car. We have no idea if he was alive or dead at the time."

"Oh my God," said Dafna earnestly.

Great acting.

"However, that is not the reason that we have called you here. Other evidence has turned up that is related to Rabbi Slater. What we are about to tell you is in the strictest confidence. We plan on releasing the information to the public on Monday afternoon and until that time you cannot tell a soul. If we discover otherwise we will prosecute and *persecute* you both," he said threateningly. "Do I make myself clear?"

"Yes, sir," I snapped out, my old Marine training showing itself.

He turned to Dafna, "And you?"

"Won't say a word," she said with a nod of her head.

"Now that we have that straight we can tell you what we found." He turned to Inspector Richards and motioned with his hand for him to speak.

"Four days ago we received a call at CID. The caller was using an electronic voice simulator and his message was 'America should be for Americans.' He then gave instructions to look in a dumpster behind the McDonalds at the Wyandotte marina, just opposite Grosse Isle. We dispatched an officer and he found a vinyl bag. He took one look into the bag and brought it into the lab. What we found in the bag was human body parts. Specifically, four human hands. All right hands."

"Oh my goodness," I responded.

I thought my acting was quite superb.

Robert De Niro, move over.

"Do you know whose hands they are?" asked Dafna in feigned shock.

Meryl Streep, you have competition.

"We have made preliminary identification for all four hands. One was from your Rabbi Slater."

"And the others?" I asked.

"Jarron, fill them in," said the Inspector to the other first lieutenant.

Lieutenant Jarron cleared his throat and said, "We think we are dealing with someone that abducts and murders his victims. All four were taken over a period of a month. The first was Muhammad Nassar, a 26-year-old graduate student at Wayne. He's originally from Chicago and went missing one week before your Rabbi. The second was your Rabbi. The fourth was two weeks after the rabbi and involved a 42-year-old woman of Vietnamese extraction, Vivian Nguyen. She worked as an administrator at the Oakland mall. I skipped the third because she worked with us, right here in the Ten Mile Post. Her name was Maria Sanchez. She was twenty-three and was Lieutenant Nealy's secretary. So that strikes very close to home and makes this whole case very personal for us."

"It must be very difficult for you," Dafna said to Nealy. "I'm so sorry."

I now noticed that Lieutenant Nealy was very tense. "Help us get this bastard," he said angrily.

The captain said, "For obvious reasons, Lieutenant Nealy will not have anything to do with the actual investigation of this case. But we have asked him to act as your liaison with the state police."

"Liaison for what? What are we supposed to do?" I inquired.

"It could be that the perpetrator's MO is similar in all four cases. Abduction using a stolen car with switched plates. We contacted our IT people and they told us that they do not have the capability to make a search similar to what *Mrs. Lackler* did. That only you ..." he said indicating Dafna, "... have the necessary experience and hardware to make such a search."

Dafna did not say a word but there was a small smile of satisfaction.

Inspector Richards continued, "We contacted *Mrs. Lackler* and asked her to help in our investigation, but she said she will only work with you, her partner."

So that is how she knew we would not be in trouble. I got into this cooperation with the state police because of her. She should have told me.

"We would like her to check and see if there were other strange cars running around where the other three were last seen. Can you do that for us?" asked Captain Forrest.

"No," said Dafna succinctly.

"No?" asked Forrest indignantly.   "But when we contacted you, you told us you would."

"What I said was that we would be happy to work *with* you," corrected Dafna. "We are looking for Rabbi Slater and his disappearance is related to these other victims. We want to be part of the complete investigation and not just be someone that you use to do computer searches. Either you keep us in the loop until this case is solved, or with all due respect, you can go look for the cars yourself."

I thought Forrest was going to bust a gut. I could see by the sudden set of his jaw and the arching of his brow that he was fuming silently. The captain had obviously worked out a carefully organized game plan of how his crew was going to conduct this investigation and now Dafna just threw a monkey wrench into his neat scenario. Forrest had to make a snap decision about how he would handle this new hurdle. He searched the faces of his fellow officers, but they were avoiding eye contact. All three seemed to be working very hard trying to stifle smiles. It was not every day that someone blackmailed their boss.

Now they know what I go through.

Slowly Captain Forrest regained his composure and made a decision. He and Inspector Richards went off to the side and conferred quietly for a minute or so. He came back and then put a forced smile on his face and said, "We have decided that it will be mutual beneficial if we could work together. That was our initial intention."

Yeah, sure.

"I'm glad to hear that," said Dafna.

"So will you join us in this investigation and look for those cars?"

"I would be happy to," said Dafna.

I quickly added, "Of course, she will need access to all the traffic cams in those areas, and all reports of stolen license plates and vehicles. And, of course, access to the DMV files."

Captain Forrest said reluctantly, "She will have them."

Inspector Richards added, "For legal and other reasons, it would be to the detriment of the state police if it got out that you, as civilians, are involved in this case. Therefore, all communication with us will be done through Lieutenant Nealy. As Captain Forrest just said, you will now be part of the investigation. We will keep Lieutenant Nealy abreast of any new developments and he will keep you informed. He will also pass along any requests you may have of us and bring us anything you uncover. Here is the file with all the information we have on the four victims," he said handing the case file to Nealy. "He will share this with you."

"What is your working theory of what makes this guy tick? What is his motive?" I asked.

"Considering the victims were one Hispanic, one Muslim, one Asian, and one Jew. And the guy said, 'America for the Americans,' the logical conclusion is that he is a white supremacy nut. But, of course that just might be a ploy to make us search in the wrong direction, so all the other possibilities are being considered," said the inspector.

"You do realize that it could be that all the victims are still alive," I suggested. "We only have the hands."

"The pathologist does not think so. The hands were taken off with a chain saw. It's all in the file," said Lieutenant Jarron.

With a chain saw? Oh my God.

"Are you happy now?" the captain asked Dafna.

"Delighted," said Dafna with a smug grin.

"When do you think we will have some results?" he asked.

"Well ... three new areas ... maybe in a day or two."

"Pass it on to us as soon as you can. Nealy will go over the file with you now," said Forrest, rising from his chair. He shook our hands and left the room along with the other officers.

When we were alone with Nealy, he turned to us and said, "Look, we got off to a bad start, and I want to apologize. What I said a few days ago was when you were sticking your noses into our business, but now that we are on the same team, I want to clear the air. I am sorry if I said things that offended you."

"Or threatened us ..." added Dafna.

I could see that Nealy was having a hard time asking for forgiveness so I said, "OK, apology accepted."

"What about you?" asked the cop.

Dafna squirmed a bit but finally said, "Me too."

Nealy smiled and said, "Great, let's get down to business."

We sat with him for over an hour, going over the files of the other three victims.

When Jarron was pointing out the ethnicity angle to the disappearances, a question had popped into my mind. I wondered how the perpetrator had been able to pick out each victim according to ethnicity. The Vietnamese woman was obvious, she must look Asian. But I thought the other three would not be so easy. Then, I saw the pictures. Rabbi Slater's beard, side locks, and suit marked him as an Orthodox rabbi, so that was easy. Maria Sanchez had the classic facial features of her Hispanic origins. No WASP in her at all. That left only Muhammad, but when I got a gander at his university ID photo it too became obvious. With his full beard and flowing *jalabiya*, Mr. Nassar was obviously a devout

Muslim. From a mile away you knew he was not a Yankee Doodle Dandy. In all four cases the victims did not come home as planned and their cars were found abandoned. There were no witnesses and no leads. Just like Rabbi Slater.

The dumpster at the McDonalds was not in the field of view of any of the surveillance cameras in the area and no one remembered any suspicious individuals going near the receptacle. They had no information as to when or how the hands got into the garbage bin.

The call to the police was made on a cellular phone that had been about two miles from central Wyandotte and then went off the air. Since the caller had used a virtual voice simulator, the caller could be anyone. Any age and any sex.

The amputated hands were now in the Wayne County Medical Examiner's Office in Detroit undergoing further tests. Initial assessment of the coroner was that when the hands were severed it was a bloodless amputation — meaning there was no blood in the limb when the cut was made through the wrist.

Very unusual.

The entire file was on a CD and Nealy had one of his men make a copy for us. When he gave me the disc he said, "Maria was a good kid. When I thought that she had just run off I bad mouthed her as being irresponsible and I feel sorry about that. This is now very personal for me and I understand why they won't let me work on the case. Once again I apologize for being a little hard on the both of you. I want us to work together to find this son of a bitch."

We left the state police post and I turned to Dafna, "You knew what this was all about before we got here and you did not tell me."

She considered what I said for a moment, nodded her head and said, "Yup, I think that pretty much sums it up."

"If we are going to be husband and wife, you can't keep secrets from me. It is rule number one for a happy marriage."

She canted her head to the side and asked sarcastically, "Do you want me to write that down so I won't forget it?"

"This is no laughing matter."

"Where do you come off lecturing me on a happy marriage? Have you ever had a happy marriage? I don't think so. But, I did. The number one rule for a happy marriage is not as you say, being completely open with each other. The number one rule is ... listen to what your spouse has to say. You don't have to agree or obey, but you have to listen."

"Yes, Dafna."

See — I am a quick learner.

23

Burglars

AS SOON as we got to Dafna's home she went down to her computer area and began banging away on her keyboard. As she worked she asked me, "What was that business about getting permission to access all the cameras and DMV. I don't need that."

"I know you don't need it, and the cops know you don't need it. But for legal purposes you need it. This way I will not have to spend the next twenty years visiting my wife in prison. So humor me."

"I like it when you say 'my wife.'"

"I do too," I said with a big smile.

Dafna spoke without looking up from her keyboard, "It seems to me that it is highly unlikely that whoever did this used the same MO."

"Look at you, using the term MO."

"Comes from all the mystery novels," she said with a shrug. "Still, why would the perpetrator go out of his way to steal a car and then another set of plates for each abduction?"

"Maybe he did, maybe he didn't. But the state police would like us to find out. So I guess we just do what they request."

Dafna checked which traffic cameras covered the major roads in the three areas where the other victims went missing. She called up the video histories of each camera and created an access to her computer. Then her program began analyzing and digesting all the video information looking for cars that should not be there.

She hit a few buttons and the screen went black.

"What's going on?" I asked.

"Now we wait," she said.

"What are you going to do until we get the information?"

"It is an awful lot of information and the computer does not need me. So, I am going to get ready for *Shabbos.* I suggest you do the same. We are guests at Rabbi Twerski's house tonight. Don't forget."

The Twerskis were a nice family. He was a young rabbi at the *yeshiva,* and she taught a kindergarten class in the day school. Their home was small, and as neat as can be expected with four little kids running around tearing the place apart. The discussion around the Friday night table was lively and interesting, but the food was not that great. To be nice I will just say that *Rebbetzin* Twerski was not in Dafna's league. It was like major league compared to little league. Luckily she recognized her limitations in the kitchen and most of the staples for the meal had been purchased pre-cooked at the kosher food mart, so they were edible but not great. She did prepare a few side dishes and I carefully avoided those.

Dafna was dressed up with a short wig and nice dress made from some shiny green material. Very pretty.

Looking good, Dafna!

Our visit to the Twerskis was over and we were walking back to the Lachler home. Dafna was wearing her red tufted down overcoat and kept her noggin warm with a big white fluffy scarf that she wrapped around her head. The girls had once again rushed ahead with their grandmother to give us some privacy.

"Does your mother have any more wedding plan surprises for me?" I asked.

"She means well. Don't be angry with her."

"I'm not angry. I just want to be ready," I said in my defense.

"Next week we are meeting with the caterer for food tasting and menu selection."

"Eating and tasting. That's something I can do."

"We were thinking that the menu would be based on the foods that you prefer so much. So the caterer is only going to make hamburgers, French fries, and pizza. This should be some wedding."

"Very funny," I said.

Shaindel and the girls had just reached their home, but they just stood on the front porch signaling silently for us to come quickly.

Dafna and I rushed to the house. "What's the matter," I asked.

"Shhh," said Shaindel holding her finger to her lips. "Look at that," she whispered.

She was pointing to the splintered door frame and the open door, through which I could see broken furniture and shards of glass.

I turned to Dafna and said quietly, "Take your mother and the girls to the Rabinowitzs and stay there."

Dafna said to her mother, "Take the girls to the neighbors."

"I want you to go with them," I insisted.

"So you can go in and play the hero on your own and possibly get hurt. Not on your life. I'm staying with you," she said defiantly. "Mom, take the girls."

Mrs. Kalin did as she was asked and when we saw them enter the adjacent house I slowly pushed the door open.

The living room was a shambles, as were the dining room and kitchen. There were shattered plates strewn about the floor. Food and groceries everywhere. I told Dafna to be silent because I thought I heard something. There was banging coming from the basement. I did not have a weapon, so I retrieved a chef's knife from the floor.

"We are not going downstairs," I commanded in a whisper. "I don't know who or what is in the basement. If I go down the stairs I will be a sitting duck. There is no other way out of there so they have to come back through here. I know it is *Shabbos,* but I am calling the cops."

"Absolutely," she said in agreement.

I grabbed the phone from the kitchen counter and called 911, giving them the pertinent information.

The banging sound from the basement stopped and soon we heard at least two people climbing the stairs. I pushed Dafna behind the wall into the dining room, "Stay here."

The basement door opened and a man dressed all in black, with a black ski mask covering his face, emerged. I could see another guy in a similar outfit coming up behind him.

I held the knife in front of me and said, "Stop right there, I am ..."

Too late.

I had not seen that the first guy had a long aluminum baseball bat behind his back. Before I could react, he whacked the back of my hand sending the knife clattering across the floor. Then he lunged at me. The other guy not far behind.

OK — my bad — time to regroup.

My martial arts training took over. They were advancing on me, so instead of moving backwards as expected I moved towards them. This put me inside the swing zone of the first guy's baseball bat. Almost without thinking, I performed a karate punch to the first fellow's

Adam's apple and he fell to the ground holding his throat. The second guy jumped over his friend and came at me. I used his forward momentum to accelerate his body and drop his torso so that his head collided with the hard granite counter top. He went down. Number one somehow got back up and apparently decided it was a good idea to get out while the getting was good by going around through the dining room to the front door. I did not see what happened but as soon as he turned the corner I heard him make a loud gasp followed by a grunt. The man rolled back into the kitchen clutching his groin.

He just met Dafna.

His agony was the result of Dafna's over three years of *Krav Magah* training at the Jewish Center. And with pointy shoes. That has gotta hurt.

The second fellow was trying to get up and I moved forward to restrain him. Problem was, in trashing the kitchen, a bag of beans had exploded. When my foot stepped on the beans it slid out from under me as if I was on ice skates. I wound up on my behind on the floor. That, normally would not hinder me much, but in my less than graceful journey to the floor my foot had also slipped through the rungs of a smashed ladder-back chair. I could not get my leg out and I could not stand. The fellow came at me but I managed to keep him off me by kicking with my free foot. He pushed my leg to the side and was about to pounce on me when he suddenly stood up tall and a surprised look appeared on his face. This immediately changed to a grimace of extreme pain as his eyeballs rolled up in their sockets and he collapsed to the floor. Standing behind the man was Dafna, ready to deliver another kick if the first one had not been sufficient. The fellow was gasping for breath and he too was clutching at his manhood.

Atta girl Dafna.

I did not want the guy on the floor to get away so I tried rolling in his direction to restrain him, but my leg was still trapped. Just then Dafna fell on top of me, grasping me by the shoulders and hugging me very tightly, as she cried out, "Are you OK? Are you hurt?"

Her hug and concern for me were genuine but I recognized that it was also a manifestation of her deflating balloon syndrome. Dafna needed the hug more than me. She was crying softly on my shoulder with her arms around my body. It would only take a moment for her to come around. She needed physical support right now.

With my foot entrapped in the chair there was little chance I could apprehend the thugs or keep them from escaping, so I did not bother to extricate myself from Dafna's bear hug. I could see that the intruders were not a threat at this moment because they were more intent in helping each other get away than they were in continuing the encounter. I watched them limp out of the house.

Being hugged by Dafna — even if we were still in our overcoats and separated by the thick layers of down — was not an unpleasant sensation.

The embrace also helped to mute the embarrassment I was feeling because I had needed Dafna to rescue me. I was supposed to be the big hero but she was the one that clobbered the bad guys.

Both of them.

We heard a car start and pull away.

After another minute or so Dafna's crying stopped and she snuffed up her tears and allowed me out of her clutches. I freed my leg and we both stood silently. I could sense that she was self-conscious about her show of weakness and the hugging business on the floor of her kitchen. I righted an overturned chair, "Nice work. If there ever was a time to kick *tuchis,* now was the time. You did a good job."

Two field goals in one night.

Dafna considered what I just said, "Yeah, I see what you mean. Pointy shoes sure make a difference."

About three minutes later a Southfield police car —
with lights flashing — pulled up in front of the house and
Dafna went out to greet the police. I heard her give the
patrolman a quick summary of what had occurred as she
escorted him into the kitchen.

It was Officer Cummings, the police officer that had
discovered Rabbi Slater's car.

What were the odds?

"Mr. Lincoln ... Good *Shabbos*. Nice to see you again,"
said the cop sarcastically.

"Always a pleasure," I answered.

Cummings had his weapon drawn and quickly
checked the other rooms on this floor. Then he made a
thorough check of the basement to be sure that there was
no further danger.

I went through the house with Dafna and saw that the
bedrooms and bathrooms were spared, so that the house
was still livable. We went down into the basement and
saw that the bad guys had been pounding against the
door of Dafna's computer center but had barely made a
dent in the heavy steel. They probably thought this was
some kind of vault containing valuables. However, to get
through that door you would need about a half ton of
TNT. The Playstations were safe and sound, working
away at Dafna's workstation, looking for the missing
vehicles.

Cummings was of the opinion that this looked like an
attempted robbery, but still wanted to know if the break-
in could be connected with a case we were working on.
We told him we could not be sure, but it was unlikely and
he wrote it up as a burglary. Having worked in Southfield
for a few years he knew that we, as Orthodox Jews, would
not sign the report on the Sabbath, so he told us to come
to the station on Sunday to add our signatures to the file.

<u>**24**</u>

Trust

DAFNA'S HOUSE was a shambles. There was debris from the break-in all over the place, but nothing could be done about it just yet. We could not clean it up until Sunday morning, because that was the earliest the insurance adjuster could come to assess all the damage. The only good side was that once the Sabbath ended at nightfall we were free to go down to Dafna's basement to see what the computers had discovered.

She did her magic with the keyboard and the screen came alive. As things booted up she explained that her program had scanned each of the traffic cameras for the period of time fifteen minutes before the disappearance of each victim and 120 minutes after. Lots of interesting stuff. There were a whole bunch of vehicles whose registration had lapsed, but these were of no interest to us. There were also quite a few with an unregistered color change, but since the year, make, model, and plate number of the car were correct these were also discarded. All the cars were cross-checked with vehicles reported stolen close to the date of the disappearance. Logic told me that it was unlikely that the perpetrator had used the same MO to snatch each of his victims. That is, steal a car and then substitute stolen plates to make his grabs. Too much trouble.

Just shows you how only thinking logically can sometimes lead you wrong.

The guy had done it four times.

For each of the victims there was a single vehicle that fit the bill exactly.

The videos showed a car with an incorrect plate number at a place and time that corresponded with each victim's disappearance. In each case, a car of that same color, make and model had been reported stolen just before the time of the disappearance and was recovered soon after, with their correct plates in place. It appeared that the abductor switched the plates on the stolen car to abduct his victims and switched them back when he abandoned the vehicle.

A different car for each abduction.

Captain Forrest had been correct — the abductor used the same MO.

Dafna collected all the pertinent video images and downloaded them to a CD. I called Nealy, but his number did not answer. I was shunted to a service that would beep him. He had mentioned that he was off duty and going up to his cabin over the week-end and that the cell phone coverage was spotty. I felt it was important to get the disc to the state police as soon as possible, so I called the Ten Mile Police Post and without revealing the purpose of my call, asked the duty officer to contact Lieutenant Jarron and give him a message to call me.

The lieutenant called back a few minutes later and arranged for an unmarked state police car to come and collect the disc. Nealy called back after twenty minutes, but I told him he did not need to return to the city because Jarron was already on top of the situation.

Because of the attempted robbery I decided it would be a good idea to start toting my little pistol in a fanny holster. I had three guns locked in my home safe and for the last two years I had taken them out only for my monthly target practice and cleaning. For firepower I relied on either my 9 mm Glock Automatic or my Smith & Wesson 38 Police Special, but for undercover work I had taken to carrying the smaller Smith & Wesson 'Chief's Special' 38 snub nose. Mary Lou's 'Baby,' was the same model and she was the one who convinced me to try it. Its small size allowed me to carry a weapon that could fire the 38 Special rounds and still be kept hidden easily. The three main disadvantages of the small gun were that it was less accurate, allowed only five rounds, and it took me longer to extract the weapon from the fanny pack. In addition it could be torture when I sat down and driving while carrying the gun was especially tricky.

I did not want to take any chances.

Eight o'clock Sunday morning, I arrived at Dafna's house to greet the insurance adjuster. The guy photographed everything from the front stoop to the back porch. He wrote down which major items had been trashed and then gave the OK to clear out the broken stuff, order new items and fix up the house. I helped the Lachlers straighten up the place for about an hour and then Dafna and I went to the Southfield police station to make our statements for the file.

At about eleven in the morning we finished all the paperwork and split up. Dafna went out to buy replacements for some of the broken items and I went back to my house. I needed to make some headway in the Alkay case. If someone associated with the case was responsible for the warning letter and/or Friday night's excitement, I wanted to find him before he tried to harm Dafna's family again. However, I realized that if I wanted to have any real level of cognitive function I needed to supply my brain with the necessary nutrients it was lacking.

I had to eat something.

I was enjoying a fresh bagel slathered with cream cheese and savoring a cup of my favorite blend of coffee, when Lieutenant Jarron called.

I never get to finish a meal in piece.

Why was Jarron calling? I was supposed to pass on everything through Nealy.

"Won't your commander's undershorts get all knotted up if he finds out you contacted me directly?" I asked.

"Absolutely, and that is the reason I'm using a throwaway phone. I got it just for you."

"What can I do for you, Lieutenant?"

"Thanks for the disc last night. It is very interesting."

"You're welcome."

"Also, in the future, I would like to ask ... when you have any more information ... I want you to contact me directly."

Big change in the game plan. His commander had specified that we go through Nealy, but he had just asked me to bypass him. "You mean cut Nealy out of the loop?"

"Not out of the loop, but I want the loop to flow in a different direction. You give me the information first, and if I say so, you can then give it to Nealy. Then he can pass on to me whatever you tell him."

What was going on here? Why did Jarron want to get the information directly instead of through the arrangement his superiors had set up? The first thing that came to mind was perhaps he did not want any delays in getting information. Perhaps. Maybe Jarron thought that Nealy could not be trusted. Could be Jarron was afraid he would alter information to protect himself or someone at his station concerning his secretary's abduction. It could also be that there was some previous animosity between the two.

My initial assessment of Jarron was that he was a hard working straight shooter. The kind of guy you wanted on your side. *I think I can trust him.*

I took a stab at it. "I take it you do not think that Nealy should be within ten miles of the investigation."

"I won't bullshit you.   Nealy used to work with Inspector Richards and he apparently called in some favors. Richards insisted I allow Nealy to be part of this investigation by his functioning as liaison.   Highly irregular."

"Have you worked with Nealy in the past?"

Jarron answered succinctly, "Yes, I have."

No elaboration. No when, what, and why. "Do you trust him?"

"He's a dedicated cop."

"Yeah, but do you trust him?"

"He's a dedicated cop."

So, I was correct about the mistrust between the two.

"How will you explain to your superiors that you are bypassing Nealy?"

"I plan on not having to explain, because they will never know."

Obviously he was asking me to keep this arrangement between us — just between us. "They won't hear about it from me."

"Good. This will be a two-way street. So, here is an update for you. We have been checking out the cars and the plates that you found. We located two of the people whose plates were lifted. They did not even know that their license plates were switched because whoever took the plates put another stolen plate on their cars. The owners never noticed that it was not their own license plates."

"The guy that did this was smart. Nobody checks their own plates."

"There is also another development," he said somberly.

"What now?" I asked tentatively.

"Last night our friend called the state police hotline and directed us to a garbage barrel at a rest stop on the I-

96. This time his message was 'Kick the foreigners out of the USA.'"

"Still no way to isolate his phone?"

"Apparently the murderer stopped at the side of the interstate ... about five miles from the rest stop ... and made his call. The phone is a throwaway just like mine, purchased with cash one month ago at the Target store near Oakland Mall. The guy uses it and then goes off the grid. He must take out the battery and we cannot make a trace."

"What did they find in the barrel?"

"More body parts. It has now definitely become a serial killer case."

"What parts?"

"Two half chests and two half pelvises."

Suddenly I felt my bagel churn around in my stomach, "Was it four different, just like the hands?"

"Oh, yeah."

All four were definitely dead.

"What's the plan?"

"There are rumors all through the state police and there is no way we can keep a lid on the case much longer. We will try to get as much information as we can before the five o'clock press conference tomorrow. I'm surprised we have been able to keep it quiet until now. This evening we will simultaneously contact each of the families and give them the bad news."

"That will be tough."

"You better believe it."

"What time?"

"Why do you want to know?"

"Dafna and I would like to be there when Mrs. Slater gets the news."

"No problem. I'll tell Nealy to coordinate that with you."

"Thanks."

"Since we now have four dead with a similar MO we have no choice but to call in the FBI. I assume once they are informed they will take over the investigation."

"Does that mean the state police are dropping the case?"

"No way. This is a Michigan state problem and we are in it ... albeit under the Feds, until it is solved."

"The Feds can be a pain in the butt. I don't envy you."

"I don't envy me either."

"Now that the Feds will be in charge, do you want us to pass the information we uncover to the FBI? Dafna has worked with them in the past."

"The Michigan State Police will be cooperating fully with the Feds and that includes putting all our resources at their disposal. That means that we give them all the information we obtain through the state police research facilities. I know that *Mrs. Lackler* is cleared to work on sensitive federal material, so I see no conflict of interest. If they don't ask us whether you are part of our research team, I see no reason to tell them."

I could see why he wanted this arrangement. Whenever the FBI comes strutting in to take over a local case, federal law requires that the local police relinquish authority. But the Fed's superior attitude usually evoked a less than enthusiastic response. Very often there is more of a competitive spirit than a cooperative one. So, if the local police are able to discover something before the Fed's massive well-oiled, well-funded, highly-manned criminal investigative machine, it was like poking a sharp stick in the eye of the dragon. It did not kill the beast, but it made you feel good to provoke a bit of discomfort.

"So, we give you guys the information we might find, and you pass it on to the FBI, making the state police look good."

"Yes, there is that," agreed Jarron.

"But, like we said, this is a two-way street and you have to keep us in the loop. We promise that anything you tell us stays with us. Is it a deal?"

"Deal. By the way how are you doing?" he asked with empathy.

"Concerning what?"

"I heard someone broke into *Mrs. Lackler's* house on Friday night. What is that all about?"

"The police assume it was a robbery attempt."

"Or maybe you stepped on someone's toes?"

"Unlikely. I just went back to working as a private investigator ... I have been ... doing other things ... for the last two years ... and all I have going right now are two cases. The missing rabbi and one other."

"What are you dealing with in the other case?"

"Product theft from a company and I am trying to catch whoever did it," I explained. "Possibly someone over there got pissed off."

"Pinching apples from the fruit stand?"

"Sort of like that, but we're talking twelve million apples."

"That's a lot of fruit."

"Apparently it could be enough for someone to want to wish me harm."

"Yup, for twelve million apples some people can become a little *not nice*. I think you are right, though. Other than that blurb in the paper about you finding the rabbi's glasses, no one really knows that you are back working on the case. The lid on this case is so tight that I cannot imagine that anyone in the know at the state police would spill the beans and the FBI has yet to be informed. Anyway ... watch your *tookas*," said the lieutenant.

"I will try to keep my *tuchis* in one piece."

A few minutes later Nealy phoned and told me about the new body parts. He also told me that officers from the state police would be going to the Slater house to inform the *rebbetzin* at about nine in the evening. I acted surprised about the new information and I am pretty sure he did not have a clue that I already had this bit of gruesome news. I asked him to call me before the state police went over so that Dafna and I could be there when the *Rebbetzin* Slater's world came crashing down. He sounded relieved and said he was glad to have our help.

I was worried about lots of things. I was worried about what would happen to *Rebbetzin* Slater when the cops dropped the bomb this evening. I was worried about the incomprehensible circus that was about to begin when the police announced the multiple murders tomorrow. I was worried about Dafna and her family. But I was just plain pissed off at myself that I did not have a clue about who at Alkay had it in for me or how they were robbing the company.

First things first. I went to Dafna's house to give her the information about the new body parts and what it meant. I could not do it over the phone.

She took the news like a champ. We would go together to the Slater house when the state police delivered the news later in the evening.

Second on the list — I had to tell *Rebbi*.

25

Dayan Emes

I WENT to the *yeshiva* and approached Rabbi Kalmonowitz before he went into a class.

He took one look at me and said somberly, "Come with me."

He knew.

I had not said a word — but he knew.

He delayed his lecture and we went to his office.

"What is it?" he asked.

I explained about the discovery of more body parts and how they indicated that Rabbi Slater was no longer alive.

"*Baruch dayan emes*," he said reverently.

The phrase meant, 'Bless God who is the true judge.'

"Amen," I responded.

"When will the authorities inform the *rebbetzin*?"

"At nine this evening," I answered. "Dafna and I will be there."

"I also want to be there when they tell her. I will bring my *rebbetzin*. It will help her. There are a number of *halachic* problems that need to be settled."

"Like what?"

"Normally the *shiva* starts immediately after the burial. However, in this case the body parts will not be released in the near future, so there cannot be a burial of any sort. *Halacha* determines that the family begins the *shiva* now. The burial will be when it will be."

"I'll call the state police and tell them you will be there," I said standing to leave.

He thought for a moment and then said, "I asked you to find out what happened to *Reb* Yechezkel and you have done that. This is now a murder investigation. So I will fully understand if you do not wish to continue with this case. There is a *mashuginer* out there and things could become dangerous. Rabbi Slater is no longer with us and finding the person who is responsible will not bring him back. I am also very concerned with the danger you are in from your other case. Both you and Dafna's family are at risk. For this reason I think you should let someone else handle the murder of Rabbi Slater and devote your efforts to solving your other case as quickly as possible."

"I'll most definitely try to solve my other case but I'm also going to work on Rabbi Slater's murder. If you want to save the *yeshiva* money and don't want me on the case anymore ... that's fine. I'll do it for free. I want this guy and I won't stop until someone finds him."

"Why are you so sure it is a man? It could be a woman."

"This guy has killed more than one person at different times and this classifies him as a serial killer. The messages he leaves indicate that he is a racist. The profilers tell us that the odds are highly in favor of it being a man."

"So if this was not a case of a serial killer and he was not a racist, then it could be a woman."

What did Rebbi mean by that?

"Well, yeah. Then it could be a woman."

"Remember what you learned in your *Talmud* class; Keep an open mind and never jump to conclusions. What you are doing now is similar to the work of a *bais din* in the time of our sages. That prestigious court had to discover all the facts in each case that came before them. To be sure they had not left any stone unturned, they would confer between themselves. They had to look at that all the evidence and testimonies from every viewpoint until they found the truth. It is a great responsibility. So solve your mysteries but most importantly ... keep safe."

"I will most definitely try," I said.

Today was Sunday and I was supposed to go to the *dojo*, but I was really not in the mood.

I went anyway.

Turned out to be a waste of time. I could not concentrate and the martial arts practice was worthless. For me and the students. A good *sensei* does not only know how to do a move very well, he must be able to sense the elements that are lacking in his student and then correct their faults. To do this requires concentration and today that was something that escaped me. In the free competition, a newly raised brown belt threw me around like an old wash rag.

What an embarrassment.

I dragged myself home and took a long hot shower. I picked up the menus for a few of the kosher take-out joints trying to decide what I would order for supper.

There was a limit as to just how much I could mooch from Dafna.

After we are married I am sure that the take-out menus will be discarded because with Dafna being the best cook in the community they will become superfluous. You may ask how is it that I, a Jewish man from a Jewish home, with a typical Jewish Oedipus complex did not automatically rank my own mother as one of the top kosher chefs. First of all, since my family never kept a kosher home, there was no way she could ever be eligible for this particular culinary category.

Secondly — and stated simply — my mother could not and did not cook. Almost twenty-five years ago my mother stopped preparing *home-cooked* meals to nurture and give sustenance to her offspring. It was not that mom shirked in her homemaking responsibilities.

Quite the opposite.

It was because she realized that she was, and still is, a total disaster in the kitchen. Apparently she could never get into the rhythm of cooking. Just imagine a person who cannot carry a tune trying to sing. Or someone who is totally uncoordinated trying to dance. That was my mother with pots and pans. Every dish she made was either under or over cooked or under or over spiced. For many years she valiantly tried to prepare our meals but nothing went right for her. Milk curdled, onions got scorched, mixtures separated, gravies stayed lumpy.

As kids, my sister and I knew that our Mom's food was not any good so we just trained ourselves to consume as little as possible of her dreadful victuals. I think she thought we were just naturally skinny kids and did not understand why the school social worker came by several times to see if we were victims of child abuse. The incident that got my mother out of the kitchen permanently occurred when I was in the sixth grade and my sister was in the tenth. Mom overheard my sister's boyfriend — a nice Catholic fellow named Patrick — we were a very ecumenical family — explain why he refused to enter our home. His exact words were, "I would rather be crucified like our Lord Jesus Christ, than have to taste any more of your mother's cooking." My father had always stoically consumed all the food she offered and to his credit, I never once heard my father complain about her cooking. But when she consulted with my dad about what Patrick had said, he confirmed that there was a problem with food preparation in our household. He convinced her to stop cooking and not to try anything more complicated than making coffee or boiling up a pot of pasta. We could afford it, so we would either get a housekeeper/cook or have the food delivered.

Mom decided on the latter.

Surprisingly, for all her incompetence in the kitchen, my mother was quite a connoisseur of good food. Her culinary aptitude showed itself in her knowledge of what was best to order from each of the dozens of take-away menus that sat on the shelf above the rarely-used range. At least five nights a week the family cuisine was either take-out from different local restaurants or pre-packaged gourmet dinners. My mother had one interesting quirk concerning this food. She never — ever — served them in the take-out packages they came in. Mom transferred everything to our own plates and serving dishes. We ate at the table with real dinnerware, cutlery, glasses and napkins. A bit strange. Once or twice a week she spiced up the menu by ordering pizza, McDonalds, or KFC and this stuff could be consumed in venues other than the dining room and did not require real plates.

A few years ago I once heard my father quip — when my mother was well out of earshot — that we were a Jewish family that had been saved by Jesus.

I was a person raised on tasty junk food and a wide variety of expensive gourmet restaurant food and I can testify that none of that stuff holds a candle to the delicious dishes created by *Rebbetzin* Kalmonowitz, Shaindel or my fiancée, Dafna. Perhaps that explains why I metamorphosize into a gluttonous fiend when I am offered their terrific home cooked food.

However, since I take after my mother when it comes to culinary skills, this evening I was on my own. So I called one of the take-out places and ordered a delivery of a couple of burgers and fries.

Nealy called at about seven and told me that two officers would be at the Slater house at nine in the evening. I told him that Dafna and I, along with the Kalmonowitzs, would be there as well.

This worked out just perfectly because I had arranged for my cousin, Steven Lincoln, my Orthodox architect/contractor cousin, to come to the Lachler home at eight o'clock. Normally he only worked on big shopping centers and malls, but he was semi-retired and he had agreed to do this small job for me. His meeting with Shaindel and Dafna went very well and he got their feedback as to what Mrs. Kalin would like in the house expansion. He explained the various steps in getting the job done, including getting the city commission to OK a zoning variance and how long it would take to complete the work. He looked at the plans for Dafna's home, which included the extension under the lawn. Since he would not need to lay a foundation he was sure (God willing and no delays) that he could have the job done before the wedding. Dafna and her family could live in the house during the construction but would have to tolerate a big mess on the front lawn and back yard until the job was completed. He would drop off plans at the end of the week and once Shaindel made her final decisions on what she wanted he would get things moving.

Shaindel was going to have her own place.

26

Shiva

DAFNA AND I left Steve with my future mother-in-law to iron out a few details and we went to the Slater home. The Kalmonowitzs and two officers of the state police, a captain and a 1st lieutenant, were already waiting there on the sidewalk. I did not recognize the police officers so I introduced myself and the Kalmonowitzs. Promptly at nine, the six of us walked up to the house and *Rebbetzin* Slater opened the door. There was a flicker of question in her eyes but when she saw Rabbi Kalmonowitz, she understood. I suppose she realized all along that something bad had happened to her husband. I guess we all did. Each of us knew that he had not disappeared voluntarily.

The police captain began by telling her in a very official manner that they were convinced that Rabbi Slater was dead. He then went on to explain about the four murders, the body parts and the messages. At first I thought it was very cruel to burden her with all the grisly details and could not see why they were subjecting her to this horrible information, but then I realized that once the media got hold of the story it was all going to come out. Better she should hear the correct version from them. The police demanded that no one reveal any of the facts of the case to anyone not connected with the official investigation until after the news conference the next day. If they must pass the news to any close family member they should also inform them of this restriction. After the press conference they were free to speak with the media or anyone else they wished.

Once the police had answered all of *Rebbetzin* Slater's questions they left. Rabbi Kalmonowitz spoke comforting words and explained why Rabbi Slater's *shiva* would start immediately even though there was no funeral. *Rebbetzin* Slater did not show any emotion. She asked pertinent questions but mostly she just sat there listening. From experience I knew that the grief would show itself later. *Rebbetzin* Kalmonowitz outlined what the community was organizing for the *shiva* and told *Rebbetzin* Slater that she would be staying with her for the night. After about an hour, Dafna and I were also able to leave.

As we climbed into my car she said, "My God, that was tough. I don't want to go through that again."

"Think about the state police. They had to do that four times tonight."

"I forgot."

"Having *Rebbi* there was certainly a help."

"For sure. What did he say when you spoke with him this afternoon?"

"He offered me the option to bow out of the case."

"He did?"

"Yeah, he is worried about us. I told him I was going ahead with the investigation." I suddenly realized that I had not really consulted with her about my decision. "Unless you want me to quit. I would not want to put your family in jeopardy."

"Are you kidding? If we can help find this guy, we have to do whatever we can."

"So you also think this is a guy?"

"Well, yeah. You know ... serial killer ... racist ... chain saw ... you explained it all to me. A guy."

"Funny, when I told *Rebbi*, he said that I had to keep an open mind. He offered the possibility that this may not be a case of a serial killer nor a racist. So it might be a woman."

"Did he say it was a woman?"

"Now, don't go looking for hidden meaning in *Rebbi's* words. There is nothing to 'take to the bank' with what he said."

"But, did he say it was a woman?" she demanded.

"No, just that it might not be a racist serial killer."

She thought for a moment. "So, if this is not a case of a serial killer nor a racist," she asked rhetorically. "We are dealing with someone who wants us to think that it is. A murderer that wants to throw us off his ... or her ... track."

"What are you getting at?"

"It could be that one of the victims was the only real target and the others are just camouflage."

"I already raised the idea with Jarron."

"Yeah, but is he doing anything about it?"

"From what it says in the file, none of the victims stands out as a prime target. All were just regular Joes. Totally unrelated. The major effort will be in searching the white supremacy groups for suspects."

"So, that means no one is really looking for a prime target."

"Basically no."

"OK, if the search is for a racist killer then I think the best ones to do the job will be the FBI."

"Couldn't you look for him as well?" I asked.

"I could, but the FBI already has all the databases available to them and gets an ongoing feed of new information. Without constant input from the field, whatever I could find would be inferior to what the FBI can do. They have all the necessary data for such a search."

"So what do you suggest we do?"

"Why don't we look into the possibility of single primary target?"

"It is highly unlikely," I said shaking my head.

"Why do you think that?"

"If the guy wanted to kill one of them, and killed the other three just to confuse us by making it look like a serial killer, why would he go to the added trouble of making it look like a hate crime? It ain't easy to specifically find a Jew, a Muslim, an Asian, and a Mexican, snatch them and then kill them. If he wanted us to think that he is a run-of-the-mill psycho serial killer, he could just kill any three people at random. Much easier."

Dafna considered what I said for a moment and then answered, "Maybe, but if we assume one of the victims was the primary target, then he did not need to search for him. Let's say the primary was Vivian, the Vietnamese lady. He knows he is going to kill her soon. So his first random victim is Muhammad and BINGO. He now has a Muslim and since he knows that he will also have an Asian he thinks up the hate crime angle. Finding a Jew and Mexican for victims would not be that tough."

"OK," I said, "but you're stretching it. So, who do you think could be the primary victim?"

"We know just about everything there is to know about Rabbi Slater, so we can pretty much rule him out as a primary target. That leaves the other three that need to be checked. Miss Sanchez was known to the state police and so, they can easily check her out. That leaves the other two. Vivian Nguyen and Muhammad Nassar. We should concentrate on them."

"I see your logic. Which would you chose?"

"Definitely Nassar."

"Why?"

"Vivian is from a local family and the state police checked out the information. Nassar was a graduate student here but he comes from Chicago. Who did the initial interview of his family?"

"The state police contacted the Skokie police and they checked out the relatives."

"And their report is the skimpiest in the file. It's not their case so they probably had no big interest. Added to that, the state police probably poisoned the Skokie cops by telling them it was a racist crime. They could have missed some vital bit of evidence. The family in Chicago needs to be interviewed again but with an open mind."

"Like ... don't jump to conclusions."

"Precisely."

"Yeah, and those are the exact words that *Rebbi* used."

"What did I tell you?"

"Stop that."

She looked at me questioningly, "You heard my thoughts on the matter, but, what do you think we should do?"

"The state police said that the family in Chicago would also be getting the information about their son's death this evening. Tomorrow afternoon, the whole world will know and then the giant media hullabaloo explodes and we won't be able to get near them. So I suggest I call them right now ... it's an hour earlier in Chicago ... and tell them we are working with the state police ... not completely untrue ... and ask to interview them tomorrow. Maybe they will go along with that."

"Sounds like a plan."

"I guess the Windy City is the next stop."

"Great, I'll make sandwiches and pack some fruit."

"Nah, I'll be fine. I can grab something on the way."

"Maybe you can, but I can't. I need real food."

"What are you talking about? You are not coming with me."

"That's what you think. We're partners."

"No, we are not.   You just assist me.   We are not partners."

"OK, have it your way.   Your partner is not going with you to Chicago."

I was relieved, "Good. I am glad you understand."

"Your assistant is going with you to Chicago.   What time do we leave?"

What did she just do?

I knew that there was no budging Dafna. I also knew that I would enjoy having her along on the four plus hour drive to Chicago.   I pointed a finger at her and said sternly, "OK, you can come. But you owe me."

She tilted her head and gave me a skeptical look from under her brow, as if she was saying, if we made a tally of who owes who, I would be the one in the red.

She was right.

27

Windy City

SINCE WE had to leave for Chicago very early in the morning I had no choice but to go to the early *minyan* at the *Bnai Israel* Synagogue.

According to *halacha,* morning prayers cannot be said before sunrise, but in a pinch they can be said when there is a lightening of the Eastern sky. The *Bnai Israel minyan* has a very loose interpretation of this rule so that they are able to organize a *minyan* when the chief rooster of the chicken coop was still getting some shut-eye and was not even contemplating a token cock-a-doodle-doo. The *Bnai Israel minyan* was not only the earliest, it was also the fastest. In and out in under thirty minutes — even with a reading from the *Torah* — lickety split.

So, I was in and out — lickety split.

After prayers I made a quick stop at home to drop off my *talis* and *tefillin* and was at Dafna's house at seven. As soon as I drove up, Dafna came trundling out of her house carrying a large picnic basket. She loaded the stuff in the back seat and we set off.

I had a surprise for her.

I drove to Ten Mile Road but instead of turning west to get to Southfield Road to reach I-94 and Chicago, I headed east to grab the I-696.

"This is not the way to Chicago. Where are we going?" she asked warily.

"You'll see."

"Am I going to like it?"

"I think so."

I travelled on I-696 going west until I turned down I-75 South to catch I-94 heading east. Then I took the Gratiot exit and went a few more blocks to arrive at Detroit City Airport. It was now officially named the Coleman A. Young International Airport, after a former mayor.

"We are going to fly to Chicago?" asked Dafna.

"That's right."

"You should have told me. I might not have had any ID with me. After 9/11, you know how strict they are. What airline are we flying?"

"I guess you could call it Ralph Air," I said as I parked the car in the lot.

"Never heard of them."

"Very small company," I said as I retrieved my small knapsack, but left the picnic basket in the car.

"What about our lunch?"

"We won't need it. We'll grab something in Chicago."

Dafna scanned the small airfield, "Where is the terminal?"

I pointed to the one and only building, "That's it."

She looked at the relatively unimposing structure, the small control tower, and the private planes parked on the concrete pads of the field, "When does our plane get here?"

"It is probably here already."

"I don't see it."

"I think it is still in the hangar. Let's find Ralph."

We entered the field's administration building and I spotted my friend Ralph Huggins. He was over at the main desk and waved to me in recognition. After finishing up some business he came over to join us.

Ralph was a 60 year old retired air force pilot and was dressed in dark green coveralls. As usual, he wore his lucky hat, a bright red Cardinal's baseball cap, "Sy Lincoln, you old son of a gun. Good to see you," he said shaking my hand. "And this must be our passenger, your fiancée."

"Yes, this is Dafna."

"Welcome to Detroit City Airport," said Ralph with a wave of his hand. "I just filed our flight plan for Chicago and the plane is all gassed up. Let's go."

Ralph headed towards the door and I started after him but Dafna held me back. She had a worried look on her face, "Is he the owner of the airline?"

"He is the owner, mechanic, and pilot. Let's go."

We followed Ralph to one of the hangers, which was actually nothing more than an oversized garage with a roll-down front. He raised the door to reveal his plane, a vintage 4-seater. "Here, give me a hand," he said passing me a rope tied to the front strut of the three wheeled plane. "OK, pull her out."

I backed up yanking hard on the rope and the plane slowly rolled out onto the airfield. As it advanced, its wings rocked from side to side.

"Am I supposed to fly in that thing?" asked Dafna anxiously. "It's just a big lawn mower with wings."

Ralph smiled and said, "This lawn mower is almost as old as I am. It's a classic 1960 4-seater Piper Pacer. I had the motor overhauled just last year. Climb in while I make the pre-flight check."

I sensed that Dafna was extremely reluctant to get into the plane and it took some good natured cajolery for her to get into the back seat. With my long legs I would be in agony if I tried to sit back there. I closed the door and told her to buckle her seatbelt.

Dafna said nervously, "What for? If this plane goes down what good would a seatbelt be? Look at the doors.

They are made out of canvas for goodness sake. This is not a plane it's an accident waiting to happen."

She was definitely stressed out. I mean — she really was worried. Very unusual for her. She was usually up for just about anything. "Dafna, calm down. Everything will be fine."

"I get bent out of shape flying commercial airliners. You know, the kind with stewardesses and soft drinks and little packages of peanuts and those other things they have ... maybe you heard of them ... safety equipment. I am going to have a nervous breakdown any moment."

"This plane has been flying for over fifty years and nothing has happened to it."

"Statistically that just means it's due to crash," she said with conviction.

Ralph climbed into the plane and as he boarded, the entire aircraft tilted to his side. Dafna let out a groan. "Are you ready for our short flight to Chicago?"

Dafna said immediately, "No, I am not. Can I get off, please?"

"First time in a light plane?" asked Ralph.

"Yes. Can you tell?" she answered.

"The white knuckles and the rapid shallow breathing are a dead giveaway."

"Did you have to say 'a *dead* giveaway'?" she replied.

"These types of planes have a better safety record than the big ones. Fewer crashes, fewer fatalities. It's got all the latest avionics. They are just plain safe. Relax and enjoy the flight."

Ralph started the engine and then taxied to the strip.

For anyone who has never travelled in a light plane, the noise of the engine is a big surprise. Even with the head sets we each wore, we still had to scream to communicate. The engine sounds were literally deafening and I knew that it was not going to get better once we were airborne. The only thing that made the noise tolerable was that after a while you got used to it.

The tower gave Ralph his clearance for takeoff. He gunned his engine and within a few seconds we were in the air.

We quickly climbed to 5,000 feet and leveled off, "I'm instrument rated but I prefer to stick to a visual flight if I can," screamed Ralph. "I don't like to go over Lake Michigan with a one engine plane so we will head down to Indiana and come around the bottom of the lake to reach Chicago. The flight will be about an hour and three quarters. Enjoy the scenery."

There were very few clouds in the sky and the scattered lakes below us sparkled as they reflected the rays of the sun still far in the east. Ralph unscrewed a thermos and poured a cup of coffee and handed it to Dafna, "Thank you," she said loudly. "It's very drafty in here. I don't think your door is completely closed."

I looked at the canvas door and saw there were gaps between the door frame and the fuselage, "I'm afraid the door is completely closed."

"Oh my," was all she said as she hunkered down in her heavy coat sipping her coffee.

The vistas seen from the air were breathtaking. It was so unlike flying at 25,000 feet. From here you could see each individual farm. The cows in the pasture. Tractors going out into the fields. You could even see the water flowing in the rivers and streams.

Terrific.

Somehow, I got the feeling that the scenery was not impressing Dafna.

She seemed catatonic, staring straight ahead.

What is wrong with her? Usually she was talking a mile a minute.

As we headed west, I noticed that there had been some snow in the area and everything was covered in a light dusting of the white powder.

Very beautiful.

The snow cover was heavier as we rounded the bottom of Lake Michigan. Really gorgeous. When the skyline of Chicago came into view Ralph called into Midway Airport and received permission to land.

"We are not flying into O'Hare?" I asked.

"Nah, I used to land at Meigs Field, on an artificial island, right on the lakeshore. That was the busiest single strip airport in the world. But Mayor Daley didn't like it, so he bulldozed the field about fifteen years ago. Midway is the closest to downtown."

Ralph made a perfect landing and taxied the airplane to the general aviation service area. He switched off the engine and turned to Dafna, "So what do you think of my plane? Wasn't that a smooth flight?"

Dafna seemed to be waking up from a trance, "What? Are we there?"

"Yes, we are. Welcome to Chicago Midway International Airport. Did you enjoy the flight?"

She looked very pale but she plastered a fake smile on her face to say, "Yes, it was delightful. Thank you very much."

What strange behavior.

"I can hardly wait for the return trip," she said blandly to Ralph. Then she leaned close to me and whispered urgently, "Shimon, get me off this flying shoebox."

When we entered the arrivals area I asked Dafna, "Is everything all right?"

"Everything is fine," she insisted and then went off to the ladies room.

I arranged with Ralph that we would head back to Detroit at about six o'clock and I would call him in the afternoon to finalize the time.

28

Drop Dead

WE GRABBED an Uber out to the Village of Skokie, a suburb just north of Chicago. Almost all the homes in the area were single family dwellings — ranches, split-levels, and two-stories. The houses were probably constructed sixty or seventy years ago but all appeared to be in good repair. A few had rather elaborate additions to the basic tract homes. There were even some with turrets and gables, but none could be considered mansions. The lots the houses sat on were not especially spacious, nor were they ghetto crowded. All the lawns and shrubbery were neat and trimmed. A nice neighborhood in the suburbs of mid-America.

The Nassar home was a two-story on North Kostner Avenue just south of Main Street. There was a big lawn, quite a few trees but no turrets.

We went up the long walk and I rang the doorbell. I heard shuffling steps approaching and a short roly-poly gentleman, aged around thirty, opened the door.

I did not need to put my detecting skills into overdrive to know that this man could not be the father of Muhammad Nassar, the twenty-six year old grad student.

I opened the screen door and announced, "We're here to see Mr. Nassar."

"I Benito, caregiver," he said with a heavy Italian accent. "Azi in living room. You be detectives. Come wit me."

He stepped back from the door to allow us to pass.

Benito was dressed in an orange sweatshirt, orange pants, and orange Keds. Very color coordinated was Benito. He probably thought that this was cutting edge chic on the Amalfi Coast, but to my eye he looked like a giant ripe mango or perhaps an oversized orange bowling pin.

We went down a short entry hall to arrive at the living room. Azi — Mr. Azzam Nassar — was sitting near the large alcove facing the street. He was wearing a loose fitting tan exercise outfit and but it was clear that he was not about to indulge in any sporting activity. How did I know? Easy ... Azi was sitting in a wheelchair. From the way his sat in the chair, with his head and body held by side supports, and the vacant look in his eyes, it was obvious that Mr. Nassar had suffered some major brain catastrophe. Stroke — head trauma — tumor — take your pick. They were all bad news. One of God's ways of reminding us how temporary we are in this world. Azi Nassar looked at us and smiled a lopsided smile. I am not sure if he was happy to see us or whether he smiled at anything that moved. There was very little flesh over the bones of his hands that were folded on a small table attached to his wheelchair. He had that ashen gray skin color that sick Middle Eastern people get. His facial features sagged, and he looked like a wilted flower.

Benito pointed us to a pair of chairs opposite the invalid, and asked if we would like something to drink.

I turned to Benito, "We did not know ..."

"That Azi not OK?"

"Yes," I said. "I called yesterday and I spoke with ... I guess you ... and you said it would be all right if we came to speak with Mr. Nassar."

Benito took a seat next to Azzam, "No me. That Fred. Night guy. You called ... he ask Azi want to speak wit you. He say yes. Azi like visitor."

"Does he know what's going on?" asked Dafna.

"With his son?" I added.

"Yes, he do. Ask yourself."

I turned towards Mr. Nassar, "Hi, my name is Sy Lincoln and this is Dafna Lachler, we are working with the Michigan State Police in the investigation of your son's murder. First let me say how sorry we are over your loss."

Azi's expression never changed but Benito said, "He say, 'Yes'. That mean he heard you."

"How can you tell? I didn't see him say anything," said Dafna.

"He no speak," said Benito stating the obvious. "Look small finger left hand. If move one time mean yes ... two mean no."

I was not sure how to progress. Questioning Mr. Nassar would take forever and in his state I was fairly sure he would tire long before we were finished. I turned to Benito, "Would it be all right if I asked you some background questions and then see if Azi agrees."

"No problem. Happy speak you, but I know not much. Only three month USA," said the caregiver.

Terrific.

I cannot speak with good old Azi and talking to my new friend Benito probably would not be much help.

Maybe coming all the way to Chicago was going to be a total waste of time.

"Benito, I read the police report and there was quite a bit of information about Muhammad. Who spoke with the police and told them all that stuff?"

"That be Sammy. Talk police."

"Who is Sammy?" asked Dafna.

"Kid Azi's," said Benito.

"Azi's kid?" asked Dafna.

"Yes, kid," he said.

"Muhammad was Sammy's brother?" I asked.

"Yes, brother. Sammy older. Twenty-eight years old."

Muhammad's file did not specifically name any siblings, but that was not unusual since the police wanted to know more about the victim. They would only investigate the family more closely if they suspected that it had some bearing on the disappearance. The report said that there was no evidence of family strife.

"How can I contact Sammy? I want to get some more information."

"Sammy know you coming. Be here any minute speak with you."

God in the heavens must have been observing my plight, because just at that moment I heard the front door of the house open and someone was approaching the living room.

The entrance to the room was behind us. Benito turned and said, "Here Sammy."

I turned to meet Muhammad's brother.

From reviewing the pictures in the file I expected that Sammy would have swarthy features similar to Muhammad or the man in the wheelchair.

I was right about the swarthy features, but was wrong about everything else.

I assumed that Sammy was Azi's son and that the name was a shortened version for Ismael or something. But one look at the person that entered the room made it obvious to me — a person trained in advanced investigatory techniques — that Sammy was not Muhammad's brother.

Sammy was a woman.

You know the expression, 'Drop Dead Gorgeous'? Or 'Arabian Princess'? She exemplified the terms.

Her long straight black hair hung down her back, she had huge — absolutely huge — hazel eyes, perfect facial features, perfect makeup, and a very good figure which she highlighted with her tight revealing outfit. Her straight tan skirt stopped way short of her knees showcasing her taupe hose encased long shapely legs. I guess she was five foot eight inches in her stocking feet, but she was wearing tan stilettos with three or four inch heels so that when I stood to greet her, she was about eye level with me. She walked without the slightest wobble and I was amazed at her skill and balance. I would not be surprised if she could run a marathon in those shoes.

Drop Dead Gordeous women — DDGs — are women that wanted to be noticed. They tweaked their natural good looks so that everyone … who was not totally blind … male or female … could not help but look at them. These women always went around in full makeup, had their hair arranged perfectly, and wore only flattering well-tailored clothes — no hand-me-down pants or baggy T-shirts, even if they were just going to answer the front door. They would never think of wearing an old faded Michigan State sweatshirt, or furry slippers around the house like Dafna does.

One of the shrinks in rehab once explained to me that I should not be judgmental of DDG's. They raised the 'sexual tension' where ever they went because they were just trying get something in this testosterone-driven society. Everything is just so much easier if you are good looking. If you are a DDG … even better.

Sammy had her DDG act down pat and she certainly had raised the 'sexual tension' in the room. At least for me.

She approached me extending her hand, "You must be Mr. Lincoln, a pleasure to meet you."

I had a problem.

In my pre-*yeshiva* days meeting someone like Sammy would have been all good. She was … as they say … easy on the eyes. But I had been a *yeshiva bocher* just a short while ago and I felt compelled to do everything in my power not to ogle her. In addition Dafna ... my fiancée ... was two feet away from me.

What to do?

Should I hope that my training as a professional investigator would allow me to overcome this sudden elevation in the 'tensions' of the room and that I would be able to control my libidinous instincts?

I hoped for the best.

I shook her hand and babbled something that sounded like, "Meeting ... pleasure ... mine." I think I pointed in Dafna's direction and mumbled, "Daffffffna."

My God — I am talking like Benito.

Sammy turned towards Dafna and shook her hand as well, "How do you do?"

Dafna smiled at Sammy and said, "I'm Mr. Lincoln's associate."

I reminded myself that I was here on the job and somehow, I got my mind to start functioning again. I turned to Benito, "I thought that Sammy was Mr. Nassar's son."

Obviously this was not the first time he had seen Sammy's effect on men. "No, no. Sammy not *son*," he said with a knowing smile.

Oh yeah — definitely not a son.

Sammy turned to me, "What would you like to know? The police were here last night. They told us we are not allowed to talk with anyone until this evening, but since you are working with the cops I'll be glad to help you in any way I can. You've got to catch the person that killed Muhammad," she said with determination.

I knew Dafna was at my side and I did not want to have to explain any reactions — primitive or otherwise. I diligently fought to keep my gaze where decorum demanded ... near my shoes.

I was almost to the point where I could jump-start my brain into functioning again when Dafna spoke up, "Ms. Nassar. Is that your name?"

"Yes, it is."

"Sammy Nassar?"

"Samira Nassar," she replied.

"Great," said Dafna, "Can we start with some background information about Muhammad."

"Sure. What do you want to know?"

"We have an outline of the nuts and bolts of his life from the Skokie police. We know when and where he was born, where he went to school and all that stuff. We need information about how he behaved in school. Who were his friends and who were his enemies — if there were any? And anything that might point to an individual that might have wanted to do him harm," said Dafna.

"The police said that it looked like a hate crime. Do you think otherwise? That someone wanted to kill my brother?"

Dafna answered with, "We are looking into all aspects of this case. We don't want to assume anything. So we are here asking for your cooperation."

"You've got it," she said.

"Did everyone call him Muhammad or did he have a nickname?" asked Dafna.

"Are you kidding? Muslims don't fool around with the name of the Prophet. No nick names. Everyone called him Muhammad. When he was in high school some of the kids called him Nassar, but that was it."

"Tell us about how Muhammad grew up. What were his interests? Start where you want and we will ask questions if anything is unclear. OK?"

Samira began talking, telling us about her brother that she obviously loved very much. She went on almost non-stop for over thirty minutes. Talking about her dead brother was obviously tough and every once in a while she would have to wipe back a tear. Mr. Nassar, sitting in his wheelchair, listened along with us and I noticed that he also shed a tear or two as his daughter spoke fondly about her brother. Dafna threw in a question where appropriate but mostly she just let Sammy tell her story.

Muhammad grew up in Skokie and went to Lincoln Junior High and then Niles West High School. He was an honor student at both schools and received a full math scholarship to Northwestern University for a BA and then masters degree. He transferred to Wayne State University for the PhD program because he was interested in an esoteric branch of mathematics that dealt in analysis of Banach Spaces — or some sort of name like that — and the country's biggest expert was at Wayne. He came home every third weekend to see his father and his girlfriend — his high school sweetheart — and she too was devastated. As a kid, he had been an Eagle Scout with a zillion merit badges. Never got in trouble with the cops. Never ran with any of the street hoodlums. Did not drink, smoke, or gamble and never had any debts. He worked part-time to help pay for his schooling as an IT and computer technician for small businesses and in people's homes.

In short, a good person without any enemies, and no reason in the world for anyone to kill him.

There was one piece of important information missing from her depiction of her brother, and Dafna had not asked about it. Muhammad had obviously been a devout Muslim, but I could not see any evidence of that in Azi or Sammy. Could that have been a bone of contention between them? I began, "I noticed that Muhammad took Islam pretty seriously ..."

Before I could finish my question she answered, "... and you want to know where we stand on that."

"Well ... yeah."

"My brother was the only born-again Muslim in the family. I am fourth generation here in Chicago. My grandfather opened the Oriental Coffee House on State Street seventy years ago. My dad ran the place until he got sick and now I am in charge. We are Muslims because we were born Muslim, but as you see," she said pointing to her revealing outfit, "We do not actively practice the faith. Don't tell the local *Imam*, but dad has a full wet bar in the basement and a slice or two of ... shall we say ... extra-non-*Hallal* meat has been known to be served in this house. Muhammad started his journey back to the faith when he was in graduate school."

"Did your religious differences create any friction in the family?" I asked.

"Well, my father would bitch about the fact that when Muhammad was home he could not have a beer when he watched the Sunday football games, but other than that, not at all."

"You said he had a girlfriend," said Dafna.

"Yes, Aisha. Nice girl. She lives up the block. I don't know how close they were of late. He was in Detroit and she stayed here in Chicago. Also, I know that they argued about his strict Muslim practices. She is more religious than us, but a lot less than he was."

Dafna asked a few more questions to complete the information and I finally got my head screwed on again and asked a couple more. Benito said that Azi was tired and needed to get some rest and wheeled him out of the living room. I then asked Sammy if she could give us a few more photographs of Muhammad. She went up to his room and brought them back for us.

No evidence that anyone wanted to kill Muhammed. No real progress.

29

Flip Attitude

WE LEFT the Nassar house and went up to Main Street. We were able to interview the owner of a small computer shop where Muhammad had been employed. He then sent us to a nearby restaurant where we were able to talk with one of Muhammad's high school pals. Obviously we could not tell them that he had been murdered so our cover story was that we were investigating his disappearance. They all gave similar accounts of who and what Muhammad Nassar had been.

We also took a chance and stopped at the home of his girlfriend. Frail diminutive Aisha was a twenty-six year registered nurse and luckily she was not on duty. She freely told us about the differences she had with Muhammad. He thought it was important that if they married she should wear a burqa — the black body sack and full veil that completely covered the bodies of religious Muslim women. She was willing to wear the head scarf but balked at the body sack and opposed the idea.   On his last visit, they had agreed that their unofficial engagement would be put on hold. There was no indication that she was angry about this decision and I could not imagine that this petite young lady — a jilted bride — traveled to Detroit and then planned and executed a complex series of murders just to do him in. Of course, it was possible that she hired someone else to do the deed but in my estimation that was a very remote possibility. My initial conclusion was that if there was a primary target, there was no evidence that it had been Muhammad Nassar, but I would keep an open mind.

My deal with Ralph was that he would fly me to Chicago if I paid for the fuel. Not cheap but less than last minute airline tickets. He had family in the Windy City and liked to visit if someone else was picking up the gas tab. On this trip he was also bringing his uncle back to Detroit and that was a bonus for Ralph. It was only two o'clock in the afternoon, so we had a few hours to kill. I gave Dafna the choice of going to one of the kosher restaurants — compared to Detroit, Chicago had many more options for kosher dining — or skipping lunch and heading to the Museum of Science and Industry to see the coal mine exhibit.

Kind of cool if you never had been there.

She chose the coal mine.

Her decision was based on several factors. She could cook rings around just about any dining establishment, so restaurant food was not a big deal for her. She was also a transplanted New Yorker where kosher restaurants were a dime a dozen. And finally, she had never really toured Chicago.

As soon as we got seated in the Uber, I thought Dafna was going to quiz me on my impressions of what we had learned after interviewing all the people who knew Muhammad Nassar. Instead she turned in her seat and looked at me seriously. "Did you find Samira attractive?"

How do you answer that? Damned if you do, damned if you don't.

"Um ... well ... I suppose so," I stammered.

"You suppose so? Is that why you could not keep your eyes off of her?"

What? How? I was looking at my shoes most of the time. Well — not all the time. I guess I had not hidden my libidinous reactions as well as I thought.

"I suppose some people would say that she is a good looking woman," I said. Then quickly added, "I say that only as an observation."

"Because you are an investigator."

"Exactly."

"So, you think she is attractive?"

"Well ... if you put it that way ... then, yes."

"What is she trying to attract?"

"What?" I asked.

"What is she trying to attract?" repeated Dafna.

"What are you asking?"

"If she is 'attractive', what is she trying to attract? Simple question."

I thought for a moment and said, "People's attention."

"All people?"

Dafna was smart. She had me cornered. "Well ... probably ... mostly men."

"Very likely ... but in today's modern world ... it could be women."

I had not thought of that, "Yeah, it could be."

"Would you like me to dress like her? You know, really sexy?"

Where did that question come from?

"Of course not," I answered quickly. "Are you jealous of her?"

Dafna thought for a moment and then said, "No. Most definitely not. I am comfortable the way I am. I just wonder if she really feels comfortable dressing the way she does."

"Like you said, she likes the attention."

"I do not know her at all, but I strongly suspect that she has a flip attitude towards sex."

"What the heck, is a 'flip attitude towards sex'?"

"You know ... casual sex. Sex without commitment. Or perhaps she uses sexuality to help get what she wants."

"Very flip."

"My question is ... is she happy? She must attract men the way a flame attracts moths."

"Could be," I said with an innocent nod of my head.

"I know I mentioned this before ... my husband, David, taught me that *halacha's* attitude is that sex is something good but it is just too intense of an experience to be allowed to run free. It has to be done in a controlled environment otherwise people get hurt. The statement that I have often heard, 'It's just sex,' is easy to say but it is hard to believe that anyone really thinks that way. There are even some people that have a philosophy of : 'If it feels good ... and does not hurt anybody ... do it'"

I tried to keep a straight face as I said, "Really? There are people like that?"

"Absolutely. But with sex you just never know who is going to get hurt. There might be some rare hedonistic people out there that consider sex to be on the same level as an indoor sport. My husband used to say that the act of total physical surrender to a partner always involves serious emotional ties. Saying such ties do not exist does not make it so. Having sex and just walking away ... after a night ... a week ... or even a month ... can lead to severe psychological stress. Sex needs commitment and boundaries."

"Like marriage," I ventured.

"Exactly. I just met Sammy ... and I like her ... but I feel she is not content. I just hope that somehow she finds happiness."

Wow! Dafna's insight amazes me.

30

Night Flight

WE PAID for our tickets and stood in line. The coal mine exhibit had not really changed in the past eighty years. Pretty amazing when you consider that when this ride was built no one could even imagine a place like Disney World. I had been through the mine a few times and for me there would be no new surprises. Still, I was bit concerned. After Dafna's reaction to the small plane, I was worried how she would react in the small cramped coal car in a dark tunnel.

Nothing happened.

We went down in the coal elevator and boarded the coal car for our trip through the black tunnels. All the while, Dafna had a naïve smile on her face and looked around in a sort of awe. Like a little kid that had just tasted ice cream for the first time. She enjoyed every minute of the ride.

This was the kind of reaction I normally expected from her.

After the coal mine we just walked around the museum looking at the exhibits and then I told her it was time to get back to the airport. Her mood changed immediately and she said in all seriousness, "When we get to the airport book me on a commercial flight."

"What's wrong?"

"I am not flying back to Detroit in that contraption," she said decisively.

"You have got to be kidding."

"The mixer in my kitchen has a bigger engine than that plane."

"Dafna, it is perfectly safe."

"I have a bad feeling about this. I keep having these thoughts that we are not going to get back home safely. Honest to goodness I do," she said with all sincerity.

"Since when have you become the psychic?"

"I just have this feeling."

"You'll be fine. Trust me."

"I trust you. It's that plane I don't trust."

I phoned Ralph and told him we should make it to the field at about 6:15. In the cab Dafna continued to demand some sort of conveyance other than 'the sardine can with a propeller.' I used every trick I knew and somehow — I have no idea how I did it — I convinced her not to bail out on me.

While we rode to the airport I used my phone to go online to see the reaction of CNN, Fox News, and NBC to the revelation that there was a serial killer in Michigan. I intended to watch the official FBI announcement when I got home. It was a hot item on all channels. I turned to Dafna, "The whole world now knows about our murderer."

"What are they saying?"

"The usual. Mostly blah blah. All the talking heads are having a field day chattering on about violent crime in America."

When we entered the general aviation area we saw Ralph waiting next to his plane. He introduced us to his uncle and they stowed his suitcase in the small cargo bay at the rear of the fuselage. Dafna whispered in my ear that it would be improper for her to sit next to a stranger in the cramped rear seat so it was decided — that is, she decided — that I would be the one that would sit next to her.

I was doomed to sit in that tiny seat.

Maybe we should have taken a commercial flight.

As Ralph made the pre-flight check, we all buckled our seat belts and put on our headphones. I was as ready as anyone could be who had his knees folded up near his chin. This was going to be a fun one and three quarter hours.

"It's getting dark," said Dafna nervously.

"Yeah, we'll be flying back at night," answered Ralph. "Don't worry. I told you I am instrument rated."

She said softly, in great despair, "Oh my."

He started the engine and radioed the tower for takeoff clearance. Once again the noise was unbelievable. We taxied out onto the tarmac and waited. He got his clearance and continued out to the runway to wait behind ten other small aircraft. We inched our way to the takeoff area. When we were finally in position he gunned the engine and the whole aircraft shuddered for about ten seconds. The brakes were released and we went speeding down the runway.

Suddenly Dafna grabbed my forearm very tightly. I could feel her nails digging into my skin.

Normally, Orthodox Jewish women did not clutch the arms of men that are not their husbands. But this was an emergency. She was in a panic and her vice-like grip was actually quite painful. Since we were both miserable, perhaps this was allowed. Extreme situations require extreme measures.

The plane raced down the field for about one hundred yards and then ever so gently we were no longer on the ground.

But just barely.

We were literally clearing the surrounding trees by only a few feet.

It looked to me that we were not gaining altitude at all.

Dafna frantically looked about at the trees passing just below the fuselage, obviously worried that we were too low.

"Ralph, how come we are not flying higher?" I asked.

"Nothing to be worried about," he said calmly.

"I'm not worried, just curious. On the inbound flight you climbed almost immediately to 5,000 feet."

"Yeah, but when we came we were one person lighter and did not have a big suitcase. So with the fuel, we are a little heavy."

"Do you mean we are overweight?" I asked worriedly.

"Just a little bit."

Dafna's ultra firm grasp was sinking deeper into my flesh and cutting off the circulation to my hand.

"You always said there is a safety factor ... so we are all right? Isn't that correct?" I ventured.

"Yeah, the safety factor ... well ... we are a little heavy even with the safety factor."

Dafna whispered loudly in my ear, "Tell him to land this plane right now. I want off."

"Ralph," I said in a friendly tone. "You know ... if we are a little heavy ... we would be glad to go back to Midway and take another plane."

"Give it another minute and we'll burn off enough fuel to be out of the red and then we will climb."

Sure enough after about thirty seconds the nose began to rise and we slowly went up to 5,000 feet for the ride back to Detroit.

Just like he said — no problem.

But Dafna was still not convinced.

I think her claws have broken skin.

The sun set in the west and night fell. The sickle shaped waning moon was reflected off the broken cloud cover and the stars shown overhead. Once again, we came around the bottom of Lake Michigan, all the while watching the red tail lights of the vehicles streaming along the interstates. When we got to central Michigan, the moonlight allowed us to see the general contour of the land. We could see the lights of a lonely farmhouse or barn sparkling in the blackness. Small towns and villages were clusters of yellow light and the occasional lake was a dark black stain surrounded by the slightly luminescent fields.

Ralph's flight plan followed I-94 back to Detroit. We heard through the headsets when the controllers of the various radar stations passed control from one beacon to the next.

For Ralph this was a routine and uneventful flight.

Dafna was catatonic.

She had not said a word or moved in her seat since her request to leave the plane over Chicago. Nor had she released my arm. I tried once to get her to give me a short respite — so I could regain some sensation in my fingers — but it was a no go.

I tried speaking to her but she did not respond.

It was obvious that she was still alive because her grip remained as powerful as a killer whale chomping down on a baby seal.

I think my arm will be crippled for life.

Far to the east I could see a bright haze on the dark horizon, indicating that we were getting closer to Detroit. The lights got brighter and soon we were over the suburbs of the city. The plane came in towards City Airport and Ralph made a wide turn to line up with the runway. He decreased the power and the plane began its descent.

Dafna's grip was now a two-handed affair, getting stronger and sinking deeper and deeper. I was sure that at any moment her fingers would clamp shut that much more and they would slice through my forearm. My amputated hand would drop to the floor of the aircraft with a thud.

The plane touched down in a perfect three point landing and Ralph decreased the throttle and braked. The aircraft slowed almost to a stop and then he taxied back to his hanger.

He cut the engine.

The silence was deafening.

Ralph turned around in his seat and said with a smile, "What did I tell you? Beautiful flying weather and a perfect flight."

Still no response from Dafna. Her grip had not relaxed.

"Dafna," I said cheerfully. "We are back in Detroit."

She seemed to be waking from a dream and said, "What?"

"Do you want to get off the plane?"

Suddenly alert, she said, "Off the plane? Yes, yes. I want to get off the plane."

She released my arm.

I could feel how the warm blood began streaming down into my frigid fingertips. There was the sensation of pins and needles, so I knew my hand was saved.

Hallelujah.

Dafna unbuckled her seat belt and scrounged around frantically for all her things. Ralph came around to her side of the fuselage and opened the door.

She scrambled out onto the tarmac and I had the distinct impression that she was considering kissing the earth in gratitude for being let out of the small plane. I followed behind her carrying my bag. I did this with my left hand, because the right was still not working properly.

Ralph was talking with his uncle and I put down my knapsack to shake his hand lefty style, "Thanks pal, you really were a lifesaver."

He shot his thumb towards Dafna, "I think your fiancée did not enjoy the flight that much. I can tell. I see that every once in a while. Don't worry, they always love it when they go up the next time."

Dafna's eyes widened in sudden panic.

She was thinking about the next time.

"Yeah, I'm sure you are right," I said with a nod of my head. "She will love it the next time."

31

Accident

WE WERE in my car headed home and I was strongly hoping that all the weirdness of the flight was behind us but Dafna was still not talking. Very unusual for her. I was worried. *Why was she so spooked by an almost perfect flight.* I figured when she was ready she would start talking again. After another ten minutes of the silent treatment I could not take it any longer and said, "I'm sorry."

"What are you sorry about?" she asked blandly.

"I'm sorry I insisted you get on that plane, because I see now that it upset you. I did not realize. So, I'm sorry."

"You're forgiven. You didn't know."

"Well, I should have figured it out. Like in sexual harassment ... if the lady says no, she means no."

"It's not your fault. You didn't know," she said solemnly.

"Didn't know what?"

"You did not know that my father was severely injured in a small plane crash eight years ago."

"How severe?"

"He never recovered. Brain injury. My mother cared for him in our home until he died a few years ago."

Oh my God. What have I done?

"I'm so, so, sorry. I really did not know."

"Of course you didn't, because my mother insists I never talk about it. When we get home, whatever happens, do not tell her I flew in a small plane."

"My lips are sealed."

"I know I behaved strangely, but between my fear of small planes and the feeling of dread I felt all day, I just could not function."

"What do you mean? Like woman's intuition? You thought something bad was going to happen to us?" I asked.

"Much more than intuition. It was like any moment … something would happen to endanger us both. It was frightening."

"Well, nothing happened and it is now behind us … so relax. In just a few minutes you will be home, safe and sound," I said trying to reassure her.

We were going about 60 mph heading north in the center lane of I-75. The weather was clear, the road was dry, and traffic was light for nine in the evening. Suddenly, about 200 feet ahead of us, a small car, travelling in the left lane, apparently misjudged the slow right curve of the highway and wandered off onto the left shoulder. It must have hit some sort of obstruction because it suddenly swerved further to the left and hit the concrete median divider. The car then spun around and careened back onto the interstate directly into a huge semi-trailer with a full trailer pup. The semi was forced to the right and the cab jackknifed on the semi-trailer. Almost immediately the semi and the pup flipped onto their side. They began sliding down the highway with sparks flying, slowly coming to a stop so that they completely blocked all four lanes of the roadway.

We were heading directly towards the truck.

My reaction was instinctive and rapid. I jammed on the brakes with all my might. I sensed the brakes grab and the start of deceleration. But, after a fraction of a second the brake pedal went mushy and I felt the rear of the car go into a bad skid to the right. I pumped the brakes but it had no effect. The rear of the car was coming around and I felt my high wheeled SUV begin to tilt to the right.

The car was still going at 60 mph and unable to stop. We were going to flip and there was nothing I could do to stop it. My SUV was already halfway to the overturned truck.

The crash was inevitable and our lives depended on the airbag system, but airbags can break bones and even kill. I yelled to Dafna, "We are going to crash. Grab the sides of your seat and push your head against the head rest."

The whole incident and crash did not take more than a few seconds but it felt like an eternity.

The SUV flipped, crunched, banged, and bumped. We were thrown about and there was a cacophony of breaking glass, steel, and concrete. Then everything stopped moving and there was silence.

I had no idea what we had hit or how we had survived the crash.

I could feel that we were upside down in the car and I immediately turned to Dafna who was hanging from her seat belt and trying to free herself.

Thank God. She did not seem to be hurt.

I was worried about possible hidden injuries, "Don't open the belt. Wait until we get some help to get out of the car. Are you all right?"

"We are alive. That makes it all right," she said thankfully.

The airbags had obviously deployed and both Dafna and I were bleeding from our noses, but nothing felt broken and there were no obvious injuries. Within moments people approached our car and although the doors were jammed shut they were able to extricate us through the shattered windows. We were banged up and bruised but both of us could walk. Then, Dafna's post trauma effect kicked in. Her balloon deflated and I hugged her close to hold her up as she cried. We hobbled over to the shoulder to wait for the emergency crews. I could see that my car was on its roof with the nose of the vehicle crushed into the underside of the semi-trailer. The rear of the car was also smashed in, as were all the doors and side panels.

I guess I do not have to worry about the unpleasant smell from the back seat anymore.

The roadway was completely blocked so we sat down on the dry winter grass. Dafna was slow to recover but I did not mind it one bit. Holding her felt very good. With the road closed and my car a wreck we were not going anywhere for a while.

Even though we both insisted we were fine, the EMT crews took us to Beaumont Hospital where we were admitted for observation. They said there was a possibility of late effects from the rapid deceleration. I was not convinced. Most likely they just wanted to run up a bigger hospital bill. Much to the consternation of the medical staff I refused being hooked up to an IV or any sort of monitor that restricted me to my bed. They finally found a wireless monitoring system and I agreed to wear the contraption since it allowed me to spend most of the evening in Dafna's room. Shaindel brought the kids to see their mom around midnight. At first I was worried that Mrs. Kalin was going to scold us once again for almost getting killed, but apparently, car accidents were not in the same category as explosions or stabbings. She was concerned but still remained pleasant. When we finally convinced them that we did not have any serious injuries they wished us well and went home.

After they left and before I returned to my room to get some sleep I said to Dafna, "Next time you get one of your premonitions ... convince me to pay it a little more attention."

Someone in my dream had a raspy voice and was saying, "Boss, wake up." When I heard it again, I realized it was not a dream. The accident came back to me and I remembered that I was in the hospital. I opened my eyes and turned toward the voice, "Good morning Mary Lou. To what do I owe this unexpected visit?"

"I got a call from Lieutenant Nealy early this morning that you were in a car crash on I-75," she stated.

"Uh ... yuh. I know that. That's why I am in a hospital," I said in return.

"That part of the highway is in his jurisdiction."

"So nice to hear he worries about me."

"Have you got any enemies I don't know about?"

"I reckon I do. I was a cop for fifteen years and PI for two. So I suppose there are a few people roaming around that do not wish me well. What does this have to do with my accident?"

"It was no accident."

"Sorry to disagree. I was there. There definitely was an accident."

"I am not talking about the semi-trailer. That was an accident. I am talking about your crash. There was enough distance between you and the semi to stop safely. Instead you skidded and flipped."

"How do you know all this? You were not there."

Mary Lou pulled a flash drive from the burlap bag on her shoulder and handed it to me, "Copy of the dash cam video of the car behind you. Take a look when you get a chance. They hauled your car into the state police garage. The mechanic found that someone cut your brake line and disabled the ABS system."

"My brakes were fine up until the accident. And how could they cut it? Isn't it made out of steel?"

"What they did was very clever. They cut the short rubber tube that connects the steel pipe to your right rear brake and then sealed it together with epoxy. The brake fluid is very corrosive but it takes time to work its way through. The bond of the epoxy gets weaker and weaker, so if you hit the brakes suddenly ... like when you are travelling at high speed ... it pops. No brakes to that wheel. Instant skid. Normally your ABS system would bail you out but whoever did it also ripped out the ABS controller on the other wheel. So no ABS. What you get is a high speed skid, flip, and crash. So who are your enemies?"

"That sounds like a complicated way to sabotage my car. How could someone do that? The car was always with me."

Well, not always. It was parked all day at Detroit City Airport. In addition, at night it sits in the open parking area in front of my condo.

"They could have spiked your brakes yesterday or even last week. The state police mechanic told me that someone who knows what they are doing could slide under your car and do it in about four minutes."

"Isn't that interesting? I suppose I am going to need another car ... can you get me one?"

"This will be your third car in nine months, boss. Your insurance is going to go through the roof ... if they give you any at all."

"How can they blame me for my car getting blown up by a crazy person or that someone sabotaged my brakes?"

"How? It's easy. You're a bad risk. In your line of work you make enemies ... they blow up your car ... you expect the insurance company to reimburse you ... ergo ... no more insurance."

"Try your best."

"Already done.   I convinced Telegraph Dodge into leasing you a SUV."

"What about insurance?" I asked.

"Luckily they will supply insurance. You can pick it up at noon. Try to keep this one for more than ten days."

We talked a bit more and she told me I had to go to the state police post to make a report and answer questions.

After Mary Lou left I went to Dafna's room and found that she was still fast asleep, so I returned to my own bed. The nurse's aide delivered my breakfast tray and I realized that I had not eaten a thing since the snacks we had in the museum in Chicago. I was starving, but first I had to say morning prayers. Shaindel had brought over my *talis and tefillin* the evening before, so I was set.

There was something that smelled very good under the metal cover on the tray and my stomach was growling. I made quick work of the prayers and dug in.

Not bad for *kosher* hospital food.

Once my blood sugar had perked up a bit I spotted the flash drive on my nightstand and realized I had no way to look at it. I went to the nurse's station and asked to use one of their computers to view the video that Mary Lou had given me. They politely refused, telling me that no outside media could be run on the hospital's system. A patient in the next room heard my request and told me that she had her laptop in her room and she would be glad to play the video for me.

The entire recording was two minutes long and started about one mile before the small car went off the road. I had been driving directly in front of the car with the camera and the incident was well documented. I watched the actual accident over and over and saw that from the beginning of the skid until we were stopped and plastered against the underside of the semi, six seconds elapsed.

The video showed that my car did a six sided flip and spin to wind up on the roof. The rear hit the concrete median divider which sent us, sliding on the roof, straight into the semi. The video was shot at thirty frames per second and I looked at every frame. I could see how the front of the SUV had accordioned into the semi-trailer and there could be no question that the engine must have been torn from its mounts. Normally that would convert the engine into an 800 pound projectile that would slam through the firewall and crush the passengers. Luckily my car had been equipped with what I had thought was a totally useless roll bar and central strut. My life, and Dafna's life, had been saved because the Bloomfield Hill Safety Division had cancelled its order.

God moves in mysterious ways.

Thinking of God made me feel disappointed in myself. I had just remembered that as we were flipping over and over I heard Dafna recite aloud, "*Shema Yisroel HaShem Elokeinu HaShem Echad.*" This means 'Hear O' Israel, God is our God, God is one.' It was the phrase used over the millennia by Jews at the time of their imminent death. Dafna had such reverent thoughts and I was embarrassed. Because as the car was going over, all I could scream was, 'Holy Shit.'

Holy — yes — but not so reverent.

But who wanted to do me harm?

It could be someone from the past, but it was more logical that it was someone from the present. I was only working on Rabbi Slater's disappearance and the Alkay Company case. Since Shaindel had sworn that she was not talking about our work to anyone, it meant that other than the police and Rabbi Kalmonowitz no one knew we were deeply involved in the Slater case. Logic had it that it must be something to do with Alkay.

So who wanted to hurt me?

Most likely it was someone who had a whole lot of money to lose.

But even if there were people that wanted to hurt me, how did they sabotage the car? The vehicle had been sitting in a busy parking lot at the airport and anyone working under my car would have been spotted. There were also several surveillance cameras around the parking lots near my condo. Still, the brakes could have been cut anytime since the car came into my possession. I had no way of knowing.

Whenever it was done, the fact remained that someone had been successful in sabotaging my car.

Perhaps someone from Alkay was not buying that I was just a security consultant and knew that I was investigating the missing product.

We had three problems.

Who killed Rabbi Slater?

How was someone stealing from the Alkay Company?

Who was trying to kill me and Dafna?

So far a big fat zero on all three.

<u>32</u>

Confer

WE WERE discharged late in the morning. Shaindel must have been worried about us, because she came to take us back home. There were aches and pains but considering we had almost gotten ourselves killed it could have been a lot worse. As soon as I got into my home, I grabbed a Coke and went online to watch the YouTube replay of the FBI's announcement from the evening before. They informed the world about a serial killer being loose in Lower Michigan and that he was delivering up his victims a little bit at a time. Special Agent Leslie Crowley, the Detroit station chief, said they had 'promising leads' and would soon be apprehending the perpetrator. Yeah, right. I am sure his *sterling performance* instilled a whole heck of a lot of confidence in the general public. I, for one, was not so confident. Standing behind Crowley were Jarron and the rest of the state police *uppity-ups*. They wisely kept in the back and remained silent.

I knew Special Agent Leslie F. Crowley.

I met him when I was a Detroit detective working an interstate murder case. This was about a half year before I was shot trying to apprehend a murder suspect and Crowley had as yet not been promoted to station chief. I must have done something right, because after we solved the case he approached me for possible recruitment. I turned the Feds down. I was too old to go to Quantico for retraining and the idea of getting shipped around the country at the whim of the Bureau was not my cup of tea. Detroit was my home and I decided to stay put.

Crowley was a straight shooter but had the tendency to keep looking over his shoulder to be sure he was doing everything by the book. He was always sucking up to the brass and I suppose that was how he made station chief. All in all, he would do a good job with the investigation. Problem was, we were not working with Crowley. Our information feed was through Jarron and the state police. Until the lieutenant passed us some new information, there was nothing Dafna or I could do about the rabbi's murder, so I decided to spend my time going through all the Alkay material for the umpteenth time.

There was something in the pictures that was just not right, but I could not figure out what it was.

I was leaning back in my chair, sipping my Coke, working all the information through my mind, when the phone rang.

Saved by the bell — because I really was not making any progress.

It was Mary Lou's husband, Andy. He told me that he had just found something in the books, but it was too complicated to explain over the phone. We agreed to meet at my office at four in the afternoon.

Mary Lou came over to drive me to the Dodge dealership to get my new car. This dark blue SUV was not as fancy as my wrecked vehicle, but appeared sturdy and reliable.

Once again I basked in the addictive new car vapors all the way to the Slater house where the *shiva* was in full swing. The ladies of the women's group had swooped in and transformed the living room into a place suitable for meeting people coming to offer condolences. All the mirrors were covered and a low stool was set up for *Rebbetzin* Slater to sit on. Women came over to help take care of her kids, prepare food, and do the housekeeping.

I was here to pick up Dafna. Even though she had just been discharged from the hospital this morning she still had found the time to come to the *shiva.*

Amazing.

My only problem was that at this moment there were no men making *shiva* calls and with the room crowded with only ultra-Orthodox women — unless the place was burning down — there was no way I could enter. I signaled from the doorway until I caught Dafna's attention and then motioned for her to join me outside. She said her goodbyes and joined me on the walk. I turned to Dafna, "When I spoke with *Rebbi,* two days ago, he said he thinks we have to give priority to the Alkay case."

"That makes sense. Now that we know for sure that someone is trying to kill you, it is only logical that it is someone connected with that case."

"That's what *Rebbi* said."

"What else did *Rebbi* say? Tell me exactly," she said with emphasis.

"Are you going to start that again? Telling me that *Rebbi's* words have a special meaning?"

"I am and I will. What did he say?" she asked again.

"I'll tell you, but if you say 'You can take it to the bank,' I will murder you."

"Mum's the word. What did he say."

"He told me to give the priority to the Alkay case."

"You said that already. What else?"

"He said that my work was like the work of the *Sanhedrin* ... no, he said *bais din.*"

"Same thing," she said correcting me.

"That they would collect all the facts in the case and then talk about what had been discovered between themselves. He used the word 'confer.' They would assess all viewpoints to arrive at the truth."

"That's it," she exclaimed.

"What's it?" I asked in response.

"We have to confer."

"You know as much about the case as I do. So, what do we confer about?"

"I have no idea," she said in exasperation.

"Maybe Andy can help. He is coming to the office at four. He thinks he might have found something."

"Who's Andy?"

"Mary Lou's husband."

"The financial wizard?"

"The same. I would like you to be there with me."

"Ah ha. At last the super sleuth realizes that he cannot get along without me," she said smugly.

"I've known that for over half a year."

"Good answer. Meanwhile, until he arrives, *Rebbi* said we should confer."

"He said the *bais din* had to confer. Not us," I corrected.

"We have a little more than two hours until Andy is due to show. You keep telling me that there is something in the pictures that is bothering you. So let's look at the photos again."

"We have both looked through the pictures a million times. What do you expect to see that you haven't seen before?"

"I have no idea, but we will do it together."

I then added, "Conferring as it were."

"Exactly," she agreed nodding her head.

We went to my office and Dafna brought up the images on my computer screen. She used some sort of computer magic and got my computer to enlarge and enhance each shot. Then we began going through them one by one. We both concentrated and checked every square inch. It was very slow going.

We were on the seventh picture when Dafna commented, "Isn't that interesting? I didn't see that before."

Her statement broke my concentration, "What is so interesting about stacks of boxes?"

"The palindrome."

"The palin-what?" I asked, not having any idea what she was talking about.

"The palindrome."

"I heard you the first time. What is a palindrome?"

"The serial number on the third box from the bottom," she said pointing to the screen.

The photo showed a pile of about twelve cartons of doors and some of the serial numbers were clearly readable. The label of the third box up showed a serial number — 'H001734437100H.'

"What is so interesting about that?"

"This is a number that is the same forwards to backwards as it is backwards to forwards. A palindrome. And it is a twelve digit one at that. Interesting."

Oh yeah. I could see that now. Leave it to Dafna to notice something like that. *I would never have picked that up in a million years.*

We got back to concentrating on the photos and we were up to the twentieth picture which showed more stacks of product. Once again, in this shot the serial numbers could be seen very clearly. I have no idea why I did it but I scanned the numbers and encountered the palindrome once more. "Here is your pal the palindrome again," I said proudly.

"Nice call," said Dafna as she studied the photo. Then she started to flip the computer screen back through the pictures we had already studied.

"What are you doing?" I asked.

"I want to see that first picture," said Dafna.

Dafna brought up the first shot that showed the palindrome and studied it for a moment. She then began enlarging the label on the box until it filled the entire screen. She turned to me and asked, "Do you see it."

I saw nothing.

The picture was larger and grainier but I still did not see anything unusual.

"All I see is a label on a box," I said.

I was still baffled.

"I think we just figured out where they squirreled away the pilfered doors and windows," she said with a satisfying smile.

"What are you talking about?"

"It appears that the pilfered doors and windows are right there in front of us," she said.

"I don't understand. We checked and found that all the serial numbers of the product we see in the photos is product legally purchased by Zeelon."

"Except I made a mistake."

"Dafna Lachler made a mistake on the computer? This should go down in history."

"Don't rub it in," she demanded angrily.

"No one is going to hear about it from me," I vowed. "So what was the mistake?"

"I had my program run the serial numbers for the doors and windows we see in the photos and each number on the boxes appeared on the manifests of the stuff sent to Zeelon. The computer checked it off as being legal but it did not note whether or not this number had shown up before."

"Of course not. It is only logical. We had quite a number of photos from all sorts of angles. The same serial number could come up as many times as it appeared in the photos because each carton may have been captured more than once, in the different pictures."

She got both pictures to appear side by side and then pointed to the screen, "When I first saw these two pictures with the palindrome I assumed we were looking at the same carton photographed from different angles. Well guess what? These are two different cartons."

"But they have the same serial number."

"Yes they do, but there are three reasons that convince me that we are looking at different cartons. First, on the wide shot of the second picture you can just make out that the carton is number four from the floor and in the first shot it is number three. Second, the serial numbers from the cartons above and below our palindrome, although not clear, are obviously not the same in both pictures. Third, if you enlarge the label of the first picture you can just see a shadow at the edge."

"And what does that mean?"

"It means that Zeelon did not use super logistics to install all the stolen merchandise first. They simply made duplicate labels using serial numbers for product they purchased legally from Alkay. They put fake labels over the labels of the stolen stuff and stored all the contraband right out in the open among the thousands of legal cartons. Zeelon knew that no one would notice that a number repeated itself."

Dafna was correct. I stared at her in awe.

"Something tells me, if we send in the cops they will find more of these double labels and the true serial numbers on the boxes might just tell them where the product came from," she said.

All this by conferring with Dafna.

Rebbi was right once again.

33

Default

I HEARD Andy arrive in the outer office. "Perhaps Mary Lou's brilliant husband can tell us how they actually stole the stuff."

When Andy left his CFO position he divested himself from his business suit in exchange for flannel shirts and corduroy pants. Today it was a bright red plaid shirt and dark brown pants. I introduced Dafna and he said he knew of many companies that had used her services.

"So what have you got for us?" I asked.

He opened his laptop and put in a flash drive to bring up an Excel file, "I transferred all the data from the last ten years of the Alkay company's internal audits into this file. At first glance everything seems to be the same from year to year. The same growth, sales, profits. Except I knew that somewhere in all this, someone was supposed to be stealing millions from the company. So I began looking for anything that had changed over the last few years. I found something."

"What?" I asked.

"The defaults."

"What is that?" asked Dafna.

"Big company like Alkay sells to thousands of customers. Developers, contractors, middlemen, you name it. Some of these companies go belly-up. They buy merchandise on their line of credit and can't pay their bills. These companies go bankrupt and suppliers that sold them merchandise are happy to get a few cents on the dollar when the bankruptcy proceedings are all through."

"This is not something new," I said.

"Hold on a second. I'll explain," he said. "Before any major company sells anyone anything on credit they check the buyer's credit rating and only sell them the amount of product that they will be able to pay for, to be sure that they don't turn out to be in default. Once a company gets a good track record ... meaning it buys stuff and pays on time ... their line of credit goes up. Then the manufacturer is willing to sell them more and more product on credit."

"But Alkay has always had a few defaulters. It has always stayed at the same percentage all these years," I said.

"Exactly right," said Andy. "That's what threw me at first. The percentage of default has been about 1—2% consistently for over ten years. But something changed," said Andy dramatically.

"What?" asked Dafna.

"Up until two years ago the number of companies that defaulted in their payments averaged around twenty-one a year. During this past year it was six clients and the year before that seven. Six or so companies each year that slowly built up their credit line and then suddenly went bankrupt. The defaulters cost Alkay 3.5 million dollars two years ago and 2.7 million this past year. The total loss to default was not any bigger than in years past but it was a bigger loss for each company. In addition, the companies that defaulted in the past were a mix of old and new companies, about fifty-fifty. In the past two years all the companies that defaulted had been incorporated in the last three years."

"That is unusual," I commented.

"Not only that," he continued. "All of these new companies ordered the same product and only that product."

"Let me guess. Zephyr style, in the Pueblo Tan color and glossy finish. Exactly what Kowalski says is being ripped off," I said.

Andy nodded his head in the affirmative.

Dafna added, "But you said that this style is their number one seller, accounting for 40% of their sales."

"That's why we couldn't find how the thieves get their hands on Kowalski's doors and windows," I explained.

Andy closed his laptop and said, "I thought you should know."

"Thirteen companies that came into business in the last three years. Just about when the Zeelon Company got the contract to construct the new hotel," said Dafna contemplatively.

"What are you getting at?" I asked her.

"If Andy is right, then they all must be connected to Zeelon and it has been running this scam for more than two years," she answered.

"Exactly," said Andy. "Methodically and slowly so that no one would notice."

"Let me use your computer," she said to me.

I vacated my spot behind the desk and she began hitting the keys of my computer.

Nothing awes me as much as watching a master craftsman at work. And that's what Dafna was. Her hands flew over the keyboard and screens flashed and disappeared. Most people would be fooled and think that Dafna could not possibly know what had been written on a screen that had only flashed open for a second. But, Dafna had a true photographic memory and she collated everything she saw. Andy was just as mesmerized as I was.

I saw the Zeelon logo come up momentarily so I could only guess that Dafna had hacked into their corporate computer system — again. She worked for twenty minutes and then hit the print button. Three typed pages flew out of the printer.

"What did you find?" asked Andy.

Dafna asked Andy in return, "Who makes money by selling to a company they know will not be able to pay?"

"No one does. You can't make money if you know you won't get paid," I stated.

"Sometimes," said Dafna. "Think again."

Andy gathered his thoughts for a moment and then said, "The salesmen would still make money. They get the same commission even if they sell to firms that ... how shall we say it ... are not financially well endowed."

"Meaning they can go bust at any minute," I said.

"Correct," he said. "That's why the manufacturer usually has an internal system ... not connected with the sales department ... to check out all companies before the first sale is made. Only when the credit clearance comes through is the sale final."

"The salesmen couldn't be in on the scam because they would lose their commissions if the companies go bankrupt," I stated.

Andy answered with, "Not necessarily. If there is a true division of authority, it would be the credit department's mistake for not uncovering the weakness of the buyer and not the sales division's fault. Very often their commissions are not touched."

"Is this common?" I asked.

"Not common, but not that rare," said Andy.

"Look at it from another angle," she said. "If someone in the credit division intentionally faked clearance reports, then those buyers get merchandise and they don't pay."

"Why would someone in the company want to do that?" I asked.

"Because whoever is part of this scam gets a kickback from Zeelon or the companies that default," said Dafna.

"I see what you are getting at. But it would have to be a really insidious plan in order to rip off Alkay on such a large scale," said Andy.

"What do you mean?" I asked.

"First the salespeople would have to avoid selling to any other questionable companies," said Andy.

"But that was how they were running the scam," I declared.

"No, the scam was only to sell to those shaky companies that were giving the kickback. If they sold to any other unstable companies then the default percentage would have gone up and we would have noticed."

"Clever," I said. "And it fits with what we found in the pictures. Some of the stuff at the hotel construction site has fake serial numbers and barcodes."

"Because that merchandise was sold to companies that defaulted," said Andy.

"And they must all be straw companies of the Zeelon Corporation," said Dafna holding out the printed pages.

The pages contained the purchasing records for the Zeelon Corporation for the last five years.

Dafna was amazing.

A bit of a criminal, but amazing.

A company Zeelon's size could buy directly from manufacturers without relying on middlemen. But the records showed that Zeelon was also buying all sorts of products from dozens of middlemen. But there were two things that made this discovery unusual. Most of the product they got from the middlemen was the exact same merchandise that they themselves were already purchasing directly from the manufacturer. One of the products that stood out was the Alkay doors and

windows in the Zephyr style in Pueblo Tan and glossy
finish. Why did they not just increase their order?
Second, the price they paid the middlemen for these
items was almost identical to the price they paid the
manufacturer. So the middlemen were not making a
profit. The only thing that made any sense was that the
middlemen were getting product from the defaulted
companies and they were actually hidden subsidiaries of
Zeelon.

"I think we found the swindle," I said with a smile.

Andy nodded his head, "It would seem so."

"I see how they did it," I exclaimed. "They bought
doors and windows from Alkay for the new hotel through
the Zeelon account and through the straw companies
owned by Zeelon. The straw companies built up their
credit line until they could make a big order and then
they declared bankruptcy and defaulted. Zeelon got
100% of the product it needed and only paid for —" I
looked to Andy.

"Well, Zeelon itself paid for 100% of their purchases,
and the straw companies probably paid for around 50%
or less. So, in the end Zeelon only paid for about 75% for
all the stuff they got."

That's a big chunk of change for a big construction
project like the New York hotel. So Albert Kowalski was
not completely correct. It was not as bad as he thought.
He was being ripped off but at least half of it was paid for.

"So who are the crooks?" I asked.

"It's got to be everyone in sales," said Andy. "And
someone in shipping. The product could not have been
delivered to the addresses of the straw companies,
because that would have increased the transportation
costs. Somehow all the merchandise was getting to
Zeelon. And someone in credit. The guys that check the
credit standing for customer accounts."

"We checked the sales manager and there was no
evidence he was getting a payoff," I stated.

"Does not mean a thing," said Andy. "He could have been getting cash and buying diamonds. It would never show up."

"What are you going to do?" asked Dafna.

"I want to catch the bastard who has been trying to kill us," I said angrily. "This is an interstate crime so it has to go through the state police, and I think they will cooperate. The sabotage of my car is also under their jurisdiction. I'll speak to Mr. Kowalski and get him on board. We'll have Net-Worth check the accounts of all the salesmen ... there are only three ... and the guys in credit and shipping. Once we have the proof we need, we'll turn it over to the state police. They will probably pull in the one with the most incriminating evidence. They'll put the screws on him until he breaks. Whoever it is will know he is going to jail and the only question is for how long. Most likely he will squeal on the rest of his crew to get a lighter sentence."

We got the ball rolling. The Net-Worth Company investigated twelve more of the Alkay employees. Two days later we had our answers. They discovered assets squirreled away for all three salesmen, and as expected, they found a fellow in credit. Someone had instructed them well and they had all done a fairly good job of hiding their ill-gained payoffs. But the Net-Worth Company was not the IRS and had no trouble getting the goods on these guys.

The weakest link in the group was the salesmen. George Jensen bought a house and put it in his wife's name. Not the best way to hide money. Calvin Yorks had an offshore account in the Maldives. It was a nice vacation spot but not a good place to hide money from Net-Worth. Bruce Alberts thought he was very smart. He used an assumed name and paid cash to purchase the houseboat that was now berthed at the Grosse Pointe Marina. It would have been almost impossible to discover the vessel if he was not paying the hefty monthly dockage fee through his personal credit card. Pretty dumb.

I felt Bruce was the best target.

I contacted Jarron and asked for his help, but he told me he was going to pass on this particular case for two reasons. One, it should go through Nealy, as the local commander for the Detroit post. Two, this was interstate crime and the FBI had to come aboard. Right now he had his hands full with the Feds.

So, I went to see Nealy and explained what we had discovered about how Alkay was being ripped off. He was impressed and contacted Lansing. They in turn notified the Attorney General's office because the case had multiple jurisdictions — so far Michigan and New York — and they brought in the FBI.

Because I was a civilian, I could not be involved directly, but Nealy — my new best buddy — kept me informed and told me how it all went down.

Three days after I contacted the state police they picked up Bruce as he was driving down I-75. They told him a cock-and-bull story that the car he was driving had been reported as stolen. He, of course, denied it, so the troopers invited him to accompany them to the station to clear up the matter. When they all got to the state police post on Ten Mile Road officers from the Criminal Investigation Division and agents from the FBI were waiting for Bruce. They laid out what they knew about his involvement in the Alkay scam. The CID and the Feds suggested he consider cutting a deal. He was advised to confer with someone that knew the law and then they allowed the salesman to call his lawyer. Four hours later, an attorney from the State Prosecutor's office arrived and arranged a plea bargain deal with the fellow. He would not be visiting the Grosse Pointe Marina for a long while.

From the information he gave the police, they discovered that the swindle was set up pretty much the way we figured. There were two surprises. The head of the marketing division was also involved and he had been the one that the Zeelon Corporation had originally contacted to set up the theft of Alkay's windows and doors. The other surprise was that everyone in shipping was in the clear. The product was being rerouted from the straw companies to Zeelon by the dispatcher of the private haulage company that transported all the Alkay merchandise. Twenty-four hours after Bruce was arrested federal agents along with the New York and Michigan State Police, made a synchronized sweep of all the suspects and confiscated records and computers. Initial examination showed that Zeelon was also running similar scams with their plumbing and furnishing suppliers.

Lots of good publicity for the FBI and the state police.

Me? I got a check from Albert Kowalski. He was delighted with the results. I was delighted with the check.

I also got a short thank-you call from the colonel of the state police. She told me how important it was for good citizens to come to the aid of their duly appointed constabulary.

God, it was so over the top patriotic and so insincere, I thought I would upchuck my cookies.

But there was one major sour note. Once everyone was arrested and all the records were checked, the FBI and the Michigan State Police told me that they were both thoroughly convinced that there was no connection between the Alkay gang and the sabotage of my car and the break-in at Dafna's house.

Someone else wanted us dead.

34

Investigate

THE SERIAL killer in Lower Michigan was still the number one story on all the TV and radio stations. The media could not get enough of it. When the Zeelon swindles were revealed, it barely got into the papers and only rated about one minute on the cable news stations. I got five seconds of glory when a CNN investigative reporter mentioned that I had assisted the police.

There is no such thing as bad publicity.

I received a dozen requests for my services in two days. I accepted seven of the cases and turned down five. The ones I accepted were those that would not keep me occupied day in and day out and were the type that would allow Mary Lou to handle a goodly amount of the clerical and investigatory work.

There were three requests for background searches of individuals who were about to be hired by big businesses. This type of investigation was known as a CV check. The things I looked for were: 1 - Was the person for real? Was the submitted CV actually from the person they claimed to be and not some stolen identity, 2 - Did they actually do what they claimed to have done? Were the accomplishments listed on the CV true and were the letters of recommendation real, 3 - Why were they looking for a new job? I had to determine how the person had interacted at their former places of employment and discover why they were changing jobs. This was standard procedure for human resources divisions of many companies.

Another was a case of industrial espionage. I was asked to discover how new catalog changes for a small electronics firm were being leaked to the competition. From my experience, most business thieves of this type were not Einsteins and I usually found the culprit without much difficulty.

There was a case of a woman who was sure that her present husband — this was her third — was surreptitiously laying the groundwork for their divorce. However, she was also convinced that in preparation for filing the papers and before their prenup agreement froze everything, he was squirreling away some of their mutual assets into some offshore account. I was asked to find the account and figure out how he was transferring the money.

Two banks requested my services to help locate individuals who had skipped town owing quite a bit of money. Standard skip cases.

The most interesting request concerned blackmail insurance. A prominent Protestant clergyman had been having an affair with one of his worshippers. The affair was over, the wife knew all about it and was forgiving. Turn the other cheek and all that. Things were just getting back to normal, when up popped the desk clerk from the Woodward Avenue motel that had been the cleric's choice for his trysts. The guy threatened to go public with some video footage of the minister and his girlfriend unless he received a sizable chunk of change. The clergyman and his wife had agreed to pay the blackmailer but they wanted to have some sort of guarantee that once they paid the money they would never hear from the creep again. Their lawyer hired me to get appropriate information on the clerk so that when he got his payoff it would be absolutely clear that there would be no further contact.

The five cases I did not accept were from lawyers who wanted me to prove infidelity of a spouse before filing divorce papers.

I turned these down for three reasons.

First, I had no idea who was trying to harm me and Dafna and until I found out, I could not be overly distracted by doing the necessary 24/7 surveillance work.

Second, I never liked this type of case. If I could keep bread on the table without adultery work, I would happily shift every one of these to other investigators.

Third, even though Rabbi Slater's murder case was now being investigated by the state police and FBI, I felt that yours truly should still be available if anything came up. The cases I did take were going to keep me quite busy, but hopefully would still leave me enough freedom to pursue any new angles that might develop.

At about the same time as my client base was blossoming someone leaked the information that the serial killer used a chain saw to cut up the bodies. The media went ape. It was so perfectly gruesome that all the ghouls in the general public crawled out from under their rocks so that they could sate their sadistic appetites by gathering as much grisly information as possible. Naturally this hot new facet of the story was picked up by all the national cable networks, and crews came to town to interview all the major players. Luckily – since Shaindel had taken her vow of silence — we were spared, because no one in the media knew that Dafna and I were actively involved. One of the sensationalist rags printed a lurid summary of the story with lots of unrelated gory photographs gleaned from an old 50's S&M archive. In an attempt at gallows humor, they suggested that if someone cut up a rabbi, it had to be a kosher butcher. That was it. The rest of the media could not help themselves and the serial killer responsible for our four murders, was dubbed the 'Kosher Butcher.'

Over the next few weeks several important things occurred.

The first was that the murderer dropped off another two packages of body parts. The message with his third bundle was 'America is being ruined. We have to stand up for our rights,' and 'Americans were here first. They should all go home,' for the fourth.

Everyone was a zealous patriot these days.

The parcels were always dropped off at spots without video surveillance and no one had seen a thing. His voice was still an electronic dub, sent via a phone that went off the air immediately after the call was made.

With the arrival of more body parts, the public switched to panic mode and began seeing gruesome parcels just about everywhere. Under trees, lampposts, cars — and all around town. Every day there were dozens of calls to the police hotline reporting the sighting of the murderer discharging another load. Usually it was just a neighbor dumping the garbage.

Secondly, the entire 'Kosher Butcher' investigation had become a jurisdictional hodgepodge. Since the murderer had bumped off four victims with the same MO, he officially was declared a serial killer and federal law dictated that the FBI had to be called in and — a big AND here — be given primary jurisdiction in handling the investigation. The state police and local units were expected to 'help.' The director, sitting in DC, was goosing Crowley and the local FBI office for results. At the same time the governor of Michigan was razzing the colonel of the state police. She in turn was pressuring Jarron. Each branch of the various law enforcement divisions had a task force of dozens of people who were checking every fact, backwards and forwards. The crime laboratories at the state police and FBI had technicians screening all the minutia of the evidence. So far, no major progress.

What were Dafna and I doing all the while?

We were investigating. In our own unique way.

Because of the lack of information concerning the actual place and method of the killings, the FBI profilers, could not come up with a clear picture of the murderer. All they could say was that statistically it was most likely that he was a middle aged male, who thought very highly of himself, was a manipulator of others, lacked remorse, did not accept responsibility for failure, and had no compunction about lying. Basically — a mean SOB. But this could also be an accurate description of your next-door neighbor. His racist messages indicated that most likely he was also a 'white supremacy nut.' So, the Feds and the state police were putting the emphasis of their investigation in finding the murderer among the multitude of skinhead, paramilitary, red-neck, and neo-Nazi groups that flourished in the great democracy of the USA. Since Dafna and I could not put in all the hours or recruit the resources that the humongous police forces had at their disposal, we completely ignored the racist aspect of the case.

We continued to concentrate on the idea that one of the victims was the main target, with the other three thrown in as window dressing to confuse the authorities. I figured if I could get some clue as to why someone wanted to murder any of the other three, I would be just that much closer to discovering who killed Rabbi Slater. Unfortunately, Jarron was not getting on board with my idea. The FBI had succeeded in convincing the lieutenant's superiors that the killer was a racist trying to make a point. So Lansing told Jarron that he should put the emphasis of his investigation on the racist angle. I tried to impress upon Jarron the great words of wisdom of the Gershwin brothers — 'It ain't necessarily so.' But, he was not buying it.

The lieutenant agreed in theory that there was a possibility that this was a simple murder case with misdirection, and that it should not be ignored, but he still refused to give me permission to personally check things out. With the FBI in charge, and them not knowing about Dafna's and my involvement in the case, the state police could get in a lot of trouble if I started sniffing around the people involved in the case. He forbade us from actively investigating the other murders.

So what did we do?

We, as law abiding citizens, must of course follow the instructions of a lieutenant in the state police but we convinced ourselves that so long as we did not personally make direct contact with people that had been involved with any of the victims, we were not violating Jarron's restrictions.

I figured we had two things that they did not have. Number one and most importantly — my fiancée, my love, my partner — Dafna. The information she was able to glean using her computer skills was absolutely amazing. Her searches were about 40% legal — the rest not so much. The second thing was my ability as an investigator. I am not a super-whiz at analyzing facts and data. I am not another Sherlock Holmes. Do not get me wrong — I am not a slouch — but that was not my forte. My specialty was functioning as a detective in the field. I got my results from walking the crime scene. Interacting with the people connected with the crime. And — working with my hunches. Dafna and I both knew that if we started our own investigation without getting clearance we might step on someone's toes — FBI — state police — and there could be repercussions.

So we did whatever we could without actually going out in the field ourselves.

As expected, Mary Lou was able to handle a large part of the work that Lincoln Investigations had taken upon itself — that was a big help — but I was still quite busy. However, whenever I had a spare moment, I tried to go over the murder books. They contained every bit of information about the four victims that had been compiled by the FBI and state police. I put emphasis on comparing the printed report of each interview with the detective's handwritten notes. Sometimes a cop would use a word or a phrase in his notes and then use something different in the material he entered into the computer. Usually, the change was not significant, but sometimes — just sometimes — the cop who did the interview had some sort of intuitive reaction to what the witness had said. Perhaps he was nervous, lying, hiding something. I burned the midnight oil and checked it all.

I dissected and analyzed every scrap of information because I wanted to get a feel of each of the people who knew the victims. Then I applied Rabbi Kalmonowitz's advice to look at the facts from every viewpoint. So far, the FBI, and the state and local police had interviewed almost sixty people for each of the victims and they were still going strong. There were hundreds and hundreds of pages of notes and reports to review. I doggedly read and reread every scrap in the file.

Dafna was trying a different tactic. She constructed a complicated database and began entering every shred of data collected on every one of the people who had been interviewed. It included where they went to school, their phone numbers, their marital status, even shoe size — everything. She was looking for a connection between them and the victims or one to the other.

So far we were both striking out.

<u>35</u>

Chametz

IT WAS NOW six weeks from our nuptials and wedding plans were in full swing. Flowers, booze, band, photographers, décor, and all the little gifties that they now give out at weddings. Thank God for Mary Lou. The work in the office kept her quite busy but even so she was also doing a whiz-bang job of organizing our wedding. Even Shaindel was crazy about her and had to admit that my administrative assistant really knew what she was talking about when it came to weddings.

Decisions were being made, but I quickly learned that the groom was not really part of the process. Nevertheless the real decision-makers kept up the façade that my input was essential. They would show me fabric, flowers or whatever and then ask, 'What do you think?' The first time I had been asked this question I was caught off guard and mistakenly expressed my true feelings by saying, 'I couldn't care less.'

As Julia Roberts said in *Pretty Woman* — 'Big mistake. Huge!'

'What, you don't care about your own wedding?' sprang simultaneously from the lips of Shaindel and Mary Lou.

So now, I mostly just nod my head and say, 'That's nice.' About the only part of the preparations for the wedding that had been fun was the menu selection. That was when I had to taste and choose between all the different dishes the caterer was offering. They had to roll me home.

There was a hullabaloo and craziness in the air but that was understandable, since the wedding was not too far off. However, we were busier still because it was also two weeks before Passover.

Purim, the holiday we celebrated two weeks ago, is my kind of holiday. Eat, drink, and be merry. Passover is an entirely different kettle of fish. And I do not mean *gefilte fish* which is one of the staples of the holiday meal. I have ambiguous feelings about this eight day holiday — also called *Pesach* in Hebrew.

The big thing about Passover is the restriction that you may not eat any kind of fermentation product of the five basic grains — wheat, barley, oats, rye, and spelt — collectively known as *chametz*. In addition you are not allowed to have them in your possession during the entire eight days. This no-*chametz* thing is a big deal, and when I say it is a restriction — it is a really *huge* restriction. Even microscopic amounts are forbidden.

But this dietary restriction is not the reason for my ambivalence towards the holiday. I could live for eight days without all my usual food items. That is relatively easy. My ambivalence stemmed from the strange way that some Jewish women have interpreted the no-*chametz* restriction to mean that they must be absolutely certain that there is not even a speck of the stuff anywhere in the entire house during the holiday.

So beginning just after Purim, every self respecting *balabusta* goes into a house cleaning frenzy which builds in intensity until *Pesach* actually arrives.

Naturally Dafna, Shaindel, and even the two girls were afflicted with this craziness and had a long — long — list of cleaning projects. Each had to be completed according to a rigid schedule. The fact that Dafna was swamped with her work as the 'Disc Lady' and from building the 'Kosher Butcher' database, did not stop her from keeping to her cleaning regime as well. Every night she found time to do another part of the house. Drawers in the guest bedroom, bookcases in the living room, boxes in the garage, etc. She even had me coming over every other day to move some heavy piece of furniture so that she could clean behind it. Apparently this manic cleaning psychosis only affected women of the Hebrew race, because — and please do not tell Dafna — I fully intended to comply with the 'no *chametz'* dictum by simply emptying out my kitchen on the day before the holiday and be done with it.

The *Pesach* cleaning psychosis definitely reached plague-like proportions in the Lachler household.

Meanwhile, the murderer dropped off a fifth package. This time the message was, 'They are ruining our great nation. Us before them.' Once again no video surveillance or witnesses. He used the same electronic voice and the phone went dead after the call.

The FBI meticulously examined each body part and carefully relegated it to the appropriate victim at the Wayne County morgue: They had Muhammad's left chest and lower leg, and right pelvis, thigh, and hand. Rabbi Slater's right thigh, pelvis, and hand were recovered, along with his left chest and lower leg. Maria's right chest, hand, and lower leg, and left pelvis, and thigh were now in the morgue. Nguyen's left chest and thigh, right lower leg, and both hands were identified. Each part was examined for blood type, and HLA tissue typing, and samples were also sent for DNA analysis. It would be quite embarrassing to find out that the murderer was sneaking in parts from a fifth, sixth, or seventh victim.

Sergeant Chandler surprised me one morning with a telephone call, "Hi Lincoln. Chandler here."

"How is the head witch of the Southfield Police Force doing?"

"As menacing as ever."

"That's what I figured. Why the call?"

"I just wanted to know how the 'Kosher Butcher' case is progressing."

She was fishing.

Like a good *yeshiva bocher* I replied by answering the question with another question, "How would I know?"

"Don't bullshit me. I know you and your girlfriend are both working with the state police."

How did she get this information?

"Is that so?" Always good to toss in another question.

"I'm just pissed off that I am out of the loop. This is probably the biggest case that will ever come my way and it had been my call to begin with. Well, at least the part about Rabbi Slater. And now the FBI and state cops are hogging all the action."

"What do you want from me?" I asked warily.

"Do you need any help?" she asked.

"You mean from the Southfield police?"

"No, from me personally. Officially the captain told us all to stay away from the case. I'm willing to help on my own time."

I began to think how we could put Chandler's offer to the best use. I would love to go over the murder books with another detective but they were restricted material. If the state police or FBI ever found out she would get canned, and Jarron and I would be up the proverbial creek. But then I thought about how Dafna was inundated with the task of entering all the information into her database. "How are you with computers?" I asked.

"I hold my own."

"Would you be willing to help Dafna with data entry?"

"Sure, I'd love to see how she makes all the magic happen."

So now, two or three times a week, on her way to or from her shift, Detective Sergeant Chandler of the Southfield Police, was coming to Dafna's house. She helped my fiancée by looking up and entering the zillion facts that had to go into the database. She saved Dafna hours of time. A byproduct of this relationship was that they became good friends. They even went shopping together.

Nice.

I also got a surprise from Lieutenant Nealy.

Working as our liaison, he was calling me every few days to pass on information about the case. Of course, he was unaware that Jarron was speaking to me directly and I already had almost everything he was giving me. I was cordial with the lieutenant, but I got the feeling that when he was speaking with me he was also fishing to see if I had any extra information about the case that I was keeping to myself. Perhaps he suspected my connection with Jarron.

Then one morning, Mary Lou came into my office and closed the door. Her hair was fire engine red and she was wearing what looked like a formal tuxedo, with bowtie and cummerbund. But the pants were cut off at the knees and under it she wore bright purple tights with yellow loafers.

I have given up trying to figure out why she dresses like that.

"There is a state police lieutenant in my office," she said warily.

"Jarron?"

"Nope, it's Nealy."

What was he doing here?

"Did he say what he wants?"

"Yeah. He wants to see you."

"So, why didn't you send him in?" I asked.

"I never met Lieutenant Nealy before. Not in person. But I get the feeling that something is not right with this guy."

Mary Lou's cop instincts had kicked in.

"What makes you think that?"

"He came into my office and was super palsy-walsy with me. We have talked on the phone but this was way over the top. His super-wide smile is as phony as a three dollar bill."

"Maybe he knows that you used to be a cop and there was a sudden rapport."

"Bull twaddle," she said decidedly. "He doesn't know squat about my past. He just sees me as some low IQ, over-age, bimbo secretary, who he thinks he can pump for information."

"What's your gut feeling about him?" I asked.

"Gut feeling ...?" she pondered for a moment. "He would send his mother up the river if she was jaywalking."

"Yup, that sounds like Lieutenant Nealy."

"I don't like people like that."

"Maybe he's just frustrated because they won't allow him to help find his secretary's murderer."

"Could be," she said with a shrug.

"Send him in."

"He wants something from you. Watch your step."

Nealy justified his visit by claiming that he had some new information and wanted to get it to me as soon as possible. This was all a load of crap, since Jarron had already passed along this new material and it was really minor. It had no real significance to the case and could have waited. Besides, if speed was of the essence — phones worked a lot faster than cars. After he delivered the information he spent the next twenty minutes asking me questions about how we solved the Alkay case, but every once in awhile he would subtly ask a question about the 'Kosher Butcher.' Of course, he got nothing from me.

Yeah, he was frustrated.

After that initial visit he began making a habit of stopping by the office two, three times a week instead of calling. It was as if he thought that we had actually become best buddies. Like we were partners in the investigation. With some of his visits he would bring Mary Lou a little gift — a mug — a small doll — useless stuff. She continued to play the part of a featherbrained secretary.

When he came by he would usually stay about twenty to thirty minutes. It took only one or two minutes to pass along whatever tidbits he had and then he would sit in my office shooting the breeze and telling cop stories. I was not sure why the good lieutenant kept stopping by. He was not getting any new information from me or Mary Lou. Perhaps dealing with speeders on the highway day in and day out was as boring as I thought it was.

Still, I enjoyed talking shop with another cop. Something I had not done since I left the force. In our discussions he passed along quite a bit about his personal life. He told me about his military career and I matched each one of his stories with something from my time in the Marines. He also spent a lot of time telling me about his kids — he had three — and on a sadder note — that his wife had demanded — wrongfully in his opinion — that he move out of their house. He was confident that the separation was only temporary and was working hard at getting his wife to see how much he loved her. Any day now she would be taking him back. What he did not know was that Jarron had given me a little addendum to the Maria Sanchez file that was off-limits to Lieutenant Nealy.

Since he had been Maria's direct boss, the detectives of the State Police Murder Task Force had evaluated him for possible involvement in her disappearance and murder. He was dropped as a possible suspect because the lieutenant had an airtight alibi. There were witnesses that testified they had been working with him at the time of the Sanchez abduction and for the other abductions as well. However the file also contained testimony obtained from Nealy's estranged wife. She stated that most people did not know that he had a violent temper and could be verbally abusive and say demeaning things. 'Never in a million years' and 'When hell freezes over' would she ever get back with him. He apparently had no insight into the status of his marriage.

Lieutenant Nealy was one screwed up individual.

I felt sorry for him.

36

No Return

IT WAS the first night of Passover and tonight we would have the first *Pesach seder*. This traditional event is celebrated by just about every Jewish family on the first two nights everywhere in the world. Even my family had a *seder* and we were just about as far away from Judaism as you could get and still consider yourself Jewish.

Rabbi Kalmonowitz had invited me and the Lachlers to join his family for both of the *seders*, but Dafna declined for the first night because they had not had a *seder* at home since her husband had passed away. She wanted to make her own *seder* and I was going to officiate.

Even though the entire *seder* is orchestrated by a special book called the *Hagadah,* at my family's *seder* we would rush through the pages of prayers and ritual parts, with the four questions, the four sons, the four cups of wine, and then move rapidly on to the terrific meal. For us the meal was the major event of the evening. But being in charge of the *seder* was a whole different ball of wax. All the 'how-to-run-a-*seder*' books emphasized that the most important aspect of the evening was to teach the youth that way back then in Egypt, God freed the Jewish people from slavery and formed our nation.

Being the guy that runs the *seder* was not so simple.

How do you keep young people interested in the convoluted Hebrew texts?

We began reciting from the *Hagadah* and drank the first cup of wine. Then when we got to the first descriptive text I took out one of the costumes I had stashed under the table — I had others. There was a Pharaoh's crown, a Moses' beard, a ladies wig and a few more items. As we read the passages from the *Hagadah,* I put on the appropriate costume and simultaneously explained what happened four thousand years ago in Egypt. The girls loved it. Even Dafna and Shaindel approved.

I asked them to visualize a typical Hebrew slave four thousand years ago — that was me. Moses tells him to grab whatever he has — clothes, food, all his possessions — and with no preparation head out into the desert. Totally insane. Did Moses really expect anyone to listen to him? To elucidate this absurd scenario I stood and portrayed a Jewish slave getting his instructions from Moses. At the same time I had Dafna and Suzie take the part of the other Hebrew slaves and requested that Shaindel and Aliza play the Egyptians. Each shouted opposing instructions about what I should do. I then swept everything that was on the table in front of me into an old knapsack, threw the bag over my shoulder, and without hesitation defiantly walked out the door saying, "I am leaving and I am not coming back."

Dafna and Suzie — the Hebrew cheering squad — said loudly, "He is not coming back."

Shaindel and Aliza — the Egyptian supporters — yelled, "You'll see. He's coming back."

Back and forth both pairs laughed and yelled, each trying to convince the other that they were correct.

Coming back — not coming back — coming back — not coming back —

When I delayed in returning, the girls started to call my name jokingly inquiring as to who would finish the *seder*. On my eventual return I explained that the *matza* we eat to this day commemorates the fact that the Jewish nation left Egypt without even taking any food. They had the utmost faith in God and just knew that he would provide. The leaving of Egypt without hesitation and our trust in God is what formed the Jewish nation. We celebrate the *seder* to remind ourselves of our heritage.

Dafna outdid herself with the meal. It was so far beyond delicious that I have no words. At the beginning of the *seder* one half of one of the three special *matzas* — the *afikomon* — is put aside to be eaten at the end of the meal. But according to an ancient custom, the kids will try to steal the *afikomon*. It was my job, as the one running the *seder*, to ransom this *matza* back from the thieving children so we could complete the meal. This was all done in good fun and kept the kids on their toes. It cost me a new video game but we finally were able to eat the *afikomon* and complete the *seder*.

Even though we finished at about one o'clock in the morning, Aliza and Suzie were still wide awake and helped clear away the cups of wine and other debris. Aliza turned to me and said, "Shimon, I never laughed so much at a *seder*. You were terrific."

Suzie added, "Yeah, it was super."

Dafna just stood there smiling, "And you were worried that you would not be able to run a *seder*. You did a great job."

I was kind of embarrassed by the compliments, "I was just trying to tell the girls about what happened with the Jewish people and Moses way back then."

"It worked great," said Suzie. "I always wondered how a people ... who were slaves ... were able to pack up everything they had and be confidant that they were not coming back. You explained it so well."

Yeah, she got it. That was the point I was trying to make.

Success.

Wow.

"I'm glad you liked it," was all I could say.

Next day, after the festival prayers at the *yeshiva,* I joined the throng waiting to approach Rabbi Kalmonowitz so that I could shake his hand and exchange holiday greetings.

When I finally got my turn he asked me, "So how was your *seder*?"

"Dafna's girls said I explained many things for them and they enjoyed it."

"Wonderful. That is the essence of the *seder*. Passing our culture on to our young. Remember, the children are the future. What is impossible today, will be solved by the young. *Gut yuntif,*" said Rabbi Kalmonowitz dismissing me as he turned to the next person in the long line.

37

Young

THE FIRST two days of Passover were on a Thursday and Friday respectively, thus the holiday was juxtaposed with the Sabbath. So that meant there was actually a three day holiday. The logistics of planning all the fancy meals were staggering, but the Lachlers were old pros at this and everything went as planned. The three day festival gave us a real break. Dafna from her computers, and me from Jarron or Nealy's information updates. Still, I was dying to know if there had been any breakthroughs.

Saturday afternoon I was at the sink helping Dafna wash up when she said happily, "This was the nicest holiday I have had in a long time."

"I'm glad."

"I was not sure that when I turned down Rabbi Kalmonowitz's invitation, things would work out so well."

"What, you did not have faith in me?" I asked in mock outrage.

"I have always had faith in you. Just, right now, I have even more."

I had not told her that I had spoken with Rabbi Kalmonowitz, "*Rebbi* wanted to know how the *seder* went."

"Really? When was this?"

"Two days ago, after services."

"You didn't tell me. What did he say?"

"I told him how the girls liked my explanations, and he said that we had to educate the young so that they will be able to solve all of our future problems."

"Were those his exact words?" she inquired.

"Would you stop it already, with *Rebbi's* exact words."

"I'm not saying a thing, but so far he has not steered us wrong."

I left Dafna and the girls to attend Saturday afternoon prayers at the *yeshiva*. When the Sabbath was over and I returned to my own place, I thought about what Dafna had said about Rabbi Kalmonowitz's exact words. She really believed that *Rebbi's* words had a hidden meaning. So, I could not help but try to reconstruct what it was that he had said. It took a while and then I remembered — 'What is impossible today, will be solved by the young.'

Was he telling me something? Which young? What was impossible? Solving the 'Kosher Butcher' case?

Nah.

Could not be.

For some reason my mind flipped back to the end of the *seder*. What did Suzie say to me? It was something about how the people of Israel had been able to leave Egypt confident that they would not return. But the Jews were slaves, so their assumption was not logical. After all, they were Pharaoh's property. The Hebrews had to have been worried that the King of Egypt was not going to let them go so easily. So, even if they somehow got out of the country, they had to realize that eventually someone was going to come and try to drag them right back into slavery. That was the essence of the miracle.

The Jews trusted in Moses and God, and they knew — they just knew — that they were not going back. They were going out and not coming back. They were leaving permanently.

Then it hit me.

Rebbi was right. It will be solved by the young.

Why did I not think of that before?

I went immediately to Dafna's house and found her — as usual — down in her computer center.

"Gut voch," I said in greeting.

"Hi," she answered.

"I just realized something."

She turned to me with a smile and said, "You just realized that you love me and cannot wait until we are married. Is that it?"

"That is not what I *just* realized. That I knew months ago."

"Then what?"

"I realized that the killer has been dropping off his packages all over the southeast corner of the lower peninsula. Five packages so far, all within thirty miles of downtown Detroit," I said.

"Some revelation. Those are the facts we all know."

"Yes, but why is he doing it?" I asked rhetorically.

"He wants to make a big show of it all."

"No, my question is, why different places?"

"So that we will not know where he lives or works," she said stating the obvious.

"Exactly," I said excitedly. "He is going to some designated spot. A place that he had identified earlier as not being under surveillance. He dumps his load and goes back home."

"Terrific breakdown of the events. Is there a point to all this?"

"He is going and coming back. Don't you see?" I asked enthusiastically.

Obviously she did not see.

This was unusual.

In high school my teachers convinced me that I was not the sharpest knife in the drawer. They never used the word 'dumb.' I've mentioned before their use of the phrase, 'He is not reaching his potential.' Like I said, they thought I was dumb.

Apparently the problem was not entirely mine and part of the blame for my lack of academic achievement could be placed on the schools. It took a while but after extensive testing with some new IQ assessment techniques I learned that I was definitely not 'dumb.' Of course my brain did not work as fast as Dafna's. I suspect there was no one in the universe that had a brain that worked as fast as my fiancée's.

"Explain, please," she said beseechingly.

"Normal people do not go and come back."

"Yes they do. Everybody does that. You go and you come back. It's called traveling."

"Of course, but not immediately, because you go somewhere for a purpose." I did not know how to proceed. "Let's say driving from point X to point Y takes five minutes.   So if you go from point X to point Y and then immediately return from point Y to point X, we can assume that at least ten minutes will have elapsed."

"Get to the *point*," she said in a pun.

"Very funny," I responded with a mocking smile. "But for most people it won't be ten minutes, because you went to point Y for a purpose and whatever you did took time. Two minutes, ten minutes, an hour."

"I understand, but how is this going to help us?"

"Why don't we have video footage of the murderer dropping off the body parts?"

"Because there were no video cameras watching the spot," she said.

"Exactly, so let's look at the video cameras we do have," I said excitedly.

"What good would that do? We will just see innocent people doing innocent things."

"Except one of them is not innocent. He is the murderer."

"Oh good. He is going to have a big sign so that we can recognize him," she said mockingly.

"No, but his car will be one of the few vehicles that will pass a particular camera going one way, and pass it again going back the other way, in exactly the correct time frame."

"Which time frame?" she asked in exasperation.

""I'll try to explain," I said slowly. "The facts are that the murderer makes his drop and then leaves the area. Once he is in a safe place ... a couple of miles away ... somewhere which won't reveal anything about him ... he calls the police. So we know more or less when the drops were made."

"It could be that he makes his deliveries ten ... fifteen ... twenty minutes before the call," she added.

"Yeah, but it won't be five or ten hours before."

"So, what time frame are you referring to?" she asked.

"The time he passes a camera to go to the drop spot, make the drop ... say two minutes ... and then drives back. That time frame."

Understanding suddenly lit up her face.

"See the *point*?" I asked with emphasis. If she could make a pun, so could I.

"Very interesting," she said as she rolled her eyes upwards in thought.

"Do you think your computer can find him?"

"That's thousands and thousands of vehicles, and hundreds of cameras, with all sorts of strange angles and lighting," she mused.

"Can the computers do it?"

"It will need a sophisticated program," she murmured into the air.

"So, can it be done?"

"Let me play a little bit," she said and went to work on her computer.

I had no idea what she was doing and I knew I would not be of any help. So, I went upstairs to join Shaindel and Mary Lou who were sitting around the dining room table working on the guest list for our upcoming wedding. I had no intention of volunteering to take upon myself any of the wedding preparations but I was not opposed to having a cup of coffee and some of the apple cake they were sampling.

"So ladies, how is it going?" I asked jovially.

"Simon Lincoln, you have been avoiding us," said Mary Lou admonishingly in her raspy voice.

This evening she was wearing a mock deerskin jacket with long fringes running up the arms and along the hem. Shiny brass beads the size of ping pong balls formed a necklace around her neck and hung down onto a bright orange silk blouse. Her legs were clad in red denim Capri shorts with knee-high lavender socks. Black high-top sneakers were on her feet. The color of her hair was hard to determine because she was wearing a black and white peaked nautical cap pulled down to her ears. I think I could make out some green locks peaking out.

Mary Lou liked to make a statement.

"I have not been avoiding you ... I have been busy."

"Boss, I'm your secretary ..."

"No, you are my administrative assistant," I said correcting her.

"You are not that busy that you could not help us make some of these tough decisions for your wedding," said Mary Lou.

Yeah, right. As if she would let me make a decision.

"Would you like some apple cake," asked Shaindel.

Would I ever. That is a decision I can make.

"Thank you, I would love some," I said taking a seat at the table.

Mrs. Kalin handed me a double-wide slab and I dug in. Even though it was a Passover recipe it had a flavor-filled crust and a sweet apple/raisin/nut filling. Wow. I could eat a ton of this.

"Who do you want to sit with your Aunt Helen?" asked Mary Lou.

Aunt Helen was a problem. She loved to talk — loudly. Her conversations were at a level where ear protectors were advised.

"Ask my mother. She will know who can tolerate her," I said.

Dafna came up from the basement, "Now we wait."

Obviously she had her Playstations hard at work.

"How long?" I asked.

"Don't know. I am really pushing it with this one. Hopefully, we will see something in 48 hours," she said grabbing herself a slice of apple cake.

I was tempted to ask for another helping of the cake but I just smiled. I made believe that my appetite for the delicious cake was sated.

It was not.

38

Defrost

MONDAY MORNING I stopped at Barnes & Noble and picked up the latest fantasy book before heading to the Wayne County Medical Examiners building in downtown Detroit. I wanted to get information from Timmy Tech and the book would help.

Lieutenant Jarron had agreed to allow me to see Timmy and he had smoothed the way. A visitor's pass was waiting for me at the reception desk. My first stop was Timmy Tech's laboratory and I found him bent over his workbench studying a specimen under some sort of microscope, "Timothy, my man, how are you doing?"

Timmy looked up and smiled, "Sy, what's going on?"

"A little bit of this and a little of that. Keeping busy. Brought you something," I said handing him the Barnes & Noble bag.

He looked inside and said, "I was about to buy this. Thanks." He took out the book and flipped through the pages for a moment, saying, "I hear you are involved with the 'Kosher Butcher' case. Just like old times."

"Yeah, they are allowing me a little peek."

"They told me you had full clearance for all the information in the file.   That's pretty impressive considering you aren't on the force anymore."

"They are just impressed with my exceptional sleuthing skills."

"Yeah, right. You must have something they want."

Absolutely, and her name was Dafna.

"Can't think of what it might be."

"How can I help you?"

"I read all the stuff that came out of this lab. I just wanted to know if there was anything else you can add?"

"I put just about everything into my reports."

"Nothing at all?"

"Well, I'm not sure if I emphasized enough the problem with the putrefaction that I mentioned with the two hands. It has been consistent with what we found in the other body parts.

"What parts are you talking about?"

"So far we have parts of the torsos for all of them, along with some of the arms, legs, feet, and hands."

"No heads or vital organs."

"Correct," he said.

"What do you mean when you said consistent?"

"The body parts from the first two victims, Nassar and Slater, show much more putrefaction."

"That makes sense, since they were snatched first," I said.

"No, that's not the reason. You see ... the victims were killed and their bodies were immediately frozen. Then the frozen corpses were cut up with the chainsaw. We are also sure that the bodies were exsanguinated before they were frozen."

"What do you mean 'exsanguinated'?"

"All the blood was drained out of the body," he stated calmly.

"How do you know that?"

"From the fluids collected from the body parts. No blood."

"So what about the putrefaction?" I asked.

"That's just it. If the body parts were frozen, we should not see any difference between the different victims."

"What is your theory?"

"Well, in those two bodies it looks more like freeze-thaw-re-freeze destruction than natural putrefaction. We are pretty sure that those two bodies thawed and refroze."

"Why would the murderer do that?"

"I can't imagine a reason for him to do that. He probably didn't know. Could have been a power outage or maybe someone left the door or the lid of the freezer open or perhaps the plug came out of the wall or a circuit breaker got tripped. Lots of reasons for that to happen."

"How long would it take to thaw a body like that?"

"It would vary on how tight the bodies were packed with other frozen items. The size of the freezer. Ambient temperature."

"Give me a ballpark figure."

"Assuming the bodies remained in a large closed chest freezer with no power, at least three days, maybe four."

I went back to Dafna's house and told her what I had learned at the medical examiner's office. I do not know what it was that I said, but something triggered her into action and she turned to her computer. Five minutes later a new screen came up on her monitor. She looked at it for a moment and then said, "We have no way of knowing if the bodies thawed because it was a problem with the freezer itself or the electric line that came into the house."

"Does not have to be a house. Could be a factory," I said.

"Yeah, but you know what I mean. I was looking to see if any of the electric companies around here had power outages. From what you told me, it was only the first two bodies that thawed and refroze. That could mean that some time after Rabbi Slater was killed and frozen and before Miss Sanchez was abducted, there could have been a power outage and the freezer warmed up."

"Logical," I said.

She pointed at her monitor and said, "So in that time frame I found that there were 245 power outages reported in the Lower Peninsula of Michigan and the adjacent areas in Ohio and the province of Ontario. Almost 90% were less than 36 hours in duration. Only twenty or so were longer than that and only one lasted four days until all the service was back. That was when a semi-trailer took out a high-tension tower of DTE Power Company in Tuscola County just outside of Caro. Power was out in a big part of Tuscola, Huron, and Sanilac counties."

"How big an area are we talking about?"

She clicked a few keys and turned back to me, "About 1,000 square miles of the Thumb. Population of over one hundred thousand people."

The lower peninsula of the State of Michigan is shaped like a mitten and the Thumb of Michigan is a huge land mass that juts out into Lake Huron, one of the Great Lakes.

"There you go. We got that pin pointed really good," I said sarcastically.

"Without any further information to narrow down where the murderer might be located, there is nowhere to begin."

"He could be in the Thumb area, but we can't find him."

"As you said, he could be. But it could also be that the freezer plug accidently came out of the wall right here in Southfield."

Very disappointing.

"Any luck with your point X ... point Y games?" I asked.

She pulled up a progress table on the screen and said, "Another two hours."

"What do we do for now?"

"I could cook us dinner," she suggested.

Dafna — a phenomenal chef — rarely cooked because when her husband passed away her mother had come from New York to help her and assumed that responsibility. But, Mrs. Kalin had taken Aliza and Suzie to a Passover show at the Jewish Center, so it would be just us two.

I have nothing but a box of *matza* in my condo. Who votes that Dafna makes magic in the kitchen? All in favor? All opposed? By unanimous vote — Dafna cooks.

Considering she made the meal with only the Passover ingredients she found in the kitchen, it was a wonder. There are certain foods that taste so much better if you eat them straight off the stove. No getting soggy or dehydrated in the fridge. No reheating.

This meal was like that.

The first course was a crispy tempura made from a variety of garden vegetables, potato starch, and Teriyaki sauce — kosher for Passover of course — they were terrific. This was followed by a tangy vegetable soup made from all sorts of leftover roots she found in the vegetable crisper. She got inspired by some chicken breasts that were hiding in the back of the meat keeper. The cutlets were passed through a bunch of spices, an egg wash and then *matza* meal, and finally were dropped into hot oil. She told me the trick was to maintain the oil at a specific temperature — and she measured it with a thermometer — I do not even own a cooking thermometer — and voila. Fluffy mashed potatoes on one side of the plate and 'schnitzel to die for' on the other. I was in heaven. And the best part was that somehow I had tricked this amazing chef into marrying me.

I felt satiated and happy. I even had a good time helping her wash the dishes and clean up the kitchen. I really liked working side by side with Dafna.

I have to watch that — it could become habit-forming.

But such a nice addiction.

The kitchen was neat and tidy and everything was back in its place, when she said, "Time to check the computer."

39

Econoline

As WE WALKED downstairs I said, "Could you explain to us stupid people what it is you did?"

"No, but I will show you."

The tower of Playstations was quiet and Dafna hit some keys and tens of different file folders came up on the computer screen. She pointed to the screen and said, "Each folder should contain the information retrieved from 131 traffic cameras around Detroit."

"How did you choose these cameras?" I asked.

"Hold your horses. I will tell you."

"I'm holding my horses."

"We assume that our murderer went specifically to a drop spot from somewhere in the Detroit area, left his little surprise package and then went back directly from there to his starting point. Therefore, he most likely returned by the same route. Are you with me so far?"

"OK, that was my starting premise."

"And a very fine premise at that," she said nodding her head in acknowledgement. "Now, it's a fact that everyone in Detroit uses the mile roads or the interstates to get anywhere. Local streets are just too slow. We have five drop zones and each can be reached by many routes.

But, logic has it that the murderer used only certain main thoroughfares. Each of these routes has traffic cameras, so the odds are he was caught on video going and coming back."

"Exactly," I said in confirmation.

"For each of the deliveries I calculated how long it would take to get from each of these various cameras to the specified drop zone."

"Which cameras?"

"The 131 cameras that are on the main roads that could lead to the different drop zones."

"So that is where the number came from," I said, finally understanding.

"Precisely."

"What was the time slot you chose?"

"Time to park the car ... watch to see everything is clear ... get out of the car ... make the drop ... return to the vehicle and go home. We know the date of each drop and I assumed that the phone call to the police was soon after the delivery. So, we know the approximate time that each drop was made. The deliveries have all been after the evening rush hour so traffic on all the roads was steady."

"I agree with you so far."

"I made another assumption that the call was made no later than one hour after the delivery."

"Once again, I agree. He probably skedadled from the drop zone and when he thought he was safely away he phoned, so that the body parts could be found as soon as possible."

"To be safe I looked at all vehicles going past each camera from two hours before the call until the time of the actual phone conversation," she said.

I nodded my head in agreement, "Stands to reason that the murderer passed the camera going to the drop zone within that two hour window."

"What I did was record every vehicle as it passed the camera leading to the drop zone in that two hour period. Then I searched to see if and when it returned to the same spot."

"Only he would be caught by the camera going in the opposite direction when he returned," I added excitedly.

"Correct," she said. "So, any vehicle that was recorded as coming and going, in the time window of double the travel time plus the drop-off time, would be suspect of being the murderer's car."

"What was your drop-off time?"

"I figured three minutes to make the drop and I added two more minutes for any extras."

I said slowly, "That means that in the two hour window you were checking each camera for a vehicle that passed the camera and returned during the five minutes which were above and beyond twice the travel time from the camera to drop zone."

"Bingo," said Dafna.

I now saw the logic in Dafna's search, "Almost everyone else ... all the other cars caught by the cameras going and coming would either have a much longer or shorter travel times or would have stopped to do something. So, not very many would show up in the time slot."

"I figure we will catch a few taxis, messengers, and some ordinary people who lived nearby that had to drop things off, but I also hope we will find something that will help us."

"Let's have a look," I said hopefully.

There were 131 cameras for the five drop zones. So that meant that there were about twenty-five cameras for each delivery. But, since the murderer had used only one road for each of them, only one camera for each drop could have captured the murderer's vehicle. That also meant that we would be wasting our time when we looked at 126 of the cameras. Dafna's computers had the job of figuring out which were the five cameras that could give us the lead we needed. We divided up the different files — one for each camera — so that each corresponded to their respective drop zone.

Then we began.

I thought we would be looking at actual video footage — like we did with the Alkay videos — but I found that her Playstations had automatically analyzed the images. Dafna's program was able to note the license plate number — it was easily available in about 50% — and the year, color, make, and model of all the vehicles. All the raw data on the cars was automatically entered into a database. It took us over four hours to go through all the files. Surprisingly there were very few vehicles that made a trip and return journey and also fell into the time slot. Most of these were registered as cabs, limousine service vehicles, delivery vans, or individuals with a nearby address.

Dafna did more computer magic, various screens came up and disappeared. Finally she announced, "None of the vehicles that fit the bill have been reported stolen. In those where we got a clear reading of the license plate numbers, none are fake. All the taxicabs we found seem to be real cabs ... and have a registered hack license, or they are registered limousine or Uber cars, so we are not dealing with a camouflaged vehicle. The delivery vans all have identifying marks and companies listed on the sides of the trucks are real companies."

"So, we have another big fat zero," I said disappointedly.

"I did not say that," said Dafna with a smile.

"What have you got?" I asked inquisitively.

"Four of the cameras," she said, pausing to point them out on the map of the greater Detroit area. "Picked up a 2014 white Ford Econoline E250 van passing at the right time."

"For every drop zone?"

"One for each of them. That is unusual. We don't have a single repeat ... that is model, make and year ... for any of the other vehicles."

"This could be something," I said excitedly. "But there was no Ford van at the fifth drop zone."

"Let me try something," she hit a few buttons and the Playstations came to life.

"What did you do?"

"I reprogrammed the computer to change the search to a seven minute time slot instead of five for these seven cameras."

"Why just these seven?" I asked.

"Because we caught the van on those other four cameras. If we assume he was coming from his home and then going back we now have the general direction of where he lives. So if he was going home from this fifth drop zone he should have passed one of these cameras. If nothing shows up, I'll try the other cameras for that drop zone."

"Can you show me what the van looks like?" I requested.

"Sure, I'll pull up all four shots," she said.

The pictures of the van came up and although they were taken at different angles it was easy to see that the van in each picture was exactly the same model and make. The pictures were not all that clear, but it was also obvious that the logo on the sides of the four vans varied.

Dafna craned her neck and hit a few keys and the pictures shifted and the elaborate advertising signs on the vans became much more distinct. We could read the words quite clearly. All four were different, "Well, it was kind of exciting for a moment. I thought we caught him," she said in disappointment.

"Don't be so sure that we didn't," I chided.

"But the vans are different," she exclaimed.

"Yes, the signs are different, but it may be the same van."

"Are you saying he repainted the truck every couple of weeks?" she asked.

"You don't paint signs any more. Those are just decals. They come off with hot water."

"You're kidding."

"Nope. Can you get a clear reading of the plate. The license plate light is out in all of the videos."

Dafna did some more magic and the plate number emerged on three of the four.

Same plate.

Whoa.

We finally got something.

Dafna ran the plate number and it came back for a white Ford van. It was registered to an Alice Sangford in Pontiac, Michigan. Dafna hit some more keys and said, "Somehow, I don't think she is our murderer."

"Why is that?"

"Alice Sangford is listed as a paraplegic who was injured in an automobile accident four years ago."

"Could be her van and somebody else is using it."

"Possibly," said Dafna.

"Can you enlarge the area near the left rear wheel?" I requested.

The pictures changed and enlarged. Each shifting to show the area I asked for. Lo and behold, there was a dent on the side of the van. An identical dent in all four.

"We got him," I said with a sense of satisfaction.

The Playstations finished their work and on the second of the seven cameras that she checked we found the white van again.

Whamo.

It was there on all five.

We still did not know who the murderer was and only had a vague suggestion as to where he lived, but we did know that he — or an accomplice — used the same van each time body parts were dropped off. Maybe he would use it again.

"The murderer has been making a delivery every week or ten days, so, he is overdue to make another drop. We have to tell the state police to be on the lookout for the white van."

"I think I can do you one better," said Dafna.

She turned back to her computer screen and began a Google search. That was about all I understood. After that I was lost. The screens changed rapidly and after twenty minutes she hit the print button to get a single sheet of paper. "How many more drops are expected?" she asked.

"Timmy Tech told me that the pathologists think it will be between two and five."

"Why the discrepancy?"

"They don't think he will drop off the heads ... the package will be too bulky. Also he may possibly cut up the legs for the same reason. And they are fairly sure that he eviscerated the bodies before freezing them."

"What do you mean 'eviscerate'?" she asked tentatively. "Do I really want to know?"

"It means he took out all the *kishkes* ... the heart, lungs, intestines ... all the innards."

"How would someone know how to do that?"

"Just about any male that is not a city boy knows how. It's what you do when you hunt a large animal. You string them up ... slit open the belly ... pull out the *kishkes* ... and that's it ... eviscerated. Takes only a couple of minutes," I said.

"Why not just keep the thing whole? Less messy."

"Because the innards swell and stink really quickly. And they don't freeze well."

Dafna then said, "OK, no *kishkes*. So, how many more deliveries from the murderer?"

"If he delivers what's still missing without the heads, and keeps the legs whole ... Timmy thinks it will be two to three more drops."

Dafna grimaced with my mentioning the heads and passed me the paper from the print-out.

On it were the names of five businesses. It read; Paragon Plumbing Supplies, Shamrock Dry Cleaners, Acme Auto parts, Pen-in-Hand Stationary, and Lister's Meat Market. There were addresses and contact information as well as a catchy slogan for the first two. The plumbing supplier had 'We Are More Than A Pipe Dream,' and the dry cleaners had 'Clean As a Whistle.'

Kind of kitschy for my taste, but what did I know.

"What's this?" I asked.

"You said that he was using decals and changes them for each drop. You can't make a decal yourself, that means he had to order them online."

"Why online?"

"If he ordered them in person, the sign company would be able to recognize him. No, it had to be via the internet."

"OK ... online."

"I also figured that to keep from appearing suspicious, he must have ordered each decal from a different firm. Now, how would he have found these different companies?" she asked rhetorically.

"If it was me, I would do a Google search."

"Exactly, so that was what I did as well. There were forty-seven places that popped up in the first pass of the search. So, I reasoned he probably used several of these places. I simply looked to see if any of these companies sent out a decal that matches any of the five decals we saw on the side of the van we spotted in our videos."

"Do you mean to say in these last few minutes you hacked into all those 47 companies?" I asked incredulously.

"Yeah," she said modestly. "I found one fairly quickly. It was from a firm in LA and they sent it to a post office box in Hamtramck. Once I had the post office box, I returned to those companies and looked for any decals that were sent to that same box. There were ten. The five we already saw on the videos ... and these other five. One from each sign company."

"How did he pay for the orders? Did he make a mistake and use a credit card?" I asked hopefully.

"Sorry. No credit cards. Bank checks from different Michigan banks."

"Crap," I said in disappointment. "Do you think there is a chance that he will use one of these decals for the next delivery?"

"Don't know. There could be more that I have not found. But why couldn't it be one of the ones we know? He doesn't have an inkling that we discovered his van. He thinks it is a safe vehicle."

Enthusiastically I said, "This could be a our big break."

40

Kegleze

I PICKED up the phone and called Jarron. I would call Nealy later. I wanted Jarron to get the alert out to all the cops in the Detroit metropolitan area.

"What are you, clairvoyant?" said the lieutenant answering the phone.

"I wanted to tell you something," I said.

"How did you know the murderer just called to tell us about another drop?"

When did this happen?

"What did he say this time?"

"Real cute. 'Make America great again.' Donald Trump is going to be furious that someone stole his slogan."

"Where is the package?"

"Somewhere in Mt. Clemens. We have a car on the way right now," he said.

"Listen, I may have a lead for you."

"What have you got?"

I told him about the white van, the plate number, and the possible advertising signs on the side of the truck. The different drop zones suggested that the murderer's home or base was somewhere in the Warren area, so I also told him on which roads he should concentrate his search. He wanted to know how we got the information before he acted, but I told him that right now it was more important he get the call out to all patrol units, because there was a good chance the murderer was still in the van at this very moment. He needed to find the van before the killer had a chance to hide the vehicle. I promised that I would fill him in after that was done.

Jarron listened to what I was saying and then went silent, so I asked, "Are you still on the line?"

"I sure am. Once I make the call it is all going to hit the fan."

"What are you talking about?"

"Crowley and all the rest of the FBI are going to want to know how we got this information and they are going to figure out that you have been helping us on the sly."

"So, what are you going to do?"

"I am going to make the APB and just take whatever crap comes my way."

Jarron said he would call me back and then hung up.

It was our first real lead on the murderer.

I hope they do not blow it.

I knew Jarron had already begun the alert, and I knew that notifying Nealy was superfluous, but to keep up appearances I placed the call. There was no answer and I was shunted to the state police switchboard who informed me that they would beep him.

Nealy returned my call twenty minutes later and I filled him in. He said he understood that time had been of the essence and that I did the right thing by getting a hold of Jarron so that he could move on the information. He also told me that he would follow the progress of the investigation and as soon as he had any information he would let me know.

Nealy did call back almost three hours later with the results of the APB, but he did not know that Jarron had already filled me in almost an hour earlier.

The van had been found.

It was abandoned in a distant parking lot of the Macy's store at the Oakland Mall. The surveillance camera showed that the van had been parked about ten minutes after the APB went out to all the local police. It also showed a man in dark clothes, walking with a distinct limp, parking the vehicle and getting on a westbound bus on Fourteen Mile Road. The camera was too far away to provide any other identifiable features. The van was now at the police lab but it looked clean as a whistle, just like it said on the Shamrock Cleaner's sign that adorned its side.

The timing of the police alert and the abandonment of the van meant that the murderer had been listening to the police frequencies. He had been alerted that we had discovered his van.

The police knew that portable police scanners were available in every Radio Shack and electronics store in the nation. But there was little they could do about it. The wonders of the media revolution.

Our one lead was blown.

Jarron told me that the state police had simultaneously dispatched four cars to investigate Alice Sangford's connection with the murders. She had not reported the vehicle stolen or missing so there was the possibility that she was an accomplice. They surrounded the house and three officers knocked at the front door. George Sangford, Alice's father, nearly had apoplexy when he saw all the armed police spread around his property.

Jarron's poetic description of the event was that the man performed a bodily function in his trousers.

George cooperated fully. The cops learned that the young woman, who had suffered for four years as a brain damaged paraplegic, had died six months earlier. Her father told the police that they had donated the wheelchair lift to a local charity and sold the van for cash almost eight weeks earlier. All he remembers was that the guy who bought it had a big bushy mustache, longish gray hair, a slow Southern drawl, and a marked limp. He guessed his age at about 60 or older and his height at about five feet ten inches. He could not be more accurate because the guy walked sort of stooped over. Like maybe he had arthritis from his bad leg or something. The dad produced a photocopy of a hand written bill of sale dated two months earlier that stated 'This is to attest that Robert Kegleze has purchased Alice Sangford's 2014 Ford van, as is, for $10,500.'

When asked how it was possible that the van was still driving on the road with their registration and plates, Mr. Sangford said that it was impossible because he still had the original registration papers and he had personally removed the license plates when Kegleze got the pink slip and took possession. Michigan law does not require the seller to report the transfer of the vehicle. It was the new owner's responsibility to go to the Secretary of State's office to get a new registration. Sangford was able to substantiate his claim by digging around in his garage and producing the old plates.

Obviously, Mr. Kegleze never went to the SOS office and had replaced the real plates that Sangford removed, with fake ones. Very smart. The guy needed a clean car to make his deliveries because a stolen vehicle would set off alarms. This way, unless he had an accident, anyone checking the plate number on the van would find that it was still registered to Alice Sangford.

The name Kegleze did not appear in any of the state's databases.

Jarron said he would send me all the written reports as soon as they were available. The father was scheduled to come to Detroit in the morning to work with the state police sketch artist to prepare a composite of 'Robert Kegleze' so it could be circulated to the law enforcement agencies. The lieutenant was really excited about finally having a suspect that he could pursue. A reward was also offered to anyone who had information about a guy with a limp who was active in the 'White Supremacy' crazies' world. I mentioned to the lieutenant that it was possible that Kegleze was not the 'Kosher Butcher' and was only a delivery boy for the body parts. The cop told me that the profilers were convinced this was all a one-man show and he would not be put off. Either way, they wanted Kegleze because he was their only real lead to the murderer.

Personally, I thought that Jarron was overly optimistic and it was way too early to celebrate.

We had handed the police the white van on a platter, and with it the possible murderer. But they had let him slip away.

Dafna and I were quite disappointed.

<u>41</u>

Conditions

TWO DAYS later, it was late Tuesday afternoon and the sixth day of Passover. Dafna and Mrs. Kalin were in the kitchen cooking like crazy for the holiday meal this evening. I was resting after partaking of a lunch made up mostly of leftovers but was still terrific — meals in the Lachler household can knock anyone for a loop — when I glanced out the window and saw Lieutenant Jarron and Special Agent Crowley, coming up the walk. Both were dressed in casual clothes. That meant no uniform for Jarron and no suit and tie for Crowley. They probably figured that this way they would be inconspicuous.

Wrong.

They both still looked like cops.

At least they tried.

But, it was not a good sign.

Jarron's prediction about everything hitting the fan was coming true.

They came up the stoop and rang the bell.

Opening the door, I was unsure how I should respond, so I smiled and offered in greeting, "Lieutenant Jarron, Agent Crowley, how nice to see you both."

"Cut the crap, Lincoln, and let us in," said Jarron somberly.

The state police lieutenant did not seem very happy.

"Please, come on in," I said holding the door wide open.

I directed them both to the living room and Jarron added, "Get your girlfriend. She is in this as well."

Very ominous.

I called out to Dafna, "You have guests."

She came in, took a gander at who was waiting for her and then instructed her mother and the girls to stay in the kitchen.

Crowley and Jarron sat on the sofa and Dafna and I sat in two upholstered chairs just opposite.

The FBI station chief began with, "First of all let me say *goot yometif* and *hag sah-may-akh.*"

Very impressive and good police technique. Start off as a good guy before you blast us away.

Dafna was surprised by Crowley, but I was able to say, "Pretty good. You said that better than me."

Jarron looked at the FBI man quizzically, "What did you just say?"

Crowley answered, "I said, 'happy holiday,' once in Yiddish and once in Hebrew."

"And happy Easter to you," said Dafna with a nod of her head.

"I don't think you guys came here so we could exchange holiday greetings," I said emphatically. "What do you want?"

Jarron had his jaw clamped tightly shut and just glared at the station chief. He motioned with his head that the FBI man should start the discussion.

Accepting the task Crowley nodded his head in return and began sternly, "I have come here, because we ... that is the FBI ... have learned that you two have had a secret role in the investigation of what has been dubbed by the media, the 'Kosher Butcher' case. We have also been informed that the upper echelons of the state police knew of your involvement and have kept this hidden from us. You two ...," he said with a gesture of his head in our direction, " ... as well as the state police, have violated about a million laws and if the federal government decides to press charges you could face serious jail time. In addition, you, *Mrs. Lackler*, would lose all your security clearances, so all your government work will dry up. You Mr. Lincoln, would lose your private investigator's license."

Aha. He said *if* they decide to press charges.

"And exactly on what will you base your decision to press charges?" I asked.

"If you agree to our conditions about any future contact with the case we will be able to avoid the embarrassment that would be caused by prosecuting you. Embarrassment to you personally and to the Michigan State Police."

Dafna seemed shaken by Crowley's words and asked meekly, "What are your conditions?"

"There are three conditions. One: You may continue your investigation of the case, but I ... meaning the FBI ... must be in the loop at all times. Whatever you tell Lieutenant Jarron, you also tell me."

"What about Nealy? Do I still keep him informed?" I asked.

"Yes, I heard about the strange arrangement with Nealy. Continue as before. I don't want anyone to know that things have changed. Two: Strict confidentiality. You will in no way or form leak to the press or any other media anything you discover. That includes your mother, Mrs. Kalin."

"For how long?" asked Dafna.

"Forever. Not a word," was his answer. "Three: Lieutenant Jarron informed me about your request to personally interrogate some of the people we have interviewed. Permission is categorically denied. You will not go within ten miles of any of those people. Do you agree to these terms?"

Dafna nodded her head in acquiescence and said softly, "Yes."

I had never seen her so cowed. Usually whenever anyone tried to restrict her, she offered fierce resistance. Strange.

Something was bothering me. Crowley's ultimatum did not add up. If we have been doing something illegal how could he let us remain on the case? Crowley was such a square and a by-the-book cop. No matter how lofty the goal he could not be an accomplice to criminal activity. So the odds were that we were not breaking any major laws and we were not facing any real jail time. Secondly, he was not closing us down. Just restricting us. So, what is it he really wants?

"And you Mr. Lincoln, do you agree?" asked the station chief.

"I'm thinking," I answered testily.

"And what great thoughts are you thinking about?" asked Jarron angrily. "Either you agree or you don't."

"OK," I said with a smile. "I don't."

"What?" exclaimed Dafna.

"Are you kidding me?" said Jarron in surprise.

"What is it you do not agree to?" asked Crowley.

"I don't agree to your conditions."

"You do realize what you will make me do?"

"Yeah," I said nodding my head. "Nothing."

"Nothing?" exclaimed Jarron. "He is going to sling mud from here to Lansing. At me and the state police. Why don't you agree?"

"Because I think Special Agent Crowley broke a whole bunch of laws if he was able to discover that you and I were working together from the get go. That was way before we discovered Mr. Kegleze."

Crowley interjected, "We did not break any laws getting that information."

Jarron looked at the FBI man and then back at me, "How did you know that the FBI knew about you working with us?"

"I guessed, but Crowley just confirmed it."

"Crap," said the station chief softly.

"You see, what he said did not make sense. I'm sure he could convince some federal prosecutor to take us to court for the violation of some esoteric federal law. Maybe it's a crime to go to the john without the teacher's permission. Something — but nothing major. Straight shooter Crowley would never work with real criminals. So I reckon your threat about yanking my private investigator's license is a bunch of malarkey. Also you threatened to take away Dafna's security clearance. Really?" I turned to Dafna, "What percentage of your income comes from your government work?"

"Police and federal?" she asked.

"Yeah," I said.

"I guess it's about one percent."

"And what percentage of your time is spent on this stuff?"

"About fifteen percent."

"So you are losing money doing the law enforcement work instead of your commercial business."

"Yes."

"So why do you do it?"

"I just feel if the government or the police need my help, I really have to be of assistance."

"So, the way I figure it, if they take away your clearance the only ones that will suffer are the police and the federal government. Interesting. I also figure that the guys at the computer-crime-stoppers branch of the FBI, or whatever they are called now, in Washington or Quantico, told Special Agent Crowley that the Michigan State Police just did not have the talent or equipment to do the sophisticated computer search to discover the cars and the MO for the murderer. They probably pointed the finger at Dafna right from the start. How am I doing so far?" I asked Crowley.

"Keep going," he said dejectedly.

"When we found the van and Kegleze, we screwed the FBI," I revealed.

"How so?" asked Jarron.

"See, now that they had to be officially informed about Dafna and me, they had to respond. They were much happier to take the position that they did not know we existed. Total deniability. That way if we messed up, it was not their fault. They could say it was not their doing and blame it all on the 'secretive' state police."

"Why?" asked Dafna.

"Special Agent Crowley did not want to have to explain why the FBI needed civilians to give them assistance. He knew that you had FBI clearance for just about any information. He also knew that I had been vetted by the FBI."

"You? When?" asked the lieutenant.

"About four years ago, when they tried to recruit me."

Dafna looked at me questioningly, "You worked for the FBI?"

"No, they just tried to recruit me. Anyway, seems to me that Crowley figured the FBI could allow us to be affiliated with the case, so long as they did not have to officially condone it."

"And then we found the van," said Dafna.

"Correct. Now we forced him to officially declare that we are part of the case. He couldn't let anyone know that he knew weeks before that non-police people were affiliated with the case and did nothing about it. So, he comes in here like gangbusters throwing around conditions. Well, I don't accept them. I want new conditions."

Crowley had been angrily rubbing his hands up and down his thighs. He looked up at me and said, "Who the hell do you think you are posing conditions to the FBI?"

"How quickly they forget. The name is Sy Lincoln. I think we have been introduced."

"Very funny," snapped Crowley.

"I am one of the partners in the crack detective team of Lincoln and Lachler. That's who is posing conditions to the FBI. I figure you can't go public with our involvement for two reasons. One, we can show that weeks ago you used illegal means to discover what we had been doing."

"No, you can't," said Crowley.

"You underestimate the computer talents of my wonderful fiancée. Believe me, she will be able to prove it seven ways from Sunday. Second, you need us."

"We don't need you," said the FBI man. "We have the largest computers, the biggest databases, and tons of experts and field agents."

"That is absolutely correct. And we both agree. Me and Dafna. That you guys are the best ones to hunt down Mr. Kegleze ... or whatever his name is ... if he is among the racist groups. You will get no competition from us on that. Thing is ... look at the scorecard."

"What scorecard?" asked Crowley angrily.

"The 'Kosher Butcher' scorecard. Dafna and I discovered the glasses, the cars used for the abductions along with the killers MO, and finally we discovered the van and Mr. Kegleze. So the Lincoln-Lachler team gets three points. FBI and state police with all the computers, databases, and field agents get zilch. Nothing. Nada. See the point? I'm sure that you guys, who work in our wonderful federal democracy, know that nowadays you cannot take people down into deep dark basements and beat the crap out of them because they did something you did not like. You have to take people to court. And they get to appear before a judge and then the media will know it all."

Jarron was smiling with understanding, "So he is not going to go public?"

"Nope," I said. "Now do you want to hear my conditions?"

The station chief was staring at the floor, obviously angry as could be, but after a moment he looked up at me, smiled and said, "I'm dying to hear them."

"It's not so bad. We accept conditions one and two. But I can't agree to your number three. Being a desk detective is not for me. I need to get out in the field. You guys did a great job of interviewing the people involved in the cases, but there are a couple of dozen loose threads that bother me. I want to pick at them until they don't bother me anymore. Crowley, we worked together on a case a few years back. You know how I do things. So here's my condition number three: Dafna and I want permission to actively interview people involved in the case."

"You can't do that," said Jarron. "You are not the police or the FBI."

"I won't say I am the FBI or police. I will simply tell them that I am working *with* the police and FBI and ask their permission to talk with them. I will send you both written reports of any interviews I conduct."

Both law enforcement officers considered the pros and cons. Jarron seemed relieved but Crowley was still angrily scrutinizing the carpet of Dafna's living room.

After a moment I asked, "Do we have a deal?"

Jarron was the first to respond, "It's OK by me and the state police have already agreed, but it is the FBI's decision."

I had called Crowley's bluff. He could accept our conditions or he would be forced to cut us off completely from the 'Kosher Butcher.' I figured he was enough of a realist to know that all the real progress in the case had come through Dafna and yours truly. It was also obvious that his bosses in Washington were getting very impatient about his lack of progress. I waited for him to respond.

Once more Crowley looked up from the floor. Nodded his head in resolve and extended his hand, "Deal."

We were back in the real detective business.

<u>**42**</u>

Big Guy

THAT EVENING was the start of the seventh day of Passover. According to Jewish tradition, on this day — a few thousand years ago — God split the Red Sea allowing the Hebrews to escape their enslavement and the pursuing Egyptians. The Hebrews got safely across but the Egyptians did not do as well. Big miracle for the Jewish people. The *Chassidic* sects commemorate the event with joyful singing and dancing on the evening preceding the seventh day and Dafna thought it would be fun if after supper we walked over to see the celebrations at the *Chassidic shteibel* in the neighboring city of Oak Park. I am not sure if the term *shteibel* is a Yiddish word or if it was borrowed from some other language. But it means a small synagogue.

Until I began my studies at the *yeshiva* I was unaware that there were different branches of ultra-Orthodox Judaism. To this day I find it difficult to tell them apart, because during the week most of the men wear similar long coats and have full beards. But on the Sabbath you can easily see the difference. For on the day of rest and on holidays the *Chassidim* sport a really cool fur hat, called a *shtreimel,* and wear a satin robe, called a *bekisheh.* Very unique.

The place was jumping — literally. Men in long black caftans and *streimelach* were singing and dancing in animated circles. Spirits were elevated, or should I say hoisted. I saw a couple of bottles of kosher for Passover plum brandy in the hands of one of the *Chassidim,* and he was filling little plastic cups and making the rounds. Even I had a couple — and I must say the booze was not half bad. Some of the *Chassidim* tried to drag me into the dancing frenzy a number of times. Even though I was just this side of being legally drunk I was able to keep myself in the cheering section and did not make a fool of myself by cavorting about on the dance floor. I watched from the sidelines sampling the cookies and pastries set up on the side table.

Wow, were they good.

Now, do not get me wrong. Dafna is a good baker, but the ingredients available on Passover are limited and that puts a crimp on the results of any baker. So, Dafna's *Pesach* stuff was good but these pastries were so much better. Like in a different universe. They were obviously homemade and if they were being served here, they had to be strictly kosher for Passover. After the holiday I had to discover the identity of this wonder baker to see if I could get some for myself.

Just — please — do not tell Dafna.

At about eleven thirty they ran out of plum brandy, the singing died out, and the *Chassidim* called it a night. Everyone dispersed and I met Dafna on the street — men and women were not allowed to be together during the dancing — and we set off walking in the direction of her home.

Dafna was ebullient and talkative. More than usual. Somehow I got the feeling that there were also a few bottles making the rounds of the ladies section. The liquor was not as potent as a good bourbon, but if you drank enough, things began to take on a more rosy hue. I definitely had a buzz on.

As we crossed Greenfield Road Dafna asked me, "Did you taste the cakes and cookies? Weren't they good?"

How do I answer that? If I say I liked them I would be leaving myself open for the inevitable — 'Better than my stuff?' I could not out and out lie and say I did not try them, because I did and they were soooo good. I decided to take the middle road, "Yes I did. They were all right, but I like what you bake much more." Always the diplomat.

"Baloney," said Dafna in disbelief. "But, that was a good answer. Ayelet Weinberg is *the* best baker in Detroit. Bar none. Not just on *Pesach.* She bakes rings around me and everyone else and she does it all in her little kitchen. Amazing. She happily gives out her recipes but no matter how carefully I prepare the dough or batter, when she does it they are so much better. It's like magic."

Ayelet Weinberg. So that was her name. Good to know. I was already thinking about how I would finagle myself a stockpile of her stuff after Passover.

We were cutting through the parking lot of one of the small commercial properties that line Greenfield Road. The area was dimly illuminated because the lights of the lot were dark. A large pale gray or tan delivery van, similar to those used by UPS, pulled into the lot just ahead of us. The vehicle had a cab in front but no windows on the body. As we passed the front of the van the passenger window slid down and we heard someone call from within, "Excuse me, could you help me."

Dark parking lot, unknown vehicle, unknown individual, late at night — my cop instincts went from neutral to full speed. I reached behind me to get my weapon but then I realized that I had left it at home in my gun safe. I figured it would not be needed on the holiday.

What an idiot.

That will not happen again.

The interior of the van was dark and all I could see was the silhouette of a big man behind the wheel. I reflexively pushed Dafna behind me and said cautiously, "Sure buddy, what's your problem."

The guy said loudly, "Just a second. I'll come around and show you."

The man took his time getting out of the van. He slammed the door and headed around the front of his vehicle to where we were standing.

The warning signals were going off. I pulled Dafna up close behind me.

There was not much light, but as he approached I could see that the man was really big — tall and wide — like a football defenseman. He was wearing baggy jeans and a quilted coat made from some kind of dark shiny material. The black baseball cap on his head was tilted down as if he were contemplating something. When he was about five feet from me he stopped, raised his large head and smiled silently. I waited a moment and then I said, "What is it exactly that you need?"

The guy nodded at me and said, "I'm supposed to deliver a message and I can't find the damn guy. Could you help me?"

The man was four or five inches taller than me and about eighty pounds heavier, but I was fairly confident that if things became messy I was skillful enough to overcome him. So far there was no evidence of any threats or weapons so I was in no rush to begin a confrontation. Still, I retained my defensive stance and asked, "Who are you looking for?"

"Fellow named Simon Lincoln."

Dafna exclaimed in surprise, "What's going on here?"

The man looked at Dafna and said, "I'm sorry. Do I make you nervous?"

"Yes, you make us nervous," I said angrily. "I don't know what your game is, but I advise you to just back off and end this little charade."

"Well, you see, I can't do that. There is this man that paid me a righteous amount of pesos to deliver this message. And, you really should not be nervous about me," he said nodding his head. "You should be nervous about my four friends standing behind you."

Too late I realized that my mind must have been clouded by the brandy and I had not sensed any other possible threats. I screwed up. I turned my head around ever so slightly and glimpsed the guy's extra large buddies. Then, I felt hands grabbing me from behind pulling me down. I toppled like a felled tree in the forest. One moment I was flying backwards, and the next I felt a terrible pain at the back of my head and then black.

I was waking up and not dead.

How did I know?

Easy.

Someone was splashing water on my face and shouting in my ear, "Lincoln, wake up!"

I figured if I had gone on to the *olam ha'bah* the welcoming heavenly angels would probably have a more amicable salutation.

Having been knocked out several times and shot in the head once, I knew that the movie version of people waking from an unconscious state was totally inaccurate. The reason a person is unconscious after head trauma is because his brain has become discombobulated. If you pour water over the guy, you would still have someone with a discombobulated brain but now he would also be uncomfortably wet.

I tried to compel my scrambled brain to process all the stimuli around me. I forced my eyes open and realized I was lying on my back on the floor of what I guessed was the inside of the big man's truck. There was illumination coming from a weak light on the roof of the vehicle. I could make out Dafna standing at the side wall held securely by two of the big guy's accomplices wearing ski masks. There were another three hovering over me. Two more with masks and the big guy himself. I tried to speak but found that my mouth was taped shut. Movement was impossible because my hands were secured together at the wrists with a plastic zip tie. The two henchmen bent over and yanked me to my feet. My head swam and I thought I might upchuck all of Mrs. Weinberg's cookies along with Dafna's fabulous dinner. *Not a good idea with my mouth taped shut.* Even though I was technically standing on my own two legs, I was still very wobbly, and if these guys were not supporting me, I probably would topple over once again.

"Now that's better," said the big man. "I haven't got all night. I was not planning on you going down for a ten count. It's messing up my schedule. I have things to do tonight."

Somehow, I could not empathize with the man's plight. I was not at all sorry that I had interfered with his plans.

"Down to business," he said decisively. "The message I was asked to deliver is: 'Stop what you are doing or there will be consequences.' I paraphrased that a little bit and changed it to 'there will be consequences.' I like that phrase. He said 'or else.' But, that has no class. Don't you agree?"

I just stared at him. *What is he talking about?* My head still hurt but it was clearing slowly.

"Now, I have no idea what it is you have been doing, but I advise you to stop. Because there is a second part of the message. The man wants me to give you a little demonstration of what he means when he says 'consequences.' Of course, he did not say, 'consequences,' what he said was, 'or else.' But you get my drift."

Terrific, my head was clearing. So now I would be awake enough to feel his goons work me over.

"The man gave me very strict instructions. Part good news and part bad. He said you were an ex-cop, so I could not kill you. I offered but he still said no. I don't know why. So the good news is you ain't gonna die. He also said that you were one mean son of a bitch and that even if I beat on you from now until next Sunday, you would not break. Just get pissed off. So I am not supposed to touch you. Therefore the bad news is that I am going to work over your girlfriend. The man said no sexual misconduct ... what a shame ... but I think you will still get the point. Bring her here," he commanded the fellows holding Dafna.

I forced myself to think. I was pretty sure that my balance was now good enough to stand on my own but I continued to lean on the two men, so that they would think that I was still totally incapacitated. They probably thought that with my hands restricted by the zip tie it was unlikely that I could do very much against five opponents simultaneously.

They were right.

Very bad odds.

I needed to improve the odds.

So far there were no weapons in sight. Most likely because of the Michigan tag-on law, which automatically adds three years of jail time to any crime committed with a lethal weapon.

That helps.

I could see that Dafna also had her hands secured with a zip tie and her mouth taped shut, but it was obvious that her eyes were wide with fear. She looked at me and I tried to transfer my thoughts into her brain. It was imperative that she make some sort of diversion. I only needed a second or two. I moved my eyes and head in a sort of mime, signaling towards the men restraining her. She signaled back with a nod of her head.

Did she really get my message?

The men forced her to stand in front of the big guy.

"I don't especially like hitting ladies. So, I hope you understand that this is just business," said the big fellow apologetically.

Dafna made a muffled laugh through the tape on her mouth.

The man holding Dafna's left arm complained loudly, "I told you I don't beat up women."

"You aren't going to hit the lady ... I am. All you got to do is hold her," said the boss.

"Same thing. I don't want no part of her getting hurt," the accomplice said defiantly.

"Ain't you the Good Samaritan? You knew we weren't going on a picnic."

"You didn't say there would be a woman."

"What the hell. Al ... switch with him. Hold the girl."

The man at my right released me and I made believe that I could not stand without his support by falling against the guy at my left. The two goons switched places.

Once Al had Dafna's arm in his grasp, the boss man took a step towards her. At that exact moment she took the heel of her left leg and drove it into Al's shin.

On holidays Dafna spiffed up and wore high heels. Tonight she was wearing 2-inch tapered heels and the steel spike went right though the fabric of the guy's pants into the flesh.

Reflexively, Al released Dafna's left arm and grabbed at his wounded leg. This allowed her to bring both her hands up quickly towards the face of the man at her right. With perfect aim she drove her thumb directly into his left eyeball.

Her *Krav Magah* instructor would be very proud of her.

The fellow who got the finger in the eye released Dafna's arm to tend to his injury. Neither man was totally incapacitated but she was giving me my two second diversion. I saw Dafna try to kick the boss in the nads but apparently her *Shabbos* dress restricted her leg and the big man saw it coming. He was able to grasp Dafna's foot and yelled, "Somebody grab her."

She was hopping around on one foot and the Good Samaritan restraining my right arm released his hold to get at Dafna. He probably figured I was too weak to be a problem.

This was my opportunity.

Once again I feigned weakness and fell forward pulling the guy on my left with me. Just as his head was coming down, I twisted to my left, and quickly raised my right knee directly into the center of his face. I heard the nose go crunch and saw his head go flying backwards as he collapsed to the floor. Something ripped when I made the move. Black *yeshiva* suits are not really made for karate.

I quickly sat down on the floor.

This was not because I needed a rest.

There are three ways to get out of a zip tie; one - use a sharp object to cut the plastic strap, two - insert a fine flat piece of metal to release the little plastic tongue that catches the grooves of the zip tie, three - use brute strength to break the little tongue. The first two were not options because I lacked the necessary paraphernalia. Usually the last would not work because humans cannot generate enough upper limb power to overcome that little bitty plastic tongue. However, there were two things in my favor. The first was that because I had been lying on my back, they had secured my wrists in the front. The second was that I did not have to rely on upper limb power alone.

Once I got to a sitting position I put my foot between my wrists and pushed with all my strength. I felt the tie bite into my flesh but after a moment it gave way and my hands were free.

The odds were getting better every second.

I scrambled forward and grabbed the boss man's pant legs and yanked backwards. This made him release Dafna's foot and sent him flying forward to land face first on the metal floor of the van, with a resounding 'bong.'

I jumped to my feet and shot a karate kick to the head of the Good Samaritan who had come around to hold Dafna. He went down. I tore the tape off my mouth and removed Dafna's as well, "Are you all right?"

"Fine ..." she said dully. Then she looked over my shoulder and exclaimed, "Watch out."

I pushed her to the side of the van to intercept Al — the one with the injured leg — as he stepped over his unconscious boss to get to me. The guy was big but slow. I anticipated his right cross and latched on to his arm. Then using his forward momentum I pulled him towards me over my hip. When he went over I heard the bones in his right arm break. He was out of the equation.

The guy that had received Dafna's thumb in his eye now tried to kick me. But in order to do that he had to put all his weight on his other foot. I did a quick leg sweep and he went crashing to the floor. He tried to get up but a quick punch to the center of his face and he went quiet. They were all down now.

I saw that Dafna's balloon was losing air quickly and she was slithering down the side of the van to the floor. She was crying softly and appeared in a state of shock. I put my arms around her and held her close, "It's OK, we're fine." She leaned against me and put her head on my shoulder. The crying became stronger as she processed what had just occurred.

I heard some noise in the van and noticed that one of the henchmen, the Good Samaritan, had begun to stir. He saw me huddled with Dafna at the side of the truck and he warily crawled to the back and opened the door. I stood up, with Dafna in my arms, and watched as he returned to help a groggy Al get out the door as well.

I had to make a quick decision. I could leave Dafna on her own and try to restrain them, but without my pistol it could be a problem. Throughout the melee no own had drawn a weapon, so the odds were that the thugs were weaponless. Right now, they all looked as if the fight was knocked out of them. With their injuries, they were not a threat to us any longer and I decided I was not going to leave Dafna even if it meant that they got away.

The Good Samaritan returned again. Keeping to the opposite wall and watching me carefully, he helped the other two get out of the truck. Rats on a sinking ship and all that.

I still had their boss who was lying unconscious in the center of the van. That was good enough for me.

I found a large carton staple on the truck floor and used it to release Dafna's hands from the zip tie.

It took about one or two minutes for Dafna's crying to abate and then she allowed me to stop a passing car and ask them to call the cops.

Dafna was her old self again. No more tears, no more fears. Only determination.

A Southfield cruiser arrived in about three minutes.

It was Officer Cummings.

Unbelievable.

He got out of his car and said, "Lincoln, we have got to stop meeting like this."

Two more police cars arrived shortly after that. The big guy was still unconscious, and they put in a call for two ambulances. When I asked why they needed two medical teams they told me the other one was for me. I had been knocked unconscious and that meant a trip to the hospital. I tried to object, but they insisted.

Cummings asked the routine questions and statements were made and reports written. Once again he told us that he knew it was a Jewish holiday and we could come in on Friday to sign all the paperwork.

I asked Cummings to call Lieutenant Nealy so that he would know about the attack. I would speak with Jarron and the FBI on my own.

Even as the reports were being written up I knew it was a waste of time. The odds of catching the accomplices were about zero. One was called Al, but there are a million Als. At least three of them would need medical attention, but even if they went to a medical facility for care, the ski masks made positive identification impossible. The only consolation was that we had their boss. In all probability he was going to say that he did not know the identity of the guy who hired him. It was probably true. This 'Kosher Butcher' was too smart. He would never have exposed himself like that.

I was pissed.

Angry with the murderer and angry with myself. I should not have been drinking. I should not have been without my weapon. I should not have let my guard down and exposed Dafna to danger.

The ambulances arrived, and the paramedics started an IV on the unconscious big guy and loaded him onto a stretcher. He was whisked away with a police escort. I did not do much better. The paramedics insisted that I had to be strapped into the stretcher. They wanted to give me an IV but I refused. I already felt like such a fool.

I asked the EMTs to let me speak with Dafna in private before they loaded me onto the ambulance. I turned to her and said, "I liked that part where we were hugging. It felt good."

She smiled uncomfortably and said, "Yes ... well ... I suppose it did ... but the support you always give me after ... we get into trouble ..."

"You mean the part where after people try to kill us I get to hug you for a bit?"

"Yeah ... exactly. I'm sorry I behaved like that."

"Don't be sorry ... I told you ... I like the hugging part."

"Exactly. That has to remain between you and me. It will not become general knowledge," she commanded.

"Mum's the word," I agreed.

"You do realize that in a month we can hug all we want," she said.

"Judaism is a tough religion."

"No, it's not. Life is tough, Judaism is what helps us get through the tough parts."

Very profound.

We certainly had a tough part tonight. I looked at her and said, "I'm sorry for what happened."

"What are you sorry about? It was not your fault. The murderer is responsible."

"But I did not prevent this from happening. They could have hurt you very badly. I feel terrible."

"Maybe you did not prevent the situation, but you certainly got us out of it."

"I could not have done it without you. When you spiked the guy in the leg and poked the other one in the eye ... you were awesome."

Dafna contemplated what I had just said and then with a nod of her head agreed, "Yeah, it feels good to be back kicking *tuchis* again."

"How did you know that I needed you to cause a distraction, just then?"

"I don't know. I looked at you and saw you being held up by those men. I also knew that that man was about to hit me. A thought came into my head that I had to do something. I could not let him hurt us without putting up a fight. I was going to do whatever I could."

"That's what saved us, it was you, not me ... partner."

"Just like old times ... *tuchis* kicking partners."

"*Tuchis* kicking almost married partners."

"Yeah, that too."

<u>43</u>

Arraignment

I WOKE the next morning with a headache that registered 9.2 on the Richter scale, so that meant the doctors kept me in the hospital for another day. SOP for head injuries. I was released on Thursday evening and it was none too soon. If normal hospital food is bad, then kosher hospital food is barely edible. Add to that the requirement for special food for Passover and you can imagine the dreadful meals I had to endure.

There was some swelling on the back of my head but otherwise I was fine. Dafna pampered me all weekend, so that was nice.

Sunday afternoon after the practice session at the *dojo*, I was sitting at a table in Dave's Burgers waiting for my order of a double hamburger with all the trimmings. My phone rang and Officer Cummings was on the line. I figured he was calling to be sure that Dafna and I would be in the courtroom for tomorrow's arraignment of the fellow we had captured at the attack.

"Yes officer, what can I do for you?"

"I'm calling about the arraignment tomorrow," he said.

"I figured as much."

"I wanted to let both of you know that you do not have to come," he said.

How strange.

"What's going on? Don't you guys need us?"

"No, we won't. The arraignment has been cancelled."

"When will it be?" I asked.

"There won't be any arraignment," he stated.

"Why not?"

"At first the guy you subdued refused to give us any information but his fingerprints identified him as Eugene Clemens and he has Detroit rap sheet a yard long. Mostly as hired muscle.   He was arrested for suspicion of homicide twice but got off both times. Works with loan sharks and makes collections for bookies when people are not eager to cover their debts. After a session with Eugene they suddenly become very eager. The doctors released him from the hospital Friday afternoon and we transferred him to the Oakland County Jail to await his arraignment. This morning they found him ... dead. So there won't be any trial."

Whoa. Wait a second.

Did he say the guy was dead?

"Please tell me he died from his head injury," I ventured hopefully.

"Wish I could. The County Sheriff says he was stuffed behind a book shelf in the corner of the common room with multiple stab wounds to the torso. There was a jailhouse shiv on the floor next to his body. His murder is being investigated but from past experience, in the end ... no one saw anything and whoever did this will never be found."

"What about the surveillance cameras?"

"Not a thing."

Cummings signed off just as the counterman called my name. Suddenly I was not hungry anymore.

Unless Eugene Clemens had been an absolute sociopath and made everyone hate him on sight, it stood to reason that he was no longer amongst the living because somebody was afraid that Eugene might have some information that could lead the authorities to discover who sent him. That person decided that the best kind of Eugene was a dead Eugene. Whoever it was, had to have far reaching tentacles to knock someone off in the county lock-up.

Suddenly finding the murderer became a prime goal. I had to do it pronto, or one of us might be the next Eugene on the list.

Monday morning my cousin Steve showed up at Dafna's house to begin the construction of Shaindel's new apartment. His crew used a backhoe and a Bobcat to clear the ground to start the work on the addition. They had to remove all the sod and landscaping to expose Dafna's existing underground extension so it could be used as a foundation for the project. I watched the men work for about an hour and it became abundantly clear that I was superfluous so I went to my office to continue my research into the murders.

Crowley was true to his word and the FBI gave me a green light to talk with some of the people that had been interviewed and I was planning how I would get this organized. After three hours I took a break to get a cup of coffee because I realized I was getting fixated on specific facts and this caused me to lose sight of the total picture. If and when I am smart enough to discern that this might be occurring, I used a mental trick that was taught to me by my first partner, Larry Patton. He told me to look at the case like a Hollywood movie. Since you knew the case backwards and forwards, you knew all the action but you did not know what the star of the film looked like. So you played the movie in your head while you checked for continuity. I would then ask myself, what did not make sense? And then sometimes the elusive actor would take form. This technique had helped me in many a case.

I ran through the movie once and noticed something. Over a week had gone by and there had been no new deliveries of body parts. It looked as if the murderer had deduced that we had some method to spot him even though there was no video surveillance in the drop area. Most likely there would be no more body parts. Without any further deliveries, how would we find the guy?

As I sat deep in contemplation, Nealy walked in to give me his latest update. He told me that the FBI had beefed up their team here in Detroit, and that the State Police Task Force had also assigned another six state troopers to find 'Kegleze.' Jarron was still in charge but now there was a captain looking over his shoulder all the time.

So far, the state police could not find a hint of a limping crazy that fit the bill in any of the local skinhead, white supremacy or Neo-Nazi groups. The FBI was not having any better luck on the national level. I, in turn, told Nealy that both Dafna and I were still up against a stone wall because we were not allowed on the street. I was lying, but he did not have to know that I would be getting a chance to play real detective. I spent the next twenty minutes using him as a sounding board for my 'out of the box' interpretations of what some of the people had said in their interviews. He was an experienced cop and his advice was helpful — but not fruitful. So far we were still batting zero. Just before he left he told me he thought he saw hopeful signs that his wife was relenting and he was going to have his family back any day now.

What misplaced confidence.

He promised to keep me in the loop.

I thought about what he had said about the cops not finding the limping, sixty-year-old 'White Supremacy' nut. So, I once again played that part of my mental movie in my brain and a bell went off. I pulled up the written report of the interview the police had conducted with Mr. Sangford, the guy who sold the van to the murderer. I had to be sure.

I called Sangford and he picked up on the fourth ring. "Hello Mr. Sangford, this is Detective Lincoln. I am working with the state police trying to locate Robert Kegleze, the guy who bought the van from you."

Hey, just like I promised I did not say I was a policeman, so that was not a lie.

My code of ethics was quite clear about that.

I never lied — unless I had to.

"Sure, how can I be of help?" he said.

"You said that Robert Kegleze had a bad limp," I stated.

"Sure did. Said it was from the military. Looked like it was mighty painful."

"Which leg did he limp on?"

"Do you mean, which one was his bum leg?"

"Yeah, which one?"

"It was his left leg," he stated with confidence.

"How can you be so sure?" I asked.

"Because he said that he misses driving a stick shift. He could not do it anymore because he could not press the clutch with his gimpy left leg."

"Thank you."

"Has someone spotted the guy?"

"Not yet, but you have been most helpful."

"You bet. Glad to do it. Just catch that bastard."

This was too important to run through Nealy and then have him leap frog it up to the Task Force. So I called Jarron's cell phone directly. He whispered that he was in a meeting and would call me right back.

Just to be sure, I used the time to look at the surveillance video that showed the van being abandoned at the Oakland mall.

Jarron returned my call about fifteen minutes later, "What've you got?"

"Stop looking for a limping Robert Kegleze."

"Why?"

"Because it is probably all a fake. There is a good chance that he is not sixty years old, does not have a mustache, and probably does not limp."

"How do you know?"

"Alice's father distinctly remembers that Robert Kegleze limped on this left leg."

"So what?"

"The guy walking away from the van is limping on his right."

<u>44</u>

Chopped Liver

OVER THE next few weeks, my time was divided between interviewing people in the 'Kosher Butcher' case, my work at Lincoln Investigations, watching my future mother-in-laws's apartment take shape, and planning my wedding which was now eight days away.

Shaindel had already let me know that she followed the old tradition that dictated I would not be allowed to see Dafna starting the week before the wedding. I guess we would keep in contact using video calls. We were both still very frustrated by our lack of progress in the murder case.

Although I was striking out with the 'Kosher Butcher', business was booming at Lincoln Investigations. Of the three original CV checks, two turned out to be bogus. The first had asked that his new employer not contact his present employer because he did not want them to know that he was thinking of changing jobs. Turns out he had already been fired because of his poor managerial skills. He thought he had successfully hidden that fact. We caught him.

The second CV was what we call very creative — more fiction than fact. One of the previous positions listed by the guy was his work as the manager of the sales department for a major firm. It turned out that the major firm was actually a mom-and-pop store in Podunk and he had been the one and only clerk. In addition, although he had indeed attended the various universities listed in the CV, he failed to mention that he had flunked out of all of them. All his academic credentials, diplomas, and recommendations were phony. The human resource divisions were super satisfied with my discoveries and they were now sending me one or two new CVs every week. Word got around and two more companies were sending us CV checks as well. Thank goodness for Mary Lou, because she did most of the work on these cases. She had a special knack for sniffing out prevaricators.

I also got the goods on the creep who was blackmailing the minister. I collected evidence proving the desk clerk's own adulterous behavior and we were able to record his blackmail threats on video. He showed up on payment day thinking he owned the goose that laid the golden egg. The minister's lawyer made it abundantly clear that if he ever approached the minister again or if the damaging video ever surfaced, he would see to it that the guy's wife learned about his extra-friendly relationships with a number of the motel's chambermaids. We would also go to the cops and charge him with blackmail. He took the money and left quietly.

As predicted, the guy who was leaking the catalog stuff to the competitors was really quite stupid. He figured no one would ever find out what he was doing because he was sending the information using a new e-mail account. The guy was really dumb — because he was doing it from his own laptop and was not even erasing his activities. He was now in jail awaiting a decision whether he would be tried in state or federal court.

We located the two guys who had skipped town owing quite a bit of money, but they were fighting extradition and as yet had not returned to Michigan. But that was the bank's problem, not mine.

With each of the successes came new business. So, it looked like Lincoln Investigations would be doing OK in the future.

The only one of the original cases still open was Mrs. Kincaid's impending divorce. Mr. Kincaid was a patent attorney by profession and thought he had an ironclad prenup in place. According to the agreement, the investment firm that they held jointly would be divided between him and his wife if and when they divorced. So he figured before the firm went on the block, he would secretly leech out as much money as he could. We had already discovered that Mr. Kincaid was secretly selling off assets and personally taking the money to the Cayman Islands. Rough estimate was that he had successfully transferred over three million dollars. Since the US border police had not caught the guy carrying large sums of cash, we assumed that he was converting the cash into bank checks or using bearer bonds. On his trips to the Cayman Islands he would always stay one night at the Marriott in Georgetown and then fly back the next day. What we did not know was which one of the 158 banks in the Cayman Islands was handling Kincaid's money — without that information we could not determine the account name he was using to stash the shekels.

The next logical step in the investigation was to have someone follow Kincaid when he made his next deposit. I recommended using a local Cayman Islands investigator since they were more familiar with the territory, but for various reasons the lawyers insisted that I be the one to go. With my upcoming nuptials and the ongoing murder investigation, I was reluctant to take the time, but then I realized that I could kill two birds with one stone.

Mr. Kincaid's work required him to appear, several times a month, before the patent court in D.C., and he would cram in his Caribbean jaunts between his court dates. What he would do was schedule court time on Monday and Wednesday mornings. He would hop down to the Caymans on Monday afternoon, and get back for another court session on Wednesday. He was due for another trip this week and I was going to follow him. There was no direct flight to the Cayman Islands from D.C. and Kincaid's Monday afternoon route always made a stop in Atlanta. I did not want to take the chance that he would spot me if I was on both of his flights, so, my plan was to make sure he boarded his D.C. flight to Atlanta and then use a different carrier to get to Georgia. From there I would be on his flight to the Caymans.

Early Monday morning, I was on the plane to Washington, D.C., because there was something else I wanted to do before flying on to the Caymans. While on board I used my iPad to read and re-read the forensic reports of all the murders. I already knew them by heart but wanted to have all the information fresh in my brain.

When I was a cop I found that it was always important to speak face to face with the pathologists and CSI personnel so that I was sure that I had every bit of information that was available from the people who had initially studied all the evidence.

It took two weeks of pestering Jarron until he finally arranged for me to get in to the Wayne County Medical Examiner's office. After meeting with them, I was fairly confident that I was now in possession of all the forensic facts that they had to give. But I was still hungry to learn more. All of the evidence that had been collected by the Wayne County Medical Examiner's office had also been examined by the pathologists at the FBI crime labs in Quantico. They probably had nothing to add — but I felt that I had to speak with them as well, and that was where I was headed today.

Crowley had not relished the idea of allowing me near Quantico but he finally set up my appointment to meet with Dr. Fisher of the Trace Evidence Unit at the FBI

Laboratory Services. She was the pathologist in charge of the bureau's analysis of the 'Kosher Butcher' evidence.

From Dulles airport I took a rental car to the FBI base. Getting into the visitor's lot was not too difficult but gaining entry to the TE unit required going through a body scan and pat down. Fisher's third floor office was at the rear of the huge building and I was stopped half a dozen times. I knew that I would have to pass through all sorts of FBI hoops and hurdles, so I had come really early. That was the reason I was still able to make it to the door of the doctor's office with five minutes to spare.

I did not want to be late.

When I entered, Dr. Fisher's secretary told me that the doctor was behind in her schedule and asked me to wait.

Only to be expected — after all, this was a super efficient government agency.

I had just gotten comfortable in a chic government-issue tan mock leather chair, and picked up a six month old travel magazine when my phone rang. I was greeted by Mary Lou's husky voice.

The caterer had just called and there was a wedding disaster in the making.

Why was Mary Lou calling and not Shaindel?

Simple reason. Mrs. Kalin was working like a one-armed paper hanger juggling all the problems of getting her new apartment habitable. She had been most reluctant to release the official reins of planning the wedding, but she also knew that she had a deadline to get out of Dafna's home and moved into her new place. So two weeks ago she relented. Mary Lou assured Mrs. Kalin that she would not make any decisions without first consulting her. She started off slow but by the end of the first week, Shaindel was relying on my administrative assistant's advice completely. Whenever Mary Lou consulted her about a problem Mrs. Kalin would usually tell her, "Whatever you think, is fine by me." She had also become the contact person for all the service providers for the wedding — food, flowers, booze, band, photographers, etc.

So, what was the disaster?

"There is a shortage of *glatt* kosher chicken livers in the entire Midwest," said Mary Lou. "They tell me there are plenty of the regular kosher. It is only the *glatt* variety that is scarce. The menu for your wedding supper calls for an appetizer of chicken liver pâté with a sweet horseradish sauce. The caterer says that this requires a two day prep time. He will not have any livers by next Sunday ... so no paté. And the printed menus say chicken liver paté. Big problem."

I had no idea why Mary Lou thought this was a big deal. I could not care less what they served for the first course. But I had noticed that certain people think stuff like this is a catastrophe. I am sure Shaindel was one of them.

"Well, what are you going to do?" I asked.

"I haven't got the slightest clue," she said. "Because I don't know the difference between *glatt* and not-*glatt* chicken liver. Is *glatt* from a chicken that has been sprinkled with holy water? Please fill me in."

This was tough enough to explain to Jewish people, how would a non-Jew comprehend the whole thing? Glatt meant that when the rabbis examined the innards of a slaughtered animal they imposed extremely rigid standards above and beyond the normal kosher guidelines.

I thought for a moment and then said, "Nothing to do with holy water. The only thing you have to know is that *glatt* means something is super kosher. The ultra-Orthodox Jews use only *glatt* stuff and modern Orthodox use the regular kosher as well."

"Yeah, that much I figured out for myself," she said in understanding. "Well, there ain't no *glatt* livers to be had. What do you want me to do?"

"Me? What do I know about these things? Ask Shaindel," I said.

"She's too busy buying furniture and is also super occupied figuring out the seating arrangements and organizing where all the guests are going to sleep on the Sabbath after your wedding. So you are it."

I forgot about the *sheva brachos.* The Sabbath celebratory meal required finding beds for the guests who lived far away because Orthodox Jews did not drive on *shabbos.* Neighbors and friends were always willing to accommodate the guests but it was quite a logistic nightmare.

Shaindel was out of the equation.

Asking Dafna was also not an option because she was swamped with work from her business and whenever she had a moment free she was priming her data-base looking for Rabbi Slater's murderer. In addition, she thought Shaindel had exaggerated greatly with all her wedding plans and refused to have anything to do with the over-the-top affair. As far as she was concerned we could have the wedding on the street in front of the synagogue and eat canned sardines for the celebratory dinner.

So what should I do with the liver disaster?

I was on my own.

"I am not a cook," I said.

"Thank goodness for that. You don't even know how to make coffee," said Mary Lou.

"But couldn't the paté be made from something else."

"Like regular kosher livers?"

"No, not that. There are some really highfalutin holy roller rabbis coming to the wedding. If Shaindel found out we used regular kosher she would kill me dead. What I meant was, how about calf's liver."

"Do you think it would work?"

"I for one would never know the difference. I am no *fine shmekker.*"

"A what?" she asked.

"A connoisseur."

"Yeah, I also don't think I could tell the difference. So, I guess we could do that. Nice call," she said happily and hung up the phone.

Problem solved.

Am I a genius or what?

<u>45</u>

Zip-Close

I HAD JUST put my phone back into my pocket when Dr. Fisher's secretary told me I could go in.

The scientist was a short slim woman with closely cropped graying curly hair and looked to be about sixty years of age. Under her tan FBI lab coat she wore baggy gray slacks and a plain white blouse. When I entered she rose from her chair and extended an open hand, "Mr. Lincoln?"

"Yes, Sy Lincoln. Thank you for seeing me," I said shaking her hand.

"Have a seat. I explained to Agent Crowley that I really have nothing to add to what we wrote in our reports. So I am afraid you are probably wasting your time."

"In that case, I doubly appreciate your seeing me, because there is a good chance that I will be wasting your time as well." That made her smile, and I went on, "Still, I wanted to talk to you about what your investigators felt when they studied all the evidence in this case not just what they wrote. Sometimes, people with a sharp eye can get a subliminal suggestion of things that would escape normal folks."

"OK, Where do you want to start?"

"At the beginning," I said knowingly.

We talked for almost an hour. The FBI had not found anything more than what the Wayne County Medical examiner had discovered. No additional prints, no incriminating trace evidence. They had even analyzed small bits of twigs, earth, and pebbles imbedded in the body parts and could corroborate that the bodies had been cut up with a chain saw while laying on the ground somewhere in Michigan.

"One last thing. Was there anything unusual about how the body parts were wrapped? It says in the report that the bags were standard Ziploc bags easily obtainable in thousands of stores."

"Funny you should mention that. First of all they were not Ziploc bags."

"They weren't?" I asked.

"No, they are Zip-Close bags. A completely different company."

"Is there a difference?"

"Oh yes. Our plastic bag expert ... "

"You guys have an expert in plastic bags?" I asked incredulously.

"Of course," she said as if stating the obvious. "Anyway, he says the bag used ... and all the body parts have been delivered in the exact same type of bag ... is known as a butcher bag."

"You're kidding me. They named the bag after this murder investigation?"

"Oh, no. That has been their name since they were introduced about six years ago as an extra strong, extra large, reclosable bag for use in the meat industry. What is interesting is that because of its extra large size and thickness it has become widely used in other industries and for crafts. You can buy this exact bag in thousands of retail outlets and online."

"So you are saying that the type of bag tells us nothing that could possibly help in this case."

"Precisely," she said with a nod of her head. "All except bag number 12."

"What is special about bag number 12?"

She consulted a file on her desk and said, "That was the one that contained Maria Sanchez's left pelvis."

That visual suddenly left me squeamish.

"What did it show?"

"On the upper right corner of the front of the bag ..."

"How do you know which is the front and which is the back on a plastic bag?"

"By our definition when this kind of bag is open the slide apparatus will be on the upper left side of the front of the bag. We do this so that we have some way to orient ourselves."

"OK, so what did you find."

"On the upper right corner of the front of the bag there was a three millimeter piece of paper glued to the bag." She passed me a photographic enlargement showing the paper fragment.

"What does this tell us?"

"These bags are marketed in packages of 10, 20, 50, and 100 bags. You can also special order them from the manufacturer, Novaplast, if you need larger quantities. The most popular sizes are the 10 and 100 packages. The smaller packages are for the craft people and the larger for meat processors. The 20 and 50 sizes come in two types of packaging. Firm cardboard or soft, depending if it is for commercial or private use. In addition there is a special pack of the 50, which comes with 49 bags fitted into the 50th bag. This is four bucks cheaper than the 50-pack that comes in a box. The hunting trade especially likes this package and it is only available online through Amazon. Our analysis of the glue and composition of that little bit of paper, on bag number 12, shows that it is the seal that closes that special fifty pack on an Amazon order."

"No kidding? That's terrific. So we know that the murderer ordered his bags on Amazon. That's a lead."

"Not really. All it shows it that bag 12 was purchased on Amazon. All the rest could have come from anywhere. However we did look into the possibility of locating the killer though Amazon and found that there were over 800 orders for that package over the last year in the state of Michigan. The murderer could have purchased it more than a year ago or come from another state. He also could have purchased the bag in a shop that sells these Amazon bags piecemeal."

"But did you look to see if any of the people connected with the case ordered these bags," I asked.

"We did better than that," she said with a nod of her head. "We checked all the orders for five years ... since these bags have been available on Amazon. Over sixty thousand orders."

"And?"

"Nothing. Not one had any connection to the case. We also looked more deeply into all orders that were within a hundred mile radius of Detroit. We included part of Ontario and Ohio."

"And?"

"Again nothing. There were about two dozen orders whose addresses were geographically close to addresses of people involved ... like a couple of blocks away ... but when we checked them out there was nothing solid."

Very disappointing.

I thought for a moment about whether there was anything else I wanted to know from Dr. Fisher. We had discussed just about every aspect of the case and so far nothing rang a bell. About the only real accomplishment I had all day was solving the *glatt* kosher liver crisis.

Why were there no internal organs? Something I could scrutinize to determine what was kosher and what was not.

Well, for one thing — none of the bodies had any innards.

Wait a second.

How come none of the bodies had any internal organs?

I had assumed that it was to make transport and freezing of the bodies easier. But maybe the guy did it to make us think that the killer was someone with hunting skills. Like a 'good old boy' redneck 'White Supremacy' crazy.

Or maybe the innards would have told us something.

What could they have possibly revealed?

I had no idea, but maybe Dr. Fischer did.

"I just had a thought," I said tentatively, "I know that there were no internal organs in any of the body parts the murderer sent."

"None so far."

"I am a bit of a dunce when it comes to forensic pathology so bear with me."

"Thank you for admitting that. Half the cops are always second-guessing us."

"My question is ... if you do a forensic analysis on a murder and you do not have the internal organs ... how does that interfere with your autopsy results?" I inquired.

"It does not interfere. We state that there are no internal organs to examine."

"So how can you be sure about the cause of death?" I asked.

"I see what you want," she stated. "As was stated in the preliminary reports, we can't be sure of anything with these murders. We don't know the cause of death. Normally, when we do an autopsy it is like opening a box of Cracker Jack and looking around for the prize." She saw my lack of comprehension and asked, "Do you know what Cracker Jack is?"

"Haven't got the slightest," I said.

"I'm just showing my age. Anyway, in our cases there was no evidence of any penetrating injuries or major trauma to the limbs. All the frozen corpses were dismembered using a chain saw. So far, there were no heads and none of the body parts indicate the cause of death. No GSWs and no penetrating injuries. Without the neck and head, we have no way of knowing if they were strangled or hung. It's possible they were poisoned, but there was no blood in the bodies and in the small amounts of body fluids that we were able to collect, nothing came up in the toxin screen. They could have been electrocuted, but there were no burn marks externally or internally. So, we know very little about how they died."

"If you had the internal organs would that have helped?"

She thought for a moment and then said, "It could have been of help if there was poisoning or asphyxiation. But otherwise it would not tell us much more. Because we know from the medical records that all the victims were extremely healthy."

"How about this ... what could the murderer hide ... by not including the internal organs?" I asked.

"Any sort of pre-existing medical condition."

"But you said they were all healthy," I questioned.

"Things like a steroid or drug abuse, dietary fetishes, anatomical aberrations and of course pregnancy."

Pregnancy. *Why did I not think of that?*

"How would you know if a dead woman was pregnant?" I asked excitedly.

"Well, finding a fetus in the uterus is pretty suggestive," she said with a straight face.

"Yeah, but you don't have a uterus. So how would you know?"

"We also do not have any blood or urine, so it is a problem."

"What about the woman's breasts. Don't they change with pregnancy?"

She thought for a moment and then said, "As a matter of fact, yes they do. But the technique to see the ultra-structural alterations of breast tissue in pregnancy is extremely new. It was only published a few months ago. Problem is you need a special type of electron microscope to see the changes. Breasts are not usually examined in an ordinary autopsy since they almost never have any bearing on the cause of death. But, I think you might be on to something."

On to what?

"Nice call," she said enthusiastically. "That should have been examined in this case. We missed that. I'm going to call Detroit and get the pathologist to do a core biopsy. If either of these women were pregnant we should see some hormonal changes in the breast tissue."

I nodded my head in agreement, accepting her compliment as if being brilliant was something I did all the time. "When can we get the results?" I asked.

"I'll have them get the samples right now and they can messenger them to us. There is a 36 hour processing time before we can examine the tissue under the electron microscope. So we should have the results about 48 hours after the material gets here. Good thinking on your part. This discussion may not have been a total waste."

46

Cayman Islands

I DROVE back to Dulles airport and watched Kincaid board his flight to Atlanta. I then hightailed it to my gate and took my flight to Georgia in pursuit. The Atlanta airport is huge and I had to hustle over to another terminal pod, but I still made the flight to the Cayman Islands in plenty of time. Naturally, Kincaid was sitting in the first class section and never looked up from his magazine as I made my way to my aisle seat in economy. I stowed my small carry-on in the overhead bin and would be ready to make a hasty exit once we landed.

It was a three hour flight to the Caymans and Kincaid was not going anywhere, so, I just leaned back in my seat and thought about the 'Kosher Butcher.'

The murderer was a clever dude.

Way too clever.

There were some questions that continued to bother me.

Did Robert Kegleze actually exist?

Did the 'Kosher Butcher' actually exist.

Oh, there definitely was a serial killer, but I was becoming more and more convinced that he was not the 'White Supremacy' crazy everyone thought he was. I had the feeling that he was just an old fashioned scumbag murderer and his other three victims were thrown in to fool the cops. If I was right, he was doing a damn good job of it.

People intentionally kill other people all the time but very often it is not planned. Premeditation is the key difference between manslaughter and murder. A murderer plans the death of the people he wishes to eliminate. This guy was definitely a murderer, but there are many motives for murder. If the murderer is not an off-the-wall psychopath — and if you can figure out the motive — you catch your murderer. In over ninety percent of the cases it involves one of three things: Sex, money and/or ego. The cops handling any murder will concentrate their investigation on family members or one of the ten people that are closest to the victim — at work, at school, in the neighborhood. One of the ten closest. Because the odds are, one of them is the murderer.

In this case the cops had checked them all.

So far, not a lead.

I sat there with the contents of all the murder books running through my mind. I considered all I had learned by personally interviewing over forty of the people affiliated with the various victims and then compared that with the information the police had collected.

Muhammad Nassar was twenty-six years old when he was murdered. He had been unofficially engaged to be married to Aisha Sootan, of Chicago, also twenty-six years old, but the wedding plans were put on hold. There was no evidence that he was fooling around, cheating on her, or doing anything that would make her angry enough to do him in. IIe was a masters graduate of Northwestern University and doing a PhD in math at Wayne State University. He worked part-time as a computer tech and lived in a rented house in Dearborn with two other Muslim men. He was not active in any fringe or extremist Muslim organizations. All his classmates at school and friends from work said he was a real go-getter and all around nice guy. Although I had personally spoken with only a few of the people interviewed by the police, I got a sense of what all the people were saying. Good old Muhammad may not have been such a great fellow. Reading between the lines, it seemed that Mr. Nassar could be a pain in the ass if he did not get his way. People who are pains in the ass can make enemies. Apparently the cops were of the same opinion and had run down just about anyone who was in contact with him on a daily basis. Not a one was a likely suspect.

Rabbi Slater I knew backwards and forwards. If anyone was destined to get the title of a *tzadik* it was the rabbi. I could not find a thing to suggest that there was any hidden information or actions that would have led someone to murder him. It could only be a crazy or a clever person acting like a crazy.

Maria Sanchez was someone I felt I also knew personally, because Nealy would talk about her all the time. The young woman had been twenty-three when she was murdered. She worked as Nealy's secretary — i.e. administrative assistant — since she graduated from junior college three years ago. Everyone in her family and all her friends had a good word for Maria. She was just nice. The young lady had been single and there was no evidence of any romantic relationships in the near past. Her folks had emigrated to the U.S.A. from Mexico almost thirty years before and she was a natural born American citizen. Her hobbies were dance and theater and she was a member of a small drama workshop in Ferndale. She was supposed to have been the co-star of a production of 'Arsenic and Old Lace' that had to be cancelled when she disappeared. Maria lived with her folks and two brothers in the Northwest section of Detroit. She was easy to get along with and was the type of individual who settled arguments and did not start them. Definitely not a pain in the ass.

Vivian Nguyen Tan Sang was the only daughter of a Vietnamese couple. The mother had worked in the U.S. embassy in Saigon before it fell to the North Vietnamese. Her father had been a colonel in the South Vietnamese army. When South Vietnam collapsed they were given visas to the U.S.A. and happily moved to America. Nguyen was born at Hutzel Woman's Hospital forty-two years ago and breezed through grade school and high school. She got a full scholarship to attend the University of Michigan's School of Business. After she received her degree, she started working as an administrative assistant in the offices of the Oakland Mall, but soon worked her way up to be the administrative supervisor. She was petite, good looking, smart, athletic, and always out to please — AKA brown-noser. Her rise in the department was rather rapid and that could have lead to pissed off coworkers. She was a divorcee with two teenage sons and her aged parents lived with her. She was the breadwinner. Her ex-husband was now living in L.A. and had proof that he was nowhere near Detroit at the time of Vivian's abduction. No recent boyfriends or girlfriends that anyone knew about. Distinct possibility that she could have had enemies, but none had turned up.

The detectives had of course looked at the 'closest ten' for every victim to see if there was anyone with a grudge. There were a whole slew of little things. Like the guy who lived next door to Muhammad who was angry about how his Muslim neighbors stacked their garbage cans on collection day. Or how Nguyen never respected the white lines in the parking lot at work. Crazy stuff. But each one of the people with a gripe had an ironclad alibi for the time of the abduction of the person with whom they found fault. I had even checked the history of Nguyen's father to see if she could possibly be the victim of someone from Vietnam trying to make payback.

Nothing.

Sometimes the 'Sex, Money & Ego' triad had nothing to do with the victim and everything to do with the murderer. A killer may get it into his mind, wrongly or rightly, that the victim was responsible for their own 'Sex, Money & Ego' problems and seek revenge. The victim might not even know the someone who was out to get him or her. Dafna was looking into that angle with her database. She was also doing computer searches on anyone that had had serious contact with any of the victims. Fifty or sixty individuals for each one. Anyone with financial problems, romantic problems, psychiatric problems, disciplinary problems and whatever else she could conjure up, went into the database. In addition to all that, she took upon herself the tedious task of going back into the GPS history of the phones of every person in the database to see if they could have been near any of the victims at the time of their abduction, or near the drop-off spots when body parts were delivered. The faintest tinkle of a warning bell on her computer would put that person under further scrutiny. So far, all the bell ringers had good alibis for the abductions.

The FBI and the state police were also batting a big zero in their search for a racist crazy. They had interviewed thousands of people affiliated with skinhead and Nazi groups from the Midwest and the rest of the USA. The search had extended to people who had a past history of any kind of affiliation with these groups. So far, the check included everyone going back ten years and they were now extending the search to go back over two decades. Since the discovery of the van, there had been no further contact with the murderer and everyone was worried that the trail would grow even colder and possibly disappear. No one wanted the 'Kosher Butcher' to become another serial killer that was never apprehended.

D.C. and Lansing were getting impatient and because of the lack of any real progress they were cutting back on personnel. The state police and FBI task forces were now half the size they had been when we had initially found 'Kegleze.' Better use of manpower they said.

So where do we go from here?

Nowhere and very fast.

I was feeling frustrated. My own investigations had not accomplished a thing. Full gas with the gear shift in neutral.

I came to the realization that the key to the whole case was whether Robert Kegleze was a real person or whether he was the murderer in disguise. The only person who had ever seen him was Alice Sangford's father. I never met Mr. Sangford in the flesh and I decided that I needed to interview him myself. As soon as I got back from the Cayman Islands that would be the first thing on my agenda.

We landed at Georgetown airport and deplaned at nine in the evening. I left Kincaid at the airport waiting for a cab to get to the Marriott. I had a car and driver standing by and was able to get to the reception desk before Kincaid. My cell phone was to my ear and I was making appropriate responses to my mock conversation, when I saw him get a key to room 311. After passing the desk clerk a twenty, I got the key to room 312 just across the hall.

Next morning was scorching hot and drippy humid, and I was sure Kincaid did not have the slightest inkling he was being followed. I had no trouble spotting him enter the Scotia Bank on Cardinal Avenue in downtown Georgetown.

Bingo.

My job was done.

I sent an e-mail with the information to the lady's attorney and quickly received a reply, 'Nice work.'

There was no need for me to return to D.C. with Kincaid and I had two hours to kill until my flight to Miami and then continue on to Detroit. I had never been in the Cayman Islands, and although the place was famous for its snorkeling, there was not enough time for me to hit the beaches. So, I just walked around the markets and souvenir shops until it was time for my shuttle to the airport. There was lots of 'stuff' made out of old coconut husks or seashells that looked cute in the shops. I did not buy any of the useless junk, because I knew that Dafna's aesthetic eye would never allow any of this kitsch in her house.

My future wife was a discerning woman. After all she had chosen me. Nothing fake or cheap in her life. Nothing like the possibly fake Mr. Robert Kegleze.

I arrived at the Cayman Islands airport quite early and used the time to call Mr. Sangford and arrange a meeting for tomorrow.

My intuition told me that he would be the key to the investigation.

47

Ticket

THE RETURN flights were uneventful and my plane landed at Detroit Metropolitan Airport late Tuesday afternoon. I drove directly to Dafna's house because I wanted to get her input about my plans to see Sangford.

Shaindel intercepted me at the door, "No way. You are not coming in. You are getting married next Tuesday and during the week before the wedding the groom cannot see the bride."

I was ready for her.

"But, that's where you are wrong," I countered.

"Where am I wrong?" She asked holding the screen door firmly shut.

"We are getting married on *Lag B'Omer*. Which will begin only with nightfall next Tuesday. So according to Jewish law that makes it Wednesday. Therefore until nightfall this evening ... which is two hours from now ... I am still not officially in the week before the wedding. Let me in," I demanded.

She held the door open in defeat and commented, "When did you become such a *Talmudic* scholar?"

Dafna was in her work center along with Sergeant Chandler and Mary Lou. The three had become good friends and functioned well together. Mary Lou had volunteered to help Dafna by taking over the clerical work for her computer business. It definitely lightened the load for Dafna because the 'Disc Lady' was still very busy solving the myriad of problems in restoring damaged or sabotaged discs referred to her company. In addition to all this, the FBI and state police kept sending updates. Chandler assisted here by entering the new information into the huge 'Kosher Butcher' database. Dafna had once explained to me that the database itself was useless. You needed the unique program she had created with her Playstations and parallel processing to sort the data.

Do not ask me what that meant.

So far the database, the Playstations and the parallel processing had not turned up anything that could lead us to the murderer.

Dafna saw me enter her computer room and looked at me quizzically, "How did you get past my watchdog mother?"

"Pure charm."

Mary Lou sniggered, "Yeah, right."

Chandler just smiled.

"No really, Mom is a real stickler for all these customs."

"I'll tell you later," I said smugly.

Mary Lou stood and said, "Well, it looks like this is going to be your last evening together until your wedding. So, I think it would be a good idea that we leave the lovebirds on their own."

Dafna stuttered angrily, "We are not l ... l... love birds."

"I see what you mean," said Chandler, as she hit the log-out button and shut down the program. "I have got to get back anyway because my husband can't function as a single parent for more than short periods of time. He is about to reach his limit."

As soon as they left the basement, Dafna turned to me and said, "OK, spill the beans. Did you find the guy's bank?   And, of course, what did they tell you in Quantico?"

I told her how I had gotten the goods on Kincaid. All I had to do now was write up the report and wait to get paid. Case closed. I then relayed to her everything I learned from Dr. Fisher. About the 'Zip-Close' bag from Amazon and the testing of the breast tissue for pregnancy.

Dafna looked at me and asked, "What made you think of checking for pregnancy?"

I wanted her to think that I am one terrific sleuth, so I was reluctant to tell her that it had all come to me because of chopped liver.   Instead I said in mock modesty, "I am just brilliant."

Hey, if I could fool Dr. Fisher.

"OK, don't tell me."

What — she did not think I was brilliant?

"Now, wait one second ..."

"Did the FBI try to track down the Amazon orders for this bag?"

"You mean the 12,000 orders last year? 800 orders in Michigan? A bag that you can pick up in Lowe's or Wal-Mart? They checked over 60,000 orders for the past five years, but without some way of whittling down the pool, it is an impossible task."

She thought for a moment and said, "I have to agree with that. So what are you going to do?"

"Tomorrow I am going to talk with Mr. Sangford. According to the reports the cops interviewed him half a dozen times, but other than speaking with him on the phone, I never questioned him myself and I want to get every scrap of information about Kegleze. Maybe the police missed something. Somehow I feel that this is the key to the case."

"Sounds good to me. What time are we going?"

Where did the 'we' come from?

"But, you can't go," I said.

"Why not? We're still partners, aren't we?"

I knew that in one week's time we would become permanent partners, but that was not the point, "We are partners, but your mother has forbidden us to see each other until the wedding?"

"When did you become such a big defender of Jewish customs?"

"It's really important to your mother ... and she will kill me."

"So I think in our unique situation we will have to adapt that particular custom and for the next week the groom ... that means you ... will not be allowed to see his future mother-in-law ... that's my mother. Me ... you are going to see."

"I don't want to be around when your mother finds out that we have been gallivanting around during the forbidden week."

"She does not have to know. I have been stuck down here for the last two months searching for the murderer and I feel he is slipping away. The new stuff they send is down to a trickle. What time are we meeting him? Don't worry ... I'll sneak out of the house. I have to do something. "

I knew the feeling, "Ten o'clock."

"Pick me up at nine at the One Stop Kosher Market."

George Sangford showed us into his living room and after offering us something to drink said, "I don't know what more I can do for you. The police questioned me ... I don't know how many times ... about the sale of the van."

"We would appreciate it if you would go over it one more time for us. We want to know everything you can remember about Robert Kegleze."

George flipped his hands open indicating he was more than eager to cooperate, "Be glad to help. Shoot."

Dafna and I spent the next hour running him through the sale of the van. Where he advertised it, how many people called inquiring about the van, what questions they asked, how many came to see the vehicle, what was the asking price, where Kegleze kept his cash, what did his wallet look like, — A zillion little questions to try and get a better picture of the man that bought the van. We wanted to glean every recollection that Mr. Sangford had of the day he made his sale. I took notes but as we progressed I could not see any kind of breakthrough that would get us closer to finding the elusive Kegleze.

We thanked George for his cooperation and were heading for the door, when I asked one final question, "Did you, at any point, feel that this guy was crooked. That there was something not right about him?"

Sangford thought for a moment and said, "Now that you mention it, there was something. Not on the day of the sale, but two weeks later, I thought maybe there could be trouble."

Unexpected answer.

"What happened two weeks after the sale? Did you remember something he said?" I asked.

"No, like I said, it had nothing to do with the day I sold the van. This was two weeks later, after a traffic ticket came in the mail."

"What ticket," I asked.

Sangford answered, "For the van."

"The van you sold?" inquired Dafna.

"Yeah, that's what we're talking about."

"A ticket from when you still owned it?" she asked.

"No, a week after I sold it. The van was caught by a red light camera and they sent the ticket to me. I knew right away I had nothing to do with the violation because it happened one week after the sale and from a town upstate that I had never visited. That's where the van went through the light. I figured the son-of-a-gun did not register the vehicle like he was supposed to and when he got a ticket they sent it to me. I thought there might be trouble."

"Have you still got the ticket?" I inquired. "It would help us if we knew where the ticket was issued."

"I don't think so. After all, it had nothing to do with me," he said shaking his head.

"Maybe you can recall the town's name." I ventured.

Sangford racked his brain, but shook his head, "Nah, can't remember."

Dafna had been looking off in the distance in deep thought but now said to Sangford, "You do realize that the ticket should have told you that he was bad news."

"Why? I had the bill of sale to prove I did not own the car anymore. So it was not me who went through the light."

She said seriously, "It has nothing to do with paying the ticket. The problem is, how did the authorities know to send you the ticket? If you took the plates off the van, how did they know you had once owned the vehicle? It had to be that the guy was driving with fake plates showing your registration."

I missed that completely. *Do I have a brilliant fiancée, or what?*

Sangford just got it, "You're right. I never put two and two together. I should have realized. I'm sorry," he said with remorse.

The guy looked as if the weight and responsibility for the four murders had just shifted onto his shoulders. Poor guy.

"You are in no way responsible for what this guy did," I told George. "When you sold your van he had already killed the four people. Even if you reported that this guy was driving around with fake plates it would not have made one bit of a difference."

"I suppose so. Still it was pretty dumb of me not to have figured that out," said Sangford.

Not so dumb, George. I had not realized it until Dafna brought it up. Still I said, "Don't feel bad. You are not trained in police work as we are. That is why we come around and ask questions."

"Well, I hope this has helped you in some way," he said.

We stood again and thanked him and then said our goodbyes. When we were in the car Dafna turned to me and said thoughtfully, "Very strange about the ticket."

Uh Oh. She was going to rub it in that I had not seen the problem about the ticket getting sent to Sangford. I am going to head this off at the pass. "I immediately noticed that bit about how the ticket got to George. I was waiting to see if you did not miss it."

She looked at me quizzically, "Miss what?"

"You were going to mention that I had not brought up the problem of how the ticket got to Sangford."

"No, that's not it," she said with a shake of her head. "My question is why did we not know about the ticket until just now?"

"Maybe the cops and the FBI are not as adept as we are and did not ask the right questions."

"That's obvious, but why didn't the ticket show up when they pulled up all the DMV records for the van? We know everything else about the vehicle. A ticket should have been front and center."

With Dafna's absolute photographic memory, if she says it was not in the records then it had to be correct. So, where had this ticket been hiding?

48

Good News

EVEN THOUGH I was no longer a full time student, I tried to make it to morning *minyan* at the *yeshiva* whenever I could. I could pray at any of the other community synagogues, but at the *yeshiva* no one was in a hurry to get to work. There was a sense of devotion in the air. As if the Almighty had stopped by to observe the services. In addition, it felt good keeping up my connection with the institution. It also allowed me to update Rabbi Kalmonowitz with any new developments in the case. Unfortunately, over the last few weeks this had become a quick affair of him looking at me across the study hall and raising his brow asking if there was some progress. I would shake my head ever so slightly and he would nod in understanding.

Things had been very slow. Nothing really new to report.

This morning he gave me a different signal and indicated with a motion of his head that he wanted to see me in his office. I quickly put away my *tallis* and *tefillin* to join him in his cramped little study. He was just hanging his frock coat on a hanger and suspending it from the peg that jutted out of the bookcase behind him. He added his large black hat to the peg and took a seat behind his cluttered desk. Remarkably, one of the chairs in front of the desk was clear of their usual stack of books and I sat down facing him.

"So, Reb Shimon, how are the plans for the wedding progressing? It is now less than a week away."

"I suppose fine. You know how it is. The women make all the decisions, so I am really in the dark."

"You should learn from this," he said with a knowing nod. "In a Jewish family it is the women who usually make all the decisions. We men must learn to keep up the charade that we have some say it what happens."

"I'll keep that in mind."

"Have you and Dafna found out anything new about who killed Rabbi Slater?

"Right now there is very little information coming in from the state police and the FBI. Even my investigation has not turned up anything that could lead to a possible suspect. Dafna is still putting everything she can into her computer search."

"It is hard for me to believe that you have not made more progress. When you informed me that you and Dafna wanted to marry, it was the same day that I asked you to look for Reb Yechezkel. I was certain that you would solve the mystery before your wedding. But here you are marrying Dafna in a few more days and the murderer still runs free. Are you sure there is no new information?" he inquired.

How did he know that I had something?

"Well, there is one thing."

"What did you find?" he asked.

"Yesterday, I went with Dafna to re-interview the man who sold the van to Robert Kcgleze — or whoever he is."

"This was yesterday?"

Obviously *Rebbi* had made the calculation that I had been with Dafna during the week that we were not supposed to be seeing each other. "Yes, yesterday," I said sheepishly.

"Very good," he said with a knowing smile. "And what did you discover?"

I told him about the red light ticket the week after Kegleze had possession of the van.

"That is very good news," he said enthusiastically.

I could not see what there was to get excited about. We did not know where the ticket was issued or the exact date and time of the violation. Even if we had this information, it would not lead us to the identity of Kegleze or where he was hiding now. "It's just a violation caught on a traffic camera. It is unlikely that it is going to solve the case."

"Of course not. But that is not the point. What is important is that the murderer made a mistake. He was driving a vehicle that he wanted to keep hidden from the authorities. He should have been super careful. And yet he made a mistake and went through a red light. On top of that, he does not even know that you are aware of this ticket."

"Why wouldn't he know?"

Rebbi looked at me in surprise, "Please, *Reb* Shimon. After almost two years in the *bais medrash?* Don't you see?"

I had to look at this like a *Talmud* problem. Why would the murderer not know about the violation? Then it hit me. Because it had not been issued to him. He was caught by a hidden camera and the actual written citation went to Sangford. That was why the murderer was unaware of the ticket.

I nodded my head in understanding, "I see, but how does this help us?"

"If he made one mistake ... then he has probably made others. I am confident that you and Dafna will uncover those mistakes and then use them to find this *rahsha*. Yes, very confidant. I am very hopeful that when you are married next week we will really have something to celebrate."

"Amen, *Rebbi,* amen."

As soon as I got home I called Dafna. Shaindel was reluctant to put her on the phone and only when I told her that it was urgent did she relent.

"And how is my *chassan* holding up," she said cheerfully as she picked up the phone.

How did she know that with each passing day I was becoming more and more apprehensive about the wedding? I was not worried about being married to Dafna. I was certain that that would be wonderful. I was just concerned about the possible screw-ups that might occur at the wedding. I had my nice Catholic administrative assistant making all the arrangements, I had a family that did not have a clue about how an ultra-Orthodox Jewish wedding was conducted, and then there was the groom who had a basic lack of knowledge concerning the intricacies of Jewish nuptials. It could be a fiasco. "I'm holding up fine, if being a nervous wreck is considered normal."

"Are you getting cold feet?"

"Not on your life. My feet are hot to trot. If you want, I will come over there right now and we can have Rabbi Kalmonowitz do a quickie service and then we elope."

"We wouldn't elope, we would have to go into the witness protection plan. My mother would kill us."

"You're probably right and I think Mary Lou would pitch in to help."

"Of course she would," she said menacingly. "So, tell me. Why the call? What was so urgent? I still have not found the traffic ticket for the van. I will text you the moment I get a break."

"I just got back from the *yeshiva* and I saw *Rebbi.*"

"You see him every day."

"Today, he wanted to speak with me."

"He asked to speak with you?"

"Yup."

"That's different, what did he say ... exactly?"

I took it for granted that Dafna wanted a verbatim report of whatever he said. She thought Rabbi Kalmonowitz was a portal of divinely inspired information. It was our job to figure out the hidden messages. Although I was not convinced it was so, I could not prove it was not true. I had to admit that his words had proven — helpful — in the past.

I related to her everything *Rebbi* had said to me. She made me go over it twice more and then re-checked specific words he had used.

"What do you think it means?" I asked.

"You keep saying that you don't believe that *Rebbi's* words are prophetic."

"I never said that I don't believe. Let's just say I am a little more skeptical than you are."

"Then why did you think it was so important to call me right away?'

She caught me.

More than once I had missed the little hints that *Rebbi* had fed us. Very often it was only Dafna who could see the inner meaning of Rabbi Kalmonowitz's remarks. I wanted her input. I did not trust myself.

I wanted it to be something I could take to the bank.

"I just thought you might be interested."

"Yeah, sure. I have a feeling you believe as well."

"So, what do you make of it?"

Dafna was silent for a moment and then said, "First of all he thinks the murderer made more than one mistake."

"If he did, they were little tiny mistakes. None of them can help us find him."

"I'll get to that," she said interrupting me. "Secondly, he thinks we can find these mistakes and that they will allow us to discover his identity."

"Wishful thinking."

"He also thinks we can do this before our wedding next week."

"In five days? We have been searching for over two months. Why will we be able to do it now?"

"Just hold on. And finally, he thinks we have to do this together."

"That won't happen. We are not supposed to be seeing each other."

"I am sure *Rebbi* knew that when he said what he said. But his words were '... you and Dafna ...'. No, we definitely have to do this together."

I knew when I was defeated. "The wrath of Shaindel is about to descend upon me and she is going to kill me dead."

"I suppose she will try, but she will have to get through me first. It is the bride's prerogative to murder the groom. Not the mother-in-law's."

"You're kidding right?"

"Do I sound like I am kidding?"

No, she did not.

"So, what are we supposed to do?"

"First of all, come over here. We have work to do and we can't do it over the phone."

"Your mother won't let me in the house."

"Let me worry about my mother. You'll be safe."

I was not so sure, but I went anyway.

<u>49</u>

Mistakes

WHEN MRS. KALIN opened the door she was not her usual affable self and said brusquely, "Your *kallah* is in the basement."

I could feel her angry stare on my back as I went down the steps.

Dafna was at her work station with her fingers flying over the keys. As I entered she looked up and said, "Hi, did you make it past Mom safely?"

"I did, but if looks could kill."

"We would both be dead."

"How did you convince her to relent?"

"I told her that Rabbi Kalmonowitz said it was all right."

"*Rebbi* never said that," I protested.

"Just a little creative interpretation.   Anyway, it worked."

"What do we do now?"

"First we work on the mistakes. As I see it, there are six. One - Rabbi Slater's glasses left at the scene. Two - the stolen cars with the switched plates. Three - the white van and discovering Kegleze ... or whoever he is.

Four - the ticket. Five - the defrosting of the frozen bodies. Six - the butcher bags ordered from Amazon."

"There was only one butcher bag ordered on Amazon."

"One is good enough."

"How do the glasses, the stolen cars or the van help us? They don't lead us anywhere? He abandoned the cars and the van and no one has seen Kegleze."

"I'm not sure how they will help either, because the FBI and state police have worked those angles every which way ... and no luck. So let's stick with the other three," she said.

"Any results with the ticket."

"Just before you arrived I discovered the reason for us not knowing about the ticket. If a violation is issued to a non-resident in a small municipality, they send out a ticket to the person listed on the registration. If they get no response they can send out another notification or file with the Attorney General's office to recognize the violation. If the AG certifies the ticket, it gets passed on to the Secretary of State's office and they notify the DMV not to allow the annual registration of the vehicle until the ticket is paid and the violation is cleared. The process takes about three or four months to get a ticket into the system, so that is why we did not know about it."

"Can you find out where the ticket was issued?"

"I am working on it. I already instigated a search of the Attorney General's data bank to see if a ticket for the van came through."

I did not need to ask if she had permission to look at this information. Little legalities like that never bothered my fiancée. I hoped that Jarron and Crowley would remember to put in a good word if and when she got caught. Dafna claimed that no one could spot her little excursions into other people's data and so far she has been correct. Let's hope her luck holds out.

The screen on her monitor was constantly changing but after five minutes it became still, "Bingo. We got it," she exclaimed.

"Where and when?"

"Municipality of Caro, Michigan, in Tuscola County on March 9th at 22:31. That's 10:31 in the evening."

"What happened on March 9th?"

With her memory she would know immediately.

"That was the night the hands were delivered."

"Where exactly was the ticket issued? Where in the city?"

Dafna checked the monitor and said, "Route 24, red light camera at corner of Cleaver Road and Elmford Drive. Near the Wal-Mart."

"How do you know it is near a Wal-Mart? Have you ever been to Caro?"

"Never, but it shows up on Google maps," she said pointing to the monitor.

A map of the city was on the screen. She is amazing.

"Which way was the van going?"

"South."

I thought for a moment and then said, "Because of the timing, we have to assume that he had the hands in the truck when he went through the red light, so that would mean he was coming from his little hidey-hole, wherever that might be. The place must be north of Caro."

"That fits with mistake number five, that the bodies defrosted. There was that big line malfunction in Caro."

"Let's be careful now. It could be, as you said, that the plug came out of the wall, here in Southfield."

"Yeah, but we now know he got a ticket in Caro so the connection with the electric line failure is looking good."

"OK, I'll buy that. But you said the power went out for over one hundred thousand people. We still have no way of narrowing it down."

Dafna thought for a moment and then began hitting her keyboard, "Maybe we do."

Her mind worked like no other.

"What are you looking for?" I asked.

"You said that your friend at the medical examiner's office told you ... "

"Timmy Tech."

"Yeah, Timmy Tech. He said that he figures if the freezers were closed it would take four days for the bodies to thaw."

"He said at least three days or more," I said, not fully understanding what she was getting at. "How does that help us?"

"Well, the problem they had at Caro was a truck that took out a DTE Power line tower. It took over 24 hours to put in a replacement. Most of that area did not have electricity for 36 hours."

"So what?"

"Don't you see?"

I had no idea what to her was so obvious, "I'm afraid I don't."

She looked at me patronizingly and said slowly, "Most of the people did not have power for 36 hours."

I was getting irritated, "You said that already."

"That also means that most people's power was restored at about 36 hours."

"Yes, that's what it usually means," I said stating the obvious. "So what?"

"It also means that the murderer was not among most of the people. Because if he was, his freezer would not have been on the fritz long enough for the bodies to defrost. He had to be in one of the pockets of customers that had a longer power outage."

She was right.

It had to be somewhere that did not get back on the power grid at 36 hours.

"How can we find the pockets of customers who did not have power for a longer time? It's hard to imagine that the power company lists which lines they fixed each day."

Dafna was way ahead of me and she was fingering new instructions into her computer. "First of all, there probably is such a list but it would be difficult to get and harder to interpret."

"Why do I think that you have a 'second of all'?"

"Because there is another way to find these pockets of customers."

"How?"

"By usage of electricity. If the line was dead those customers would not have been using electricity. I am looking at their electricity usage."

"Their electric bills?"

"Not their bills. That would be a monthly charge. I am looking at their DTE Power company daily electric usage. I am checking in the counties that the line served ... Tuscola, Huron, and Sanilac."

I just had a thought, "I think I can make your job easier."

"How?"

"You don't have to look in Sanilac county."

"Why not?"

"Because he got the ticket on route 24. If he was in Sanilac, he would not be coming through Caro to get to the Detroit area. He would have used route 25 along the lake or 53 going south. So stick with the area north of Caro."

"Good point. That does help."

Even though Dafna's super computers could sift the information rapidly, it still took quite a bit of time to enter the complicated databases of the electric company without being detected. After about four hours, a map appeared on the monitor with clusters of homes and municipalities. Beside each cluster was a number that said how many customers were in the group and how many hours power was out until service had been restored. She played with the image a bit and only the clusters that had been without power for more than 72 hours remained on the screen. There were about four thousand customers distributed in the various clusters.

When she was satisfied with the image she said, "That's the best I can do."

"You think the murderer is in one of those homes?"

"I don't know, but we don't have anything better to go on."

I knew what she had not mentioned, so I added it, "And *Rebbi* said."

"Yeah, and *Rebbi* said," she agreed.

"OK, now let's look at the last mistake. The butcher bag from Amazon. Were there any bags ordered from any of these homes?"

"If I remember correctly, there were over 800 orders for Michigan over the past year. With another thousand or so if you included Indiana, Ohio, and Ontario. Let's see how many for this area of the Thumb." Dafna hit some keys and I could see the Amazon logo appear and disappear from the screen. She had obviously entered into the ultra-secure customer database for the enormous company. *Just shows you that ultra-secure is not really ultra-secure.* For Dafna, that meant it took just a little longer.

Finally, a long list of names appeared on the screen. "My results show there were one hundred and seventy people in the Thumb that ordered Amazon butcher bags during the year before the first delivery of body parts. Unfortunately, the stuff could have been ordered two years ago or even the year before that. But let's take a look at the six months before the murders."

She hit a few keys and said, "Sixty-two orders. Now let's see if any of the orders were from one of the houses that were without power for the extended period of time."

The computer made a short whirling sound and then went silent. Dafna turned from the screen and said, "Nada. Nothing. Not one order from any of these houses."

"Well, we tried," I said without much conviction.

"I thought we had something," she said sadly.

"Sometimes the perpetrator gets lucky and we don't. You don't always solve every case."

"But, *Rebbi* said," she said disappointedly.

"Even if *Rebbi* said."

"He said we would find the murderer before our wedding."

"No. what he said was that he was very hopeful that we would be able to find the 'Kosher Butcher.' Looks like his confidence was a bit exaggerated. So let's just put the whole thing out of our minds until after the wedding and try to be happy."

Dafna was silent for a moment and then said, "Yeah, let's just try to be happy. Do you know why our wedding is being held on *Lag B'Omer*."

"Well, sort of. The *omer* is the seven week period from Passover to *Shavuot* (Pentecost) and during this period, two thousand years ago, twenty-four thousand students of Rabbi Akiva died of disease. So, because there were so many deaths in that short span of time it became a tradition not to schedule happy celebrations or weddings during the *omer*. The exception is on *Lag B'Omer*, the 33rd day, because that was the day the students stopped dying."

"That's right," she said. "The sages say that the reason the students died was because they did not respect each other. Murder is just about the greatest disrespect there is. I want to catch this guy."

"So do I," I agreed. "I thought we had something for a moment."

"Do you know how they celebrate *Lag B'Omer* in Israel?"

"You mean they do it differently in the Holy Land?"

"Oh, yeah. On the night of the holiday they have big bonfires and all the kids have homemade bows and they shoot arrows into the flames."

"Why do they do that?"

"I have no idea, but if I had one of those bows and arrows I would try to find this guy and shoot him dead. I want to be happy on my wedding day and nothing would make me happier than to see this guy behind bars ... or worse."

I knew the feeling. I also wanted to catch him. Very badly. For a moment I felt we were on the verge of discovering something that would lead to his identity.

Once again nothing.

Wait one second.

What did she just say.

Bows and arrows.

When did the Jewish people go in for hunting?

They did not.

But other people do.

"How many orders for the Thumb for the last six months?"

"Sixty-two," she answered immediately.

"But there were one hundred and seventy for the year ..." I said waiting for an answer.

Dafna got my reasoning, "Why didn't we see half of the orders in six months. We only had sixty-two."

"And the answer is?"

"I don't know," she said shaking her head.

"Because of hunting season. Dr. Fisher at the FBI told me the 50 pack butcher bags ... the one with the little stickum thing on the 50th bag ... was popular with hunters who ordered it through Amazon. Deer hunting season starts in the fall."

"I didn't go back far enough."

"Right. Do it again."

Dafna got back to the computer and searched the earlier orders. Within a few seconds a single name and address came up on the screen:

Francois Gillet, West Kinde Road, Caseville, Michigan, 48445. The bags had been purchased with a debit card made out to F. Gillet, on August 19th the year before.

We had a solid lead.

<u>50</u>

Caseville

"WHO THE HELL, is Francois Gillet?" I exclaimed loudly.

Dafna was busy with her keyboard and said, "Give me a moment."

After about five minutes, she pointed to the screen and said, "The debit card was issued to Francois Gillet by the Valley Bank of Helena, in Helena, Montana. Property records show a home on Hummingbird Court, in Helena belonging to a Mr. Gillet and that is the address listed on his bank account. He is still registered to vote and as of his payment last month he has all his state and city taxes up to date. According to his Blue Cross record he is a 79 year old Vietnam War veteran. He graduated from Helena High School and served in the Green Berets and has two Purple Hearts and a Bronze Star. He has a badly injured leg from a war wound but still was the owner-mechanic of his own garage in Helena. His wife passed away 18 years ago and he is now listed as retired and living alone in Helena."

"You got all that in five minutes?" I asked in amazement.

"If I had some more time I could have gotten more, but I figured you wanted the basics right away."

Amazing.

"If he lives in Montana, why does he have a house in Caseville? Does he live here part time?"

"One sec," she said hitting the keys.

Screens came up and disappeared until the monitor showed a carefully ruled form with a colored map and the Caseville city logo at the top of the page. She pointed to the screen and said, "The property is a house and the twelve surrounding acres along the Pigeon River, about one mile west of Caseville. It was purchased in cash from the previous owner six years ago. There is no outstanding mortgage and the place is held by Mr. Gillet free and clear. All taxes are up to date and were paid with that same debit card that ordered the bags from Amazon."

At age 79 he was too old to be Kegleze, but the bum leg and Green Beret training fit for the serial killer. I could feel — it was more than a hunch — that this guy was crucial to the whole case. We had to get in contact with him. "Do you have a phone number for Francois Gillet?"

"Yes ...," began Dafna. She quickly changed her tone and said, "Never mind. You don't need the phone number."

"Are you kidding? Of course we do," I said emphatically. "We have to speak with this guy. Maybe he can lead us to Kegleze."

"Could be. But it won't do you much good."

"Why not?"

"Because Mr. Gillet died last year in St. Peter's Health Hospital in Helena. Here is a copy of his discharge summary," she said hitting the print button.

"He was not exactly discharged from the hospital."

"I would say that dying is the ultimate discharge," she said handing me the printout.

I looked at the paper and turned to Dafna, "Then who has been using his debit card to pay his taxes in Montana?"

"Somebody that did not want to report his death."

"Why do you say that?"

"Because he is still listed as a registered voter and someone paid the taxes on the house in Caseville just last month."

Strange.

If he was dead, why did the authorities not know about it? Perhaps someone did not want his will to go through probate. Inheritance problems? Who knew?

"The person with the debit card is the murderer," I declared confidently.

"Maybe yes and maybe no," countered Dafna.

"Of course he is. Just look how everything leads to him. The van got the ticket in Caro on the first night body parts were delivered. The house is in the area where there was a power outage. And, his was the only place without power that ordered those bags from Amazon," I argued loudly.

"You are not thinking logically."

"What do you mean? I just showed you how it has to be him."

"Calm down," she said waving a prone palm in front of my face to cool my enthusiasm. "I did not say that the guy who is walking around with Mr. Gillet's debit card is not the 'Kosher Butcher,' but you have to accept the fact that it may not be him. You and I both know that the bodies could have defrosted for all sorts of reasons and had nothing to do with the power line being knocked out. There were also another thousand or so people in the rest of the state that ordered these bags from Amazon. We found this guy through a bunch of what-if assumptions. If one of the assumptions is wrong, then he is not the one."

"But *Rebbi* said ..."

"Ah ... that's it. *Rebbi* said. I can just see how quickly a Michigan jury will be convinced by what *Rebbi* said."

I thought for a moment. "We need evidence."

"Of course we do."

"Problem is we can't let this guy know we are on to him. We have got to get into his house. Both of them," I said.

"What do you mean, 'both of them'? There is only one house up in Caseville."

"The murderer has got to have another home near Detroit."

"Why do you say that?" she asked.

"Do you remember how we deduced that the guy had to live in the Warren area when we were searching for the van?"

"Yeah, because he made his drop-off points as far as possible from where he lives."

"Exactly. But I always had difficulty with that."

"Why? That makes sense."

"Well, besides there being over a million people in that area, there was just no place in the Warren area that a murderer could have gutted and chain sawed his victims. There are just too many people around. Even if there was a meat packing plant, it would have been a nightmare to try to hide the bodies."

"It is a nightmare."

"And he did this four times," I said making a point. "No, it makes more sense that he did the butchering somewhere out in the boonies like Caseville, but has another home near here. He probably transferred the packages down here at his leisure and went from there to make the deliveries whenever he wanted."

"Except for the first one," said Dafna.

"Why not the first one?"

"Because he came from Caro with the first one. We have the red light ticket to prove it. We got lucky because he delivered the first package way down river in Wyandotte."

"Yeah, you are right," I realized.

"But I think you are correct. He must have another home here."

"This guy is smart."

"Or lucky."

"Or both," I agreed. "But if he gets an inkling that we know about his place in Caseville, he is going to disappear."

"What are we going to do?"

"I'm going to call Jarron and try to convince him to approach a judge to get a search warrant for the house in Caseville."

I called the lieutenant and laid out all we had. The ticket, the power outage, and the Amazon bags. His initial response was, "You have got to be kidding. It looks like you pulled this guy's name out of a hat. And you want me to ask a judge for a search warrant based on this?"

"Yeah, I do," I said sincerely. "It's true that we made a lot of assumptions, but that is what detective work is all about. I can only investigate the leads that I get because there is nothing else. And my gut tells me this is the place."

The policeman thought for a moment and said, "We haven't got anything else in the fire. Why not? The judge is going to think that I am crazy but I'll give it try."

"Should I call Nealy and Crowley to let them know what's going on?"

"Not on your life. It's bad enough I am going to make a fool of myself with the judge. I don't want them to know about it. If by some miracle the judge grants the warrant we'll fill them in. I'll call you back."

Twenty minutes later I closed my phone and turned to Dafna, "Jarron was shot down. The judge says there is not enough evidence to issue the warrant. The cops will start running Gillet through the system to see if anything comes up, but no warrant for now."

"I told you so. You can hardly blame the judge ... even Jarron was not convinced."

"At least he tried," I said despondently.

"So now what?"

"The judge wants something that ties Gillet's house with the 'Kosher Butcher.'"

"Like what?"

"Like someone seeing the van at the house. Or maybe spotting someone that looks like Kegleze in the area."

"Yeah, right. No problem," she said sarcastically.

"I'm not giving up. I'm sweet on this."

"What does that mean? You're sweet on this?"

"It means I feel that this house is the place. It makes sense."

"Only if all the assumptions we made are correct."

"I know they are."

"Based on what?" she asked.

"*Rebbi* said we would find his mistakes and discover his identity. This is where the mistakes lead."

"Back to *Rebbi* again. You have become more of a believer than me. We've been through this before. What are we going to do?"

"I'm going to get the proof we need so that the judge will issue the warrant."

"How are you going to do that?"

"Tomorrow is Friday ... a short work day because of *Shabbos*. I have to do it tonight. If I don't go right now, I won't be able to leave until Saturday night. So, I'm going to Caseville tonight."

"You mean, *we're* going to Caseville," she insisted.

"You are staying here. It could be dangerous," I said adamantly.

"Hold on there, buddy. You are forgetting something."

"What?"

"You know as well as me that this could all be a wild goose chase. So, what convinced you to go to Caseville?" she asked rhetorically. "What's the reason?"

"You know the reason. *Rebbi* said so."

"He also said that *we* ... you and I ... are going to find the murderer. I'm coming along."

"What about your mother? She is going to have a conniption fit."

"Let me worry about that," she said dismissingly. "When will you pick me up?"

I looked at my watch and could hardly believe it was already five o'clock in the afternoon. We had spent over eight hours together looking for the murderer and it had seemed like mere moments. I loved being with this woman. I truly did.

"Travel time is going to be about three hours so it will be well after nightfall when we get there. Wear dark clothes. I'll pick you up at seven."

"Good. I'll need at least an hour to calm down my mother. I'll make a thermos of coffee and on the way we'll stop and pick up some doughnuts."

"Doughnuts? You never eat store bought doughnuts."

"I know, but detectives on a stakeout need doughnuts. It's a law or something."

"We are not going on a stakeout. But, if you want, get doughnuts for yourself. For me ... if your mother is still talking to you ... bring me some of her strudel."

51

Bloody Nail

WAZE TOLD me that I-75 north through Saginaw was fifteen minutes faster than Highway 24 because of roadwork. But I took the slower option anyway, because I wanted to see the red light camera in Caro that gave the van the ticket.

I saw that the apparatus was set up to catch violators coming into town from the north and I made a mental note to get a copy of the picture from the Caro Police Department that showed the vehicle going through the light. We might need it to prove the connection between the house in Caseville and the white van.

A little after 10 p.m. we made it to Caseville — a lovely hamlet on the shore of Lake Huron on the west side of the thumb — and stopped at the Marathon station to fill the gas tank. Most of the businesses were already closed and it looked like the town was the kind of place that rolled up the sidewalks at the stroke of midnight. Very likely nothing would be open when we wanted to leave. We got some snacks, used the restrooms, and then headed out towards Mr. Gillet's house.

The whole municipality was ten blocks north to south and three wide. We drove east from the lake out of town and as soon as we left the last home we hit flat Michigan farm land.

As I drove down West Kinde Road, I said, "I wish I could have seen this area two hundred years ago."

"What for? There was no one here."

"That's exactly it. This was all pristine forest. As far as the eye could see."

Dafna looked around at the absolutely flat land with only the occasional glint of a light in a distant farmhouse. "Forest here? What happened to the trees?"

"The timber barons happened to the trees. They came in and cut down every tree, log, and matchstick they could lay an axe to and then shipped it all to the east and Europe."

"The good old entrepreneurial system at its finest."

"The rape of Michigan."

"And Ohio, and Indiana, and Illinois. Need I go on?"

It only took a couple of minutes to reach the GPS coordinates for Gillet's place. It was just east of the bridge that crossed the meandering Pigeon River. The house could not be seen from our position because it was situated in a heavy stand of trees that ran along the river. A dirt trail branched off north from the paved road into the trees on this side. I stopped the car to reconnoiter. The land was flat and West Kinde Road was straight as an arrow. That meant there was a clear line of sight right to the horizon in both directions. The nearest farm was about one half mile away. We could not drive up the dirt track without revealing our approach to anyone in the house and we could not park the car on the road without someone stopping to investigate.

"We have a problem," I said to Dafna.

"What's the problem? Let's just drive up and take a look at the house."

"We can't do that," I said looking for her to understand.

Dafna thought for a minute and said, "I see what you mean. Where can we leave the car without it being spotted?"

"We have only one choice. We go back to town and park the car at one of the bars. That's about the only place it won't be noticed."

"How do we get back here?"

"We walk. It's just about a mile."

As we walked back from town I explained to Dafna what we could and could not do once we got to the house. "First of all, getting caught is not an option. We cannot let anyone see us."

"Why not?"

"Because we do not have a warrant to search the premises."

"Aren't we allowed to ask him questions?"

"Sure, but that tips our hand. Since we cannot arrest him, if he gets suspicious he will just disappear. Also, even if we find anything we cannot take it as evidence."

"What? If we find something incriminating we have to leave it there?"

"Exactly, because a judge could rule that the evidence was obtained illegally and the guy may walk."

"The constitutional protection against search and seizure. The Bill of Rights."

How did she know that? Never mind. She just knows things.

"Yeah, exactly," I said.

"But isn't evidence suppressed only if it's the cops that obtained it illegally?" she asked.

"In theory, you are correct. But his lawyer could argue, that since we have been working with the cops, any evidence we might find could also be considered inadmissible. So we can't leave any traces that we were there. Because if this is the guy, and he does go to court, his lawyer will have a good basis to have the whole case thrown out."

"OK, I get it. Don't get caught and don't let anyone know we were here."

"Precisely."

Twenty-five minutes later we were back at the dirt track on West Kinde Road. According to Google maps, the narrow access road was about a quarter of a mile long and ended in a clearing. At that point there should be a few structures on a small bluff above the river. I felt we would be OK to walk down the road because the track curved through the property and at the first hint of a vehicle's headlights we would have enough warning to hide among the trees. It took five minutes to reach the clearing and it looked like no one was home. The whole place was dark but there was a full moon and I could make out a small wood frame house with a garage — a necessity for the Michigan winters — and two wooden sheds behind the house. One large, one small. We stayed close to the trees and circled the clearing. I could see that the garage door was up and had room for at least two cars. Right now there were no vehicles at all.

I whispered to Dafna, "The garage is open so it looks like whoever lives here stepped out for a bit. I don't know how much time we have so keep a sharp lookout."

"Are you going to search the house?"

"If we have time, yes. But most likely if the butchering of the victims was done here, he did it near the sheds. We will start there. But first, put these on."

I helped her don latex gloves and then we set out.

Staying in the high weeds near the trees, we got up close to the door of the larger shed. It had rained two nights before and the earth in front of the shed was soft. I could see that we would be leaving footprints but there was little I could do about that. The door to the shed was old but sturdy and there was a new steel hasp with a large Yale lock securing the entrance.

"Can you pick the lock?" she asked quietly.

"I know all the super duper detectives in the mystery books can pick just about any lock in about four seconds. But this baby has double faced pins. Can't be picked without really special equipment."

"So how do we get in?"

"This is upstate Michigan. Most people don't even lock their front doors. Come with me."

We went to the side of the shed and tried the first window. Sure enough it slid up easily and I glanced inside. The shed appeared to be one large square space and there was a sturdy table just under the sill. I moved aside some of the items on the surface — memorizing their position so I could put them back when we left. After hoisting myself up, I clambered through the window onto the table and slid off to stand on the floor. Then I offered Dafna a hand so that she could get in.

"Stand here and keep a lookout. If you see car lights approaching we have to get out of here and pronto."

There was an odd smell to the shed that I could not quite identify. I hit the flashlight button on my cell phone and directed the beam around the shed.

I almost dropped the phone.

The whole place was built for processing game. There was a heavy wide butchering table in the center and a large meat hook hung from the ceiling. Along the sides were four huge chest freezers and three more tables. The one near the door held rolls of butcher paper and a stack of Zip-Close plastic bags. Just like the ones the murderer used.

This could simply be the place to which all the guys in the area brought their game during hunting season, but I got the feeling that the carving up of the victims had been done in this room. I now recognized the elusive odor I had smelled before. It was old dried blood. I saw traces all over the floors and tables.

I apprehensively opened the first chest freezer and peered inside.

The cooler was crammed with plastic wrapped packages of all sizes. Each was sealed and carefully marked as venison, telling the cut of meat and date the animal was shot and processed.

"Did you find anything?" asked Dafna.

"Just deer meat."

One down three to go.

Freezer number two had more of the venison packages.

I opened the third freezer and saw that this was different. It was not as crowded and there were oddly shaped plastic wrapped packages inside four large plastic sacks — like the kind used for bagging fallen leaves. I opened one of the big bags to extract a rounded package and juggled it around. Suddenly I realized that a pair of human eyes were staring back at me.

Oh my God.

The package slipped from my hand and fell back into the freezer with a thud, as I exclaimed, "Holy shit. We got him."

"Got who?" asked Dafna coming towards me from the window. "What did you find?"

"Stay where you are," I commanded. "You don't want to see this."

"What did you find?"

"There are more body parts in here."

"So Mr. Gillet is the murderer," she said with satisfaction.

"Not Gillet. He's dead. The guy that lives here."

"What do we do now?"

"I want to take some pictures and get a hold of Jarron."

I heard Dafna exclaim, "Oh my God."

"What's the matter?" I asked worriedly.

"I'm sorry. I was not paying attention. There is a car coming up the road."

I turned off my light and watched as a vehicle pulled into the garage.

This was the guy.

All I could see were headlights, and so I could not identify the driver and had no idea what type of vehicle he was driving.

We did not have much time. The guy would spot our footprints and come to investigate.

"Quick, out the window and get into the trees," I said pushing her towards the window.

She scampered up onto the table and out the window and was soon hidden in the undergrowth of the trees. I hopped onto the table and quickly began to slide head first out the widow. There was a sudden intense stabbing pain in my right side. I felt with my hand and discovered that there was a large metal spike jutting out of the window frame and it had ripped a gash in my side. What was worse was that the head of the nail was still stuck in my flesh and was hung up on my pelvic bone. I was suspended in the air hanging upside down impaled on the nail. Although I could just touch the ground with my hand, I could not move and did not have enough leverage to free myself. The pain was excruciating and I wanted to scream out but miraculously I kept silent. There were footsteps approaching the shed. I tried to reach for my pistol at the small of my back but was unsuccessful. Without help I knew I was not going to get away. Once the person entered the shed he would see my legs through the open window.

I blew it.

The guy would probably kill me and then escape.

A silent prayer for help went through my mind.

I could hear the man fidgeting with the lock and hasp.

Suddenly I felt hands pushing me upwards.

Dafna had returned for me. I had no idea how she sensed I was in trouble. Intuitively she knew where the problem was and reached under my body with her hand. She bent over under me and then straightened up so that all my weight was now on her back. Once I got some of my bulk off the nail she was able to jerk my body off the spike. I tumbled forward right on top of her, making quite a bit of noise. Luckily my fall occurred at the same moment that the shed's old door swung open. The scraping of the door on the floor boards and the loud screeching of the hinges hid the sounds of my fall.

We huddled silently just under the shed's window with my one hand over Dafna's mouth and the other covering the bleeding wound in my side. We heard someone walking around the room opening and closing the freezers. I sensed him just above us at the open window and I held my breath. Luckily the table kept him away from the window so he could not look directly down, because if he did he would surely have seen us. He closed the window and left the shed. The door was locked and he walked back to the house and went inside.

I waited with Dafna at the side of the shed for a good five minutes. When my pulse had returned to normal, I signaled silently to head into the trees. Once we were hidden from the house we made our way as quietly as possible to the road.

When we hit the paved road, Dafna turned to me and asked, "Now, what do we do?"

"First we call, Jarron. He has to get moving on this."

She pointed to the blood seeping through my fingers, "First we take care of that hole in your side."

Dafna was in her tough girl mode. No meltdown in sight. Way to go!

Meanwhile, my side hurt like the dickens, but I was fairly certain that nothing vital had been injured. Still if I kept losing blood, I could be in serious trouble, "You are worried about me. Isn't that sweet?"

"I'm not worried about you. It's the hole in your sweatshirt. You're missing a whole piece of it. Clothes are expensive. If you don't know how to take care of your clothes maybe I should just find another *chassan*."

I looked down and said seriously, "Oh crap, no."

"I was only making a joke. Don't take me seriously."

"No, it's not that. There is a good chance that a piece of my sweatshirt, soaked in my blood, is hanging from that big nail on the wall of the shed."

"I suppose there is."

"Don't you see? That means his lawyer may be able to prove illegal entry and could possibly get him off scot-free. I might have blown the whole case against this guy."

"But he did it. We can prove it."

"No we can't. Not if the prosecution can't use the evidence in the shed."

"So what are we going to do?"

"Call Jarron. I'll worry about the rest later."

<u>52</u>

Stitches

AS WE began our walk back to town I called the lieutenant and he answered on the third ring, "This better be good Lincoln. I just fell asleep."

"We found him."

"Who did you find?"

"Me and Dafna took a little trip to Caseville and guess what this guy has in the shed behind his house?"

"Stop playing games. What did you find?" he asked anxiously.

"He has a meat processing plant in the shed and body parts in the freezer. This is the guy. Just like I said."

"It could be just 100% pure beef in the freezer. How can you be sure?"

"I saw a human head."

His exact words were, "Holy shit."

"That's just what I said."

"You were right. Do you also do fortune telling?"

I do not, but maybe Rebbi does.

"Only as a hobby."

"Where are you guys right now?" he asked.

"We are on the road walking back to town?"

"Where is your car?"

"It's in town ... you'll understand once you get here."

"OK, so who is he? We know it can't be Gillet because he is dead. Is it anyone we know?"

"Can't say, because I never got to see him. We were still in the shed behind the house when he got back home and got real busy bugging out of the place. I don't even know what kind of car he is driving now. Sorry."

"Can you stay hidden near the house and watch to see if he leaves the property?"

"I would like to do that but I have this hole in my side and I have to get some medical care."

"Are you injured?"

"Walking wounded, but I need to get it treated, so I can't stick around."

"Absolutely, I'll get a hold of the local cops and see if they can help. You go to the hospital."

"Jarron, one more thing."

"What's that?"

"I got this wound diving out of the window. There could be a piece of me and my sweatshirt, hanging from a nail on that shed."

He thought for a minute and then said, "We'll take care of it."

"How?"

"I don't know. But we will."

"How are you going to convince a judge this time?"

"I now have a witness that saw what looks like a suspicious meat processing facility on the property."

"But you can't tell him that I went in."

"Of course not. You saw everything through the window. He'll buy it. And if he does not ... then I will wake up every judge in the state until I get my warrant."

He said he would call Crowley and arrange things with the FBI. As soon as he knew when they would make the raid on the property he would call me back.

I terminated the connection and turned to Dafna as we walked, "Did you hear?"

"I heard enough from your side of the conversation," she said. "Jarron is going in. Good."

"Yeah ... I can't believe it. After so long."

"You did it. You caught the murderer," she said with pride.

"First of all, no one has been caught yet. And secondly, *we* caught the murderer. Me and my partner."

"Partner for life, and don't you forget it. We make it official in a few days," she emphasized.

My wound hurt but at least the bleeding had slowed to a trickle. Once we got to town we picked up my car and then I stopped a passing vehicle to ask about where I could get medical aid. At first, the driver was frightened by all the blood on my clothes but then told me that there was a small hospital in Pigeon, Michigan, about eight miles south of Caseville.

The young doctor in the E.R. saw all the blood on the back of Dafna's jacket and wanted to treat her first, but she insisted that she was fine and that I was the one who needed attention. He said my wound was not deep but there was a six inch jagged skin tear. The medic injected local anesthesia and went to work. I am no expert, but the young doc demonstrated an obvious lack of experience with the needle and thread. I have seen burlap sacks with a better stitching job. Sixteen stitches, two antibiotic pills, and one tetanus shot later, we checked out of the hospital and drove back to Caseville to wait for the good guys to show up.

I tried calling Nealy to let him know that we might be very close to catching Maria's killer, but once again I was shunted to his service, which would beep him. I told them to tell him there was no rush. I knew there was nothing he could do until after the cops made the raid.

When we got back to Caseville, Crowley called to say the FBI and the troopers were on the way. He added, "Nice work. Where are you just now?"

"We're on Main Street in Caseville at the Boathouse Bar & Grill."

"Tossing back a few beers are we? It's a little early for that. Wait until we catch the bastard."

"It's a little too early for anything. The place is closed. Everything in town is closed. We're sitting in the parking lot waiting for you guys. When will you be here?"

"The state police woke up a judge in Bad Axe and he is issuing the search warrant as we speak. The state and county police will meet us in Caseville at 5:30 a.m. I want you to be there to fill us in with whatever you know. We will move out to the house as soon as everyone is on sight."

"Can we come along when you go in?" I asked tentatively.

"Negative to that. If everything is as you say, the real cops have to make the bust. We will call you once the place is secure."

I had not expected any other answer. If the case ever went to court, having civilians along on a search or arrest could become a legal nightmare, especially if one of us got hurt or we hurt someone. We would just have to wait.

With the coming of dawn, Chuck's Coffee Shop opened for business. We sat drinking coffee and munching on some stale packaged cookies ... they were the only items with a kosher certification. A little after eight in the morning we got the call that we could come out to the house.

The road leading up to the clearing was now swarming with police and FBI vehicles. The crime scene people had roped off the entire area. Technicians in hazmat suits were going over every inch of the place with a fine-toothed comb. A Huron County sheriff's deputy barred the way and would not let us on the scene until he got clearance from Crowley. Then we were told to walk only on the designated paths so as not to contaminate the area. Someone had set up a small folding table with a few stools and Agent Crowley was sitting there filling out paperwork. A government operation is judged by the amount of its paperwork.

As soon as he saw us he motioned to two other chairs, "Have a seat. You guys deserve it."

"Where is Lieutenant Jarron?" asked Dafna.

"He is inside supervising the whole circus. Jarron called us in just like he was supposed to. But the son of a gun knew that the FBI had no way of getting teams in here for at least another six hours. Since time was of the essence, we had to let the state boys do the job. Sneaky guy."

"Just like you," I said.

"Maybe."

"No maybe about it."

"It's going to take at least half a day just to bag and tag everything on the property and then we have to wait for the county coroner to come and give us his clearance. We even found a chain saw in the other shed with suspicious material lodged in the teeth. Won't be until late afternoon when we can start moving stuff to the lab."

"Did you get him?" I asked expectantly.

"Nope. There was no one here. Garage was empty."

The guy must have seen my blood and sweatshirt on the nail and was able to get away.

"Crap. I messed up," I said dejectedly.

"Why so sad. Is it because of some nail on the window?"

"You know about that?"

"Yeah, Jarron told me."

"Yeah, because of that. I could kill myself."

"Don't go killing anyone just yet. This guy has done enough of that already. Anyway, Jarron said they checked carefully for that nail. Looked high and low for something with blood and a piece of a sweatshirt. They found nothing."

I could not believe my ears. *How could they not have found it?*

Crowley then reached into his pocket and surreptitiously slid a small opaque plastic bag across the table towards me, "A little present from Jarron."

I covered the bag with my palm and when no one was looking, peeked inside the little sack. Within was a large nail covered in blood and torn piece of a navy blue sweatshirt.

I could understand why Jarron made the nail disappear. He was — shall we say — a creative policeman. But Special Agent Crowley? The agent in charge of the FBI's office in Detroit, Mr. Go-By-The-Book, follow all the rules and procedures, never take short cuts — how could he go along with this? Then I realized that this murderer had been Jarron's and Crowley's personal nemesis for over two months. They wanted him very badly. Apparently, for the first time in his life, Mr. FBI found a reason to bend the rules a little. Now that there was no nail, there was not even the slightest possibility of claiming illegal search and seizure and all the evidence would be valid.

I'll buy that.

"I am so glad to hear there was no nail," said Dafna in an understanding tone.

"So am I," said Crowley.

Dafna asked eagerly, "The guy was obviously not Francois Gillet because he passed away in Montana last year. So who was this man?"

"We made a quick check of the entire property but amazingly there is absolutely nothing in the house or shed that says who he is. Not an envelope, not a bill. Nothing. But he left all sorts of trace evidence and tons of fingerprints so we will eventually be able to tie him to this house and the bodies."

"I guess we have to wait to see if his prints are in the system."

"I didn't say that," said the FBI agent.

What was he not telling us?

"Do you already know who he is?" I asked.

"The local cops never heard of anyone called Francois Gillet and did not know that the place was listed under his name on the county records. When Jarron contacted the locals and told them that the state police were preparing the raid this morning, they thought that Gillet must be some sort of tenant to the guy that they thought owned the place. So without telling us, they called the fellow they knew as the owner and asked if he ever heard about some person named Gillet. They even told him that the police were nosing around looking for the guy. That's why he disappeared. It had nothing to do with the nail."

"Why would the cops do that? It does not make sense," said Dafna.

"Because they knew that the guy who owns this house is also a cop. This little piece of property is known by the locals as *Nealy's place.*"

"Our Lieutenant Nealy?" asked Dafna incredulously.

"One and the same," said the FBI man.

I was flummoxed.

Nealy was the 'Kosher Butcher.'

How could that be? What could be his motive? I suddenly realized that I almost contacted him to tell him about the raid.

He had fooled us from the get-go.

I felt like killing the bastard.

53

Truck Scales

IT WAS a little past ten when we left the house and the lab techs were still buzzing around like a swarm of bees. Someone had obviously leaked the story and there were now numerous TV trucks parked along West Kinde Road. Nealy's identity had as yet not been released to the press, but the newscasters were telling the world what they knew or guessed about the raid and its connection with the 'Kosher Butcher.'

Nealy was nowhere to be found and no one knew where he could be.

Dafna and I were heading back to Detroit because there was nothing for us to do in Caseville and when they lit the candles this evening it would be the Sabbath before our wedding. Big deal for an ultra-Orthodox Jewish couple.

The trip home was going to take two and a half hours and both of us had not slept a wink. I turned to Dafna, "It's really important that you talk to me while I am driving so that I don't get drowsy."

"No problem, you can rely on me," she said enthusiastically.

Ten minutes later, Dafna's head sort of lolled over against the side window and she fell fast asleep.

She meant well.

I also could have used forty winks but we did not have any time to spare, so I just concentrated on the road and drove.

When we reached Pontiac on I-75 and my head was nodding from fatigue, my cell phone rang. I did not recognize the number and hit the speaker, "Hello?" I said questioningly.

"Hello, is this Mr. Lincoln."

Who calls me 'Mr. Lincoln?'

"Yeah, this is Sy Lincoln."

"This is Lieutenant Jarron from the state police."

What the heck? *Why was he calling me on a different phone? And what was with the 'Mr.?'*

I answered warily, "How can I help you, Lieutenant?"

"The state police would like to check something with you."

'The state police' — that meant his bosses and not him. "So this is an official call?"

"Absolutely," he said seriously.

I understood. The call was being recorded for the state police *uppity-ups*. Someone was covering their behind about something. I answered directly, "Shoot. I am all ears."

"The state police will be issuing a statement that Lieutenant Nealy is suspected of being the serial killer. They will be stating that he had nothing to do with the 'Kosher Butcher' investigation. Since you and *Mrs. Lackler* were involved as well, the state police want to be certain that you saw things the same way."

I get it. They wanted us to forget that the brass in the state police had insisted that Dafna and I pass on every bit of information we collected through Nealy. We were also to ignore the fact that he had intimate knowledge of the entire investigation all along. That could be very embarrassing. So, the state police were going to cover up the whole thing and they wanted my cooperation.

"Let me get this straight. The state police want us to say that the entire investigation was conducted without Nealy knowing anything about it."

"Absolutely correct. And the state police would appreciate your help in this matter."

Reading between the lines, if I cooperated and did not spill the beans, I would receive a 'Get-Out-Of-Jail-Free' card from the state police. They would owe me one. That could be very helpful for a private investigator in the state of Michigan. It was very tempting.

Considering the fact that if not for a fluke, I would have been the one who tipped off Nealy, I really could not be hypocritical about them having been fooled. He hoodwinked me as well.

"Yeah, I agree with the state police's statement. My whole team will say that you guys caught Nealy because of your superb police work and that you were able to keep him isolated from the investigation."

"I was sure you would see it that way. The state police thanks you. We'll be in contact," he said and broke the connection.

I figured the last bit meant he would call back and explain what that was all about.

Time to wake Dafna. My fiancée was still fast asleep and I had to loudly call out her name a few times.

She woke and looked around at the passing scenery trying to figure out where she was, then turned to me, "Are we home yet?"

"Another half hour."

"I'm sorry I fell asleep, but I'm not like you. I need at least a few hours of sleep."

"I know. I woke you because I thought you would like to know about an interesting call that I just got."

I then related the gist of the phone conversation with Jarron.

"Why did you agree? The state police are the ones who messed up."

"Because they really could not be blamed. Yeah, procedure says that Nealy should not have been allowed access to any part of the case, but he fooled me as well. When we first met, I may not have liked the guy but that was because I thought he was obnoxious, and not because I suspected him of being the killer. The state police are going to be eating plenty of humble pie from the state administration and there is no use slinging any more mud on them. Besides, this means the state police will owe me one."

"OK, I am cool with that," she agreed. "But you still haven't explained why you woke me up. I was having this terrific dream about how we were married already."

"Sorry about that. I figure Jarron is gonna call back soon to explain what's happening. I thought you would like to hear what he has to say. Until he calls, maybe you want to tell me what you were dreaming about."

"You really want to know?"

"I sure do."

"Dream for yourself," she said with a knowing smile.

Five minutes later my phone rang again, only this time it was Jarron's throwaway phone. I hit the speaker button and heard him say, "Lincoln, just wanted to let you know about that last call."

"Sounds interesting. Just so you know, Dafna is here with me."

"I figured she would be. Good afternoon, Mrs. *Lackler*."

"Good afternoon to you too, Lieutenant."

"So, what happened?" I asked.

"This went all the way up to the colonel. She is so pissed and everyone is walking on eggshells. When it all comes out, the whole force will look like a bunch of idiots. Inspector Richards got reamed out really good for letting Nealy be the go-between between you guys and us. It's bad enough that a state police lieutenant is a murderer, but if the media ever found out about his involvement in the case the force would never live it down."

"What about you? I know that you did not want Nealy in the investigation, but shit rolls downhill. You were in charge."

"Actually, I'm going to come out of this OK. Seems I had the foresight of writing an official memo to my boss telling him that I objected to having Nealy around."

"I get it. You told them that you will follow their orders, but you think they are wrong. Smart move."

"Not so smart. Just lucky. It's not a very good idea to tell your commanding officer that you think he is wrong. Could have backfired on me."

"I have been there myself. Have you released his name yet?"

"Just about to. All morning the brass kept on insisting that we could not name Nealy as the murderer because none of us made a positive ID of him at the Caseville house."

"But the locals all thought that a cop named Nealy was the owner of the Caseville property."

"I think the colonel was hoping for a miracle and maybe we would find it was some other cop with the name Nealy."

"That's crazy," said Dafna. "Another cop named Nealy being the serial killer? No way."

"So what convinced them?" I asked.

"I sent some men to search the house he's renting in Warren."

"He lives in Warren?" asked Dafna.

"Yeah, just like you said. Don't say 'I told you so,'" warned Jarron.

"Never said a word," I replied smugly.

"Anyway, we found more body parts in his basement freezer. So, they had no choice."

"Are you still in Caseville?" I asked.

"I'll be here until late tonight. Meanwhile, I have men looking at everything in his file. Maybe it will tell us where he could be hiding."

"I wanted to ask you, how was it that he had such a great alibi for the abductions. Your own men said that they saw him at work."

"At the specific times that the victims were grabbed he had been the SDO for Southeast Michigan, but he had not been at the Ten Mile Station."

"I don't speak state police lingo. What's an SDO," asked Dafna.

"Senior Duty Officer. So he was taking calls at the station, at home, or wherever he happened to be. He also traveled around the district as needed. The people who alibied him simply said that they had been working those evenings and that they had been in contact with him."

"So they never really saw him. That's bad police work," I commented.

"Don't rub it in. When we checked with them today they admitted that they could not verify exactly where Nealy was when he spoke with them.

"What about the fact that when I did a GPS trace on his cell phone, it showed he was nowhere near the victims?" Dafna asked.

"A few years ago Nealy told his superiors that he was often in areas with poor cell phone reception so they also allowed him to use a beeper. When he was on duty, SOP for contacting him was to try his cell and if he did not respond immediately, to beep him. He would call back on a landline shortly after."

Dafna nodded her head in understanding, "So that meant he could easily have left his cell phone at home, and then abduct the victims or move the body parts and the GPS trace would show that he never left his house."

"Exactly."

"So when he was SDO for the night ... was he wandering around with dead bodies in his car?" she inquired.

"Looks that way," he said

"Holy crap. What a sicko," I said in disgust.

"Definitely," agreed Jarron.

"I have another question," I said. "If he had Gillet's debit card and basically had his identity, why did he create Kegleze to buy the van?"

"We still can't be certain that there is no Kegleze, but it looks like you are right and the guy is purely Nealy's invention. Crowley thinks he made up Kegleze. He wore the disguise and developed a limp just to buy the van. That way, when the time was right, he could dump the van without leaving any connection with himself."

"Have you figured out Nealy's relationship with Gillet?"

"Do you know about Nealy's wife, Lynne?"

"Yeah, he told me she threw him out. He was always talking how she was just about to come back to him. Boy, was he off-base. She hates him. Hell, she was the smart one. She dumped him last year."

"Yeah, I guess she was. Anyway, did you know she comes from Montana?"

"Are you kidding me? Is she related to Gillet?"

"His only kid. She told us that Nealy had been handling her father's finances for years."

"So she was Lynne Gillet before she married," I stated. I pronounced the name like the razor company, Gillette.

"Yeah," answered Jarron. "But the name is French and the correct pronounciation is like 'Jelly' with a long 'ay' sound at the end."

"Jell ... ay," I said.

"But, she said that back in Montana no body could get it right. Everyone used a hard 'G' and her name always came out so it sounded like 'Gill-it.'

"Did you ask her why her dad is still listed on the voting rolls even though he passed away?" asked Dafna.

"Her divorce lawyer advised her to hold off on settling her father's estate until after she is totally separated from Nealy. Hopefully, that way all the assets in Montana won't be considered communal property," said Jarron.

"But, how come she never mentioned the house in Caseville when she was interviewed?" I wanted to know.

"Two reasons," he said. "Firstly, no one asked her. Nealy was not a suspect. Secondly, when we asked her today, she said she doesn't know anything about a house in Caseville. Whenever Nealy would go up north he always said he was going to some cabin he was renting."

"So, how did he get the old man to buy a house here in Michigan?"

"We don't think he did."

"But the place is registered to Gillet."

"You had no way of knowing this, but about six years ago the state police ran an internal investigation on Nealy."

"I never saw anything about it in the file."

"You wouldn't. It was a 'need-to-know' type of thing."

"What was the charge?"

"No charge, just a suspicion. Someone was leaking the 'Truck-Scale' schedule to a couple of the shipping companies."

"What's a 'Truck-Scale' schedule?" asked Dafna.

I turned to her and said, "It means that if trucking companies know which truck scales are going to be open on a particular day, they could re-route their overweight trucks around the scales."

"Exactly. We're talking six to seven figure corruption," said the lieutenant.

"That's a lot of overweight trucks," commented Dafna.

"Yup."

"So what happened with the investigation?" I asked.

"Nealy looked guilty, but we had no evidence. The brass dropped the investigation because we could never find any proof that he had received any money from the trucking companies."

"No money trail equals no conviction," I said.

Jarron added, "It looks like we just found the money."

"That explains why he did not report Gillet's death to the authorities," said Dafna.

"Why?"

"Since Nealy is separated from his wife ... if Mr. Gillet is officially dead, there is no way that his wife ... who is Gillet's daughter ... would not inherit the house," she said knowingly. "After all, it was still in her father's name. Even if she never knew about the house she would still get it. Nealy would lose it all."

"He would lose all the payoff money he received from the trucking companies," said Jarron.

"Has anyone figured out why he killed all those people?" I asked. "I never thought he was a racist."

"Nealy was certainly not a card carrying liberal, but he was no racist," declared the cop. "So, guess what? Your suspicions were correct once again."

"We suspected everyone and everything," I said. "Which particular suspicions are you talking now?"

"Dr. Fisher from Quantico called Crowley an hour ago."

"You're kidding me. The breast samples?" I asked eagerly.

"Yup, the electron microscope analysis of the breast tissue from the two women indicates that Maria Sanchez was about four months pregnant when she was killed."

"Nealy must have been boffing her and she got knocked up," I explained.

"A very interesting turn of phrase," said Dafna sarcastically.

Jarron added, "We figure she must have confronted him and he went nuts. He was always talking about getting back with his wife. If Maria spilled the beans it would ruin his chances for reconciliation."

"The guy was delusional," I said.

"And he did not want to lose the property in Caseville," added Dafna.

"So I have to admit that you were right all along," said the cop. "There was only one target and the rest were camouflage."

"What a sick bastard."

54

Off Limits

WE PULLED up to Dafna's house. I turned towards her and said, "I want to thank you."

"For what? I slept the whole way back and you had to drive all by yourself. You must be dead tired."

"Not for that."

"Then what?" she inquired.

"For insisting on coming with me up to Caseville. Because of you they are going to catch the murderer."

"I didn't do anything. You were the one who figured out Nealy's mistakes and I just processed them through the computer. And when we were at the house, you did all the searching. I was just along for the ride."

"You forgot one little item."

"What did I forget?"

"The little matter of the nail in my side."

"It was not serious. Only a few stitches."

"Yeah, but I was stuck on that nail, hanging upside down. If you didn't come back to help, Nealy would have seen me dangling out that window."

"So what if he saw you. It would only have meant that he knew we were on to him a little earlier. He disappeared anyway."

"That was never the problem."

"So what was?"

"I was stuck upside down ... I could not reach my weapon ... Nealy had already killed four people ..."

Suddenly Dafna understood, "He would have killed you. Oh my God. I didn't realize."

"Yeah, and you saved me. If you had not been there ..."

"Look, I told you once before that no one gets to murder you but me."

"I look forward to that."

Dafna smiled contentedly for a moment and I was worried that maybe some air was leaking out of her balloon, when she looked at me and said, "If *Rebbi* had not said that we both had to go to find the murderer ... "

"Yup, no wedding in four days. So, thank you. You saved my life, Mrs. Soon-to-be Dafna Lincoln."

Dafna smiled in satisfaction and said, "No problem, that's what soon-to-be brides do for their soon-to-be grooms."

Dafna was fine.

"Speaking of brides and grooms, what are the chances that your mother will relent and give us a short reprieve so that I can see you tonight?"

"The chances are zero. Once I go into the house, I suspect it will become off limits to you. She thinks it brings bad luck. But there is a strong possibility that I will want to take a walk around the block this evening. If you just by chance happen to be on the street at that time I suppose I would have to say hello to you ... just to be polite."

"At what time were you thinking of being polite?"

"What do you say to about ten o'clock?"

"I'll be there ... just to be polite."

Before we went into Dafna's house we stashed our blood stained jackets in the rear seat of my car and I replaced my torn and stained shirt with the new T-shirt I had purchased in Caseville. Then we arranged the rest of our clothes to hide any residual blood stains.

The wrath of Shaindel — remember?

Dafna walked right in and to my great surprise, Mrs. Kalin let me in as well. However it was not because she had relented on the 'one week rule,' it was just that she wanted to begin her harangue without making a spectacle for all the neighbors to see.

She had seen the police press conference on her TV and although our names were never mentioned she immediately knew that Dafna and I must have been up to our necks in the raid. Not only had we violated the 'one week no peek' rule for the bride and groom, we had put ourselves in danger once again.

The words — crazy — nuts — *meshugah* — were repeated every few sentences. She was quite angry for about fifteen minutes until she noticed the blood that had soaked through my bandage onto my new T-shirt and saw the crimson stains on Dafna's shoes. Then she went ballistic.

Dafna kept on insisting that we were fine and my wound was just a scratch, but it still took almost another twenty minutes until Shaindel calmed down to the level of just being angry. When Dafna mentioned that we had not had anything real to eat for almost twenty-four hours, she finally ended her scolding. She even agreed to allow me to dine with them. Her exact words were, "You are already here. And where are you going to get any food so late on a Friday?"

The meal was a slightly strained affair, but, however awkward the situation it did not prevent me from enjoying the fluffiest most succulent mushroom and onion omelets I had ever tasted. Yes, I said omelets. Plural. I could not help myself. Those were followed by rich creamy chocolate brownies and a latte. A delight.

The way to a man's heart and all that.

Once the meal was finished I went back to my condo to change my bandage and clean up for the arrival of the Sabbath. I also called Mary Lou and Sergeant Chandler to fill them in. They deserved it and I had a request to make of them. Nealy had already instigated a few acts of mayhem towards us — he sabotaged the brakes of my now defunct SUV, had Eugene attack us and then had him killed in the Oakland County jail, and had also sent the goons who broke into Dafna's house. Even though he was in hiding he could still be after us and I did not want to take any chances. I figured I could take care of myself but I wanted someone to watch over Dafna and her family.

Before we discovered that Nealy was the murderer I had been looking over my shoulder, now I was looking over both shoulders and behind every tree.

Dafna's family might be in jeopardy.

It took awhile but I was finally able to explain to Mrs. Kalin about the possible danger to the Lachler family. Reluctantly, she agreed that I could take my meals with them, but under no circumstances would it be appropriate for the groom to sleep in the same house as the bride. So about one half hour before the lighting of the candles — the act that signifies the arrival of the Sabbath — I was waiting outside the Lachler home for Mary Lou and Andy Evans to arrive. I hardly recognized Mary Lou because she was dressed — normally. A simple matching cream colored skirt and blouse and flat black shoes. Her hair was an ordinary light brown. Andy's flannel shirt and corduroy pants had been left in the closet and he wore a white shirt, striped tie, and a plain gray suit. Mary Lou and Andy were going to be the week-end house guests of Dafna and her family. They would experience a *Shabbos* for the first time and Mary Lou — along with 'Baby' — would watch over the house.

<u>55</u>

Aufruf

THIS WAS my *aufruf Shabbos* — where I, the prospective groom, was called up to the *Torah* in the synagogue.

The *aufruf* came off without a hitch. It was great. There were even short periods of time during the Sabbath that I was able to forget that someone might be trying to kill us.

I had been fairly sure that Nealy would not try to get at us right in the middle of the *bais medrash,* but I did not take any chances. So, I took basic precautions and carried my snub nose wherever I went. As soon as I arrived in the synagogue I slipped my pistol into my pew. It was still close at hand if I needed it and the only time I left my seat was when I was called to the *Torah.*

Which was still a risky move, because in Orthodox circles, when the groom finishes his *aliya* he comes under fire. Not from bullets — from bags of candy — the kids scamper about joyfully collecting the swag. Lest you think the groom comes out of this unscathed, I know one groom who had his new gold watch shattered by flying sweets and more than one groom got a nougat in the eyeball. I survived my candy fusillade virtually unharmed because I had been wearing my black fedora. One package of bonbons blew my hat right off my head. I figure that little sucker had been traveling at a velocity and force that would have sent a bare headed man to the hospital with a concussion.

Mary Lou was somewhere in the woman's section. I suspect she came equipped with a hunting sling shot.

She is big on ethnic rituals.

All during the Sabbath, the festive meals were stupendous. Even Mary Lou, a voracious eater, could not stuff in another bite.

Late in the afternoon a FedEx truck pulled up to the house to deliver a small flat box for Dafna, and the driver required a signature. Mary Lou signed for her and opened the package to find an envelope inside. She read the enclosed letter and looked up at me with a grim expression.

"What is it?" asked Dafna.

"We'll get the bastard," said Mary Lou threateningly, passing the letter to Dafna.

If Mary Lou was using cuss words, she was plenty ticked off.

I looked over Dafna's shoulder and read the letter. It was an enlarged photocopy of our wedding invitation. On it was written in red Magic Marker, "You ruined my marriage — I will ruin yours."

Mary Lou called Jarron and a state police car came to collect the letter so they could examine it in the crime lab. I could not see how it could aid them in finding Nealy.

At first we all were wondering how he had gotten one of our invitations, but later on Jarron called Mary lou and told her that the photographic specialists found that it had been taken from the Facebook page Shaindel had set up for the wedding. Chandler called after the Sabbath to tell us that the Southfield police would be patrolling the area around Dafna's house until Nealy was caught.

Nothing we could do but wait. The search for Nealy was in the hands of the FBI and state police. But in truth — we were all in the hands of God.

The manhunt was on. Nealy's picture was being shown on all the TV news shows.

Sunday morning one of the local stations offered a reward for any information that would lead to the arrest of the 'Kosher Butcher.' Every ten minutes another concerned citizen would call the hotline with a 'definite' sighting of the murderer.

None of them were Nealy. He was still invisible.

I spent the whole day helping Shaindel move stuff into her new apartment. My cousin Steve had done a fantastic job.

Monday morning Fox News scooped the other networks with information about the state police's internal investigation of Nealy's 'truck-scale' corruption. The tagline for the story was that the 'Kosher Butcher' was known to be a criminal years ago, but the Michigan State Police did nothing about it.' I am sure Jarron and his colonel loved that.

The FBI kept a low profile but I knew from Crowley that they had imported a whole bunch of agents to help search for Nealy.

We were all getting ready for our wedding. It was a madhouse of last minute crises, but Mary Lou's experienced hand dealt with them quickly. I hate to think of the pandemonium we would have had if it was Shaindel who had to deal with these problems. I was busy finishing the last reports for the clients whose cases could not be kept on hold for the next fortnight. If anything urgent came up Mary Lou would handle it.

Early Tuesday morning — my wedding day — I got a call from Sergeant Chandler. She and Mary Lou had been tag-teaming the security of the Lachler home. One of them was there at all times. Chandler — who had spent the night watching over Dafna's family — said that Mary Lou had just called saying that she was stuck on the road with a flat tire and no spare. Andy was on the way to help and she figured she would be only a few minutes late. Chandler had to be at the Southfield police station at eight o'clock and asked me to fill in until Mary Lou arrived. I immediately agreed and went over to Dafna's house.

I had just turned off the ignition when Shaindel came charging out to intercept me, "Where do you think you are going? You are not coming in here. Maybe I was just a big softy about you not seeing Dafna for the week before the wedding, but this is your wedding day and you will not be seeing your bride until the *chupah* tonight."

"But I have to ..." I began.

"Whatever you need to do you will do it over the phone," she insisted.

"Someone has to watch the house until Mary Lou gets here," I argued.

"Then you can watch from the car, but you are not coming into the house."

"What about breakfast?" I asked hopefully.

"What about it? You are supposed to be fasting today," said Mrs. Kalin chastisingly.

Ouch, I forgot all about that. A Jewish couple's wedding day is like a minor version of *Yom Kippur* — the holiest day of the Jewish calendar — and the bride and groom were expected to fast until after the wedding ceremony. Luckily, because of Chandler's call, I had not followed my usual morning routine of making an after *minyan* bagel shop stop to get my usual half-dozen. If I had, I would have already polished off at least three or four.

"I forgot," I said sheepishly,

"Well, unforget. This is your wedding day. Find someplace else to be," she said shooing me away from the door.

"I need to protect Dafna."

"I know that. But Mary Lou will be here any minute, so you can wait in your car," said Mrs. Kalin.

Five minutes later Mary Lou pulled up. She walked over to my car and asked, "Have they found Nealy?"

"Not yet, and I can't think of anything we can do to help. It's all in the hands of the FBI and state police."

"Boss, did you ever think that maybe the state police are not really giving it their all?"

"Like, maybe they want to protect one of their own?"

"Yeah, like that. It has been known to happen," she said.

"I think Jarron is the real thing. He wants to get that bastard almost as bad as I do."

"I hope you're right. And stop cussing. I will watch your bride for you. Go get dressed or whatever a Jewish groom does on the day of his wedding."

Shragai Halperin, my *bais medrash* study partner for the past two years, was with me for the rest of the day. My first stop was the men's *mikvah.* An Orthodox Jewish man is expected to enter his marriage in a state of purity and I was supposed to immerse myself in the waters of the ritualarium. Usually it is the women who use the ritualarium. Married women cannot be intimate with their husbands during their monthly menstrual cycle and must go to the *mikvah* before they can return to their husband. People in the know assured me that these little bouts of abstinence and return, make for many mini honeymoons and increase the bond between husband and wife.

An interesting way of looking at it. I hope they were correct.

The actual dip was not that bad. The water was warm and the place was clean and bright. Did I mention you do it in the nude? It was a little strange to be skinny dipping in the oversized bathtub but it was for less than twenty seconds, so I was in and out in a flash.

I got dressed and checked my phone and saw that Dafna had called while I was in for my dunking. I called her back, "Hi Mrs. Lachler ... but not for much longer."

"Yup, not much longer."

"You called. What's up?"

"Crowley just got off the line. Someone spotted Nealy in a Battle Creek mini mall. Security cam at the entrance confers. The state police have road blocks around the city. Looks like they may be about to catch him."

"I'll believe that when he is in jail."

"You got him. I'm proud of you," she said with admiration.

"We both got him."

Dafna thought for a moment and then said, "Yeah, we really did."

"See you tonight."

"Are we seeing each other tonight?" she asked coyly.

"Either you or somebody else, it really does not matter," I said jokingly.

"You try that buster and you are dead."

<u>56</u>

Nuptials

So HOW was my wedding?

I guess it was terrific.

My memory is a bit foggy.

I must explain why I say 'my wedding' and not 'our wedding.'

Guests and family at an ultra-Orthodox Jewish wedding are under the false impression that when the bride and groom get hitched it is a single solitary wedding. That may be true of a regular Orthodox Jewish wedding. But for the ultra-Orthodox it is actually two weddings that occur simultaneously.

One for the groom and one for the bride.

Before the wedding ceremony, both the *chassan* — that's me — and the *kallah* — that's Dafna — are kept in separate rooms and then the nervous groom, accompanied by his parents, gets to see his bride for the first time that day — or week — or ever — when he pulls the bridal veil over his bride's face and he is whisked off to the *chupah*. She then follows to join her soon-to-be husband.

Lots of loud singing and energetic dancing.

Once under the marriage canopy, the groom finally gets to say something but it is only the prescribed words in Hebrew for 'With this ring I thee wed.'

That's it.

No one says 'I do' or 'I don't.' No one has to 'forever hold their peace.'

The rabbi recites a whole bunch of blessings. The bride and groom get a few measly sips of wine. The marriage contract is read aloud before all the guests, but the text is all in Aramaic so there are only a handful of people who understand what is going on. The finale of the event is when the groom stomps down and breaks a glass — carefully wrapped so no one gets hurt — to remind the assembled of the destruction of the Jewish Temple in Jerusalem 2,000 years ago. With the ceremony completed everyone screams *mazel tov* and the orchestra begins playing wild Jewish music.

More loud singing and energetic dancing.

So far the couple have not even said 'Hello' or 'How are you?' to each other.

Now comes the *yichud*. The couple is taken to a separate room and stay there alone — just the two of them — for about fifteen minutes. In the super-ultra-Orthodox circles, where the matches are made by the family, this is often the first time that the couple have ever been in the same room together with no one else present.

Everything I just described probably happened at my wedding as well. I say probably because I was so nervous that everything became one big blur. All evening there was someone at my side telling me what was required. Whatever they told me to do, I did. I remember lots of *yeshiva bucherim* jumping and dancing to the beat of the loud music. But the what, where, how, and when is a total morass. I have been told by other recent grooms that this is the norm and you discover what happened at your own wedding by watching the video.

Somehow we both made it to the *yichud* room. It was the first time the entire evening that I had a chance to look at Dafna. She was so beautiful in her cream colored dress. Cream colored because it was a second marriage — some sort of custom. Tevye, of Fiddler on the Roof fame, asked, 'Why do Jews have a custom for everything?' His answer was, that he does not know — and that was also a custom.

I looked at her and suddenly realized.

She was now Mrs. Dafna Lincoln.

My wife.

The first order of business was to smile at each other and then I said, "Hello, Mrs. Lincoln."

She replied, "Hello, Mr. Lincoln."

Then we hugged and kissed. I will not go into the details for fear of being indelicate. But it felt good. Really good. Second order of business was to attack the cakes, soft drinks, and assorted goodies someone had laid out for us to break our fast. Once we finished stuffing our faces and could feel the sugar high take effect, we returned to the hugging and kissing — taking care not to smudge her makeup — and then we were called back to the festivities.

Once out of the *yichud* room, the real dancing began. This was not your rumba, twist, waltz, cha cha, fox trot, type dancing. It is not in any way similar to ballroom dancing or any other type of dancing common to the Western world. The music, which is of a repetitive cadence, came blasting out of giant loudspeakers at a volume that allowed the music to be heard on the moon. Circles of high stepping men and women danced to this music with unflagging energy. I say men and women — but not together. There was a solid partition erected in the middle of the hall and the men danced with the groom and the women with the bride.

You may ask, where did all these frolickers come from? After all, our wedding was quite small — only two hundred sit-down guests — a small Jewish wedding. The answer is that all the *bocherim* from the *yeshiva* and all the girls from the girl's high school wanted to come. Dafna gives a computer class to the girls and she is one of their favorite teachers. To feed the hungry hordes of youngsters the caterer prepared buffet tables at the sides of the hall laden with finger food — fried chicken, chicken wings, *knishes,* little hamburgers and hot dogs, herring, *gefilte fish,* even sushi — which allowed the prancing youth to replenish their energy stores.

Jewish wedding dancing is almost impossible to describe, but imagine a feeding frenzy of about two hundred hungry sharks. Throw in some bloody chum. Put it all to music and have them go in circles. Get the picture?

I was supposed to be in the middle of all this, dancing right along with them. But most of those guys were twenty years younger than me and had double my stamina. I could dance for maybe ten minutes and then I needed to rest to catch my breath and get my strength back. I was also afraid that at any moment I would tear out the stitches and reopen the wound in my side. So give me a break.

The dancers would have continued on all night without a pause but the caterer insisted that he had to serve the meal. The waiters brought out the liver paté appetizers. For this, I was allowed to sit with Dafna on the dais for about ten minutes. Once the first course was finished — voom — everyone was back on the dance floor.

My heart rate was up near cardiac arrest level and I was sweating like a — pardon the expression — pig, and I had to take another break to grab something to drink. Glass of Coke in hand, I was leaning against a post when a woman came out from behind the partition calling me, "Lincoln, how are you holding up?"

I nearly dropped my cup. Never in a million years would I have recognized the woman talking to me if it was not for her voice. The lady wore a shoulder length dark brown fall wig and a long sleeved sequined blue dress that went from her neck to the floor. A typical *rebbetzin.* But not so typical.

I could not believe it.

"Sergeant Chandler, you look lovely."

She did a half curtsy, "What do you say, not bad for a *shiksa?*"

"Thanks for watching Dafna."

"I would not miss her wedding for the world. Glad to do it," she said patting her purse.

She was obviously armed and guarding Dafna for me, "I appreciate it."

"Did you see Mary Lou?" she asked.

"No, where is she?"

"Right over there," she said pointing to a slim woman with short brown hair and a sedate gray pants suit.

"That's Mary Lou?" I asked incredulously.

"The one and only."

"Are you kidding me. Wow."

Only Mary Lou could get away with wearing a pants suit at an ultra-Orthodox Jewish wedding.

"By the way, the menu says your first course was supposed to be chicken liver paté. I tasted it. It's not. The caterer switched it for calf's liver. Ask for your money back."

"I most certainly will."

There went my brilliant idea that no one would notice.

I saw that my mom and dad were having a great time. They were at the open bar with family and friends, tossing back potent *le'chaims.* As the evening progressed they were becoming happier and happier. Even my Aunt Helen was enjoying herself. They finally found someone who was willing to listen to her yapping all evening. What she did not know was that she was seated next to

Dafna's Aunt Bela, who was as deaf as a doornail and refused to wear a hearing aid.

After the service staff got the entrée on the tables, the band started playing an especially hectic tune. I was surprised to see my dad join the revelers in the very middle of the circles. He was obviously drunk and shucked off his tuxedo jacket to kick up his heels with the most energized of the young bucks. He seemed to be really enjoying himself but I noticed that his face was getting very flushed. When it began approaching fire engine red I decided to grab him and usher him to the sidelines. If he did not take a break we would need the CPR crew.

It took a few moments for him to catch his breath and then he said, "Terrific wedding. We should do this more often. I need a drink."

Off he went to get more liquid fortitude.

I took a peek over the partition and saw that Dafna was dancing with her mother and her two daughters, along with Mary Lou and Sergeant Chandler.

How odd and how nice.

The music, dancing, and frolicking went on until almost midnight, maybe later. I do not know when they actually stopped because I left with Dafna to go to the hotel. Mary Lou would be the last to leave and she would settle all the outstanding accounts. No one could do it better.

Ultra-Orthodox newlyweds do not go on honeymoons because they are required to participate in the week of special celebratory meals — the *sheva brachos.* Family and friends organize these meals and they are sort of like mini-wedding receptions. Some — not so mini. These celebrations help smooth the transition — for both the bride and groom — from being single individuals, who only think about themselves, into considerate life partners.

A new groom had many new things to learn. He had to discover toilet seat etiquette. Dealing with frilly undergarments. Improve on personal hygiene. And a slew of other things that required patience and effort.

So we were not going anywhere for the next week. The days and nights for the next seven days were carefully planned. But tonight was different. Tonight Dafna and I would be together as man and wife for the first time. I booked a suite at the fancy Courtyard Detroit Hotel in Southfield and ordered bouquets of flowers to be spread around the rooms. Jarron left word that he would have police in and near the hotel to watch for Nealy. I hope they were watching really good, because when I got to the hotel and carried Dafna across the threshold of our suite — I am a big romantic at heart — the 'Kosher Butcher' was the farthest thing from my mind.

<u>57</u>

Baby-Baby

I WILL not describe our wedding night because that is no one's business but ours. Suffice it to say that being intimate with someone you love, respect and admire is an unbelievable experience. Better than anything I could have imagined.

Dafna was gorgeous, smart, friendly, witty, a phenomenal cook and homemaker, and in the intimacy department — wowee.

And I was able to trick her into marrying me.

Am I a lucky bastard or what?

There was a mile wide smile plastered across my face when I awoke at seven thirty the next morning. Dafna had a similar smile and that made me feel even better. We both began dressing. She wanted to get back to her house to see her girls and prepare our wedding brunch. I had to get to morning prayers because I knew from experience, that when the groom did not make it to *minyan* the morning after his wedding, he was the target of wisecracks for the rest of the week. We would be spending the next five nights at the hotel so we did not have to pack anything. At 8:15 a.m., I retrieved my Smith

& Wesson 38 snub nose from under the pillow on the bed and tucked it into my fanny pack.

Just then there was a knock on the door. I extracted my pistol and motioned for Dafna to go towards the bathroom away from the door. I stood to the side and asked, "Who is it?"

"Room service," was the reply.

"We did not order anything from room service."

"I've got an order for coffee and Kosher sweet rolls and bagels, for Mr. and Mrs. Simon Lincoln in the honeymoon suite," said the fellow outside the door.

Who could have made the order?

Then it dawned on me. Mary Lou. She thinks of everything.

I peeked through the spy hole and could make out a short service person and a cart. I warily unfolded the security latch on the door and opened the door a crack. A young waiter stood in the hall with a rolling table loaded with coffee utensils and baked goods. There was no one else in the hall.

I replaced my pistol and opened the door to allow the guy to wheel the cart into the room.

The fellow received a five dollar tip before he left.

I closed the door behind him.

There was a thermos of coffee, bagels and pastries along with a note from the rabbi of the hotel certifying that all the baked goods were strictly kosher.

"Very nice," said Dafna.

"Yeah, I suppose it is. We'll have something to *nosh* later on."

"We better get moving," she said.

"You ready, Mrs. Lincoln?" I asked Dafna.

"I like the sound of that," she said standing on her tiptoes to kiss my cheek.

"And I like that," I said returning the kiss.

I heard the electronic door lock whir behind me and I turned to see the door begin to open. I looked towards the intruder to say, "What the hell ..."

How stupid of me. I had forgotten to flip closed the security latch.

When the door opened fully I saw a tall man standing in the doorway. He was wearing a black suit with a white ecumenical collar. His gray unmempt hair was long and he had black rimmed glasses. There was a silver headed walking stick in his left hand and a Glock 9 mm automatic in his right. I was baffled for a moment but then I figured it out. Nealy had come to pay us a visit.

"How convenient. You're both being here for me. Put your hands behind your heads and step back towards the bed," he said waving his pistol.

I positioned Dafna behind me as we moved deeper into the room. Nealy walked in and kicked the door closed.

"Do something," Dafna urged behind me.

Nealy laughed and said, "Your boyfriend ... excuse me ... your husband does not have too many options."

If we were going to get out of this alive I needed to buy time. So, I looked at him and said seriously, "You are going to shoot us. Isn't that right?"

"Don't give him any suggestions," said Dafna.

"What kind of question is that?" asked a surprised Nealy.

Just then the bedside phone rang.

I was expecting the call.

I extended my hand towards the phone and Nealy said, "What the hell do you think you're doing? Don't touch that phone."

In acquiescence I raised my hands again and let the phone ring, "OK, if that is what you want. You are the boss. But if I don't answer the phone, you can be pretty sure that someone is going to come to see why, really quickly."

Nealy thought for a moment and said, "Answer it, but no funny stuff. Tell them everything is hunky dory in here."

I lifted the phone to hear Mary Lou ask, "Boss, are you OK? The video camera showed that after the hotel waiter left your room a priest with a cane came down the hall and he did not come from the elevator."

"That is so thoughtful," I answered. "I look forward to receiving that complimentary bowl of fruit this afternoon. It is so nice of you and your staff to think of us."

Nealy whispered, "Who is it?"

I put my hand over the microphone and said, "Hotel manager."

"Get rid of him."

I heard Mary Lou anxiously ask, "There's trouble, isn't there?"

"Absolutely," I said with a broad smile. "And send special regards to Baby."

I hung up the phone and Nealy asked, "Who's Baby?"

"The manager's poodle," I told him.

"Very cute doggy," added Dafna.

"If you two are finished, get back to where you were," commanded Nealy.

"And I asked you, are you going to shoot us?"

Dafna reasoned, "You do have a record for killing lots of people. So, it is a fair question."

"Are you both totally crazy? I am holding a gun. What do you think?" he said angrily.

"I just wanted to be sure," I said nodding my head in understanding. "See ... I want to ask a favor from you."

"A favor ... now?" said Nealy in exasperation.

"Yeah, a favor. I don't know what to say ... this is my best suit. And if you shoot me, there is going to be blood all over it. So, they will lay me out at the funeral in my other suit. The collar is frayed and really tacky. I don't want people to remember me like that. So, the favor is ...

could I please take off my jacket so it won't get messed up?"

I was certain Nealy's knowledge of Jewish funeral customs did not include the fact that Jews never have open casket type services. I just wanted him to consider the question because I needed to buy time.

He thought for a second and said, "OK, but real slow. No fast moves. Take off your jacket."

I undid the buttons and as I withdrew my right arm from the sleeve I lifted the back flap. I wanted Dafna to see my pistol and hopefully take it while I blocked Nealy's line of sight. I felt her remove the whole fanny pack as I extricated my other sleeve and folded the jacket. I turned slowly and placed the jacket over Dafna's hands, hiding the gun. I turned back to Nealy and said, "Thank you. I really appreciate that courtesy."

"You're not going to get away with this," Dafna said in warning.

"Oh really, and why is that? Do you think I didn't recognize the cops downstairs? Two in the lobby and three walking around. They might as well be wearing signs. No, you two are going to pay for what you did to me."

I felt Dafna stiffen with anger as she tried to come around me, but I held her back. I did not want her to get too close and make Nealy feel threatened. I also did not want him to see the weapon hidden in her hands.

Dafna was in a rage and leaned towards Nealy to say loudly, "What we did to you? All we did is catch you. You killed four people and chopped them into little pieces ... all because you can't face up to the fact that you got your secretary pregnant. Don't you think that you are the one who is responsible for what happened to you and not us?"

"That little *chikeetah* said she was going to go to my wife and say I raped her," said Nealy vehemently. "I would never have gotten my family back."

"Maybe that little *chikeetah* said no and you did rape her?"

Nealy tensed with Dafna's accusation, and the veins on his neck began to bulge. I could not reach for my pistol without him seeing me. I needed a distraction. "Dafna, stop talking. He has got a gun," I warned.

"I don't care," she said. "Rape is rape."

"She wanted it," he responded loudly.

"It was still rape," she insisted just as loudly.

Because of the vociferous exchange I had not heard the activation of the door lock but just over Nealy's shoulder I could see the door open slowly. In the doorway stood Mary Lou holding 'Baby' in a two-handed grip. She moved forward slowly and silently.

Nealy waved his gun at us, "I liked you. I thought you were a nice guy. But, what is it with you people? It isn't enough that you control all the banks and the stock markets? You have all the movie studios and all the newspapers. Why do you have to stick your noses into things that are not your business? It is because of you people, that Jesus died," he said in anger.

Mary Lou was maybe six feet from Nealy when she said in her distinctive raspy voice, "Drop your weapon Nealy, or I will shoot you in the back right where you stand."

Nealy did not move or speak at first and then said without turning his head, "Well, well, well. If it isn't Mary Lou. You've come to save your boss. How commendable. I cannot believe that anyone would allow you to handle a gun. I don't want you to get a twitchy finger so I am going to drop my pistol and turn around real slow."

Nealy opened his hand on the grip so that the weapon dangled from his right index finger. He raised the stick in his left hand and began to turn. I was watching him carefully and saw the way the gun was still hanging from his finger. It was a cop trick. All he needed to do was close his grip and fire. Nealy tensed and I could see that he was about to make the move I had been watching for.

He was going to shoot as he turned.

Five things happened at once — I screamed, "Mary Lou shoot!," I grabbed Dafna and pushed her to the floor under me, I extracted my weapon from her hands, Nealy turned, threw the stick at Mary Lou and fired his gun three times. At the same time both Mary Lou and I did a double tap, firing our guns twice in rapid succession. Mary Lou from a one knee stance and me from the floor.

Lots of noise, smoke, and then silence.

Because Mary Lou had dropped to one knee, Nealy's bullets went over her head. All four of our bullets hit the cop central mass, sending him to the floor like a stone.

Dafna was on the floor crying softly and saying, 'Oh my God' over and over. She was in meltdown mode. I pulled my wife into my embrace to comfort her.

My wife needed a few moments.

Nealy was gasping for breath and Mary Lou approached to kick his gun away. She looked down at him and said, "You got it all wrong. It is because of people like you that Jesus died."

I pulled out my cell phone and dialed 911. I requested that they send the police and an ambulance. Mary Lou looked at me and asked, "Boss, do we have to call for an ambulance for scum like this?"

"Yeah, it's the Christian thing to do."

Dafna pulled away from me and through her tears asked Mary Lou, "How did you know he would be here?"

"I didn't. I have been sitting in a room down the hall. Your husband had us put in our own remote video cameras for the lobby and this corridor, just to be safe. I figured it was a good idea, because if your wedding night was anything like what I had with Andy, a Panzer Division could have driven through our room and we would not have known a thing. When I saw that a priest appeared from nowhere, I called."

"So that was you on the phone?" asked Dafna. "Not the manager?"

"No, just me."

"So we are not going to get a complimentary bowl of fruit?" Dafna asked jokingly through her tears.

Dafna was becoming herself again.

I asked Mary Lou, "Why did you drop to one knee? That move saved your life. That is not standard police practice."

"You guys were in my line of fire. Couldn't take the chance if I missed. The Lord moves in mysterious ways."

Absolutely.

<u>58</u>

Blessing

THE COPS began arriving after about five minutes and the paramedics got there after six. The first one through the door was — I should have known — good old Officer Cummings with his gun drawn.

When Cummings saw that it was me he said, "Oh come on. Give me a break."

"Always a pleasure to see you, Cummings," I responded.

Nealy was barely breathing but he was not dead. The paramedics immediately started an IV and quickly transported him to the hospital.

Jarron came in twenty minutes later with the third wave of state police. While statements were being taken from all of us, Crowley made his appearance, suit and all. 'Baby', Nealy's pistol, and my weapon were all appropriated by the state police and would be returned when all the facts of who shot whom were figured out.

Our suite had multiple bullet holes, a big blood stain in the carpet, a colossal mess left by the paramedics, and the CSI team would be there for hours. So the hotel moved us into the adjoining suite for the rest of our stay. We spent the next two hours in our new accommodations telling our story to various investigators until Jarron and Crowley came in and asked everyone else to leave.

Crowley began, "The FBI and the big shots from the state police will be organizing a press conference at noon. They will commend the state and local police for their hard work. But you and I know that you were really the ones who solved the whole thing. I'm sorry we can't give you any of the credit. But, there is too much political hay to be harvested from this kind of a case. Just so you know, you made a friend and I owe you guys."

"Same for me," said Jarron.

"You sure do owe us," I said. "The next time I get a speeding ticket on the interstate you are going to hear from me."

"Talk to the troopers. I don't do speeding tickets," said the FBI man.

Jarron looked hurt, "Hey, what do you think I am? A crooked cop? I don't fix speeding tickets."

"Then what good are you?" I said jokingly. "Take care, both of you. We need all the good cops we can get."

Jarron and Crowley said their goodbyes and left the room, leaving us alone for the first time since Nealy had come to pay us a visit. I turned to Dafna and asked, "How are you holding up?"

She looked up at me and demanded quietly, "Give me a hug."

Uh oh. Perhaps the morning events were affecting her again, "Are you having one of your ... episodes?"

"What? You can only hug me if we get blown up or shot at?" she inquired. "We're married now. It's allowed."

"No ... it's not that ... it's just ... ," I stammered.

"Shimon, I'm waiting. What does it take to get a hug around here?"

Yeah — it was allowed. It finally sank in.

I pulled her into my arms.

It felt very good.

Completion.

We swayed back and forth in our embrace and then there was a knock on the door.

My cop craziness went into overdrive. Perhaps Nealy had an accomplice. Maybe there really was a Kegleze. I reached for my pistol but then remembered that the state police had taken it to sort out the shooting.

I pulled Dafna over to the corner of the room. "Stay here," I commanded.

"What's wrong with you?" she asked. "Why don't you just go see who is at the door?"

"I do not have my weapon. We can't take any chances."

"Last time I checked, Nealy was shot to pieces and on his way to the hospital. It is unlikely that Kegleze even exists. There are six lab techs in our old room right next door and there are cops marching back and forth. Do you really think another bad guy is going to come waltzing in just to get us?"

She was right. I overreacted just a bit.

Maybe more than a bit.

I walked over to the door and asked, "Who is it?"

"Reb Shimon, it is Rabbi Kalmonowitz. Can I come in?"

Rebbi was here? It could not be.

I looked through to peephole and discovered that it was indeed the *Rosh Yeshiva*.

I opened the door wide, "Please come in."

The rabbi strode into the room in his long black frock coat and black hat. There was a wide smile on his face as he pumped my hand and said, "*Boruch HaShem* you are both all right."

The official police statement, released to the media, said that Nealy had been apprehended by the state police and the FBI. Our part in catching him would remain a secret known to only a few. There was no way that *Rebbi* could possibly know that Mary Lou and I had been the ones who brought him down. I was not going to tell him because there was no reason for him to be worried about us.

I motioned to one of the chairs near our small sofa, "Please have a seat. There was never any need for concern. The state police and the FBI were watching over us. They did a good job. They caught him, didn't they?"

Dafna added, "*Rebbi,* we're fine."

"Yes, you are fine. Both of you are fine wonderful people. You are both *giborim.* And both of you have a bit of a problem with telling the *emes,*" said *Rebbi,* looking at me and then Dafna.

How did he know?

Dafna just nodded her head accepted *Rebbi's* words.

I began, "I can assure you ..."

"Yes, I can assure you as well that I am in your debt. I asked you to look into Reb Yechezkel's disappearance and in the end you put your lives in jeopardy and were even shot at. The whole community thanks you."

Somehow, he knew. It was useless to deny what had happened, so I said simply, "You're welcome."

"I had to come and to thank you immediately. I did not want to wait until this evening. Don't forget, you are both guests at our house tonight for *sheva brochose.* Thank you again."

With that he rose, shook my hand again and began heading for the door. Dafna got up as well and called out, "Rabbi Kalmonowitz?"

He turned and said, "Yes, Dafna. Or should I say Mrs. Lincoln? What do you want?"

"For you, it will always be Dafna," she said with a smile. "You said that you are in our debt."

"That is correct. What you did was an enormous help to all of us," he responded.

"Well, if you think you have a debt to us ... perhaps you would like to redeem that debt?"

The rabbi cocked his head to the side and with a smile on his face asked, "What did you have in mind?"

What was Dafna doing?

"How about you give us a *brocha*? Your personal *brocha*," she said emphatically.

She was pressuring *Rebbi*. *Unbelievable.*

"You know that *brochos* are more commonly given by the *Chassidic* rabbis. In our *yeshiva* world we do not give *brochos*. Each person should pray for God's help by himself and rely on his or her own merit," he answered.

"Yeah, I know that," said Dafna nodding her head. "But giving us a *brocha* would sure be a good way to work off your debt."

Rebbi chuckled and said, "You strike a hard bargain."

"Do we have a deal?" she inquired.

"Yes we do," said Rabbi Kalmonowitz solemnly. He closed his eyes and began rocking gently back and forth in deep concentration. Then he recited aloud some Hebrew sentences that I recognized as the classic priestly blessing. When he concluded the prayer he became silent but continued the rocking and the concentration. After about a minute, he opened his eyes and said, "Debt is paid. You got your *brocha*. Now it is up to *HaKodesh Baruch Hoo* to see if he agrees."

"If you made the *brocha,* how can we go wrong?" I said.

Dafna looked at Rabbi Kalmonowitz and asked, "What was the *brocha* you made for us?"

Rebbi smiled and said, "I asked God to allow you to establish a *bayis ne'eman* and as it builds and grows it should be a blessing and an honor to all of the people of Israel."

"Amen," I said.

"Thank you," said Dafna smiling gratefully.

Rabbi Kalmonowitz looked at us and said, "If there is nothing else, I have got to get back to the *yeshiva*. See you both tonight."

Rebbi left and we were once again on our own. I turned to Dafna, "I can't believe you fenagled a *brocha* out of *Rebbi* like that."

"Are you angry with me?"

Yes, I suppose I am. She should not have done that. I have a good mind to — I don't know what. "That was not a nice thing to do."

She said enthusiastically, "Yeah, but we did get a *brocha* from *Rebbi*."

"I was so embarrassed."

"I won't do that ever again," she said with a coy smile.

Why do I get the feeling that she was not completely sincere.

"Are you being honest with me?" I asked insistently.

She was silent for a moment and then looked up at me to say, "Shimon ... I think I am having an episode."

"What kind of episode?"

"That kind of episode," she said meekly.

I quickly took her in my arms and we just stood there. My anger faded away. I suspect she knew that would happen. Sneaky. But who cares.

After a few moments I asked in a soft voice, "I am not too sure if I really understand *Rebbi's* blessing. You claim that his words have a special meaning."

"You know I do," she whispered in return.

"If I remember correctly, the word *bayis* means house or home. So when he says it should build and grow, does it mean we have to build an extension onto the house? Or perhaps the extension we built for your mother is enough. What do you think?"

"The word *bayis* also means family. I think that is what he was referring to."

Suddenly it dawned on me. "Do you really think he means for our family to get bigger?" I asked. "Like, I will become a dad?"

Dafna pushed my shoulders back so that she could look me straight in the eye to say knowingly, "You can take it to the bank."

BIOGRAPHY

Born in London, England, Melvyn Westreich was raised in New York City. He attended Yeshiva University and completed his medical degree and residencies at Wayne State University, in Detroit. After completing his studies he moved to Israel and eventually became the chairman of the Department of Plastic Surgery at the Assaf HaRofeh Medical Center of Tel Aviv University, Sackler School of Medicine, the President of the Israel Association of Plastic Surgery and the Chairman of the Board of Plastic Surgery of Israel. His interests include travel, photography, gardening and he has a *mishigas* about Japanese Gardens. He presently lives on Kibbutz Yavne, in Israel, with his wife Ada. *The Kosher Butcher* is his second published novel.

According to His Deeds

The sages say that first marriages are made in heaven, but for the second time around it is an entirely different story. Meet Steven Lincoln, Shimon's widower contractor cousin and Ayelet Weinberg, the widow who is such a fantastic baker. Can two people that come from such different worlds make a match? Perhaps Rabbi Kalmonowitz has the answer in Melvyn Westreich's new novel - **According to His Deeds**

Prologue

Might as well end this three way conference call. There was no way I was going to win. Once again my paranoia was getting the best of me and my son, David, and Rabbi Schlussel were not going to relent. "Enough already. Enough already. I'll go," I said in defeat. "Just stop *noodging* (pestering) me."

"Good," said a triumphant Rabbi Schlussel. "You were a hard nut to crack, Mr. Lincoln."

"Rabbi, please call me Steve. Mr. Lincoln was my father."

David added, "Dad, we were not *noodging* you. We were just trying to show you the benefits of going."

"Yeah, just like Don Corleone made offers you couldn't refuse," I stated.

"Who is Don Corleone?" asked the rabbi.

"Rabbi Schlussel, he was talking to me. That was my father's attempt at a joke," said David. "Dad ... you know you need help."

"I don't know anything of the kind," I replied.

"Mr. Lincoln … Steve," said the rabbi correcting himself. "The meetings at the Jewish Center will do you good."

"Rabbi, don't start all over again. I said I was going."

My son added, "It's been two years since mom died. You have to have a positive attitude about this for it to work."

"You have enough positive attitude for the both of us and you live seven hundred miles away in Atlanta," I said.

"Yeah, but I'm not the one who will be going to the meetings," responded David.

"Don't I know it," I replied.

"Rabbi, tell my father how important it is for him to be positive about the meetings."

"Attitude is essential … absolutely," said the rabbi with certainty.

"I said I would go … but attitude is not part of the agreement. Take it or leave it."

"We'll take it!! We'll take it!!" exclaimed Rabbi Schlussel and my son in unison.

∞

"So, Ayelet, it is agreed? You will be going to the meetings?" asked *Rebbetzin* Kalmonowitz over the phone.

I begin to protest, "But, the meetings at the Jewish Center … men and women sit together."

"Who suggested that you go to these meetings?"

"*Rav* Kalmonowitz," I answer humbly.

"Exactly," said the *rebbetzin*. "And do you think that the *Rosh Yeshiva* does not know that the meetings are mixed?"

"Well …"

"Of course he knows," interjected *Rebbetzin* Kalmonowitz. "So, if the *Rosh Yeshiva* suggests you go to the meetings, at least take it into consideration."

Funny, how whenever the *rebbetzin* speaks about her husband she always refers to him as the *Rosh Yeshiva*

(Head rabbi at the highest Torah academy) or *Rav* Kalmonowitz. She never uses his first name or calls him 'my husband'. He is the most respected Torah scholar in the community and had been my Rephael's mentor. If Rabbi Kalmonowitz suggests something it means I really do not have a choice.

Still it is very odd.

The *frum* (ultra Orthodox) community does not exactly boycott the Jewish Center, but they avoid their social gatherings because of the lax rules regarding male and female co-participation. In addition, the meetings are usually at night. That will be a problem.

"*Rebbetzin* ... aren't the meetings at night?"

"Yes, but *Rav* Kalmonowitz will take care of that. Go down to the JCC tomorrow and register."

There is no use arguing.

"Yes, *rebbetzin*," I respond meekly.

"Ayelet, *vet zayn gut* (things will get better)." Just before she hung up she added as a benediction, "*HaKodesh Baruch Hoo* (Almighty God) should bless you and your children."

"Amen," I say, hoping that things would indeed get better.

Glossary of terms

agunah   a state of Jewish legal limbo which creates
                    a situation where a woman cannot
                    remarry because even though her
                    marriage has been dissolved she is still
                    legally married. This can occur when a
                    husband refuses to give a divorce or the
                    whereabouts of the husband are
                    unknown. The majority of Jewish
                    marriages end by either the death of a
                    spouse or a divorce decree issued by a
                    Jewish court. The problem is that in
                    order to finalize a Jewish divorce the
                    husband must send or personally
                    administer the divorce papers - the *get*.
                    Without an available husband there are
                    huge difficulties. Such a situation could
                    happen if the husband disappears
                    mysteriously or in cases of desertion
                    and/or abandonment. Since the *get*
                    cannot be administered, the marriage is
                    not formally dissolved and the wife
                    becomes an *agunah*. The worst type of
                    agunah is where the woman is granted a
                    divorce by a Jewish court, but her
                    husband — who is available — simply
                    refuses to perform the actual divorce
                    ceremony. Judaism frowns on such
                    behavior and Jewish courts deal

stringently with these recalcitrant men. In Israel they are even sent to prison.

aliya — the honor of being called upon to recite a portion from the *Torah*

aufruf — Yiddish for 'call up' - refers to the *aliya* of a bridegroom on the Sabbath before his wedding.

bais din — Jewish court

bais medrash — *yeshiva* study hall

balabustas — Jewish homemakers

bayis ne'eman — a true home

bima — raised altar in synagogue

bocher — young man or student (plural - *bocherim*)

Borsalino — hat manufacturer brand name

boruch HaShem - blessing to God

bris — Also called *bris milah.* Jewish ritual circumcision of eight day old male infants.

brocha — blessing

challah — traditional braided white bread served on festive occaisions, as a pair of loaves.

charedi	(someone that follows) ultra-Orthodox Judaism
chassan	bridegroom or fiancé
chilul HaShem	denigration to the name of God
chupah	marriage canopy
daven	v. to pray
davening	prayers
emes	truth
frum	ultra-Orthodox Jews
frumies	slang for ultra-Orthodox Jews
get	Jewish bill of divorce
giborim	heroes
gut voch	Yiddish for good week
gut yuntif	Yiddish for happy holiday
KaKodesh Baruch Hoo - Almighty God	
halacha	Jewish law
HaShem	God

kibitz   v. to advise or comment, usually unasked
                  for advice. One who gives such advice is a
                  kibitzer.

kiddush HaShem - sanctification of God's name

Knaidelach   dumpling made from eggs and *matzah*
                  meal, usually served in soup.

maariv   see *shacharis*

mashuginer   mad man

matza   a dry flat bread, made from unfermented
                  dough

Megilah   The Book of Esther written on a
                  parchment scroll

Mensch   (good) human being

mincha   see *shacharis*

minhag   custom

minyan   prayer quorum of at least ten Jewish men

mishloach manose - sending of food parcels on the Purim
                  holiday, also called *shlach manose*. These
                  packages are not given as charity but are
                  gifts of friendship. According to *halacha*
                  you can fulfill the requirement by giving
                  any two types of prepared foods to any
                  two friends. But no woman in the *yeshiva*
                  world does this. They usually give tens —

sometimes more than a hundred — of parcels, each containing baked goods, fruits, sweets, snacks, beer, spirits, hard liquor, condiments, jams and a wide variety of exotic foods. Just about any kind of kosher food or drink could be found in the parcel.

mitzvah	religious requirement or meritorious deed (plural - *mitzvahs*).
neshama	soul
noodge	v. *to pester*
olam ha'bah	the world to come - heaven - as opposed to this world - *olam ha'zeh*
olam ha'zeh	the world we live in - as opposed to the world to come - *olam ha'bah*
Passover	see *pesach*
Pesach	Or Passover - eight day Jewish holiday in the spring. The four middle days are less stringent. During the holiday no fermentation products of the five basic grains — wheat, barley, oats, buckwheat, and spelt — collectively known as *chametz* — are allowed. In addition you are not allowed to have them in your possession during the entire eight days, so that householders perform a rigid cleaning of the entire house before the

holiday and only foods with special 'Kosher for Passover' certification are allowed. Traditionally, *Matza* is eaten instead of bread or pasta.

rahsha   evil person

Rav   short form for the word rabbi

Reb   version of rabbi, but is usually an honorary title put before the name

rebbetzin   a rabbi's wife

Rebbi   version of Rabbi, but usually signifies one's teacher or rabbinical authority

rosh yeshiva   head rabbi of *yeshiva*

sandek   the person that holds the young child on his lap during the *bris milah*. Considered big honor.

sanhedrin   highest Jewish court in ancient Israel

sechel   intelligence

seder   Hebrew for order or arrangement - Used to describe the traditional family meal on the first night of *Pesach* and a study session in the *yeshiva*.

sefer   text on *Torah* subject

seudah   special meal

Shabbos the Jewish Sabbath - Saturday

shacharis There are three prayer sessions in the Jewish day; *shacharis, mincha, and maariv.* The big one is *shacharis* in the morning, and the last two are usually done in tandem, just before and after sunset. Although all prayers can be said privately, it is considered more meritorious for them to be recited in a *minyan.*

sheva brachos Hebrew for seven blessings. In the week after a wedding the bride and groom are treated as royalty. Festive meals are planned which culminate in the recital of the *sheva brachos.*

shiduch match - usually matrimonial (plural - *shiduchim*)

shiksa non Jewish woman

shiva seven days of mourning which usually commence after the burial

shlach manose see *mishloach manose*

shlep v. Yiddish for carry with effort

shtick trickery

siddur prayer book

simcha happiness or celebration

Ta'anis Esther   the Fast of Esther - one of the minor fast days. Orthodox Jews have six fast days in the year. Two biggees — *Yom Kippur* and *Tisha B'Av* (The ninth day of the Jewish month of Av) and four minor ones. The Fast of Esther is one of the lesser fasts and is in memory of the fast days that Queen Esther asked of the Jews of Shushan — the Capital of Persia — 2,500 years ago. From sunrise to sunset no food or drink.

tfilas haderech - traveler's prayer

Torah   The holy scroll containing the first five books of the Bible. Also refers to all aspects of religious Jewish life and study.

Tuchis   buttocks

tzadik   righteous person (plural - *tzadikim*)

yeshiva   Academy teaching religious Jewish subjects

yeshiva bocher   student in a *yeshiva*

yeshiva gedola   highest *Torah* study center

yichud   seclusion in a private area of a man with a woman

Made in United States
North Haven, CT
16 October 2022

25530104R00286